THE ZAPPA TOUR ATLAS

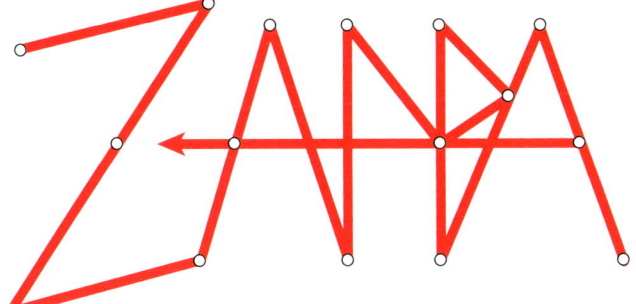

MICK ZEUNER
WITH KLAUS KÜHNER & ANDREW GREENAWAY

THE ZAPPA TOUR ATLAS

WITH ANNOTATED DISCOGRAPHY

WP
WYMER
PUBLISHING
Bedford, England

Imprint

First published in Great Britain in 2019
by Wymer Publishing
Bedford, England
www.wymerpublishing.co.uk
Tel: 01234 – 326691
Wymer Publishing is a trading name of Wymer (UK) Ltd.

First edition.
Copyright © 2019 Mick Zeuner / Klaus Kühner / Andrew Greenaway / Wymer Publishing.
ISBN: 978-1-912782-17-8

Edited by Jerry Bloom.

The Author hereby asserts his rights to be identified as the author of this work in accordance with sections 77 to 78 of the Copyright, Designs & Patents Act 1988.

All rights reserved. No part of this publication maybe reproduced or transmitted in any form or by any means, electronic or mechanical, including photocopying, or any information storage and retrieval system, without written permission from the publisher.

This publication is sold subject to the condition that it shall not, by way of trade or otherwise, be lent, re-sold, hired out or otherwise circulated without the publishers prior consent in any foml of binding or cover other than that in which it is published and without a similar condition including this condition heing imposed on the subsequent purchaser.

A catalogue record for this book is available from the British Library.

Printed by Replika Press.

Book conceived, researched, coordinated and supervised by Amaretto Mick Zeuner
Cover design, interior design and typeset by Klaus Kühner
Maps © Klaus Kühner
Photos © Guy Bickel 15, BBC 17, Corneliu Cazacu 11, Klaus Kühner 9, 16, Juliane Rudolph 12, 16, Rimbert Schickling 251, Mick Zeuner 8, 9

"Gone far too soon, this book is my tribute to the man who, when he wasn't out on the road playing his beautiful music, was at home creating even more."

– Mick Zeuner

Contents

CONTENTS

DA WORDZ 8
Foreword *by Robert Martin*........................... 11
Preface *by Mick Zeuner* 12
The Authors 16
Statistics 18

DA MAPZ 26

DA DISCZ 132
Albums reviewed *by Andrew Greenaway* 134

Acknowledgements 248

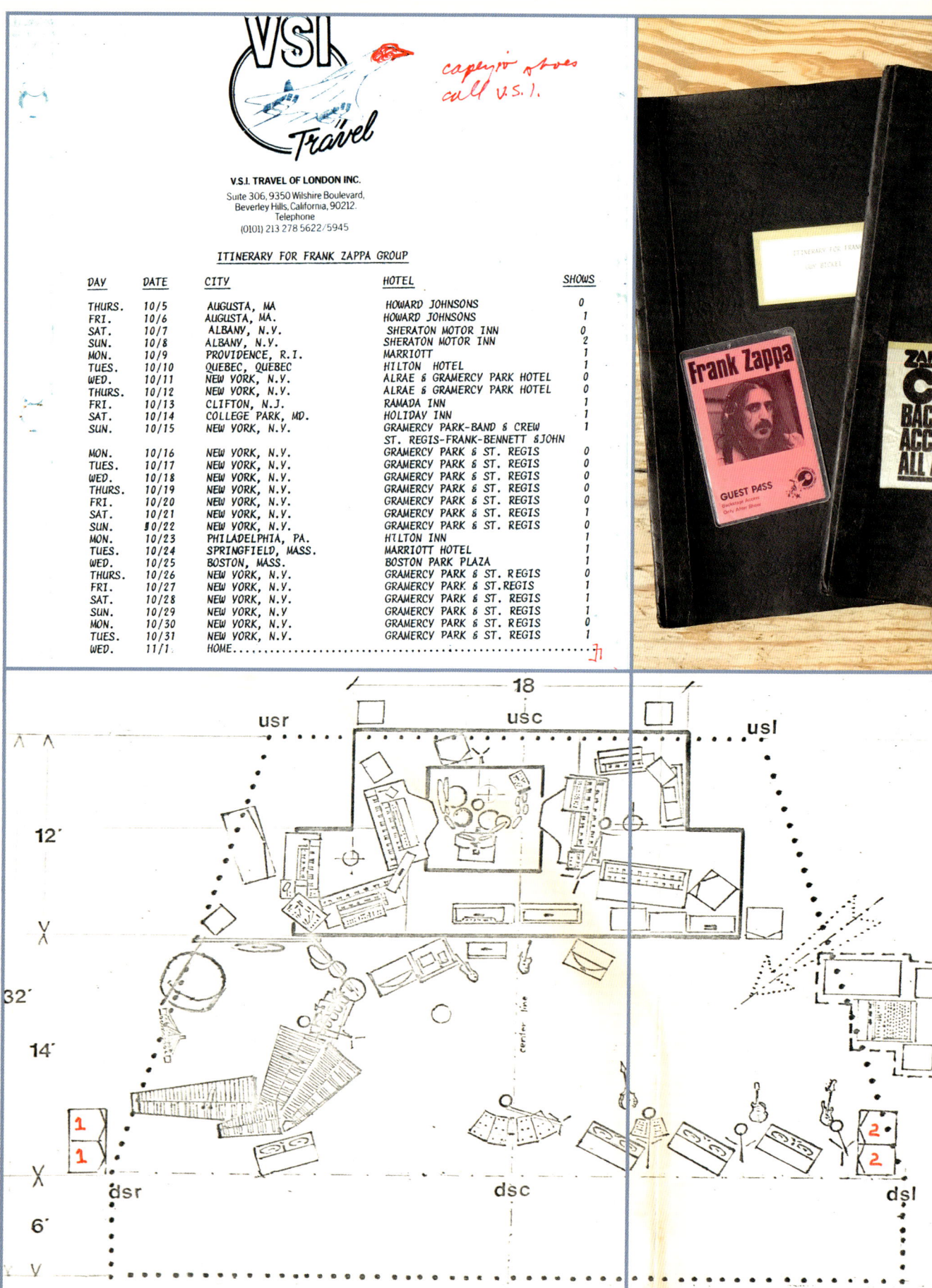

VSI Travel

V.S.I. TRAVEL OF LONDON INC.
Suite 306, 9350 Wilshire Boulevard,
Beverley Hills, California, 90212.
Telephone
(0101) 213 278 5622/5945

capeyio shoes call v.s.i.

ITINERARY FOR FRANK ZAPPA GROUP

DAY	DATE	CITY	HOTEL	SHOWS
THURS.	10/5	AUGUSTA, MA	HOWARD JOHNSONS	0
FRI.	10/6	AUGUSTA, MA.	HOWARD JOHNSONS	1
SAT.	10/7	ALBANY, N.Y.	SHERATON MOTOR INN	0
SUN.	10/8	ALBANY, N.Y.	SHERATON MOTOR INN	2
MON.	10/9	PROVIDENCE, R.I.	MARRIOTT	1
TUES.	10/10	QUEBEC, QUEBEC	HILTON HOTEL	1
WED.	10/11	NEW YORK, N.Y.	ALRAE & GRAMERCY PARK HOTEL	0
THURS.	10/12	NEW YORK, N.Y.	ALRAE & GRAMERCY PARK HOTEL	0
FRI.	10/13	CLIFTON, N.J.	RAMADA INN	1
SAT.	10/14	COLLEGE PARK, MD.	HOLIDAY INN	1
SUN.	10/15	NEW YORK, N.Y.	GRAMERCY PARK-BAND & CREW ST. REGIS-FRANK-BENNETT & JOHN	1
MON.	10/16	NEW YORK, N.Y.	GRAMERCY PARK & ST. REGIS	0
TUES.	10/17	NEW YORK, N.Y.	GRAMERCY PARK & ST. REGIS	0
WED.	10/18	NEW YORK, N.Y.	GRAMERCY PARK & ST. REGIS	0
THURS.	10/19	NEW YORK, N.Y.	GRAMERCY PARK & ST. REGIS	0
FRI.	10/20	NEW YORK, N.Y.	GRAMERCY PARK & ST. REGIS	0
SAT.	10/21	NEW YORK, N.Y.	GRAMERCY PARK & ST. REGIS	1
SUN.	10/22	NEW YORK, N.Y.	GRAMERCY PARK & ST. REGIS	1
MON.	10/23	PHILADELPHIA, PA.	HILTON INN	1
TUES.	10/24	SPRINGFIELD, MASS.	MARRIOTT HOTEL	1
WED.	10/25	BOSTON, MASS.	BOSTON PARK PLAZA	1
THURS.	10/26	NEW YORK, N.Y.	GRAMERCY PARK & ST. REGIS	0
FRI.	10/27	NEW YORK, N.Y.	GRAMERCY PARK & ST.REGIS	1
SAT.	10/28	NEW YORK, N.Y.	GRAMERCY PARK & ST. REGIS	1
SUN.	10/29	NEW YORK, N.Y	GRAMERCY PARK & ST. REGIS	1
MON.	10/30	NEW YORK, N.Y.	GRAMERCY PARK & ST. REGIS	0
TUES.	10/31	NEW YORK, N.Y.	GRAMERCY PARK & ST. REGIS	1
WED.	11/1	HOME		

DA WORDZ

ZAPPA
Band – setup
summer – falltour '78

Foreword

Like the cartographers who chronicled the explorations of Magellan hundreds of years ago, with this volume, Mick Zeuner has memorialized for us the world travels of one of the most profound and prolific musical explorers who ever lived, Frank Zappa. As a member of Frank's band for every tour from 1981 on, I was fortunate to have participated in many of those journeys, both musically and around the globe.

To the great delight of music fans the world over, one of Frank's joys in life was to play his music live with hand picked musicians whose skills and creative capacities were in tune with his own. The road, and the ensembles Frank assembled to navigate it with him, both influenced his astounding creative output.

Freak Out!, Frank's first album, was released in 1966, the year I graduated high school. The following year, Frank's touring brought him to Philadelphia where I saw him play with The Mothers at The Spectrum in 1967. Seven years later, in 1974, I saw him at The Spectrum again with a different line up of amazing musicians. Seven years after that, I joined the band and became a full participant in Frank's musical and geographical journeys. From 1981 until Frank passed in 1993, those odysseys were far reaching and hugely influential on me and countless others whose lives were touched by Frank's music, and his restless, probing mind. In our world travels, we played in Berlin before The Wall fell – and through Frank's musical journeys, one can only imagine how many walls fell in the lives of his world-wide listeners.

He once said that touring can make you crazy, but looking back, my experience of touring with Frank is filled with joyful memories and deep personal and musical growth. My world travels with Frank brought an incredible array of unique and wonderful people into my life, some of whom were my bandmates, and countless thousands of whom were fellow travelers in the experience of the human condition that Frank was so adept in describing. I am supremely grateful to call Frank a friend and generous mentor – and thankful that this book now exists to chronicle the wide and influential journey of his life.

Robert Martin
Los Angeles, June 2018

Preface
Mick Zeuner

Preface

or

How This Book Came To Be

On reaching the age of twelve and dropping the needle of my record player onto the grooves of the newly released LP, Studio Tan, I was infected with the Zappa virus. By the time of his European tour at the start of the Eighties, I was already a big fan.

I had been lucky enough to experience live shows at an early age in Bremen, from Queen (January 1979 & December 1980) and Led Zeppelin (May 1980), but I couldn't grab a ride to Zappa's concerts in the local Civic Hall in 1980 and 1982 due to the fact that I grew up about 12½ miles (20 km) away in the province just outside of Ganderkesee.

Even in 1984, when I finally became an adult, I still wasn't able to see Frank Zappa live. The 125 mile (200 km) journey to the concert in Ahlen/Westfalen wasn't the problem; rather, it was the fact that I had to take an important exam for my vocational school in Bremen the day after. But my mate Reiner Keuchel captured the show illegally on a cassette and handed it over to me on his return. Of course, this was only a weak substitute for the missed show. He told me of the heavy downpours – especially during the evening of this open air event – which turned the entire Motocross stadium into a mud pit. Other artists playing that day were Rory Gallagher, The Waterboys, Blancmange and The Alarm. This Golden Summernight Festival, headlined by FZ, was rolling on to the open air stage at Loreley near St. Goarshausen on the Rhine the following day.

Almost four years passed before Frank's next European tour was announced. It became the 1988 big band tour, the success of which had already been heard of from Zappa's American North Eastern fans. In those pre-internet days, I hastily called the telephone hotline (which could be found on every concert poster) to get information about every stop of the European leg. It was immediately clear to me which shows from this tour I would attend: Berlin (April 12th), Bremen (April 24th), and Hamburg (May 6th).

In order to grasp the extent of the Broadway The Hard Way tour across my home continent, I snatched a map of Europe, fixed it to a cork board, and placed small pins higgledy-piggledy in the locations of the approximately 40 tour stops. Finally, I connected the pins with red wool, starting with the first concert in Central France on April 9th and ending at the tour's grand finale in Genoa, Italy, two months later.

As the tour went on, I followed the stops almost daily on my homemade construction. The idea of a tour atlas with exact details containing all of Zappa's concerts and tours began to sprout inside my head.

After attending those three gigs in 1988, I was only able to see Frank one last time: at the Alte Oper in Frankfurt on Saturday, September 19, 1992.

Around this time, The Torchum Never Stops appeared: four fan-compiled scrapbooks detailing the official and unofficial Zappa/Mothers and related discographies, bibliographies and more. The fourth volume had a Frank Zappa tour chronology, the first I had ever seen. I wanted to ask the authors if they could envision a fifth edition with a tour atlas. Such was my eagerness for this to happen that I made a trip to the South of Germany in my old Peugeot 205 to discuss my idea with 'Torture Team' members Reinhard Preuss and Willi Jäger. Unfortunately they were struggling – mentally and, more significantly, financially – with their reference book so much so that it was impossible for me to enlist their help. Additionally, there were too many gaps in their lists, and the necessary maps were not readily available.

Over the next 20 years, I kept trying to obtain the maps that would enable me to move this project forward. Because Zappa toured mainland Europe during the time of the Iron Curtain, the border lines needed to be correct in the tour atlas as many had been altered in the intervening period. I searched in countless antique shops for atlases from the 1970s or 1980s in Hamburg and Berlin, and with my friend Andrew Greenaway in London, but with no success.

During Zappanale (an annual open air music festival held in the former East Germany, featuring various bands performing Zappa music and more since 1990) I spoke with my Dutch friend and cartographer Luuk de Goede about this problem. He told me that it would be very risky to use maps for this atlas without the permission of the copyright holders. Furthermore, he felt no publisher could be persuaded to seek the necessary legal clearances.

Almost resigned to the probability that my project would never reach fruition, I spoke with Carola Trabert about my idea during the intermission of a Grandmothers concert in Hamburg's Nochtspeicher, when Klaus Kühner bumped into us. I had gotten to know Klaus from previous Zappanale festivals, and this conversation about my crazy vision of a tour atlas with detailed cartographic depictions of all concerts that Zappa had played since the foundation of the Mothers led to a breakthrough: not only was Carola a trained compositor with many years of experience, but Klaus was – besides being a qualified graphic designer and cartographer – an owner of the rights to the necessary maps. On this evening – November 11, 2014, a day I'll always remember – Carola, Klaus and I decided to grasp the nettle, take the bull by the horns and do the funky Alfonzo.

The next weeks and months consisted of working on the structure and layout of the book. The process was rather sluggish, because Carola lived in Göttingen 150 miles (250 km) away, which forced us to communicate every little detail via email. This three-way constellation turned out to be too cumbersome, so we decided to continue the project without Carola. (Carola, I thank you from the bottom of my heart for everything you did for me, for us, and for the eventual realization of this book. Without your inspiration and your contagious enthusiasm I would have never gotten this far. Thank you!)

Next, my soul mate, long time friend and brother from another mother, Andrew Greenaway, clambered onboard and offered to write a short but (even for insiders) informative discography; this sat fantastically alongside the map section of the book (on which Andrew has also helped).

Klaus and I then spent the next two years puzzling over the collected tour information and how best to insert it graphically into the maps of North America, Europe and the Pacific Rim. Klaus quickly and professionally modified the maps of Europe so that the borders were set to the time when the tours actually took place.

Over the past decades, I continuously cannibalized tour dates from books and internet sources. My association with the Arf Society (organizers of the Zappanale) led to me befriending some of Zappa's traveling companions, and a few of them gladly supported the completion of the tour lists. I would especially like to thank Robert Martin (who sang and played keyboards, sax and French horn for Frank between September 1981 and June 1988), who let me peep into his itineraries and readily agreed to write the book's foreword.

Thanks as well go to: Denny Walley, for stuffing up the cracks of the 1979 tour list; Arthur Barrow for spotting the moldy watermelons in our easter hay; Bob & Candy Zappa, Mark Pinske, Massimo Bassoli, Maury Baker, and the late Robert "Frog" Camarena, for intriguing background information; the members of our Little Houses Zappa Used To Live In Research Chat Group: Luc Peersman, Corné van Hooijdonk & Stanley Hope; Chris Opperman for services above and beyond the call of duty; and Guy Bickel, roadie from the second European and US tours of 1978, who very kindly handed me his original itineraries, including stage lay-out plans, passes and doo-dads of all sorts. Guy also shot the photo of Frank which can be seen below; it was taken at the Electric Ballroom, London, UK, at the end of August 1978, where the band rehearsed for the fall tour through Europe and North America's East Coast – the first to feature Ike Willis. Thank you very much, Guy: you are really a hammer!

I would also like to express my gratitude to: Andrew Greenaway and Klaus Kühner, my exceptional partners on this book; my family, Kerstin & Finja Zeuner (FZ!) and Annette Ernst; and my friends Dan Sefton & family, Mary Jayne & Stephen Chillemi, Dave Mitchell & Ngaio McKay, Jerry Outlaw & Deborah Serrano, Jon Singley & Barbara Rossi, Alex Pasut, Angel Tejeda & family, Reinhard Preuss, Eike Hagen, Marcel Koeslin and Christian Eckhardt.

And finally: thanks to Frank, without whom I would not have driven all of the above to distraction these past thirty odd years. YOUR music is the best!

Mick Zeuner
Hamburg, October 2018

The Authors

Mick Zeuner (*1966) – Zappologist, collector, merchant, globetrotter, multi-instrumentalist, executive producer of the Zappanale CD sets 2002–2005 & 2015, and father of a girl initialed FZ. Lives in Hamburg, Germany.

FZ shows attended

Apr 12, 1988	Germany	Berlin	Deutschlandhalle
Apr 24, 1988	Germany	Bremen	Stadthalle IV
May 06, 1988	Germany	Hamburg	CCH, Saal 1
Sep 19, 1992	Germany	Frankfurt	Alte Oper

DZ shows attended

Jun 02, 2006	UK	London	Royal Albert Hall
May 27, 2009	Germany	Hamburg	Große Freiheit 36
Nov 06, 2010	UK	London	Roundhouse
Nov 18, 2011	UK	Gateshead	The Sage
Oct 28, 2015	Denmark	Aarhus	Train
Jul 15, 2017	Germany	Bad Doberan	Zappanale #28

Klaus Kühner (*1958) – Cartographer, graphic designer, writer, artist, traveler, and Zappa fan since 1974. Lives in Hamburg, Portugal, and on life's trail.

FZ shows attended

Feb 23, 1978	Germany	Münster	Halle Münsterland
Mar 21, 1979	Germany	Eppelheim	Rhein-Neckar-Halle
Jun 25, 1980	Germany	Mannheim	Eisstadion
Jun 06, 1982	Germany	Mannheim	Rhein-Neckar-Stadion
May 06, 1988	Germany	Hamburg	CCH, Saal 1
Sep 23, 1992	Germany	Berlin	Philharmonie

DZ shows attended

May 27, 2009	Germany	Hamburg	Große Freiheit 36
Jul 15, 2017	Germany	Bad Doberan	Zappanale #28

Andrew Greenaway (*1958) – Husband, father, broadcaster, webmaster at www.idiotbastard.com, author of Zappa The Hard Way (Wymer Publishing, 2010), The Beatles ... The Easy Way (Wymer Publishing, 2014), Frank Talk: The Inside Stories Of Zappa's Other People (Wymer Publishing, 2017), FZ88 (Wymer Publishing, 2019) and contributor to 1001 Songs You Must Hear Before You Die (Octopus Books, 2010) and The Greatest Albums You'll Never Hear (Octopus Books, 2014). Lives in the Thames Delta, UK.

FZ shows attended

Feb 16, 1977	UK	London	Hammersmith Odeon
Jan 27, 1978	UK	London	Hammersmith Odeon
Feb 28, 1978	UK	London	Hammersmith Odeon
Feb 18, 1979	UK	London	Hammersmith Odeon (late show)
Jun 17, 1980	UK	London	Wembley Arena
Jun 19, 1982	UK	London	Hammersmith Odeon (late show)
Apr 18, 1988	UK	London	Wembley Arena

DZ shows attended

May 01, 1991	UK	London	The Marquee Club
Jul 07, 1993	UK	London	The Marquee Club
Jun 02, 2006	UK	London	Royal Albert Hall
Jun 04, 2006	Ireland	Dublin	Vicar Street
Sep 25, 2007	UK	London	Shepherd's Bush Empire
Jun 14, 2009	UK	London	Shepherd's Bush Empire
Jul 22, 2010	UK	Brighton	The Brighton Centre
July 24, 2010	UK	London	High Voltage Festival, Victoria Park
Nov 06, 2010	UK	London	The Roundhouse
Nov 10, 2012	UK	London	The Roundhouse
Nov 11, 2013	UK	London	Shepherd's Bush Empire
Oct 17, 2015	UK	London	Bush Hall
Oct 18, 2015	UK	London	Royal Festival Hall
Jul 15, 2017	Germany	Bad Doberan	Zappanale #28
Oct 10, 2017	UK	London	Royal Festival Hall
Oct 13, 2017	UK	Bexhill-On-Sea	De La Warr Pavilion

Statistics

Frank Zappa Tour Statistics – General data	
Total number of shows	app. 1800
Total number of venues	app. 800
Total number of tunes	app. 750
Total number of tours	50
Total number of countries	20
Total number of continents	4

Countries visited	
USA	app. 1250
Germany	123
Canada	90
France	65
United Kingdom	60
Italy	35
Denmark	27
Sweden	26
Netherlands	22
Australia	17
Austria	17
Belgium	17
Switzerland	15
Finland	9
Norway	9
Spain	9
Japan	4
Luxembourg	2
Yugoslavia	2
New Zealand	1

Shows per musician

		total shows played	%
1.	Roy Estrada	720	37.0
2.	Don Preston	633	32.6
3.	Jimmy Carl Black	618	31.8
4.	Bunk Gardner	552	28.4
5.	Ray Collins	499	25.7
6.	Ian Underwood	497	25.6
7.	Ray White	476	24.5
8.	Tommy Mars	453	23.3
9.	Ike Willis	398	20.5
10.	Ed Mann	388	20.0
11.	George Duke	367	18.9
12.	Robert Martin	345	17.7
	Scott Thunes	345	17.7
	Chad Wackerman	345	17.7
15.	Napoleon Murphy Brock	327	16.9
16.	Bruce Fowler	314	16.2
17.	Tom Fowler	293	15.1
18.	Terry Bozzio	287	14.8
19.	Jim "Motorhead" Sherwood	249	12.8
20.	Ruth Underwood	247	12.7
21.	Arthur Barrow	239	12.3
22.	Art Tripp	219	11.3
23.	Steve Vai	191	9.9
24.	Chester Thompson	176	9.1
	Peter Wolf	176	9.1
26.	Aynsley Dunbar	166	8.5
27.	Ralph Humphrey	164	8.4
28.	Patrick O'Hearn	163	8.4
29.	Vinnie Colaiuta	155	8.0
30.	Howard Kaylan	149	7.7

contd.

		total shows played	%
	Mark Volman	149	7.7
32.	Allan Zavod	133	6.8
33.	Jeff Simmons	131	6.7
34.	Denny Walley	130	6.7
35.	Walt Fowler	103	5.3
36.	Buzz Gardner	102	5.2
	André Lewis	102	5.2
38.	David Logeman	84	4.3
	Jean-Luc Ponty	84	4.3
40.	Adrian Belew	83	4.3
41.	Paul Carman	81	4.2
	Kurt McGettrick	81	4.2
	Mike Keneally	81	4.2
	Albert Wing	81	4.2
45.	Jim Pons	75	3.9
46.	Eddie Jobson	68	3.5
47.	Bob Harris #2	62	3.2
48.	Warren Cuccurullo	47	2.4
49.	Sal Marquez	45	2.3
50.	Captain Beefheart	36	1.9
	Tom Malone	36	1.9
52.	Earle Dumler	31	1.6
	Tony Duran	31	1.6
	Glenn Ferris	31	1.6
	Malcolm McNab	31	1.6
	Dave Parlato	31	1.6
57.	Jim Gordon	30	1.5
58.	Norma Jean Bell	28	1.4
	Bob Harris #1	28	1.4
60.	Gary Barone	23	1.2

contd.

		total shows played	%
	Bianca Odin	23	1.2
62.	Dweezil Zappa	12	0.6
63.	Billy Mundi	10	0.5
	James "Bird Legs" Youmans	10	0.5
65.	Max Bennett	9	0.5
66.	Don "Sugarcane" Harris	8	0.5
	Kin Vassy	8	0.5
68.	Mike Atlschul	7	0.4
	Jerry Kessler	7	0.4
	Jay Migliori	7	0.4
	Joanne McNab	7	0.4
	Charles Owens	7	0.4
	Tom Raney	7	0.4
	Ray Reed	7	0.4
	L. Shankar	7	0.4
	Ken Shroyer	7	0.4
77.	Lou Marini	5	0.3
	Don Pardo	5	0.3
79.	Mike Brecker	4	0.2
	Randy Brecker	4	0.2
	Dave Samuels	4	0.2
82.	Barry Leef	3	0.2
	Nigey Lennon	3	0.2

Note: For special guests who appeared during only one or two shows, see gig lists that follow.

Most-played songs

1.	City Of Tiny Lites	320
2.	Cosmik Debris	296
3.	Pound For A Brown	265
4.	Bobby Brown	244
5.	The Illinois Enema Bandit	233
6.	Montana	226
7.	Easy Meat	222
8.	The Meek Shall Inherit Nothing	208
9.	Dancin' Fool	205
10.	I Ain't Got No Heart	202
11.	Black Napkins	199
12.	Chunga's Revenge	194
13.	Why Does It Hurt When I Pee?	192
14.	Keep It Greasey	188
15.	Honey Don't You Want A Man Like Me?	187
16.	The Black Page	185
17.	Joe's Garage	183
18.	Camarillo Brillo	177
19.	Penguin In Bondage	175
20.	Bamboozled By Love	174
21.	King Kong	170
22.	The Torture Never Stops	159
23.	Dinah-Moe Humm	156
24.	Advance Romance	154
25.	Stinkfoot	150

Most-played venues		
1.	Palladium, New York, NY	25
2.	Hammersmith Odeon, London, UK	20
3.	Fillmore West, San Francisco, CA	18
	Fillmore East, New York, NY	18
5.	Auditorium Theatre, Chicago, IL	15
6.	Tower Theatre, Upper Darby, PA	13
7.	Boston Music Hall, Boston, MA	12
8.	Felt Forum, New York, NY	11
	Falkoner Teatret, Copenhagen, Denmark	11
	Berkeley Community Theater, Berkeley, CA	11

Countries by year								
Country	'66	'67	'68	'69	'70	'71	'72	'73
NORTH AMERICA								
Canada	'66	'67	'68	'69	'70	'71	'72	'73
United States	'66	'67	'68	'69	'70	'71	'72	'73
EUROPE								
Austria			'68		'70	'71		
Belgium				FZ	'70			'73
Czechoslovakia								
Denmark		'67	'68		'70	'71	'72	'73
Finland								'73
France			'68	'69	'70			'73
West Germany		'67	'68		'70	'71	'72	'73
Hungary								
Italy						'71		'73
Luxembourg								
Netherlands		'67	'68		'70	'71	'72	'73
Norway								'73
Spain								
Sweden		'67	'68		'70	'71		'73
Switzerland						'71		'73
United Kingdom		'67	'68	39	'70	'71	'72	'73
Yugoslavia								
PACIFIC								
Australia								'73
Japan								
New Zealand								

'74	'75	'76	'77	'78	'79	'80	'81	'82	'84	'88	'91	'92
'74	'75	'76	'77	'78		'80	'81		'84			
'74	'75	'76	'77	'78		'80	'81		'84	'88		
'74		'76		'78	'79	'80		'82	'84	'88		
'74		'76	'77	'78	'79	'80		'82	'84	'88		
											FZ	
'74		'76	'77	'78	'79	'80		'82		'88		
'74		'76	'77							'88		
'74		'76	'77	'78	'79	'80		'82	'84	'88		
'74		'76	'77	'78	'79	'80		'82	'84	'88		FZ
											FZ	
'74								'82	'84	'88		
								'82	'84			
'74		'76	'77	'78	'79	'80		'82	'84	'88		
'74		'76	'77		'79	'80		'82	'84	'88		
'74		'76			'79				'84	'88		
'74		'76	'77	'78	'79	'80		'82	'84	'88		
'74		'76		'78	'79	'80		'82		'88		
'74			'77	'78	'79	'80		'82	'84	'88		
	'75											
		'76										
		'76										
		'76										

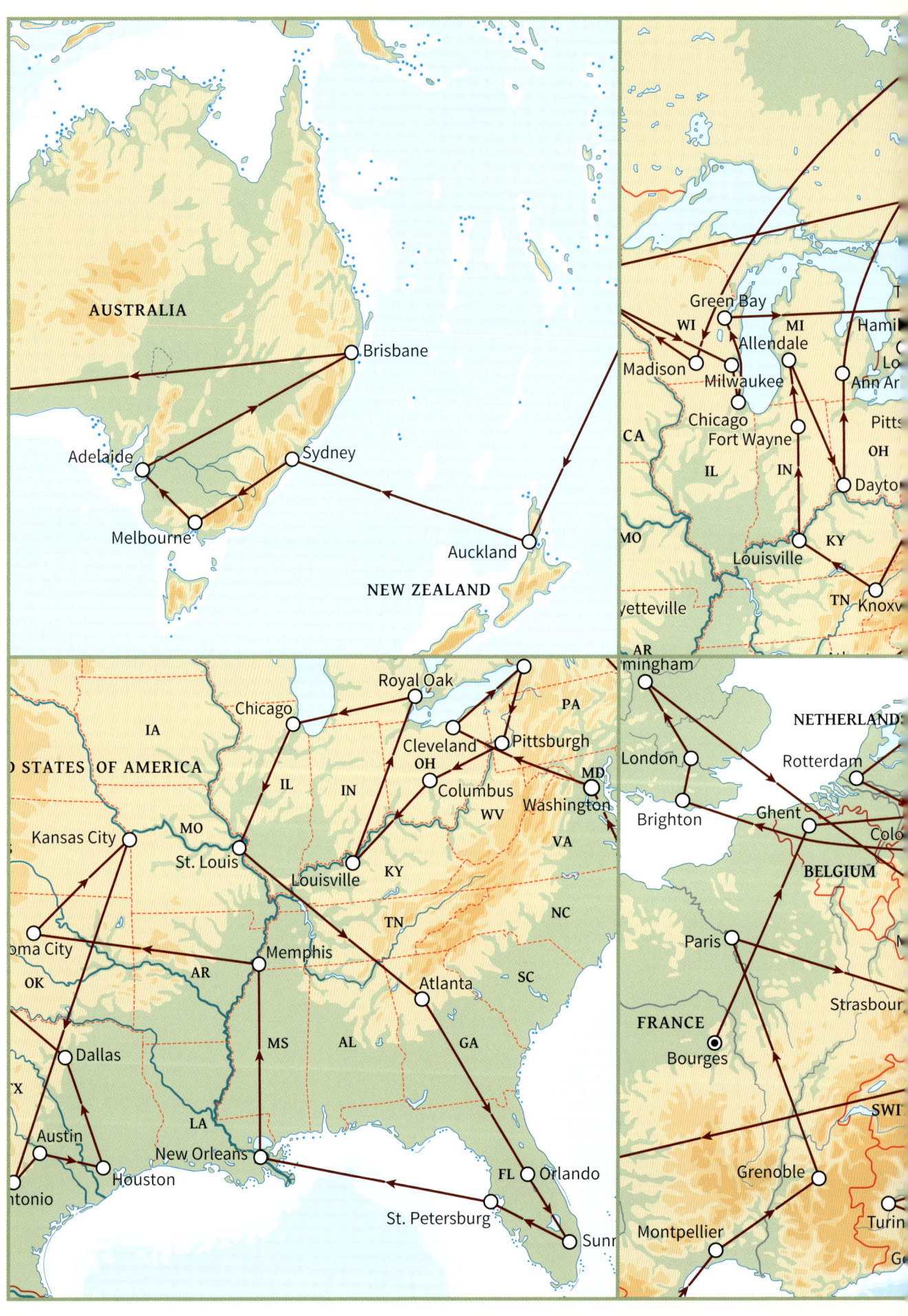

DA MAPZ

27

Zappa's Life Tour
1940–1993

Dates	#	Location
ca. 1940–1942	1	Park Heights Ave, Pikesville, Baltimore, MD
ca. 1942–1944	2	Edgewood Arsenal, Aberdeen, MD
ca. 1944–1945		Opa-locka, Miami-Dade County, FL
ca. 1945–1951	3	Pulaski Highway, Edgewood, MD
1951–1952	4	Monterey, CA
1952–1953	5	Pacific Grove, CA
1953–1954	6	257 W Oak Park Drive, Claremont, CA
1954–1955	7	El Cajon, CA (near San Diego)
1955–1956	8	Clairemont, San Diego, CA
1956		Lancaster, CA (in duplex close to center)
1956–1957	9	45438 Third Street East, Lancaster, CA
1957–1958	10	233 W Oak Park Drive, Claremont, CA
1958–1960	11	487 St Augustine Ave, Claremont, CA
1960	12	247 Brooks Ave, Claremont, CA
1960–1961	13	625 N Euclid Ave, Ontario, CA
1961–1964	14	314 W G Street, Ontario, CA (with **Kathryn J. "Kay" Sherman**)
1964–1965	15	8040 Archibald Ave, Cucamonga, CA (Studio Z)
1965	16	Formosa Ave, L.A., CA (for a few months)
1965–1966	17	1819 W Bellevue Ave, Echo Park, L.A., CA (Little house I used to live in)
1966–1968	18	8404 Kirkwood Drive, L.A., CA (with **Adelaide Gail Sloatman**)
1966–1967	19	Apartment 3-C, 180 Thompson Street, Greenwich Village, New York City, NY
1967–1968	20	54 Charles Street (near 7th Ave S), West Village, New York City, NY
May 05–Sep 05, 1968	21	2401 Laurel Canyon Blvd., L.A., CA (log cabin)
Sep 05, 1968–Dec 04, 1993	22	7885 Woodrow Wilson Drive, L.A., CA (UMRK)
Dec 1970–Apr 1971		56 Ladbroke Grove, London, UK (before, during and after 200 Motels)

North American Tours
1966

Frank Zappa guitar, vocals **Ray Collins** vocals, tambourine **Henry Vestine** guitar (Jan thru Mar) **Elliot Ingber** guitar (Mar thru Aug) **Del Casher** guitar (mid 1966) **Van Dyke Parks** keyboards (mid 1966) **Roy Estrada** bass, vocals **Jimmy Carl Black** drums

Jan 31– Feb 02+05	Los Angeles	CA	The Trip (feat. **Jim Guercio**?)
Feb 05	Los Angeles	CA	The Trip (feat. **Jim Guercio**?)
Feb/Mar		TX	10-day engagement (feat. **Jim Guercio**?)
Mar/Apr	Los Angeles	CA	
Apr 07–16	Waikiki	HI	Da Swamp
May	San Diego	CA	Jazzville
May 03 05	Los Angeles	CA	The Trip
May 06–26	Hayward	CA	Frenchy's
May 27–29	San Francisco	CA	Fillmore Auditorium
Jun 03+04	San Francisco	CA	Fillmore Auditorium
Jun 24+25	San Francisco	CA	Fillmore Auditorium
Jul	Bethesda	MD	"Kerby Scott Dance Party" WDCA-TV show
Jul	Washington	DC	Roundtable Restaurant, Georgetown
Jul 12	Windsor	Canada	"Swingin' Time" CKLW Channel 9 TV show
Jul	Warren	MI	Motor City Roller Rink
Jul 16	Southfield	MI	"Club 1270" WXYZ-TV Channel 7, Detroit
Jul	Dallas	TX	"Sump'n Else" WFAA-TV show
Jul 23	Los Angeles	CA	Danish Center "GUAMBO"
Aug 13	Los Angeles	CA	Shrine Exposition Hall "Son Of GUAMBO"*

Frank Zappa guitar, vocals **Ray Collins** vocals, tambourine **Don Preston** keyboards **Roy Estrada** bass, vocals **Jimmy Carl Black** drums **Billy Mundi** drums

Sep	Los Angeles	CA	Lindy Opera House
Sep 09	San Francisco	CA	Fillmore Auditorium
Sep 10	San Francisco	CA	Scottish Rites Temple
Sep 17	Los Angeles	CA	Shrine Exposition Hall (feat. **Del Casher**?)*

* feat. *9 unidentified musicians* on *trumpets (3), trombone, tuba, tympani (2) and French horns (2)*

Frank Zappa guitar, vocals **Ray Collins** vocals, tambourine **Jim Fielder** guitar **Bunk Gardner** woodwinds **Don Preston** keyboards **Roy Estrada** bass, vocals **Jimmy Carl Black** drums **Billy Mundi** drums

Sep 27– Oct 02	Los Angeles	CA	Whisky a Go Go – 2 shows (Sep 27–29, Oct 02) 3 shows (Sep 30, Oct 01)
Oct 23	Los Angeles	CA	Hullabaloo – *questionable*
Oct 29	Santa Barbara	CA	Earl Warren Showgrounds
Nov 07	Los Angeles	CA	Student Union Grand Ballroom, UCLA
Nov 23–26	New York	NY	Balloon Farm
Nov	New York	NY	Village Theater
Dec 02+03	New York	NY	Balloon Farm
Dec 04	Island Park	NY	Action House
Dec 09	East Lansing	MI	Student Union, Michigan State University
Dec 16+17	New York	NY	Balloon Farm
Dec 23–31	New York	NY	Balloon Farm

1st North American Tour
1967

Frank Zappa *guitar, vocals* **Ray Collins** *vocals, tambourine (thru June)*
Sandy Hurvitz *vocals (mid 1967)* **Jim Fielder** *guitar, bass (thru Feb)*
Bunk Gardner *woodwinds* **Jim "Motorhead" Sherwood** *baritone sax (from Sep on)*
Don Preston *keyboards* **Ian Underwood** *keyboards, woodwinds (from mid 1967 on)*
Roy Estrada *bass, vocals* **Jimmy Carl Black** *drums, trumpet, vocals*
Billy Mundi *drums*

Jan 07–21	Montreal	Canada	New Penelope
Jan	Los Angeles	CA	*questionable*
Feb 03+04	Los Angeles	CA	Lindy Opera House
Feb 14	New York	NY	Ballroom, Hilton Hotel
Feb 17–19	San Francisco	CA	Fillmore Auditorium
Feb	Sacramento	CA	
Mar 03–05	San Francisco	CA	Fillmore Auditorium
Mar 23–Apr 03			
	New York	NY	Garrick Theatre*
Apr	Baltimore	MD	University Of Maryland
Apr 06–19	New York	NY	Garrick Theatre
Apr 20–23	Boston	MA	Commonwealth Armory
Apr 24–May 01			
	New York	NY	Garrick Theatre
Apr 28	New York	NY	Infinite Poster
May 02–21	New York	NY	Cafe au Go Go*
May 20	New York	NY	Village Gate
May	Toronto	Canada	*questionable*
May 24–Sep 05			
	New York	NY	Garrick Theatre feat. **Jimi Hendrix** & **Mitch Mitchell** (July)**
Jun 28	New York	NY	Village Theater
Aug 13–16	College Park	MD	University of Maryland
Sep	Cincinnati	OH	
Sep	Chicago	IL	International Amphitheater – *questionable*
Sep	Detroit	MI	*questionable*
Sep	New York	NY	Town Hall
Sep	Miami	FL	*questionable*

* 2 shows weeknights, 3 shows weekends
** 2 shows Sun, Tue, Wed, Thu, 3 shows Fri, Sat

European Tour
1967

Frank Zappa *guitar, vocals* **Ray Collins** *vocals, tambourine*
Jim "Motorhead" Sherwood *baritone sax* **Bunk Gardner** *woodwinds*
Ian Underwood *keyboards, woodwinds* **Don Preston** *keyboards*
Roy Estrada *bass, vocals* **Jimmy Carl Black** *drums, trumpet* **Billy Mundi** *drums*

Sep 23	London	UK	Royal Albert Hall – with members of the **London Philharmonic Orchestra**
Sep 24	Amsterdam	Netherlands	Concertgebouw
Sep 25 or 26	Hamburg	Germany	
Sep 27	Copenhagen	Denmark	Falkoner Teatret
Sep 29	Gothenburg	Sweden	Konserthallen, Liseberg
Sep 30	Stockholm	Sweden	Konserthuset
Oct 01	Copenhagen	Denmark	Falkoner Teatret – 2 shows
Oct 02	Lund	Sweden	Olympen

CANADA
WA
OR
ID
MT
ND
MN
SD
WI
WY
NV
UT
NE
IA
Chicago
San Francisco
CA
CO
UNITED STATES OF AMERICA
IL
KS
MO
Pasadena
AZ
NM
OK
AR
MS
TX
LA
MEXICO

2nd North American Tour
1967

Frank Zappa *guitar, vocals* **Ray Collins** *vocals, tambourine* **Jim "Motorhead" Sherwood** *baritone sax* **Bunk Gardner** *woodwinds* **Ian Underwood** *keyboards, woodwinds* **Don Preston** *keyboards* **Roy Estrada** *bass, vocals* **Jimmy Carl Black** *drums, trumpet, vocals* **Billy Mundi** *drums*

Oct	New York	NY	Garrick Theatre – *questionable*
Oct 28	Rochester	NY	War Memorial Theater
Oct 31	New York	NY	Town Hall
Nov 03	Baltimore	MD	Eastern High School
Nov	Hamilton	NY	Colgate University – *questionable*
Nov	New Haven	CT	Yale University – *questionable*
Nov	Providence	RI	*questionable*
Nov 24	Boston	MA	Psychedelic Supermarket
Nov 25	Boston	MA	Psychedelic Supermarket
Dec 01	Detroit	MI	Ford Auditorium
Dec 02	Ann Arbor	MI	Fifth Dimension – 2 shows
Dec 03	Ann Arbor	MI	Fifth Dimension
Dec	Chicago	IL	International Amphitheater
Dec	Buffalo	NY	*questionable*
Dec 09	Pasadena	CA	Civic Auditorium
Dec 14	San Francisco	CA	Fillmore Auditorium
Dec 15	San Francisco	CA	Winterland
Dec 16	San Francisco	CA	Winterland
Dec 20	New York	NY	Mineola Theatre – 2 shows
Dec 22	New York	NY	Town Hall
Dec 23	New York	NY	Town Hall
Dec 26	Philadelphia	PA	Trauma
Dec 27	Philadelphia	PA	Trauma
Dec 28	Philadelphia	PA	Trauma
Dec 29	Philadelphia	PA	Trauma
Dec 30	Philadelphia	PA	Trauma
Dec 31	Philadelphia	PA	Trauma

CANADA
Vancouver
Seattle
WA
OR
ID
MT
ND
MN
SD
WI
WY
Farmington
Sacramento
Berkeley
San Francisco
NV
UT
NE
IA
Chicago
Monticello
Denver
CO
IL
IN
Fresno
CA
KS
MO
Louisvi
UNITED STATES OF AMERICA
Santa Barbara
San Ber'dino
Los Angeles
Torrance
Fullerton
Anaheim
AZ
OK
AR
San Diego
Phoenix
NM
Tucson
MS
TX
LA
MEXICO

1st North American Tour
1968

Frank Zappa guitar, vocals **Ray Collins** vocals, tambourine **Bunk Gardner** woodwinds **Jim "Motorhead" Sherwood** baritone sax **Ian Underwood** keyboards, woodwinds **Don Preston** keyboards **Roy Estrada** bass, vocals **Jimmy Carl Black** drums **Billy Mundi** drums (Jan 28) **Art Tripp** drums, percussion (from Feb 24)

Date	City	State	Venue
Jan 28	Toronto	Canada	Convocation Hall, University Of Ontario
Feb 01	Boston	MA	Boston Tea Party – questionable
Feb 18	Fall River	MA	Durfee Theatre
Feb 24	Hamilton	NY	Reid Athletic Center, Colgate University
Feb 25	Syracuse	NY	War Memorial Theater
Feb 29	New York	NY	The Statler Hilton
Mar	Boston	MA	Psychedelic Supermarket – questionable
Mar 15+16	Miami Beach	FL	Thee Image
Mar 17	Louisville	KY	Kaleidoscope – 2 shows
Mar 22–24	Philadelphia	PA	Electric Factory – 2 shows on Mar 24
Apr	Sacramento	CA	Memorial Auditorium – questionable
Apr 03	Fullerton	CA	questionable
Apr 09	Chicago	IL	International Amphitheater – questionable
Apr 10	Detroit	MI	Grande Ballroom – questionable
Apr	Philadelphia	PA	Arena – questionable
Apr 19+20	New York	NY	Fillmore East – 2 shows each night
Apr 26	Cincinnati	OH	Taft Auditorium – 2 shows
Apr 27	Chicago	IL	Coliseum
Apr 28	Detroit	MI	Grande Ballroom – 2 shows
May 03	Denver	CO	The Dog
May 04	Phoenix	AZ	Star Theatre
May	Berkeley	CA	Community Theater
May 10+11	Los Angeles	CA	Shrine Exposition Hall
May 17	Torrance	CA	Blue Law – questionable
May 18	Hallandale	FL	Gulfstream Race Track
May 19	Hallandale	FL	Wreck Bar – Jam session with **Jimi Hendrix, Noel Redding, Arthur Brown, John Lee Hooker, Jimmy Carl Black** & **FZ**
May	Miami Beach	FL	Thee Image – questionable
May 25	Fresno	CA	Selland Arena
May 29	Farmington	UT	Lagoon
May 31	San Bernardino	CA	Swing Auditorium
Jun 01	San Diego	CA	Community Concourse
Jun 03	Los Angeles	CA	Shrine Exposition Hall – questionable
Jun	Santa Barbara	CA	questionable
Jun 06	San Francisco	CA	Fillmore West
Jun 07+08	San Francisco	CA	Winterland
Jun	Seattle	WA	questionable
Jun	Vancouver	Canada	Agrodome – questionable
Jun	Phoenix	AZ	Veterans Memorial Coliseum – questionable
Jun 14	Tucson	AZ	
Jun 15	Anaheim	CA	Convention Center
Jun 21	Monticello	IN	Indiana Beach Ballroom
Jun 22	Sacramento	CA	Memorial Auditorium
Jun 25	Los Angeles	CA	*Steve Allen TV show* (broadcast date: Jul 24)
Jun 27	Los Angeles	CA	Wrigley Stadium
Jun 28–30	Los Angeles	CA	Cheetah

CANADA
UNITED STATES OF AMERICA
MEXICO
Vancouver
Seattle
WA
OR
ID
MT
ND
SD
MN
WI
WY
NE
IA
NV
UT
CO
CA
KS
MO
IL
AZ
NM
OK
AR
TX
MS
LA
Lake Geneva
Milwaukee
Elgin
Chicago
St. Louis
Pasadena
Santa Monica
Los Angeles
Phoenix
Dallas
Houston

2nd North American Tour
1968

Frank Zappa *guitar, vocals* **Ray Collins** *vocals, tambourine (until Aug 10)*
Bunk Gardner *woodwinds* **Jim "Motorhead" Sherwood** *baritone sax*
Ian Underwood *keyboards, woodwinds* **Don Preston** *keyboards*
Roy Estrada *bass, vocals* **Jimmy Carl Black** *drums* **Art Tripp** *drums, percussion*

Jul	Santa Monica	CA	*questionable*
Jul 14	Los Angeles	CA	Cheetah – "GUAMBO 2"
Jul 23	Los Angeles	CA	Whisky a Go Go
Jul 26+27	St. Louis	MO	
Aug 03	New York	NY	Wollman Rink, Central Park – 2 shows
Aug	Baltimore	MD	*questionable*
Aug 08	Providence	RI	Rhode Island Auditorium
Aug 09+10	Milwaukee	WI	The Scene
Aug	Lake Geneva	WI	Playboy Club – *questionable*
Aug 14–17	Chicago	IL	Kinetic Playground
Aug	Elgin	IL	*questionable*
Aug 24	Seattle	WA	Center Arena
Aug 25	Vancouver	Canada	Kerrisdale Arena
Aug	Phoenix	AZ	Celebrity Theater – *questionable*
Aug 30	Dallas	TX	Memorial Auditorium
Aug 31	Houston	TX	The Catacombs
Sep 09	Los Angeles	CA	*Joey Bishop TV Show*
Sep 15	Pasadena	CA	Rose Bowl
Sep 17	Los Angeles	CA	*questionable*

NORWAY
IRELAND
UNITED KINGDOM
DENMARK
Copenha
Hamburg
NETHERLANDS
Bremen
London
Amsterdam
Essen
BELGIUM
Frankfurt
Paris
W. GERMANY
FRANCE
Munich
SWITZERLAND
PORTUGAL
SPAIN
ITALY
MOROCCO
ALGERIA
TUNISIA

European Tour
1968

Frank Zappa *guitar, vocals* **Bunk Gardner** *woodwinds* **Jim "Motorhead" Sherwood** *baritone sax* **Ian Underwood** *keyboards, woodwinds* **Don Preston** *keyboards* **Roy Estrada** *bass, vocals* **Jimmy Carl Black** *drums* **Art Tripp** *drums, percussion*

Sep 27	Essen	Germany	Olympia-Kino am Wasserturm
Sep 28	Essen	Germany	Grugahalle
Sep 29	Frankfurt	Germany	Kongresshalle
Oct 01	Stockholm	Sweden	Konserthuset
Oct 03	Copenhagen	Denmark	Tivolis Koncertsal – 2 shows feat. **Don Cherry**
Oct 05	Hamburg	Germany	Musikhalle – 2 shows
Oct 06	Bremen	Germany	Beat Club – *TV show*
Oct 09	Munich	Germany	Deutsches Museum, Kongresssaal
Oct 10	Paris	France	*TV studio*
Oct 12	Vienna	Austria	Konzerthaus – 2 shows
Oct 16	Berlin	Germany	Sportpalast
Oct 20	Amsterdam	Netherlands	Concertgebouw – 2 shows
Oct 23	London	UK	Colour Me Pop – *TV show*
Oct 25	London	UK	Royal Festival Hall – 2 shows
Oct 26	Paris	France	Olympia

CANADA
WA
OR
ID
MT
ND
MN
SD
WI
WY
NV
NE
IA
Berkeley
UT
CO
IL
MO
CA
KS
UNITED STATES OF AMERICA
Los Angeles
Fullerton
AZ
OK
AR
NM
Phoenix
MS
TX
LA
MEXICO

3rd North American Tour
1968

Frank Zappa *guitar, vocals* **Lowell George** *guitar, vocals* **Jim "Motorhead" Sherwood** *baritone sax* **Buzz Gardner** *trumpet* **Bunk Gardner** *woodwinds* **Ian Underwood** *keyboards, woodwinds* **Don Preston** *keyboards* **Roy Estrada** *bass, vocals* **Jimmy Carl Black** *drums* **Art Tripp** *drums, percussion*

Nov 08	Fullerton	CA	Titan Gymnasium, Cal State College feat. **Wild Man Fischer**
Nov	Toronto	Canada	
Nov 29	Phoenix	AZ	Veterans Memorial Coliseum
Nov 30	Berkeley	CA	Community Theater
Dec 01	Berkeley	CA	Community Theater – *questionable*
Dec	Philadelphia	PA	Spectrum Theater
Dec 06	Los Angeles	CA	Shrine Exposition Hall
Dec 07	Los Angeles	CA	Shrine Exposition Hall

CANADA
Vancouver
Seattle
WA
OR
ID
MT
ND
MN
SD
WY
NE
IA
Appleton
WI
Chicago
IL
IN
San Francisco
CA
NV
UT
CO
UNITED STATES OF AMERICA
KS
MO
Los Angeles
Fullerton
San Diego
AZ
NM
OK
AR
MS
TX
LA
MEXICO

1st North American Tour
1969

Frank Zappa guitar, vocals **Lowell George** guitar, vocals until May 23
Jim "Motorhead" Sherwood baritone sax **Buzz Gardner** trumpet **Bunk Gardner**
woodwinds **Ian Underwood** keyboards, woodwinds **Don Preston** keyboards
Roy Estrada bass, vocals **Jimmy Carl Black** drums **Art Tripp** drums, percussion
(same as 2nd North American Tour 1968)

Jan 17	San Francisco	CA	Winterland
Jan 18	San Francisco	CA	Winterland
Jan 24	Los Angeles	CA	Shrine Exposition Hall
Jan 25	Los Angeles	CA	Shrine Exposition Hall
Jan 31	Boston	MA	War Memorial Auditorium feat. **Roland Kirk** and **Joe Habao Texidor**
Feb 07	Miami Beach	FL	Thee Image
Feb 08	Miami Beach	FL	Thee Image
Feb 11	Philadelphia	PA	Electric Factory
Feb 12	Philadelphia	PA	Electric Factory
Feb 13	New Haven	CT	Woolsey Hall, Yale University
Feb 14	New York	NY	McMillin Theater, Columbia University – 2 shows
Feb 15	Madison	NJ	Drew University
Feb 16	Stratford	CT	Ballroom – 2 shows
Feb 21	New York	NY	Fillmore East – 2 shows
Feb 22	New York	NY	Fillmore East – 2 shows feat. **Shirley Ann**
Feb 23	Toronto	Canada	Rock Pile – 2 shows
Feb 28	New York	NY	The Factory, Bronx
Mar 01	Westbury	NY	Westbury Music Fair
Mar 02	Philadelphia	PA	Arena
Mar	Allentown	PA	
Mar	Baltimore	MD	
Mar	Charlotte	NC	Park Center
Mar	Providence	RI	
Mar	Boston	MA	
Mar	Hartford	CT	Hartford Ballroom
Mar	Rochester	NY	War Memorial Theater
Mar	Montreal	Canada	
Mar	Toronto	Canada	Convocation Hall
Mar	Chicago	IL	
Mar 15	Fullerton	CA	Cal State University
Mar 22	Los Angeles	CA	Thee Experience
Mar 31	Los Angeles	CA	Aquarius Theatre feat. **Ray Collins**
Apr 12	San Diego	CA	Community Concourse feat. **Ray Collins**
Apr 18	Vancouver	Canada	Agrodome
Apr 19	Seattle	WA	Arena / Eagles Auditorium
Apr 25	New York	NY	Colden Center, Queens College, Flushing
Apr 26	Allentown	PA	Memorial Hall, Muhlenberg College
Apr 27	Baltimore	MD	Civic Center
Apr	Boston	MA	War Memorial Auditorium – *questionable*
May 02	Buffalo	NY	Clark Gymnasium, SUNY Buffalo feat. **Paul Simon** and **Art Garfunkel**
May 04	West Hartford	CT	Physical Education Center, University of Hartford
May 17	Detroit	MI	Ford Auditorium
May 19	Toronto	Canada	Massey Hall
May 23	Appleton	WI	Memorial Chapel, Lawrence University
May 24	Toronto	Canada	Rock Pile – 2 shows feat. **André**

NORWAY
IRELAND
DENMARK
Newcastle
Manchester
UNITED
KINGDOM
Birmingham
Bristol
London
NETHERLANDS
Portsmouth
Amougies
BELGIUM
W. GERMANY
Paris
FRANCE
SWITZERLAND
PORTUGAL
SPAIN
ITALY
MOROCCO
ALGERIA
TUNISIA

European Tours
1969

Frank Zappa *guitar, vocals* **Jim "Motorhead" Sherwood** *baritone sax*
Buzz Gardner *trumpet* **Bunk Gardner** *woodwinds* **Ian Underwood** *keyboards,*
woodwinds **Don Preston** *keyboards* **Roy Estrada** *bass, vocals*
Jimmy Carl Black *drums* **Art Tripp** *drums, percussion*

May 30	Birmingham	UK	Town Hall – 2 shows
May 31	Newcastle	UK	City Hall – 2 shows
Jun 01	Manchester	UK	Palace Theatre – 2 shows
Jun 03	Bristol	UK	Colston Hall – 2 shows
Jun 05	Portsmouth	UK	Guildhall – 2 shows
Jun 06	London	UK	Royal Albert Hall feat. **Kanzas J. Canzus,** **Dick Barber** and **Noel Redding**
Jun 07	Paris	France	Olympia – 2 shows
Oct 23	London	UK	Speakeasy – **FZ & Beefheart** jammed with **Juicy Lucy**
Oct 24	Amougies	Belgium	Actuel Festival*
Oct 25	Amougies	Belgium	Actuel Festival*
Oct 26	Amougies	Belgium	Actuel Festival*
Oct 27	Amougies	Belgium	Actuel Festival*
Oct 28	Amougies	Belgium	Actuel Festival*

* **FZ** was the MC and jammed with **Pink Floyd** (Oct 25), **Archie Shepp, Aynsley Dunbar's Retaliation, Caravan, Black Cat Bones, Blossom Toes, Sam Apple Pie,** and **Captain Beefheart & The Magic Band**

CANADA
WA
OR
ID
MT
ND
MN
Minneapolis
SD
WI
Fontana
WY
Highland Park
Chicago
IA
NE
NV
UT
Denver
CO
UNITED STATES OF AMERICA
IL
CA
KS
MO
TN
Los Angeles
AZ
OK
AR
NM
MS
TX
LA
Houston
MEXICO

2nd North American Tour
1969

Frank Zappa *guitar, vocals* **Jim "Motorhead" Sherwood** *baritone sax* **Buzz Gardner** *trumpet* **Bunk Gardner** *woodwinds* **Ian Underwood** *keyboards, woodwinds* **Don Preston** *keyboards* **Roy Estrada** *bass, vocals* **Jimmy Carl Black** *drums* **Art Tripp** *drums, percussion*

Jun 13	New York	NY	Fillmore East – 2 shows
Jun 14	New York	NY	Fillmore East – 2 shows
Jun 27	Denver	CO	Mile High Stadium
Jun 28	Charlotte	NC	Coliseum feat. **Roland Kirk** and **Duke Elligton** (?)
Jun 29	Miami	FL	Jai Alai Fronton feat. **Roland Kirk** and **Joe Habao Texidor** (?)
Jul 03	Houston	TX	The Catacombs
Jul 05	Newport	RI	Festival Field feat. **Miles Davis** (?)
Jul 08	Boston	MA	The Ark
Jul 11	Philadelphia	PA	Spectrum Theater
Jul 12	Laurel	MD	Laurel Race Track
Jul 13	Minneapolis	MN	Tyrone Guthrie Theater
Aug 01	Chicago	IL	Aragon Ballroom
Aug 02	New York	NY	Wollman Rink, Central Park – 2 shows feat. **Maryanne**
Aug 03	Atlantic City	NJ	Atlantic City Race Track
Aug 06	Highland Park	IL	Ravinia Outdoor Music Center
Aug 08	Framingham	MA	Carousel Theatre
Aug 09	Fontana	WI	Majestic Hills Ski Resort
Aug 10	Warrensville Heights	OH	Musicarnival
Aug 13	London	Canada	Wonderland Gardens
Aug 15	Ottawa	Canada	National Arts Center – 2 shows
Aug 16	Montreal	Canada	Canada Bandshell, Man and His World – 2 shows
Aug 17	Montreal	Canada	Canada Bandshell, Man and His World – 2 shows
Aug 18	Montreal	Canada	Canada Bandshell, Man and His World
Aug 19	Ottawa	Canada	*CJOH-TV Show*
Sep 24	Los Angeles	CA	Thee Experience
Nov 28	Los Angeles	CA	Thee Experience
Nov 29	Los Angeles	CA	Thee Experience

CANADA
WA
OR
ID
MT
ND
MN
WY
SD
WI
NV
UT
CO
NE
IA
IL
KS
MO
CA
AZ
NM
OK
AR
TX
LA
MS
UNITED STATES OF AMERICA
MEXICO
Berkeley
El Monte
Los Angeles
San Diego
San Antonio
Minneapolis
Appleton
Madison
Beloit
Chicago

1st North American Tour
1970

Frank Zappa guitar **Ian Underwood** keyboards, alto saxophone **Max Bennett** bass
Ed Greene drums

Feb 08	San Diego	CA	Sports Arena
Feb	Los Angeles	CA	Thee Experience – questionable

Frank Zappa guitar, vocals **Don "Sugarcane" Harris** violin, keyboards, vocals
Ian Underwood keyboards, alto saxophone **Max Bennett** bass
Aynsley Dunbar drums

Mar 07	Los Angeles	CA	Olympic Auditorium
Mar	Los Angeles	CA	UCLA – questionable
Mar	Los Angeles	CA	Ash Grove – questionable
Mar 20	Los Angeles	CA	Hollywood Palladium

Frank Zappa guitar, vocals **Ray Collins** vocals **Jim "Motorhead" Sherwood**
baritone saxophone **Ian Underwood** alto saxophone **Don Preston** keyboards
Jeff Simmons bass, vocals **Aynsley Dunbar** drums **Billy Mundi** drums

Apr 19	Berkeley	CA	Community Theater
Apr	El Monte	CA	Legion Stadium – questionable
Apr	Fort Lauderdale	FL	Auditorium – questionable
Apr	Miami	FL	questionable
Apr	Minneapolis	MN	questionable
Apr	Madison	WI	questionable
Apr	Beloit	WI	questionable
May 05	Appleton	WI	Cinderella Ballroom
May 06	Chicago	IL	Auditorium Theater – 2 shows
May 07 or 11	Cincinnati	OH	
May 08	New York	NY	Fillmore East – 2 shows
May 09	New York	NY	Fillmore East – 2 shows
May 10	Philadelphia	PA	Academy Of Music
May 15	Los Angeles	CA	Pauley Pavilion, UCLA feat. **George Duke** and members of the **Los Angeles Philharmonic Orchestra** conducted by **Zubin Metha**

Frank Zappa guitar, vocals **Mark Volman** vocals, guitar **Howard Kaylan** vocals
Ian Underwood keyboards, alto saxophone **George Duke** keyboards, trombone
Jeff Simmons bass, vocals **Aynsley Dunbar** drums

Jun 12	San Antonio	TX	Municipal Auditorium
Jun 13	Atlanta	GA	Atlanta Stadium

NORWAY
IRELAND
UNITED KINGDOM
DENMAR
NETHERLANDS
London
Shepton Mallet
Amsterdam
Uddel
BELGIUM
W. GERMANY
LUX.
FRANCE
SWITZERLAND
AU
Valbonne
PORTUGAL
SPAIN
ITALY
MOROCCO
ALGERIA
TUNISIA

1st European Tour
1970

Frank Zappa guitar, vocals **Mark Volman** vocals, guitar **Howard Kaylan** vocals
Ian Underwood keyboards, alto saxophone **George Duke** keyboards, trombone
Jeff Simmons bass, vocals **Aynsley Dunbar** drums

Jun 18	Uddel	Netherlands	Piknik – *VPRO TV*
Jun 19	Amsterdam	Netherlands	Paradiso – unscheduled gig after closing – according to an eyewitness, **FZ** did NOT play
Jun 20	London	UK	Speakeasy
Jun 28	Shepton Mallet	UK	Bath Festival
Jul 25	Valbonne	France	Riviera Festival

Edmonton
Calgary
Vancouver
Seattle
WA
Spokane
CANADA
Portland
Eugene
OR
MT
ND
MN
ID
SD
Minneapolis
WI
Appleton
Lake Geneva
Highlan
Park
Beloit
WY
IA
Chicago
San Rafael
NV
San Francisco
UT
NE
IL
Indianapol
CO
UNITED STATES OF AMERICA
CA
KS
MO
Santa Monica
AZ
OK
San Diego
NM
AR
MS
TX
LA
San Antonio
MEXICO

2nd North American Tour
1970

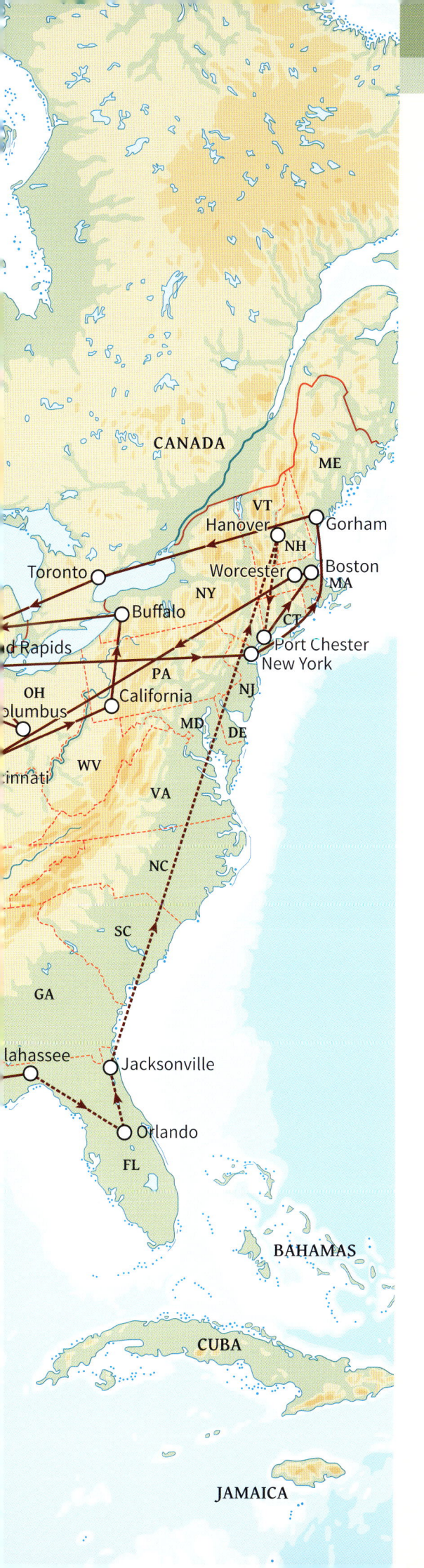

Frank Zappa guitar, vocals **Mark Volman** vocals, guitar **Howard Kaylan** vocals
Ian Underwood keyboards, alto saxophone **George Duke** keyboards, trombone
Jeff Simmons bass, vocals **Aynsley Dunbar** drums

Jul 01	Highland Park	IL	Ravinia Outdoor Music Center
Jul 03	Indianapolis	IN	Middlearth
Jul 04	Indianapolis	IN	Middlearth
Jul 05	Minneapolis	MN	Tyrone Guthrie Theater – 2 shows
Aug 21	Santa Monica	CA	Civic Auditorium
Sep	Calgary	Canada	Jubilee Auditorium
Sep 17	Spokane	WA	Coliseum
Sep 18	Edmonton	Canada	Kinsmen Field House
Sep 19	Vancouver	Canada	Coliseum
Sep 20	Seattle	WA	Moore Theater – 2 shows
Sep 22	Portland	OR	Pamplin Sports Center
Sep	Eugene	OR	questionable
Sep 25	San Rafael	CA	Pepperland
Sep 26	San Rafael	CA	Pepperland
Oct 04	San Diego	CA	Peterson Gym, San Diego State College
Oct 08	San Antonio	TX	Memorial Center, Trinity University
Oct 09	Tallahassee	FL	Tully Gymnasium, Florida State University
Oct	Orlando	FL	Sports Stadium
Oct	Jacksonville	FL	Auditorium
Oct	Hanover	NH	Dartmouth College
Oct 16	Port Chester	NY	Capitol Theatre
Oct 17	Port Chester	NY	Capitol Theatre
Oct 18	Boston	MA	Boston Tea Party – 2 shows
Oct 19	Worcester	MA	Clark University
Oct 21	Cincinnati	OH	Music Hall
Oct 22	California	PA	Hamer Hall, California State College
Oct 23	Buffalo	NY	Kleinhans Music Hall
Oct 24	Beloit	WI	Fieldhouse, Beloit College
Oct 25	Minneapolis	MN	Depot – 2 shows
Oct	Appleton	WI	Cinderella Ballroom
Oct	Lake Geneva	WI	
Nov 05	San Francisco	CA	Fillmore West
Nov 06	San Francisco	CA	Fillmore West
Nov 07	San Francisco	CA	Fillmore West
Nov 13	New York	NY	Fillmore East – 2 shows feat. **Joni Mitchell** (late show)
Nov 14	New York	NY	Fillmore East – 2 shows feat. **Grace Slick**
Nov 15	Gorham	ME	University Of Maine
Nov 18	Toronto	Canada	Massey Hall
Nov 19	Grand Rapids	MI	Fountain Street Church – 2 shows
Nov 20	Columbus	OH	Veterans Memorial Auditorium – 2 shows (?)
Nov 21	Chicago	IL	Auditorium Theatre – 2 shows (?)

NORWAY
IRELAND
Manchester
Liverpool
UNITED
KINGDOM
DENMAR
NETHERLANDS
Amsterdam
Rotterdam
London
Hambu
Düsseldorf
Brussels
BELGIUM
W. GERMANY
LUX.
Frankfurt
Paris
FRANCE
Munich
SWITZERLAND
PORTUGAL
SPAIN
ITALY
MOROCCO
ALGERIA
TUNISIA

2nd European Tour
1970

Frank Zappa *guitar, vocals* **Mark Volman** *vocals, guitar* **Howard Kaylan** *vocals*
Ian Underwood *keyboards, alto saxophone* **George Duke** *keyboards, trombone*
Jeff Simmons *bass, vocals* **Aynsley Dunbar** *drums*

Nov 26	Liverpool	UK	Mountford Hall
Nov 27	Manchester	UK	Free Trade Hall
Nov 29	London	UK	Coliseum – 2 shows feat. **Stephen Stills** (late show)
Dec 01	Stockholm	Sweden	Konserthuset
Dec 02	Copenhagen	Denmark	K.B.-Hallen
Dec 04	Hamburg	Germany	Musikhalle
Dec 05	Frankfurt	Germany	Kongresshalle
Dec 06	Amsterdam	Netherlands	Concertgebouw – 2 shows
Dec 08	Düsseldorf	Germany	Rheinhalle
Dec 10	Rotterdam	Netherlands	De Doelen
Dec 12	Vienna	Austria	Konzerthaus
Dec 13	Munich	Germany	Circus Krone
Dec 15	Paris	France	Palais Gaumont feat. **Jean-Luc Ponty**
Dec 16	Brussels	Belgium	Paleis voor Schone Kunsten

Edmonton
Vancouver
CANADA
Winnipeg
WA
OR
ID
MT
ND
MN
WI
Madison
SD
WY
NV
UT
NE
IA
Chicago
IL
CA
CO
UNITED STATES OF AMERICA
KS
MO
Claremont
AZ
NM
OK
AR
TN
MS
TX
LA
MEXICO

1st North American Tour
1971

Frank Zappa *guitar, vocals* **Mark Volman** *vocals, guitar* **Howard Kaylan** *vocals*
Ian Underwood *keyboards, alto saxophone* **Bob Harris #1** *keyboards*
Jim Pons *bass, vocals* **Aynsley Dunbar** *drums*

May 18	Claremont	CA	Bridges Auditorium, Pomona College
May 21	Chicago	IL	Auditorium Theatre – 2 shows
May 22	Delaware	OH	Selby Field, Ohio Wesleyan University
May 23	Columbus	OH	Ohio Theater
May 25	Detroit	MI	Olympia Stadium
May 27	Madison	WI	Field House, University Of Wisconsin
May 29	Rochester	MI	Baldwin Pavilion, Oakland University
May 30	Cleveland	OH	Public Hall
Jun 01	Scranton	PA	Watres Armory
Jun 02	Pittsburgh	PA	Civic Arena
Jun 03	Harrisburg	PA	State Farm Show Arena
Jun 05	New York	NY	Fillmore East – 2 shows feat. **Don Preston** (both shows)
Jun 06	New York	NY	Fillmore East – 2 shows feat. **Don Preston** (both shows), **John Lennon** and **Yoko Ono** (late show)
Jun 30	Boston	MA	Fenway Theater – 2 shows
Jul 02	Quebec	Canada	Le Colisee
Jul 03	Ottawa	Canada	Civic Center Arena
Jul 04	Montreal	Canada	Centre Paul Sauve
Jul 05	Montreal	Canada	CHOM-FM Studios *radio broadcast*
Jul 08	Winnipeg	Canada	Arena
Jul 09	Edmonton	Canada	Kinsmen Field House
Jul 10	Vancouver	Canada	Agrodome

CANADA
UNITED STATES OF AMERICA
MEXICO
Seattle
WA
Spokane
Portland
OR
ID
MT
ND
MN
SD
WY
Wi
Milwaukee
Eureka
NV
NE
IA
Sacramento
Berkeley
UT
Denver
CO
Indianapo
IL
IN
CA
MO
KS
Kansas City
St. Louis
Los Angeles
AZ
NM
OK
AR
MS
TX
LA

2nd North American Tour
1971

Frank Zappa *guitar, vocals* **Mark Volman** *vocals, guitar* **Howard Kaylan** *vocals*
Ian Underwood *keyboards, alto saxophone* **Don Preston** *keyboards* **Jim Pons**
bass, vocals **Aynsley Dunbar** *drums*

Aug 07	Los Angeles	CA	Pauley Pavilion, UCLA feat. **Jimmy Carl Black**
Aug 25	Berkeley	CA	Community Theater feat. **Nigey Lennon**
Aug 27	Seattle	WA	Paramount Northwest Theatre – 2 shows (?) feat. **Nigey Lennon**
Aug 28	Portland	OR	Memorial Coliseum
Aug 29	Spokane	WA	Kennedy Pavillion, Gonzaga University feat. **Nigey Lennon**
Oct 01	Sacramento	CA	Memorial Auditorium
Oct 02	Eureka	CA	Municipal Auditorium
Oct 04	Virginia Beach	VA	Minidome Civic Auditorium – 2 shows
Oct 06	Boston	MA	Music Hall – 2 shows
Oct 08	New Haven	CT	Arena feat. **George Duke**
Oct 09	Northampton	MA	John M. Greene Hall, Smith College
Oct 11	New York	NY	Carnegie Hall – 2 shows
Oct 13	Toronto	Canada	Massey Hall
Oct 15	Providence	RI	Loew's State Theater
Oct 16	Stony Brook	NY	Stony Brook Gym, SUNY – 2 shows
Oct 17	Baltimore	MD	Lyric Theatre – 2 shows
Oct 19	Indianapolis	IN	Coliseum
Oct 20	Milwaukee	WI	Milwaukee Arena
Oct 21	St. Louis	MO	Fox Theatre
Oct 23	Kansas City	MO	Cowtown Ballroom – 2 shows
Oct 24	Denver	CO	Arena, University of Denver

NORWAY
IRELAND
UNITED KINGDOM
London
Aarhus
DENMARK
Odense
NETHERLANDS
Hamburg
Rotterdam
BELGIUM
Düsseldorf
W. GERMANY
Frankfurt
FRANCE
Munich
SWITZERLAND
Montreux
Milan
PORTUGAL
SPAIN
ITALY
MOROCCO
ALGERIA
TUNISIA

European Tour
1971

Frank Zappa *guitar, vocals* **Mark Volman** *vocals, guitar* **Howard Kaylan** *vocals*
Ian Underwood *keyboards, alto saxophone* **Don Preston** *keyboards*
Jim Pons *bass, vocals* **Aynsley Dunbar** *drums*

Nov 19	Stockholm	Sweden	Folkets Hus – 2 shows
Nov 20	Aarhus	Denmark	
Nov 21	Copenhagen	Denmark	K.B. Hallen – 2 shows
Nov 22	Odense	Denmark	
Nov 23	Düsseldorf	Germany	Rheinhalle
Nov 24	Berlin	Germany	Deutschlandhalle
Nov 25	Berlin	Germany	Deutschlandhalle
Nov 26	Hamburg	Germany	Musikhalle
Nov 27	Rotterdam	Netherlands	The Ahoy
Nov 28	Frankfurt	Germany	Jahrhunderthalle – 2 shows
Nov 29	Munich	Germany	Circus Krone
Dec 02	Vienna	Austria	Konzerthaus
Dec 03	Milan	Italy	
Dec 04	Montreux	Switzerland	Casino – venue burned down that night
Dec 10	London	UK	Rainbow Theatre – **FZ** was pushed from the stage; the planned second show went ahead with just the support band, Cochise

EUROPE

UNITED KINGDOM — London
NETHERLANDS — The Hague
BELGIUM
FRANCE
LUX

CANADA

WA, OR, ID, MT, ND, MN, WI, SD, WY, NE, IA, IL, NV, UT, CO, KS, MO, CA, AZ, NM, OK, AR, MS, TX, LA

UNITED STATES OF AMERICA

Los Angeles

MEXICO

1st North American & European Tour
1972

Frank Zappa guitar, vocals **Tony Duran** guitar **Malcolm McNab** trumpet
Sal Marquez trumpet **Tom Malone** tuba, trumpet **Jay Migliori** saxophone
Ray Reed saxophone **Charles Owens** saxophone **Mike Altschul** piccolo,
bass clarinet **Earle Dumler** oboe, sarrusophone **Ken Shroyer** trombone
Glenn Ferris trombone **Bruce Fowler** trombone **Jerry Kessler** cello
Joanne McNab bassoon **Ian Underwood** keyboards **Dave Parlato** bass
Ruth Underwood percussion **Tom Raney** percussion **Jim Gordon** drums

Sep 10	Los Angeles	CA	Hollywood Bowl
Sep 15	Berlin	Germany	Deutschlandhalle
Sep 16	London	UK	Oval Cricket Ground
Sep 17	The Hague	Netherlands	Houtrust Hallen
Sep 22	New York	NY	Felt Forum
Sep 23	New York	NY	Felt Forum
Sep 24	Boston	MA	Music Hall

CANADA
Vancouver
Seattle
WA
Portland
OR
ID
MT
ND
MN
SD
WI
WY
IA
NV
UT
NE
UNITED STATES OF AMERICA
Lincoln
IL
San Francisco
CA
CO
KS
Kansas City
MO
Wichita
AZ
NM
OK
AR
MS
TX
LA
MEXICO

2nd North American Tour
1972

Frank Zappa *guitar, vocals* **Tony Duran** *guitar* **Malcolm McNab** *trumpet*
Gary Barone *trumpet (substituted by* **Charles Lloyd** *flute on Nov 05)*
Tom Malone *tuba, trumpet, trombone, saxophone* **Earle Dumler** *oboe, saxophone, sarrusophone* **Glenn Ferris** *trombone* **Bruce Fowler** *trombone*
Dave Parlato *bass* **Jim Gordon** *drums (substituted by* **Maury Baker** *on Nov 05)*

Oct 27	Montreal	Canada	Forum
Oct 28	Syracuse	NY	Onondaga County War Memorial Theater
Oct 29	Binghamton	NY	Men's Gym, Harpur College
Oct 31	Passaic	NJ	Capitol Theatre – 2 shows
Nov 01	Waterbury	CT	Palace Theatre
Nov 03	Richmond	VA	Mosque – 2 shows
Nov 04	Charlotte	NC	Park Center Arena
Nov 05	Columbia	SC	Township Auditorium feat. **Maury Baker & Charles Lloyd**
Nov 07	Commack	NY	Long Island Arena
Nov 10	Philadelphia	PA	Irvine Auditorium, University Of Pennsylvania – 2 shows
Nov 11	Washington	DC	DAR Constitution Hall – 2 shows
Nov 12	Providence	RI	Palace Theatre
Nov 30	Wichita	KS	Century II
Dec 02	Kansas City	MO	Cowtown Ballroom – 2 shows
Dec 03	Lincoln	NE	Pershing Auditorium
Dec 08	Vancouver	Canada	Agrodome
Dec 09	Portland	OR	Paramount Northwest Theatre – 2 shows
Dec 10	Seattle	WA	Paramount Northwest Theatre
Dec 15	San Francisco	CA	Winterland

CANADA
WA
OR
ID
MT
ND
MN
SD
WY
NV
UT
CO
NE
IA
IL
UNITED STATES OF AMERICA
CA
KS
MO
AZ
NM
OK
AR
MS
TX
LA
MEXICO
Appleton
WI
Milwaukee
Chicago
Indianapolis
San Francisco
Fresno
Los Angeles
San Diego
Phoenix
Tucson
Oklahoma City
Memphis
Arlington
Austin
Houston

1st North American Tour
1973

Frank Zappa guitar, vocals **Jean-Luc Ponty** violin **Sal Marquez** trumpet, vocals (from Mar 24) **Kin Vassy** vocals (Apr 07 thru May 01) **George Duke** keyboards, vocals **Ian Underwood** woodwinds, synthesizer **Bruce Fowler** trombone **Tom Fowler** bass **Ruth Underwood** percussion **Ralph Humphrey** drums

Feb 23	Fayetteville	NC	Cumberland County Auditorium
Feb 24	Durham	NC	Cameron Stadium, Duke University
Feb 26	Atlanta	GA	Municipal Auditorium
Feb 27	Athens	GA	Stegeman Coliseum, University of Georgia
Feb 28	Macon	GA	Macon Coliseum
Mar 02	Tampa	FL	Curtis Hixon Hall
Mar 03	Hollywood	FL	Sportatorium
Mar 04	Daytona Beach	FL	Peabody Auditorium – 2 shows
Mar 05	Dania	FL	Pirate's World
Mar 06	Memphis	TN	Ellis Auditorium
Mar 07	Columbus	OH	Veterans Memorial Auditorium
Mar 09	Oklahoma City	OK	Civic Center Music Hall
Mar 10	Austin	TX	Armadillo World Headquarters – 2 shows
Mar 11	Arlington	TX	Texas Hall Auditorium
Mar 12	Houston	TX	Music Hall
Mar 23	Los Angeles	CA	Hollywood Palladium feat. **Ricky Lancelotti**
Mar 24	San Diego	CA	Sports Arena feat. **Don Preston**
Mar	Fresno	CA	Selland Arena
Mar 30	San Francisco	CA	Winterland
Mar 31	San Francisco	CA	Winterland
Apr 07	Phoenix	AZ	Celebrity Theatre – 2 shows
Apr 08	Tucson	AZ	McKale Center, University Of Arizona
Apr 27	Princeton	NJ	Dillon Gymnasium, Princeton University
Apr 28	Philadelphia	PA	Spectrum Theater
Apr 29	Lancaster	PA	Franklin + Marshall College or
	State College	PA	Rec Hall, Penn State University
May 01	Kent	OH	Memorial Gymnasium, Kent State University
May 02	Indianapolis	IN	Coliseum
May 03?	Appleton	WI	Lawrence University Chapel
May 04	Toronto	Canada	Maple Leaf Gardens
May 05	Rochester	NY	War Memorial Auditorium
May 06	Pittsburgh	PA	Syria Mosque
May 08	Boston	MA	Music Hall
May 09	Passaic	NJ	Capitol Theatre
May 11	Milwaukee	WI	Milwaukee Arena
May 12	Detroit	MI	Cobo Hall
May 13	Cincinnati	OH	Music Hall
May 16	Chicago	IL	Auditorium Theatre
May 17	Albany	NY	Palace Theatre or
	Hempstead	NY	Hofstra University
May 18	Uniondale	NY	Nassau Coliseum
May 19	Annapolis	MD	Great McGonigle's Seaside Park
May 20	Providence	RI	Civic Center
May 21?	Quebec	Canada	Hilton Hotel – *questionable*

MONGOLIA

N. KOREA

S. KOREA

JAPAN
Kyoto
Osaka
Tokyo

CHINA

INDIA
BANGLA-
DESH
BURMA
N. VIETNAM
LAOS
THAI-
LAND
S. VIETNAM
CAMBODIA

TAIWAN

PHILIPPINES

BRUNEI
MALAYSIA

INDONESIA

PAPUA NEW GUINEA

AUSTRALIA

Brisbane
Adelaide
Sydney
Melbourne

NEW ZEALAND

Pacific Tour
1973

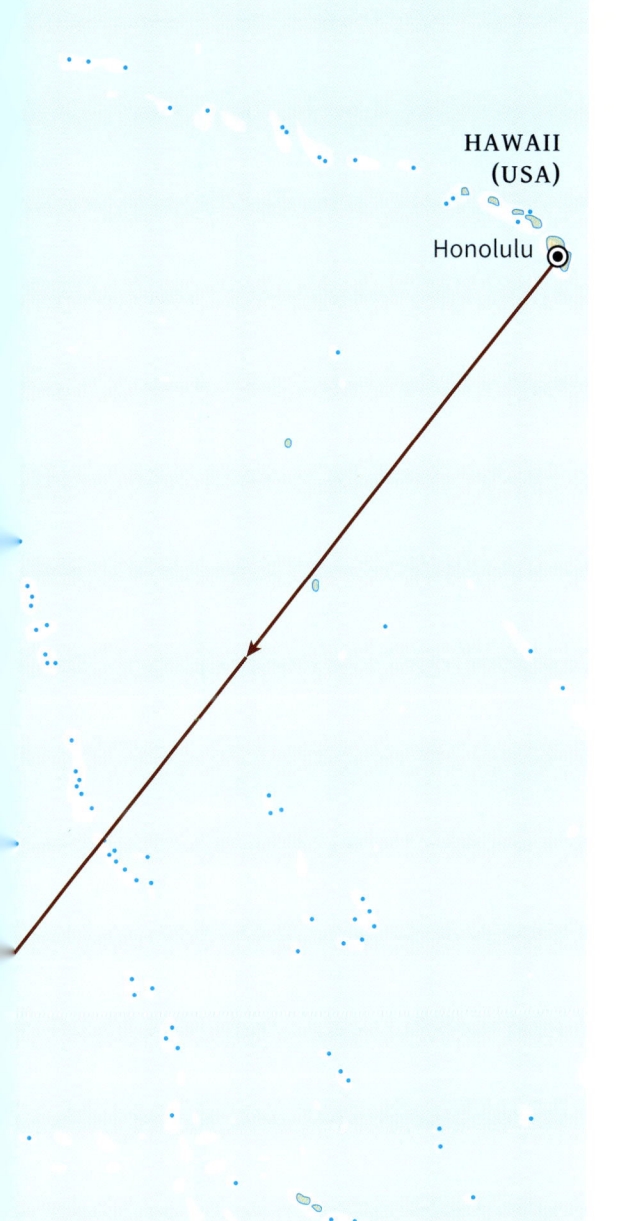

Frank Zappa *guitar, vocals* **Jean-Luc Ponty** *violin* **George Duke** *keyboards, vocals*
Ian Underwood *woodwinds* **Bruce Fowler** *trombone* **Tom Fowler** *bass*
Ruth Underwood *percussion* **Ralph Humphrey** *drums*

Jun 15	Honolulu	HI	Civic Center
Jun 21	Brisbane	Australia	Festival Hall
Jun 24	Sydney	Australia	Hordern Pavilion
Jun 25	Sydney	Australia	Hordern Pavilion
Jun 26	Sydney	Australia	Hordern Pavilion feat. **Barry Leef**
Jun 28	Melbourne	Australia	Festival Hall
Jun 29	Melbourne	Australia	Festival Hall feat. **Barry Leef**
Jul 01	Melbourne	Australia	Festival Hall
Jul 04	Adelaide	Australia	Apollo Stadium
Jul 08	Sydney	Australia	Hordern Pavilion feat. **Barry Leef**

NORWAY
Sandvik

IRELAND

UNITED KINGDOM
Liverpool
Birmingham
London

NETHERLANDS
Amsterdam
Brussels
BELGIUM
LUX.
Paris
FRANCE

DENMARK

W. GERMANY
Cologne
Frankfurt
Offenbach
Freiburg
Munich
Zurich
SWITZERLAND

PORTUGAL
SPAIN

Antibes
Bologna
Verona
ITALY
Rome

MOROCCO
ALGERIA
TUNISIA

European Tour
1973

Frank Zappa *guitar, vocals* **Jean-Luc Ponty** *violin* **George Duke** *keyboards, vocals*
Ian Underwood *woodwinds, keyboards* **Bruce Fowler** *trombone* **Tom Fowler** *bass*
Ruth Underwood *percussion* **Ralph Humphrey** *drums*

Aug 18	Copenhagen	Denmark	K.B. Hallen
Aug 19	Gothenburg	Sweden	Konserthallen Liseberg
Aug 21	Stockholm	Sweden	Sollidenscenen, Skansen
Aug 23	Helsinki	Finland	Finlandia-talo – 2 shows
Aug 26	Sandvika	Norway	Kalvoya Festivalen
Aug 28	Freiburg	Germany	Stadthalle
Aug 29	Antibes	France	also shown as Milan, Italy
Aug 30	Bologna	Italy	Stadio Communale
Aug 31	Rome	Italy	Palasport
Sep 01	Verona	Italy	*questionable*
Sep 02	Zurich	Switzerland	Mehrzweckhalle Wetzikon
Sep 03	Munich	Germany	Deutsches Museum
Sep 05	Offenbach	Germany	Stadthalle
Sep 06	Cologne	Germany	Musikhalle
Sep 07	Frankfurt	Germany	Festhalle (?)
Sep 08	Brussels	Belgium	Vorst Nationaal
Sep 09	Amsterdam	Netherlands	Concertgebouw – 2 shows
Sep 10	Paris	France	also shown as Lille, France
Sep 11	Liverpool	UK	Liverpool Stadium
Sep 13	Birmingham	UK	Town Hall – 2 shows (?)
Sep 14	London	UK	Empire Pool Wembley

CANADA
WA
OR
ID
MT
ND
MN
WI
SD
WY
NE
IA
Chicago
UNITED STATES OF AMERICA
NV
UT
CA
CO
IL
KS
MO
Nashv
Los Angeles
AZ
Phoenix
NM
OK
AR
MS
TX
Austin
LA
MEXICO

2nd North American Tour
1973

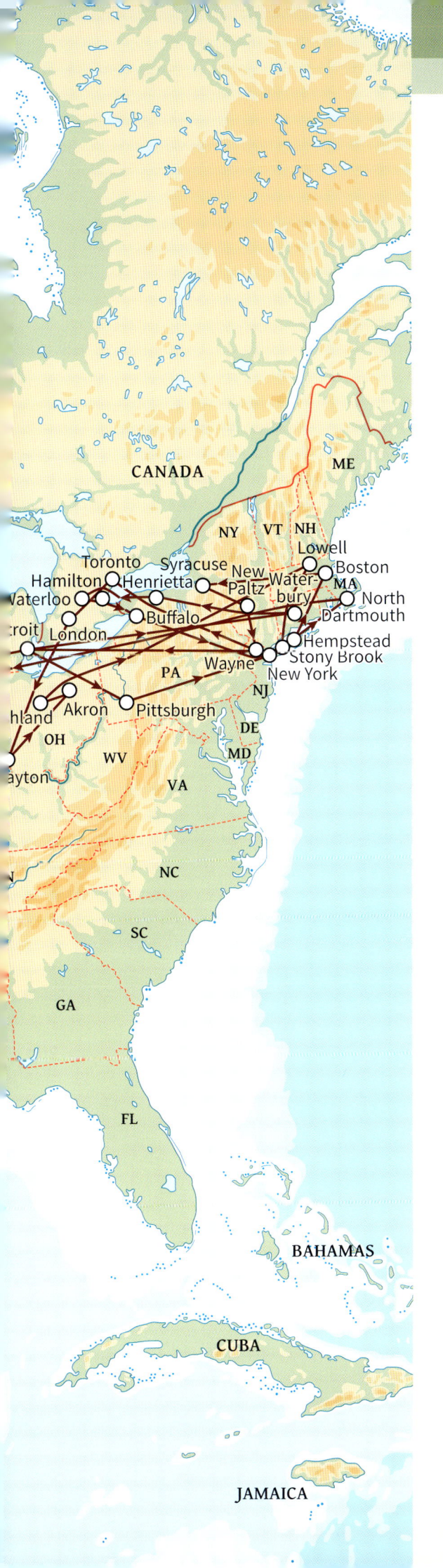

Frank Zappa *guitar, vocals* **Napoleon Murphy Brock** *tenor sax, vocals*
George Duke *keyboards, vocals* **Bruce Fowler** *trombone* **Tom Fowler** *bass*
Ruth Underwood *percussion* **Ralph Humphrey** *drums* **Chester Thompson** *drums*

Sep 17	Nashville	TN	Tennessee State Fair – 2 shows – *questionable*
Oct 26	Austin	TX	Armadillo World Headquarters – 2 shows
Oct 27	Austin	TX	Armadillo World Headquarters – 2 shows
Oct 31	Chicago	IL	Auditorium Theatre – 2 shows
Nov 02	Detroit	MI	Masonic Auditorium
Nov 03	Pittsburgh	PA	Carnegie Mellon University – 2 shows
Nov 04	New York	NY	Whitman Auditorium, Brooklyn College – 2 shows
Nov 06	Hempstead	NY	Hofstra University – 2 shows feat. **Bruce Chapin**
Nov 07	Boston	MA	Orpheum Theater
Nov 09	Syracuse	NY	Onondaga County War Memorial Auditorium
Nov 10	New Paltz	NY	Elting Gym, SUNY
Nov 11	Wayne	NJ	William Paterson College – 2 shows feat. **Irma Coffee**
Nov 14	Detroit	MI	Masonic Auditorium
Nov 16	Waterbury	CT	Palace Theatre
Nov 17	Henrietta	NY	Dome Arena
Nov 18	Waterloo	Canada	University Of Waterloo
Nov 19	Hamilton	Canada	
Nov 21	Buffalo	NY	Memorial Auditorium
Nov 22	New York	NY	Avery Fisher Hall –2 shows
Nov 23	Toronto	Canada	Massey Hall – 2 shows
Nov 24	London	Canada	London Arena
Nov 26	Dayton	OH	Field House, University of Dayton (?)
Nov 27	Akron	OH	Civic Theater
Nov 28	Ashland	OH	Meyers Convocation Center, Ashland College
Nov 30	Lowell	MA	Costello Gym, Lowell Technical Institute
Dec 01	Stony Brook	NY	Stony Brook Gym, SUNY – 2 shows
Dec 02	North Dartmouth	MA	Gymnasium, Southeastern Massachusetts University
Dec 08	Los Angeles	CA	Roxy – soundcheck / invite-only show feat. **Jeff Simmons**
Dec 09	Los Angeles	CA	Roxy – 2 shows
Dec 10	Los Angeles	CA	Roxy – 2 shows
Dec 14	Phoenix	AZ	Celebrity Theatre – 2 shows

CANADA
Vancouver
Seattle
WA
Portland
OR
MT
ND
MN
ID
Boise
SD
WI
WY
Sacramento
Berkeley
NV
NE
IA
Salt Lake City
UNITED STATES OF AMERICA
UT
IL
Denver
CA
CO
Colorado Springs
Kansas City
KS
MO
Santa Barbara
Los Angeles
Oklahoma City
OK
AR
Memphis
AZ
NM
MS
Dallas
TX
LA
Austin
Houston
MEXICO

1st North American Tour
1974

Frank Zappa *guitar, vocals* **Napoleon Murphy Brock** *tenor sax, vocals*
Jeff Simmons *guitar, harmonica, vocals* **George Duke** *keyboards, vocals*
Bruce Fowler *trombone* **Tom Fowler** *bass* **Ruth Underwood** *percussion*
Ralph Humphrey *drums* **Chester Thompson** *drums*

Feb 15	Sacramento	CA	Memorial Auditorium
Feb 16	Berkeley	CA	Community Theater
Feb 17	Santa Barbara	CA	Robertson Gymnasium, UCSB
Feb 23	Los Angeles	CA	Shrine Auditorium **feat. Ruben Guevara, Robert "Frog" Camarena, Johnny Martinez**
Mar 01	Atlanta	GA	Fox Theatre
Mar 02	Memphis	TN	*questionable*
Mar 04	Austin	TX	Coliseum
Mar 05	Dallas	TX	Convention Center
Mar	Louisville	KY	Freedom Hall – *questionable*
Mar 08	Kansas City	KS	Soldiers And Sailors Memorial Hall
Mar 09	Oklahoma City	OK	Travel and Transport Building, State Fairgrounds
Mar 10	Houston	TX	Sam Houston Coliseum
Mar 14	Vancouver	Canada	Agrodome
Mar 15	Seattle	WA	Paramount Theatre
Mar 16	Portland	OR	Paramount Theatre
Mar 18	Salt Lake City	UT	Terrace Ballroom
Mar 19	Boise	ID	*questionable*
Mar 21	Colorado Springs	CO	*questionable*
Mar 23	Denver	CO	Coliseum

CANADA

UNITED STATES OF AMERICA

WA, OR, MT, ND, MN, ID, SD, WY, NV, NE, IA, UT, CO, CA, KS, MO, AZ, NM, OK, AR, TX, MS, LA, IL, IN

Marquette, Eau Claire, WI, Milwaukee, Rap..., DeKalb, Chicago, So... Be..., Indianapo..., Louisv...

MEXICO

2nd North American Tour
1974

Frank Zappa *guitar, vocals* **Napoleon Murphy Brock** *tenor sax, vocals*
Jeff Simmons *guitar, harmonica, vocals* **George Duke** *keyboards, vocals*
Don Preston *synthesizer* **Bruce Fowler** *trombone* **Walt Fowler** *trumpet*
Tom Fowler *bass* **Ralph Humphrey** *drums* **Chester Thompson** *drums*

Apr 19	Allendale	MI	Fieldhouse, Grand Valley State Colleges
Apr 20	Toledo	OH	Sports Arena
Apr 21	Marquette	MI	Northern Michigan University
Apr 23	Milwaukee	WI	Riverside Theater – 2 shows
Apr 24	Indianapolis	IN	Convention Center
Apr 26	Eau Claire	WI	University Of Wisconsin
Apr 27	DeKalb	IL	Carl Sandburg Auditorium, Northern Illinois University
Apr 28	Big Rapids	MI	Ferris State College
Apr 30	College Park	MD	Ritchie Coliseum, University Of Maryland
May 01	Binghamton	NY	Broome County Veterans Memorial Arena
May 03	Geneva	NY	Geneva Theater
May 04	Washington	DC	Constitution Hall – 2 shows
May 05	Catonsville	MD	Gymnasium, UMBC
May 06	Williamsburg	VA	College Of William + Mary – *questionable*
May 07	Louisville	KY	Convention Center
May 08	Edinboro	PA	Edinboro State College
May 10	Flint	MI	I.M.A. Auditorium
May 11	Chicago	IL	Auditorium Theatre – 2 shows
May 12	South Bend	IN	Athletic & Convocation Center, Notre Dame University

CANADA
WA
OR
ID
MT
ND
MN
WI
SD
WY
NV
UT
NE
IA
UNITED STATES OF AMERICA
San Carlos
CA
CO
KS
Normal
IL
St. Louis
MO
Santa Monica
Los Angeles
San Diego
AZ
Phoenix
NM
OK
Little Rock
AR
Memphis
Tuscaloc
MS
Mob
TX
LA
Chalmett
MEXICO

3rd North American Tour
1974

Frank Zappa guitar, vocals **Napoleon Murphy Brock** tenor sax, vocals
Jeff Simmons guitar, harmonica, vocals (Jun–Jul 03?) **George Duke** keyboards, vocals **Tom Fowler** bass (Jun–Jul 03?) **Mick Rogers** bass (Jul 10)
Ruth Underwood percussion **Chester Thompson** drums

Jun 21	Los Angeles	CA	DiscReet Rehearsal Studio (the 'Premore' shoot)
Jun 28	Quebec	Canada	Centre Municipal des Congres, Hilton Hotel – 2 shows
Jun 29	Montreal	Canada	Place des Nations, Man + His World Expo
Jul 01	Ottawa	Canada	Civic Center Arena
Jul 02	Detroit	MI	Cobo Hall
Jul 03	Normal	IL	University Union Auditorium, Illinois State University
Jul 05	St. Louis	MO	Ambassador Theater – 2 shows
Jul 06	Little Rock	AR	Robinson Memorial Auditorium
Jul 09	Memphis	TN	North Hall, Ellis Auditorium
Jul 10	Mobile	AL	Municipal Auditorium
Jul 12	Miami	FL	Jai Alai Fronton
Jul 13	St. Petersburg	FL	Bayfront Center feat. **Lance Loud**
Jul 14	Tuscaloosa	AL	Morgan Auditorium, University Of Alabama – 2 shows
Jul 15	Chalmette	LA	St. Bernard Civic Auditorium feat. **Hurricane Brass Band**
Jul 17	Phoenix	AZ	Celebrity Theater – 2 shows
Jul 19	San Carlos	CA	Circle Star Theatre
Jul 20	San Carlos	CA	Circle Star Theatre
Jul 21	San Carlos	CA	Circle Star Theatre
Aug 08	Los Angeles	CA	Shrine Auditorium
Aug 11	San Diego	CA	Golden Hall feat. **Tom Waits**
Aug 16	Santa Monica	CA	Civic Auditorium
Aug 17	Santa Monica	CA	Civic Auditorium
Aug 27	Los Angeles	CA	*KCET-TV Studios* – 2 shows

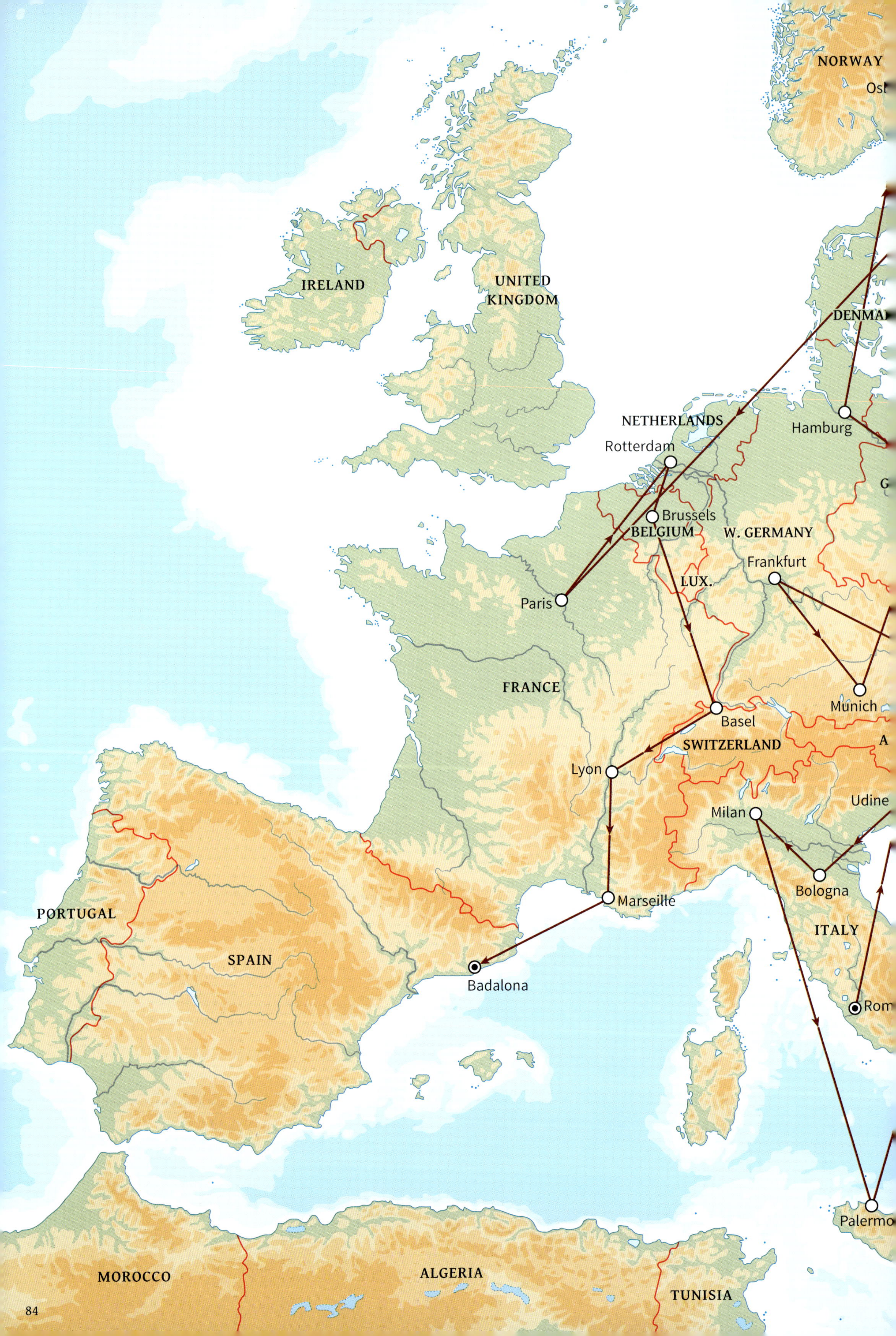
NORWAY
IRELAND
UNITED
KINGDOM
NETHERLANDS
Rotterdam
Hamburg
Brussels
BELGIUM
W. GERMANY
Frankfurt
LUX.
Paris
FRANCE
Munich
Basel
SWITZERLAND
Lyon
Udine
Milan
Bologna
Marseille
ITALY
PORTUGAL
SPAIN
Badalona
Palermo
MOROCCO
ALGERIA
TUNISIA

European Tour
1974

Frank Zappa *guitar, vocals* **Napoleon Murphy Brock** *tenor sax, vocals*
George Duke *keyboards, vocals* **Tom Fowler** *bass* **Ruth Underwood** *percussion*
Chester Thompson *drums*

Sep 06	Rome	Italy	Palazzo Dello Sport
Sep 07	Udine	Italy	Palasport
Sep 08	Bologna	Italy	Stadio Comunale
Sep 09	Milan	Italy	Velodromo Vigorelli
Sep 10	Palermo	Italy	
Sep 11	Vienna	Austria	Kurhalle – 2 shows
Sep 12	Frankfurt	Germany	Jahrhunderthalle – 2 shows
Sep 13	Munich	Germany	
Sep 14	Berlin	Germany	Deutschlandhalle
Sep 16	Hamburg	Germany	Congress Centrum Hamburg
Sep 18	Oslo	Norway	Njaardhallen
Sep 19	Stockholm	Sweden	Kungliga Tennishallen
Sep 20	Copenhagen	Denmark	K.B. Hallen
Sep 22	Helsinki	Finland	Kulttuuritalo – 2 shows
Sep 23	Helsinki	Finland	Kulttuuritalo
Sep 25	Gothenburg	Sweden	Konserthuset – 2 shows
Sep 26	Paris	France	Palais des Sports
Sep 27	Paris	France	Palais des Sports
Sep 28	Rotterdam	Netherlands	Sportpaleis Ahoy
Sep 29	Brussels	Belgium	Ancienne Belgique
Oct 01	Basel	Switzerland	Festhalle Mustermesse – 2 shows
Oct 02	Lyon	France	
Oct 03	Marseille	France	Salle Vallier
Oct 04	Badalona	Spain	Nuevo Pabellón, Club Joventud

CANADA
WA
OR
ID
MT
ND
MN
SD
WY
NV
UT
CA
CO
NE
IA
WI
St. Paul
Madison
Chicag
Naperville
Fort Wayne
UNITED STATES OF AMERICA
Lincoln
IL
KS
MO
Louisv
Long Beach
AZ
NM
OK
AR
MS
TX
LA
MEXICO

4th North American Tour
1974

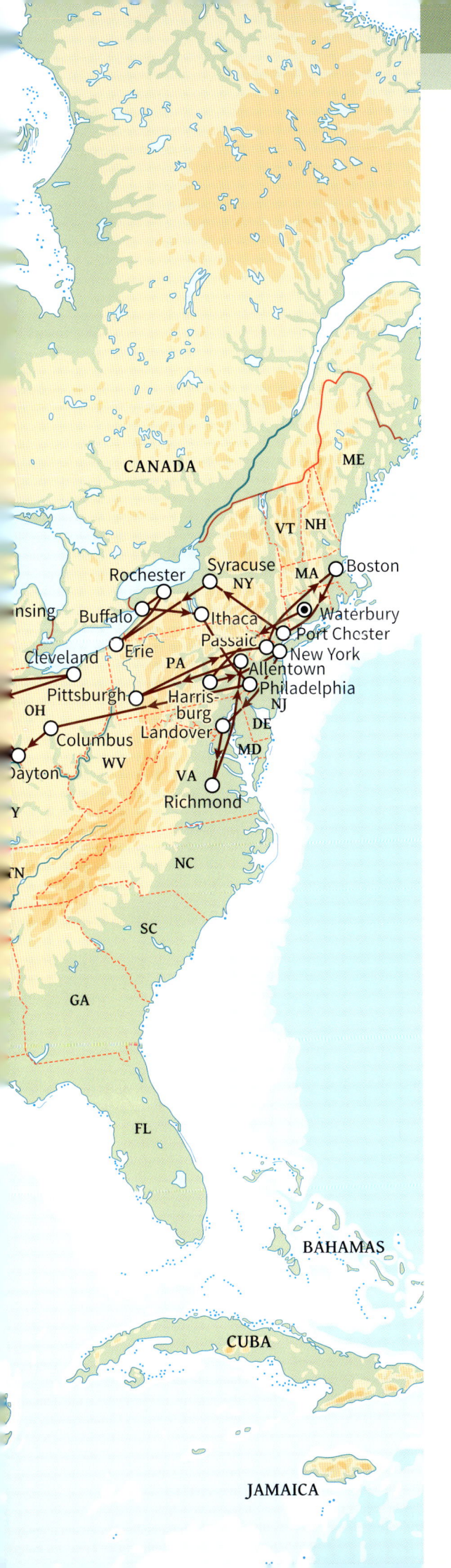

Frank Zappa guitar, vocals **Napoleon Murphy Brock** tenor sax, vocals
George Duke keyboards, vocals **Tom Fowler** bass **Ruth Underwood** percussion
Chester Thompson drums

Oct 28	Waterbury	CT	Palace Theatre – 2 shows
Oct 29	Harrisburg	PA	State Farm Show Arena
Oct 31	New York	NY	Felt Forum – 2 shows feat. **Bruce Fowler** (late show)
Nov 01	Landover	MD	Capital Centre
Nov 02	Richmond	VA	Richmond Coliseum
Nov 05	Allentown	PA	Agricultural Hall
Nov 06	Pittsburgh	PA	Syria Mosque – 2 shows
Nov 08	Passaic	NJ	Capitol Theatre – 2 shows
Nov 09	Boston	MA	Orpheum Theater – 2 shows feat. **Tom Waits**
Nov 10	Port Chester	NY	Capitol Theatre – 2 shows
Nov 11	Syracuse	NY	Onondaga County War Memorial Auditorium
Nov 12	Erie	PA	Gannon Auditorium, Gannon College
Nov 14	Rochester	NY	War Memorial Auditorium
Nov 15	Buffalo	NY	Memorial Auditorium
Nov 16	Ithaca	NY	Ben Light Gymnasium, Ithaca College
Nov 17	Philadelphia	PA	Spectrum Theater
Nov 19	Columbus	OH	Veterans Memorial Auditorium
Nov 20	Dayton	OH	Hara Arena
Nov 22	Fort Wayne	IN	Coliseum
Nov 23	East Lansing	MI	Jenison Fieldhouse, Michigan State University
Nov 24	Madison	WI	Dane County Memorial Coliseum
Nov 25	Louisville	KY	Freedom Hall
Nov 26	Lincoln	NE	Pershing Municipal Auditorium
Nov 27	St. Paul	MN	St. Paul Civic Center Arena
Nov 28	Chicago	IL	Hat Trick Arena
Nov 29	Naperville	IL	Field House, North Central College
Nov 30	Naperville	IL	Field House, North Central College
Dec 03	Cleveland	OH	Public Hall
Dec 31	Long Beach	CA	Long Beach Arena feat. **James 'Bird Legs' Youmans**

CANADA
WA
OR
ID
MT
ND
MN
WI
SD
WY
NV
UT
CA
CO
NE
IA
UNITED STATES OF AMERICA
KS
MO
IL
IN
OK
AR
MS
LA
TX
AZ
NM
MEXICO
Claremont
Phoenix
El Paso
Austin
St. Louis
Chicago
South Bend
Normal
Indianapol
Evansvil
Kalamazo

1st North American Tour
1975

Frank Zappa guitar, vocals **Captain Beefheart** soprano saxophone, harmonica, vocals **Napoleon Murphy Brock** tenor saxophone, vocals **Denny Walley** guitar **George Duke** keyboards, vocals **Bruce Fowler** trombone **Tom Fowler** bass **Terry Bozzio** drums

Apr 11	Claremont	CA	Bridges Auditorium, Pomona College – 2 shows
Apr 18	New Haven	CT	Veterans Memorial Coliseum
Apr 19	Passaic	NJ	Capitol Theatre – 2 shows
Apr 20	Kutztown	PA	Keystone Hall, Kutztown State College
Apr 22	Syracuse	NY	Onondaga County War Memorial Auditorium
Apr 23	Syracuse	NY	Gifford Auditorium – Lecture with **FZ, Captain Beefheart** and **George Duke**
Apr 24	Albany	NY	Palace Theatre
Apr 25	Uniondale	NY	Nassau Veterans Memorial Coliseum
Apr 26	Providence	RI	Alumni Hall, Providence College
Apr 27	Boston	MA	Music Hall – 2 shows
Apr 29	Trenton	NJ	Jones County Civic Center
Apr 30	Johnstown	PA	War Memorial Arena
May 02	Hampton	VA	Hampton Coliseum
May 03	Baltimore	MD	Civic Center
May 04	Charleston	WV	Civic Center
May 06	Normal	IL	Union Auditorium, Illinois State University
May 07	Frankfort	KY	Capitol Plaza/CPA Sports Center
May 09	South Bend	IN	Morris Civic Auditorium – 2 shows
May 10	Indianapolis	IN	Convention Center
May 11	Chicago	IL	International Amphitheater
May 13	St. Louis	MO	Kiel Opera House
May 14	Evansville	IN	Roberts Municipal Stadium
May 16	Cincinnati	OH	Cincinnati Gardens
May 17	Kalamazoo	MI	Wings Stadium
May 18	Detroit	MI	Cobo Hall
May 20	Austin	TX	Armadillo World Headquarters
May 21	Austin	TX	Armadillo World Headquarters
May 23	El Paso	TX	County Coliseum feat. **Jimmy Carl Black**
May 25	Phoenix	AZ	Celebrity Theater – 2 shows
May 26	Phoenix	AZ	Celebrity Theater

90

2nd North American Tour
1975

Frank Zappa & The Abnuceals Emuukha Electric Orchestra

Sep 17	Los Angeles	CA	Royce Hall, UCLA
Sep 18	Los Angeles	CA	Royce Hall, UCLA
Sep 19	Los Angeles	CA	Royce Hall, UCLA (private)

Frank Zappa guitar, vocals **Napoleon Murphy Brock** tenor saxophone, vocals **André Lewis** keyboards, vocals **Roy Estrada** bass, vocals **Terry Bozzio** drums, vocals **Norma Jean Bell** alto saxophone, vocals (Nov 01–Dec 09)

Sep 27	Santa Barbara	CA	Robertson Gymnasium, UCSB
Sep	Oakland	CA	Paramount Theatre
Oct 01	Vancouver	Canada	War Memorial Gymnasium
Oct 02	Spokane	WA	Convention Center
Oct 03	Portland	OR	Paramount Theatre
Oct 04	Seattle	WA	Paramount Theatre – 2 shows
Oct 08	Oklahoma City	OK	Civic Center Music Hall
Oct 10	San Antonio	TX	Municipal Auditorium
Oct 11	Houston	TX	Hofheinz Pavilion, University Of Houston
Oct 12	Dallas	TX	Convention Center
Oct 14	Kansas City	KS	Soldiers And Sailors Memorial Hall
Oct 15	Fayetteville	AR	Barnhill Arena, University Of Arkansas
Oct 16	New Orleans	LA	The Warehouse
Oct 17	Durham	NC	Duke University
Oct 18	Atlanta	GA	Municipal Auditorium – 2 shows
Oct	St. Petersburg	FL	Bayfront Center
Oct 23	Boston	MA	Music Hall
Oct 24	Providence	RI	Palace Theatre
Oct 25	Passaic	NJ	Capitol Theatre – 2 shows
Oct 26	Hempstead	NY	Hofstra University Playhouse – 2 shows
Oct 29	Waterbury	CT	Palace Theatre – 2 shows
Oct 31	New York	NY	Felt Forum – 2 shows feat. **Norma Jean Bell**
Nov 01	Williamsburg	VA	William & Mary Hall, College Of William & Mary Tribe
Nov 02	College Park	MD	Cole Field House, University Of Maryland
Nov 03	Philadelphia	PA	Spectrum Theater
Nov 05	Henrietta	NY	Dome Arena
Nov 07	Pittsburgh	PA	Civic Arena
Nov 08	Knoxville	TN	Civic Coliseum
Nov 09	Louisville	KY	Louisville Gardens
Nov 14	Fort Wayne	IN	Memorial Coliseum
Nov 15	Allendale	MI	Grand Valley State University Fieldhouse
Nov 16	Dayton	OH	Hara Arena
Nov 18	Ann Arbor	MI	Crisler Arena, University Of Michigan
Nov 21	Zagreb	Yugoslavia	Sportska Dvorana
Nov 22	Ljubljana	Yugoslavia	Hala Tivoli
Nov 25	Madison	WI	Dane County Coliseum
Nov 26	St. Paul	MN	Civic Center
Nov 28	Milwaukee	WI	Milwaukee Auditorium
Nov 29	Chicago	IL	Auditorium Theatre
Nov 30	Chicago	IL	Auditorium Theatre – 2 shows
Dec 02	Green Bay	WI	Brown County Arena feat. **Darryl Dybka (?)**
Dec 04	Toronto	Canada	Maple Leaf Gardens feat. **Darryl Dybka (?)**
Dec 05	London	Canada	London Arena feat. **Darryl Dybka** and **Ralphe Armstrong**
Dec 06	Ottawa	Canada	Civic Arena
Dec 07	Hamilton	Canada	Physical Education Complex, McMaster University feat. **Eddie Jobson**
Dec 08	Montreal	Canada	Forum feat. **Eddie Jobson**
Dec 09	Quebec	Canada	Centre Municipal des Congrès de Quebec, Hilton Hotel
Dec 26	Oakland	CA	Paramount Theatre
Dec 27	San Francisco	CA	Winterland
Dec 29	San Diego	CA	Golden Hall
Dec 31	Inglewood	CA	The Forum

MONGOLIA
N. KOREA
JAPAN
Kyoto
Tokyo
S. KOREA
Osaka
CHINA
INDIA
BANGLA-
DESH
BURMA
N.
VIETNAM
LAOS
TAIWAN
THAI-
LAND
S.
VIETNAM
PHILIPPINES
CAMBODIA
BRUNEI
MALAYSIA
INDONESIA
PAPUA
NEW GUINEA
AUSTRALIA
Brisbane
Perth
Adelaide
Sydney
Melbourne
Auckland
NEW ZEALAND

Pacific Tour
1976

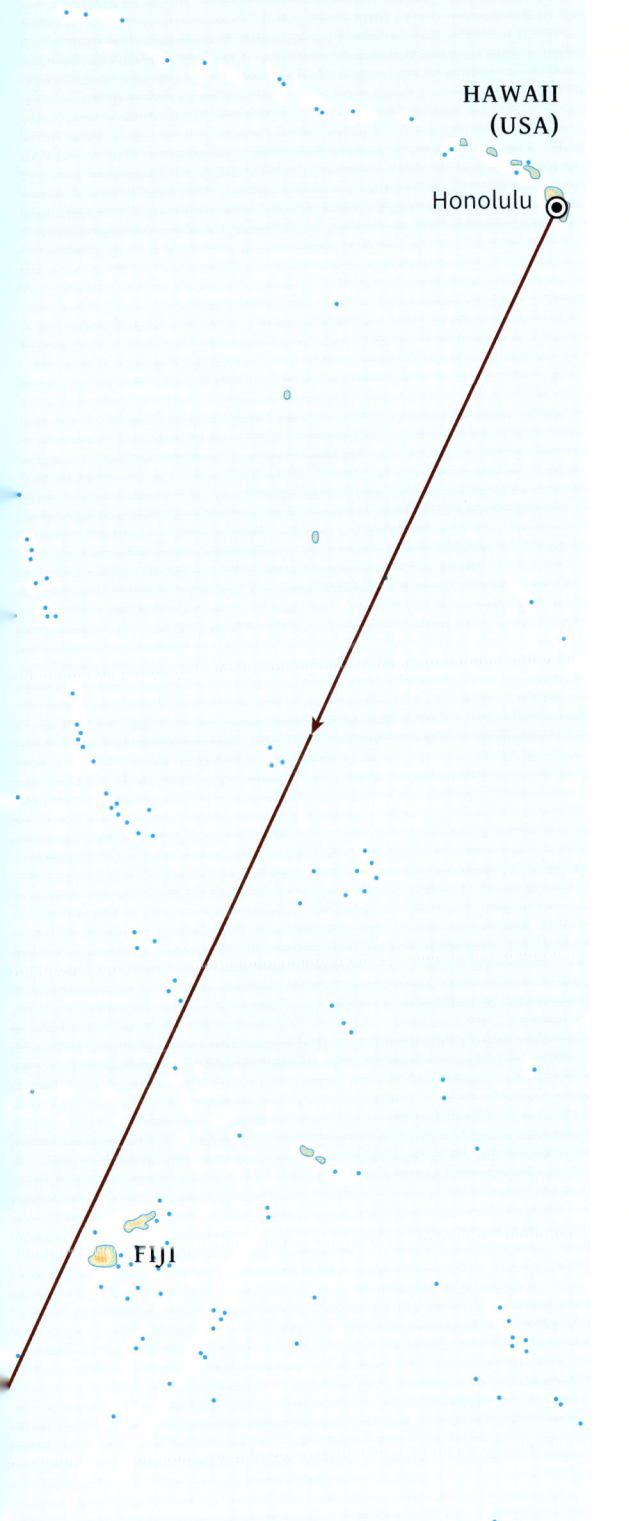

Frank Zappa *guitar, vocals* **Napoleon Murphy Brock** *tenor sax, vocals*
André Lewis *keyboards, vocals* **Roy Estrada** *bass, vocals*
Terry Bozzio *drums, vocals*

Jan 11	Honolulu	HI	Arena
Jan 16	Auckland	New Zealand	Town Hall – 2 shows
Jan 20	Sydney	Australia	Hordern Pavilion feat. **Norman Gunston**
Jan 21	Sydney	Australia	Hordern Pavilion
Jan 22	Melbourne	Australia	Festival Hall
Jan 23	Melbourne	Australia	Festival Hall
Jan 24	Adelaide	Australia	Apollo Stadium
Jan 25	Adelaide	Australia	Apollo Stadium
Jan 26	Brisbane	Australia	Festival Hall
Jan 28	Perth	Australia	W.A.C.A. Ground
Feb 01	Tokyo	Japan	Asakusa Kokusai Gekijo
Feb 03	Osaka	Japan	Kosei Nenkin Kaikan
Feb 04	Kyoto	Japan	Daigaku Seibu Kodo
Feb 05	Tokyo	Japan	Nippon Seinen-Kan

NORWAY
Os
IRELAND
UNITED
KINGDOM
Aarhus
DENMA
Hamburg
NETHERLANDS
Amsterdam
Hanover
G
Essen
Brussels
Cologne
BELGIUM
W. GERMANY
Paris
Saarbrücken
Ludwigshafen
Offenburg
Munic
FRANCE
Zurich
SWITZERLAND
AU
Lugano
PORTUGAL
SPAIN
ITALY
MOROCCO
ALGERIA
TUNISIA

European Tour
1976

Frank Zappa *guitar, vocals* **Napoleon Murphy Brock** *tenor sax, vocals*
André Lewis *keyboards, vocals* **Roy Estrada** *bass, vocals*
Terry Bozzio *drums, vocals*

Feb 13	Vienna	Austria	Kurhalle – 2 shows
Feb 14	Munich	Germany	Deutsches Museum
Feb 15	Ludwigshafen	Germany	Friedrich-Ebert-Halle feat. **Davey Moire**
Feb 17	Cologne	Germany	Sporthalle
Feb 18	Hanover	Germany	Niedersachsenhalle
Feb 19	Essen	Germany	Grugahalle
Feb 20	Hamburg	Germany	Congress Centrum Hamburg
Feb 21	Aarhus	Denmark	Vejlby-Risskov Hallen
Feb 23	Oslo	Norway	Njaardhallen
Feb 24	Stockholm	Sweden	Konserthuset – 2 shows
Feb 25	Stockholm	Sweden	Konserthuset – *questionable*
Feb 26	Helsinki	Finland	Messukeskus
Feb 29	Copenhagen	Denmark	Falkoner Teatret – 2 shows
Mar 02	Lund	Sweden	Olympen – 2 shows
Mar 03	Copenhagen	Denmark	Tivolis Koncertsal – 2 shows
Mar 04	Berlin	Germany	Deutschlandhalle
Mar 06	Amsterdam	Netherlands	Jaap Edenhal
Mar 07	Brussels	Belgium	Vorst Nationaal
Mar 08	Paris	France	Palais des Sports
Mar 10	Saarbrücken	Germany	Saarlandhalle
Mar 11	Offenburg	Germany	Oberrheinhalle
Mar 12	Zurich	Switzerland	Kongresshaus – 2 shows
Mar 13	Lugano	Switzerland	Palasport Mezzovico

CANADA
WA
OR
ID
MT
ND
MN
SD
WI
WY
IA
DeKalb
Chicago
NV
UT
NE
UNITED STATES OF AMERICA
IL
CA
CO
KS
MO
Nashville
AZ
NM
OK
AR
MS
TX
LA
Houston
New Orleans
MEXICO

North American Tour
1976

Frank Zappa *guitar, vocals* **Ray White** *guitar, vocals* **Eddie Jobson** *keyboards, violin* **Patrick O'Hearn** *bass* **Terry Bozzio** *drums, vocals* **Lady Bianca Odin** *keyboards, vocals (Oct thru Nov 11)*

Oct 11	Houston	TX	Hofheinz Pavilion, University Of Houston
Oct 12	New Orleans	LA	McAlister Auditorium, Tulane University – 2 shows
Oct 14	Tampa	FL	Fort Homer Hesterly Armory
Oct 16	Coral Gables	FL	The Patio, University Of Miami
Oct 17	Atlanta	GA	Omni Coliseum
Oct 18	Nashville	TN	Gymnasium, Vanderbilt University
Oct 19	Johnson City	TN	Freedom Hall Civic Center
Oct 22	Buffalo	NY	Memorial Auditorium
Oct 23	Plattsburgh	NY	Field House
Oct 24	Boston	MA	Music Hall – 2 shows
Oct 27	Pawtucket	RI	Leroy Concert Theater – 2 shows
Oct 29	Philadelphia	PA	Spectrum Theater
Oct 30	New York	NY	Felt Forum
Oct 31	New York	NY	Felt Forum – 2 shows
Nov 04	Landover	MD	Capital Centre
Nov 05	Pittsburgh	PA	Syria Mosque
Nov 06	Troy	NY	Fieldhouse, Rensselaer Polytechnic Institute feat. **John Smothers**
Nov 07	Springfield	MA	Civic Center
Nov 09	Ottawa	Canada	Civic Centre
Nov 10	Montreal	Canada	Forum
Nov 11	Quebec	Canada	Le Colisee
Nov 12	Erie	PA	Erie County Fieldhouse
Nov 13	Toledo	OH	Sports Arena
Nov 15	London	Canada	London Gardens
Nov 16	Toronto	Canada	Maple Leaf Gardens
Nov 18	DeKalb	IL	Evans Fieldhouse, Northern Illinois University
Nov 19	Detroit	MI	Cobo Hall feat. **Ralphe Armstrong**, **Don Brewer, Howard Kaylan** and **Mark Volman**
Nov 20	Cleveland	OH	Public Hall
Nov 22	Columbus	OH	Veterans Memorial Auditorium
Nov 24	Chicago	IL	Auditorium Theatre
Nov 25	Chicago	IL	Auditorium Theatre
Dec 06	New York	NY	The Bottom Line – **FZ** was a special guest on **The Flo & Eddie Show**
Dec 11	New York	NY	*Saturday Night Live* feat. **John Belushi, Don Pardo, Ruth Underwood, Tom Malone, Lou Marini, Ronnie Cuber, Don Grolnick, Alan Rubin, Mauricio Smith, David Shaw, Cheryl Hardwick** and **Bob Cranshaw**
Dec 26	New York	NY	Palladium*
Dec 27	New York	NY	Palladium*
Dec 28	New York	NY	Palladium*
Dec 29	New York	NY	Palladium*

*feat. **Don Pardo, Ruth Underwood, Tom Malone, Mike Brecker, Randy Brecker, Lou Marini, Ronnie Cuber** and **Dave Samuels**

NORWAY
Os

DENMARK
Copenha

Glasgow
Edinburgh

IRELAND
UNITED KINGDOM

Stafford

London

NETHERLANDS
Amsterdam

Hamburg

Düsseldorf
Brussels
BELGIUM
Cologne
W. GERMANY

Paris
Wiesbaden
Neunkirchen am Brand

FRANCE
Böblingen

Munich

SWITZERLAND
A

PORTUGAL
SPAIN
ITALY

MOROCCO
ALGERIA
TUNISIA

98

European Tour
1977

Frank Zappa guitar, vocals **Ray White** guitar, vocals **Eddie Jobson** keyboards, violin **Patrick O'Hearn** bass **Terry Bozzio** drums, vocals

Jan 13	Copenhagen	Denmark	Falkoner Teatret – 2 shows
Jan 15	Stockholm	Sweden	Konserthuset – 2 shows
Jan 16	Oslo	Norway	Ekeberghallen
Jan 21	Gothenburg	Sweden	Scandinavium
Jan 23	Helsinki	Finland	Kulttuuritalo – 2 shows
Jan 24	Hamburg	Germany	Congress Centrum Hamburg
Jan 25	Neunkirchen am Brand	Germany	Hemmerleinhalle
Jan 26	Munich	Germany	Olympiahalle
Jan 27	Düsseldorf	Germany	Philipshalle
Jan 28	Brussels	Belgium	Vorst Nationaal
Jan 30	Wiesbaden	Germany	Rhein-Main-Halle – 2 shows
Jan 31	Böblingen	Germany	Sporthalle
Feb 02	Paris	France	Pavillon de Paris feat. **Sugar Blue**
Feb 03	Paris	France	Pavillon de Paris
Feb 05	Amsterdam	Netherlands	Jaap Edenhal
Feb 06	Cologne	Germany	Sporthalle
Feb 07	Berlin	Germany	Deutschlandhalle
Feb 09	London	UK	Hammersmith Odeon
Feb 10	London	UK	Hammersmith Odeon
Feb 12	Stafford	UK	New Bingley Hall
Feb 13	Glasgow	UK	Apollo Theatre
Feb 14	Edinburgh	UK	Playhouse Theatre
Feb 16	London	UK	Hammersmith Odeon
Feb 17	London	UK	Hammersmith Odeon

100

North American Tour
1977

Frank Zappa guitar, vocals **Adrian Belew** guitar, vocals **Tommy Mars** keyboards, vocals **Peter Wolf** keyboards **Patrick O'Hearn** bass **Ed Mann** percussion **Terry Bozzio** drums, vocals

Sep 08	Tempe	AZ	Activities Center, Arizona State University
Sep 09	San Diego	CA	Open Air Amphitheater, San Diego State University
Sep 10	Las Vegas	NV	Aladdin Theatre for the Performing Arts
Sep 11	Tucson	AZ	Community Center Arena
Sep 13	Austin	TX	Armadillo World Headquarters – 2 shows
Sep 14	Houston	TX	Music Hall – 2 shows
Sep 16	Dallas	TX	Convention Center Auditorium
Sep 17	Baton Rouge	LA	Assembly Center, Lousiana State University
Sep 18	Atlanta	GA	Fox Theatre
Sep 20	Des Moines	IA	Veterans Memorial Auditorium
Sep 21	Mount Pleasant	MI	Rose Arena, Central Michigan University
Sep 23	Champaign	IL	Assembly Hall, University Of Illinois
Sep 24	Iowa City	IA	Field House, University Of Iowa
Sep 25	Bloomington	MN	Metropolitan Sports Center
Sep 27	Milwaukee	WI	Milwaukee Auditorium
Sep 29	Toronto	Canada	Maple Leaf Gardens feat. **Howard Kaylan** and **Mark Volman**
Sep 30	Detroit	MI	Cobo Hall
Oct 01	Carbondale	IL	Southern Illinois University Arena
Oct 02	St. Louis	MO	Quadrangle, Washington University
Oct 05	Columbus	OH	Veterans Memorial Auditorium
Oct 06	Buffalo	NY	Memorial Auditorium
Oct 08	Allentown	PA	Memorial Hall, Muhlenburg College
Oct 09	Cleveland	OH	Public Hall
Oct 17	Hartford	CT	Civic Center
Oct 18	Poughkeepsie	NY	Mid Hudson Civic Center
Oct 20	Boston	MA	Music Hall – 2 shows
Oct 21	Portland	ME	Cumberland County Civic Center
Oct 22	Montreal	Canada	Forum
Oct 23	Pawtucket	RI	Leroy Concert Theater – 2 shows
Oct 24	Philadelphia	PA	Spectrum Theater
Oct 26	Quebec	Canada	Colisee de Quebec
Oct 28	New York	NY	Palladium – 2 shows
Oct 29	New York	NY	Palladium – 2 shows
Oct 30	New York	NY	Palladium feat. **Roy Estrada, Phil Kaufman** and **Thomas Nordegg**
Oct 31	New York	NY	Palladium feat. **Roy Estrada**
Nov 04	Chicago	IL	Uptown Theatre – 2 shows
Nov 05	Pittsburgh	PA	Stanley Theater – 2 shows
Nov 06	Ann Arbor	MI	Hill Auditorium
Nov 10	Louisville	KY	Louisville Gardens
Nov 11	Kansas City	MO	Uptown Theater – 2 shows
Nov 14	Denver	CO	Auditorium Arena
Nov 15	Salt Lake City	UT	Salt Palace
Nov 18	Sacramento	CA	Memorial Auditorium
Nov 19	Stanford	CA	Maples Pavilion, Stanford University feat. **Carol Bozzio**
Nov 20	Los Angeles	CA	Pauley Pavilion, UCLA
Dec 31	Los Angeles	CA	Pauley Pavilion, UCLA feat. **Roy Estrada**

NORWAY
IRELAND
DENMARK
UNITED KINGDOM
NETHERLANDS
London
Rotterdam
Münster
Hambu
Düssel-
dorf
W. GERMANY
G
Brussels
Cologne
BELGIUM
Frankfurt
Neunkirche
am Brand
Paris
Eppelheim
FRANCE
Colmar
Munich
Zurich
Bern
SWITZERLAND
A
Lyon
PORTUGAL
SPAIN
ITALY
MOROCCO
ALGERIA
TUNISIA

1st European Tour
1978

Frank Zappa guitar, vocals **Adrian Belew** guitar, vocals
Tommy Mars keyboards, vocals **Peter Wolf** keyboards **Patrick O'Hearn** bass
Ed Mann percussion **Terry Bozzio** drums, vocals

Jan 24	London	UK	Hammersmith Odeon
Jan 25	London	UK	Hammersmith Odeon
Jan 26	London	UK	Hammersmith Odeon
Jan 27	London	UK	Hammersmith Odeon
Jan 29	Frankfurt	Germany	Festhalle – 2 shows
Jan 30	Hamburg	Germany	Congress Centrum Hamburg – 2 shows
Feb 01	Düsseldorf	Germany	Philipshalle
Feb 02	Munich	Germany	Rudi-Sedlmayer-Halle
Feb 03	Vienna	Austria	Stadthalle
Feb 04	Zurich	Switzerland	Hallenstadion
Feb 05	Bern	Switzerland	Festhalle
Feb 06	Paris	France	Pavillon de Paris, Porte de Pantin
Feb 07	Paris	France	Pavillon de Paris, Porte de Pantin
Feb 08	Paris	France	Pavillon de Paris, Porte de Pantin – *questionable*
Feb 09	Paris	France	Pavillon de Paris, Porte de Pantin
Feb 10	Lyon	France	Palais des Sports
Feb 11	Colmar	France	Parc des Expositions
Feb 13	Rotterdam	Netherlands	The Ahoy
Feb 14	Cologne	Germany	Sporthalle
Feb 15	Berlin	Germany	Deutschlandhalle
Feb 17	Copenhagen	Denmark	Falkoner Teatret – 2 shows
Feb 18	Gothenburg	Sweden	Scandinavium
Feb 19	Stockholm	Sweden	Konserthuset – 2 shows
Feb 23	Münster	Germany	Halle Münsterland
Feb 24	Eppelheim	Germany	Rhein-Neckar-Halle
Feb 25	Neunkirchen am Brand	Germany	Hemmerleinhalle
Feb 26	Brussels	Belgium	Vorst Nationaal
Feb 28	London	UK	Hammersmith Odeon
Mar 01	London	UK	Hammersmith Odeon

NORWAY
IRELAND
DENMARK
UNITED
KINGDOM
Stevenage
NETHERLANDS
Bremen
BELGIUM
W. GERMANY
Saarbrücken
FRANCE
Ulm
Munich
SWITZERLAND
PORTUGAL
SPAIN
ITALY
MOROCCO
ALGERIA
TUNISIA

2nd European Tour
1978

Frank Zappa *guitar, vocals* **Ike Willis** *guitar, vocals* **Denny Walley** *guitar, vocals*
Tommy Mars *keyboards, vocals* **Peter Wolf** *keyboards* **Arthur Barrow** *bass*
Ed Mann *percussion* **Vinnie Colaiuta** *drums*

Aug 26	Ulm	Germany	Friedrichsau Festplatz
Sep 03	Saarbrücken	Germany	Ludwigsparkstadion
Sep 04	Bremen	Germany	Stadthalle
Sep 05	Malmö	Sweden	Folkets Park
Sep 07	Berlin	Germany	Deutschlandhalle feat. **L. Shankar**
Sep 08	Munich	Germany	Circus Krone
Sep 09	Stevenage	UK	Knebworth Festival

CANADA

WA
OR
ID
MT
ND
MN
SD
WI
Milwaukee Kalar
WY
IA
NE
UNITED STATES OF AMERICA
Chicago So
NV
UT
Be
CA
CO
IL
KS
MO
Bloomingto
AZ
OK
AR
NM
MS
TX
LA

MEXICO

North American Tour
1978

Frank Zappa guitar, vocals **Ike Willis** guitar, vocals (thru Oct 14) **Denny Walley** guitar, vocals **Tommy Mars** keyboards, vocals **Peter Wolf** keyboards **Arthur Barrow** bass, acoustic guitar **Patrick O'Hearn** bass (from Oct 13) **Ed Mann** percussion **Vinnie Colaiuta** drums

Sep 15	Miami	FL	Jai Alai Fronton – 2 shows
Sep 16	St. Petersburg	FL	Bayfront Center
Sep 17	Atlanta	GA	Fox Theatre – 2 shows
Sep 19	Columbus	OH	Veterans Memorial Auditorium
Sep 20	Buffalo	NY	Memorial Auditorium
Sep 21	Poughkeepsie	NY	Mid Hudson Civic Center
Sep 22	South Bend	IN	Notre Dame University
Sep 23	Pittsburgh	PA	Stanley Theater – 2 shows
Sep 24	Bloomington	IN	Assembly Hall, Indiana University
Sep 25	Kalamazoo	MI	Wings Stadium
Sep 26	Milwaukee	WI	Milwaukee Arena
Sep 28	Detroit	MI	Cobo Hall
Sep 29	Chicago	IL	Uptown Theatre – 2 shows
Sep 30	Cincinnati	OH	Swingos Celebrity Inn
Oct 01	Cleveland	OH	Public Auditorium
Oct 03	Toronto	Canada	Maple Leaf Gardens
Oct 04	Montreal	Canada	Forum
Oct 06	Augusta	ME	Civic Center
Oct 08	Albany	NY	Palace Theater – 2 shows
Oct 09	Providence	RI	Civic Center
Oct 10	Quebec	Canada	Le Colisee
Oct 13	Passaic	NJ	Capitol Theatre – 2 shows
Oct 14	College Park	MD	Cole Fieldhouse, University Of Maryland
Oct 15	Stony Brook	NY	SUNY – 2 shows
Oct 21	New York	NY	*Saturday Night Live* feat. **John Belushi, Lew Del Gatto, Howard Johnson, Tom Malone, Lou Marini** and **Alan Rubin**
Oct 23	Philadelphia	PA	Spectrum Theater
Oct 24	Springfield	MA	Civic Center
Oct 25	Danvers	MA	North Shore Coliseum
Oct 27	New York	NY	Palladium – 2 shows feat. **L. Shankar** (both shows)
Oct 28	New York	NY	Palladium – 2 shows feat. **L. Shankar** (both shows)
Oct 29	New York	NY	Palladium
Oct 31	New York	NY	Palladium feat. **L. Shankar, Warren Cuccurullo** and **Nancy**

108

European Tour
1979

Frank Zappa guitar, vocals **Ike Willis** guitar, vocals **Denny Walley** guitar, vocals
Warren Cuccurullo guitar **Tommy Mars** keyboards **Peter Wolf** keyboards
Arthur Barrow bass **Ed Mann** percussion **Vinnie Colaiuta** drums

Date	City	Country	Venue
Feb 10	Birmingham	UK	Odeon Theatre
Feb 11	Birmingham	UK	Odeon Theatre
Feb 12	Manchester	UK	Apollo Theater
Feb 13	Newcastle	UK	City Hall
Feb 14	Glasgow	UK	Apollo Theater
Feb 16	Brighton	UK	Brighton Centre
Feb 17	London	UK	Hammersmith Odeon
Feb 18	London	UK	Hammersmith Odeon – 2 shows
Feb 19	London	UK	Hammersmith Odeon
Feb 21	Brussels	Belgium	Vorst Nationaal
Feb 23	Paris	France	Hippodrome de Pantin
Feb 24	Paris	France	Hippodrome de Pantin – 2 shows
Feb 25	Cambrai	France	Palais Des Grottes
Feb 27	Rotterdam	Netherlands	The Ahoy
Feb 28	Hamburg	Germany	Congress Centrum Hamburg
Mar 01	Copenhagen	Denmark	Falkoner Teatret – questionable
Mar 02	Oslo	Norway	Ekeberghallen
Mar 03	Stockholm	Sweden	Johanneshovs Isstadion
Mar 05	Copenhagen	Denmark	Falkoner Teatret
Mar 06	Gothenburg	Sweden	Scandinavium
Mar 08	Strasbourg	France	Hall Rhénus, Parc des Expositions
Mar 09	Dijon	France	Palais des Sports
Mar 11	Lyon	France	Palais des Sports
Mar 12	Montpellier	France	Palais des Sports
Mar 13	Barcelona	Spain	Palacio de los Deportes
Mar 14	Madrid	Spain	Pabellón de Deportes de la Ciudad Deportiva del Real Madrid – 2 shows
Mar 16	Pau	France	Parc des Expositions
Mar 17	Bordeaux	France	Parc des Expositions
Mar 18	Nantes	France	Grand Palais de la Beaujoire
Mar 19	Brest	France	Parc de Penfeld
Mar 21	Eppelheim	Germany	Rhein-Neckar-Halle
Mar 22	Passau	Germany	Nibelungenhalle
Mar 23	Graz	Austria	Liebenauer Stadion
Mar 25	Dortmund	Germany	Westfalenhalle
Mar 26	Hanover	Germany	Eilenriedehalle
Mar 27	Wiesbaden	Germany	Rhein-Main-Halle – 2 shows
Mar 29	Cologne	Germany	Sporthalle
Mar 30	Neunkirchen am Brand	Germany	Hemmerleinhalle – 2 shows
Mar 31	Munich	Germany	Rudi-Sedlmayer-Halle – 2 shows
Apr 01	Zurich	Switzerland	Hallenstadion

CANADA
Vancouver
Seattle
WA
Portland
Eugene
OR
MT
ND
MN
ID
SD
WI
WY
Berkeley
Sacramento
NV
NE
IA
Stanford
Omaha
Boulder
UNITED STATES OF AMERICA
UT
IL
CA
CO
Kansas City
KS
MO
Wichita
San Ber'dino
Los Angeles
AZ
OK
San Diego
NM
AR
Phoenix
MS
TX
LA
New Orleans
MEXICO

1st North American Tour
1980

Frank Zappa *guitar, vocals* **Ike Willis** *guitar, vocals* **Ray White** *guitar, vocals*
Tommy Mars *keyboards* **Arthur Barrow** *bass* **David Logeman** *drums*

Mar 25	Seattle	WA	Center Arena / Rainbow Tavern
Mar 26	Vancouver	Canada	Pacific Coliseum
Mar 27	Eugene	OR	McArthur Court, University Of Oregon
Mar 29	Portland	OR	Paramount Theatre – 2 shows
Mar 30	Sacramento	CA	Memorial Auditorium
Apr 01	Berkeley	CA	Community Theater – 2 shows
Apr 03	Stanford	CA	Maples Pavilion, Stanford University
Apr 04	San Diego	CA	Sports Arena
Apr 05	San Bernardino	CA	Swing Auditorium
Apr 06	Los Angeles	CA	Sports Arena
Apr 08	Phoenix	AZ	Celebrity Theatre – 2 shows
Apr 10	Boulder	CO	Events Center, University Of Colorado
Apr 11	Wichita	KS	Henry Levitt Arena, Wichita State University feat. **Craig "Twister" Steward**
Apr 12	Omaha	NE	Civic Auditorium Music Hall – 2 shows
Apr 13	Kansas City	KS	Soldiers And Sailors Memorial Hall – 2 shows
Apr 15	New Orleans	LA	Saenger Performing Arts Center – 2 shows
Apr 17	Tampa	FL	Jai Alai Fronton
Apr 18	Sunrise	FL	Sunrise Musical Theatre – 2 shows
Apr 19	Gainesville	FL	Gymnasium, University of Florida – 2 shows
Apr 20	Atlanta	GA	Fox Theatre – 2 shows
Apr 22	Norfolk	VA	Fieldhouse, Old Dominion University
Apr 24	Syracuse	NY	Manley Field House, Syracuse University
Apr 25	Piscataway	NJ	Athletic Center, Rutgers University
Apr 26	Troy	NY	Fieldhouse, Rensselaer Polytechnic Institute
Apr 27	Bethlehem	PA	Stabler Arena, Lehigh University
Apr 29	Upper Darby	PA	Tower Theatre – 2 shows
Apr 30	Hanover	NH	Dartmouth College
May 02	Providence	RI	Civic Center
May 03	Boston	MA	Music Hall – 2 shows
May 04	Portland	ME	Cumberland County Civic Center
May 06	Columbus	OH	Veterans Memorial Auditorium
May 07	Cincinnati	OH	Fieldhouse, University Of Cincinnati
May 08	New York	NY	Mudd Club
May 09	Uniondale	NY	Nassau Veterans Memorial Coliseum – 2 shows
May 10	Upper Darby	PA	Tower Theater – 2 shows feat. **L. Shankar**
May 11	Baltimore	MD	Civic Center

NORWAY
Drammen
DENMARK
Kiel
Hambu
IRELAND
UNITED KINGDOM
London
NETHERLANDS
Rotterdam
Bremen
Hanover
Düsseldorf
Dortmund
Brussels
Cologne
BELGIUM
W. GERMANY
Frankfurt
Neunkirche am Brand
Rouen
Paris
Mannheim
Nantes
Offenburg
Sindelfingen
FRANCE
Mulhouse
Munich
Zurich
SWITZERLAND
Geneva
Clermont-Ferrand
Vienne
Orange
PORTUGAL
SPAIN
ITALY
MOROCCO
ALGERIA
TUNISIA

European Tour
1980

Frank Zappa guitar, vocals **Ike Willis** guitar, vocals **Ray White** guitar, vocals
Tommy Mars keyboards **Arthur Barrow** bass **David Logeman** drums

May 23	Brussels	Belgium	Vorst Nationaal
May 24	Rotterdam	Netherlands	The Ahoy
May 26	Berlin	Germany	Deutschlandhalle
May 27	Bremen	Germany	Stadthalle
May 28	Kiel	Germany	Ostseehalle
May 30	Copenhagen	Denmark	Forum
May 31	Drammen	Norway	Drammenshallen
Jun 01	Stockholm	Sweden	Eriksdalshallen – 2 shows
Jun 02	Gothenburg	Sweden	Scandinavium
Jun 04	Hamburg	Germany	Congress Centrum Hamburg feat. **Joachim Kühn**
Jun 05	Hanover	Germany	Eilenriedehalle
Jun 07	Cologne	Germany	Sporthalle – 2 shows
Jun 08	Dortmund	Germany	Westfalenhalle
Jun 09	Düsseldorf	Germany	Philipshalle
Jun 10	Paris	France	Palais des Sports
Jun 11	Paris	France	Palais des Sports – 2 shows
Jun 13	Clermont-Ferrand	France	Chapiteau Place du 1er Mai
Jun 14	Nantes	France	Palais de la Beaujoire
Jun 15	Rouen	France	Chapiteau Place du Boulingrin
Jun 17	London	UK	Wembley Arena
Jun 18	London	UK	Wembley Arena
Jun 20	Orange	France	Theatre Antique
Jun 21	Geneva	Switzerland	Le Patinoire des Vernets
Jun 22	Zurich	Switzerland	Hallenstadion
Jun 23	Offenburg	Germany	Oberrheinhalle
Jun 25	Mannheim	Germany	Eisstadion
Jun 26	Neunkirchen am Brand	Germany	Hemmerleinhalle
Jun 27	Vienna	Austria	Stadthalle
Jun 28	Sindelfingen	Germany	Messehalle
Jun 30	Vienne	France	Theatre Antique
Jul 01	Mulhouse	France	under canvas
Jul 02	Frankfurt	Germany	Festhalle
Jul 03	Munich	Germany	Olympiahalle

114

2nd North American Tour
1980

Frank Zappa guitar, vocals **Ike Willis** guitar, vocals **Ray White** guitar, vocals **Steve Vai** stunt guitar **Bob Harris #2** keyboards, trumpet, vocals **Tommy Mars** keyboards **Arthur Barrow** bass **Vinnie Colaiuta** drums

Oct 10	Tucson	AZ	Main Auditorium, University of Arizona – 2 shows
Oct 12	Albuquerque	NM	Johnson Gymnasium, UNM feat. **Jimmy Carl Black**
Oct 13	Phoenix	AZ	Celebrity Theatre – 2 shows
Oct 14	El Paso	TX	Special Events Center, University of Texas
Oct 16	Austin	TX	Armadillo World Headquarters – 2 shows
Oct 17	Dallas	TX	Convention Center Arena
Oct 18	Tulsa	OK	Brady Theater – 2 shows
Oct 19	Oklahoma City	OK	Zoo Amphitheater
Oct 21	Houston	TX	Sam Houston Coliseum
Oct 22	Memphis	TN	Ellis Auditorium
Oct 24	Hartford	CT	Civic Center
Oct 25	Buffalo	NY	Memorial Auditorium
Oct 26	Stony Brook	NY	SUNY – 2 shows
Oct 27	Charlottesville	VA	Kidsworld (?)
Oct 28	Albany	NY	Palace Theater
Oct 30	New York	NY	Palladium
Oct 31	New York	NY	Palladium
Nov 01	New York	NY	Palladium – 2 shows
Nov 04	Washington	DC	*questionable*
Nov 05	London	Canada	London Gardens
Nov 06	Montreal	Canada	Forum
Nov 07	Upper Darby	PA	Tower Theatre – 2 shows
Nov 08	Providence	RI	Ocean State Performing Arts Center
Nov 10	Richfield	OH	Richfield Coliseum
Nov 11	Toronto	Canada	Maple Leaf Gardens
Nov 13	Pittsburgh	PA	Stanley Theater – 2 shows
Nov 14	South Bend	IN	Athletic + Convention Center, Notre Dame
Nov 15	Carbondale	IL	Southern Illinois University Arena
Nov 16	Madison	WI	Dane County Coliseum
Nov 18	St. Paul	MN	Civic Arena Bowl
Nov 20	Green Bay	WI	Brown County Veterans Memorial Arena
Nov 21	Normal	IL	University Union Auditorium, ISU – 2 shows (?)
Nov 22	Louisville	KY	Louisville Gardens
Nov 23	St. Louis	MO	Kiel Opera House – 2 shows
Nov 25	Milwaukee	WI	Milwaukee Auditorium
Nov 26	Detroit	MI	Masonic Auditorium – 2 shows
Nov 28	Chicago	IL	Uptown Theatre – 2 shows
Nov 29	Chicago	IL	Uptown Theatre – 2 shows
Nov 30	Des Moines	IA	Civic Center
Dec 02	Fort Collins	CO	Moby Gym, Colorado State University
Dec 03	Salt Lake City	UT	Terrace Ballroom – 2 shows
Dec 05	Berkeley	CA	Community Theater – 2 shows
Dec 07	Las Vegas	NV	
Dec 08	Santa Barbara	CA	Arlington Theater
Dec 09	San Diego	CA	Civic Theater
Dec 11	Santa Monica	CA	Civic Auditorium – 2 shows

CANADA
UNITED STATES OF AMERICA
MEXICO
WA
OR
ID
MT
ND
MN
SD
WY
WI
NE
IA
IL
NV
UT
CO
CA
KS
MO
AZ
NM
OK
AR
MS
TX
LA
Vancouver
Seattle
Portland
Eugene
Reno
Sacramento
Berkeley
Santa Cruz
Santa Barbara
Santa Monica
San Diego
Las Vegas
Salt Lake City
Boulder
Mesa
Tucson
Albuquerque
Norman
Tulsa
Dallas
Austin
Houston
New Orleans
Kansas City
St. Louis
Minneapolis
St. Paul
Milwauk
DeKalb
Chicago
Champaign
Bloomingt

North American Tour
1981

Frank Zappa guitar, vocals **Ray White** guitar, vocals **Steve Vai** stunt guitar
Robert Martin keyboards, tenor sax, vocals **Tommy Mars** keyboards
Scott Thunes bass **Ed Mann** percussion **Chad Wackerman** drums

Date	City	State	Venue
Sep 27	Santa Barbara	CA	Event Center, UCSB
Sep 28	Sacramento	CA	Memorial Auditorium
Sep 29	Santa Cruz	CA	Civic Auditorium – 2 shows
Oct 01	Portland	OR	Paramount Theatre – 2 shows
Oct 02	Seattle	WA	Seattle Center Arena
Oct 03	Vancouver	Canada	Pacific Coliseum
Oct 04	Eugene	OR	McArthur Court, UO feat. **Artis the Spoonman**
Oct 06	Reno	NV	Centennial Coliseum
Oct 07	Las Vegas	NV	Aladdin Theater For The Performing Arts
Oct 09	Tucson	AZ	Main Auditorium, Univ. of Arizona – 2 shows
Oct 10	Mesa	AZ	Mesa Amphitheater
Oct 11	Albuquerque	NM	Johnson Gymnasium, UNM
Oct 13	Norman	OK	Lloyd Noble Center, University Of Oklahoma
Oct 14	Tulsa	OK	Brady Theater
Oct 16	Dallas	TX	Convention Center
Oct 17	Houston	TX	The Summit
Oct 18	Austin	TX	Erwin Center, University Of Texas
Oct 20	New Orleans	LA	Saenger Performing Arts Center – 2 shows
Oct 22	St. Petersburg	FL	Bayfront Center
Oct 23	Sunrise	FL	Sunrise Musical Theatre – 2 shows
Oct 24	Gainesville	FL	O'Connell Center, University Of Florida
Oct 25	Atlanta	GA	Fox Theatre – 2 shows
Oct 27	Columbus	OH	Veterans Memorial Auditorium
Oct 29	New York	NY	Palladium
Oct 30	New York	NY	Palladium feat. **Artis the Spoonman**
Oct 31	New York	NY	Palladium – 2 shows
Nov 01	New York	NY	Palladium
Nov 03	Upper Darby	PA	Tower Theater – 2 shows
Nov 04	Providence	RI	Ocean State Theatre, PPAC – 2 shows
Nov 05	Hartford	CT	Civic Center
Nov 06	Hartford	CT	Civic Center
Nov 07	Boston	MA	Case Center, Boston University – 2 shows
Nov 08	Montreal	Canada	Forum
Nov 09	Toronto	Canada	Maple Leaf Gardens
Nov 11	Buffalo	NY	Shea's Performing Arts Center – 2 shows
Nov 12	Albany	NY	Palace Theatre
Nov 13	Syracuse	NY	Manley Field House, Syracuse University
Nov 14	Troy	NY	Rensselaer Polytechnic Institute
Nov 15	Owings Mills	MD	Painter's Mill Star Theatre – 2 shows
Nov 17	New York	NY	The Ritz – 2 shows feat. **Al di Meola** and **Brian Peters** (early show)
Nov 19	Cleveland	OH	Public Hall
Nov 20	Cincinnati	OH	Riverfront Coliseum
Nov 21	Champaign	IL	Assembly Hall, University Of Illinois
Nov 22	Bloomington	IN	Indiana University Auditorium
Nov 23	Chicago	IL	Park West Club – 2 shows
Nov 24	Pittsburgh	PA	Stanley Theatre – 2 shows
Nov 25	Detroit	MI	Cobo Hall
Nov 27	Chicago	IL	Uptown Theatre – 2 shows
Nov 28	Minneapolis	MN	Northrop Auditorium
Nov 29	St. Paul	MN	Civic – questionable
Dec 01	Milwaukee	WI	Milwaukee Auditorium
Dec 02	DeKalb	IL	Chick Evans Field House, NIU
Dec 04	St. Louis	MO	Kiel Opera House – 2 shows
Dec 05	Kansas City	MO	Municipal Auditorium
Dec 06	Boulder	CO	Event Center, University Of Colorado
Dec 07	Salt Lake City	UT	Terrace Ballroom – 2 shows
Dec 10	Berkeley	CA	Community Theatre – 2 shows
Dec 11	Santa Monica	CA	Civic Auditorium – 2 shows feat. **Ahmet Zappa, Craig "Twister" Steward** and **Nicolas Slonimsky** (early show), **Ike Willis** (late show), **Lisa Popeil** (both shows)
Dec 12	San Diego	CA	Fox Theatre – 2 shows

118

European Tour
1982

Frank Zappa guitar, vocals **Ray White** guitar, vocals **Steve Vai** guitar
Robert Martin keyboards, tenor saxophone, vocals **Tommy Mars** keyboards
Scott Thunes bass **Ed Mann** percussion **Chad Wackerman** drums

May 05	Aarhus	Denmark	Vejlby-Risskov Hallen
May 07	Stockholm	Sweden	Johanneshovs Isstadion
Max 08	Drammen	Norway	Drammenshallen
May 10	Gothenburg	Sweden	Scandinavium
May 11	Copenhagen	Denmark	Brondby-Hallen
May 12	Berlin	Germany	Deutschlandhalle
May 14	Brussels	Belgium	Vorst Nationaal
May 15	Rotterdam	Netherlands	The Ahoy
May 17	Paris	France	Hippodrome de Pantin
May 18	Paris	France	Hippodrome de Pantin
May 19	Paris	France	Hippodrome de Pantin
May 21	Cologne	Germany	Sporthalle feat. **Peter Eggers**
May 22	Düsseldorf	Germany	Philipshalle
May 23	Kiel	Germany	Ostseehalle
May 28	St. Etienne	France	Palais des Sports
May 29	Fréjus	France	Arènes de Fréjus
May 30	Cap d'Agde	France	Arènes du Cap
Jun 01	Bordeaux	France	La Patinoire
Jun 02	Rennes	France	La Salle d'Omnisports
Jun 03	Dijon	France	Palais des Sports
Jun 05	Schüttorf	Germany	Vechtewiese Open Air
Jun 06	Mannheim	Germany	Rhein-Neckar-Stadion
Jun 08	Hamburg	Germany	Congress Centrum Hamburg
Jun 09	Bremen	Germany	Stadthalle
Jun 10	Essen	Germany	Grugahalle
Jun 11	Frankfurt	Germany	Alte Oper – 2 shows
Jun 12	Frankfurt	Germany	Alte Oper – *questionable*
Jun 13	Würzburg	Germany	Feste Marienberg
Jun 15	Differdange	Luxembourg	Centre Sportif
Jun 17	Lille	France	Foire de Lille (cancelled after soundcheck)
Jun 18	London	UK	Hammersmith Odeon feat. **Dweezil Zappa**
Jun 19	London	UK	Hammersmith Odeon – 2 shows
Jun 22	Metz	France	Le Parc des Expositions
Jun 23	Böblingen	Germany	Sporthalle
Jun 24	Zurich	Switzerland	Hallenstadion feat. **Dweezil Zappa**
Jun 26	Munich	Germany	Olympiahalle feat. **Moon and Dweezil Zappa**
Jun 27	Ulm	Germany	Donauhalle
Jun 28	Vienna	Austria	Stadthalle feat. **Dweezil Zappa**
Jun 29	Linz	Austria	Sporthalle
Jul 01	Geneva	Switzerland	La Patinoire des Vernets
Jul 02	Turin	Italy	Campo Sportivo
Jul 03	Bolzano	Italy	Stadio Comunale
Jul 04	Bologna	Italy	Quartiere Fieristico
Jul 05	Genoa	Italy	Stadio Ferraris
Jul 07	Milan	Italy	Parco Redecesio
Jul 08	Pistoia	Italy	Stadio Comunale
Jul 09	Rome	Italy	Ex Mattatoio di Testaccio
Jul 12	Naples	Italy	Stadio San Paolo feat. **Massimo Bassoli**
Jul 14	Palermo	Italy	Stadio Comunale La Favorita feat. **Massimo Bassoli**

CANADA
WA
OR
ID
MT
ND
MN
SD
WY
NE
NV
UT
CA
CO
KS
MO
AZ
NM
OK
AR
TX
MS
LA
IA
WI
IL
Minneapolis
West Allis
Madison
Chicago
Indianapolis
Omaha
Des Moines
Denver
Santa Fe
Phoenix
Berkeley
Santa Cruz
Santa Barbara
Los Angeles
San Diego
Columbia
UNITED STATES OF AMERICA
MEXICO

1st North American Tour
1984

Frank Zappa guitar, vocals **Ike Willis** guitar, vocals **Ray White** guitar, vocals
Napoleon Murphy Brock tenor saxophone, vocals (Jul 17 – Aug 1)
Robert Martin keyboards, tenor saxophone, French horn, vocals
Allan Zavod keyboards **Scott Thunes** bass **Chad Wackerman** drums

Date	City	State	Venue
Jul 17	Los Angeles	CA	Palace Theater
Jul 18	Los Angeles	CA	Palace Theater
Jul 19	Los Angeles	CA	Palace Theater
Jul 20	Los Angeles	CA	Palace Theater feat. **Dweezil Zappa**
Jul 21	Los Angeles	CA	Palace Theater
Jul 22	Los Angeles	CA	Palace Theater feat. **George Duke, Johnny "Guitar" Watson, Aynsley Dunbar, Bruce Fowler** and **Denny Walley**
Jul 24	San Diego	CA	Open Air Amphitheater, San Diego State University
Jul 25	Santa Cruz	CA	Civic Auditorium
Jul 27	Berkeley	CA	Greek Theater
Jul 29	Santa Barbara	CA	County Bowl
Jul 31	Phoenix	AZ	Celebrity Theater – 2 shows
Aug 01	Santa Fe	NM	Paolo Soleri Amphitheatre
Aug 02	Denver	CO	Turn Of The Century – 2 shows
Aug 04	Denver	CO	Turn Of The Century – 2 shows
Aug 05	Omaha	NE	Civic Auditorium Music Hall
Aug 07	Des Moines	IA	Civic Center
Aug 08	Minneapolis	MN	Northrop Auditorium
Aug 10	West Allis	WI	State Fairgrounds
Aug 11	Madison	WI	Oscar Mayer Theatre, Madison Civic Center
Aug 12	Cuyahoga Falls	OH	Blossom Music Center
Aug 13	Holmdel	NJ	Garden State Arts Center
Aug 15	Toronto	Canada	Canadian National Exhibition Grandstand
Aug 16	Wantagh	NY	Jones Beach Theatre
Aug 18	Chicago	IL	Pavilion, University Of Illinois
Aug 19	Cincinnati	OH	Cincinnati Gardens
Aug 22	Indianapolis	IN	Vogue Theater – 2 shows
Aug 23	Rochester	MI	Meadowbrook
Aug 24	Rochester	MI	Meadowbrook
Aug 25	New York	NY	The Pier
Aug 26	New York	NY	The Pier
Aug 27	Syracuse	NY	State Fairgrounds
Aug 29	Poughkeepsie	NY	Mid Hudson Civic Center
Aug 30	Columbia	MD	Merriweather Post Pavilion
Aug 31	Salem	MA	Winter Island
Sep 01	Saratoga Springs	NY	Saratoga Performing Arts Center
Sep 02	Columbia	TN	Bam Webster Farm

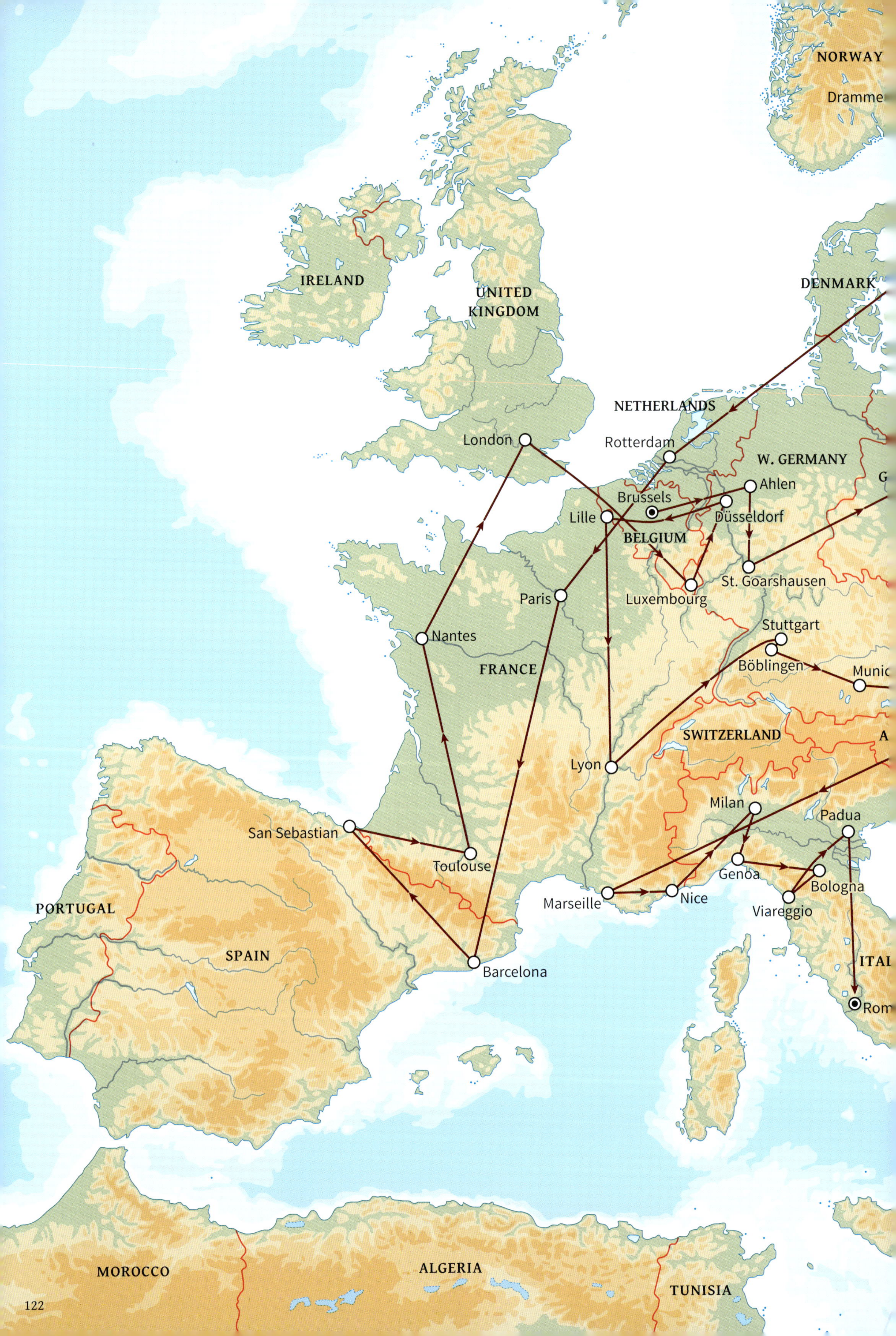
NORWAY
Dramme
IRELAND
UNITED KINGDOM
DENMARK
NETHERLANDS
London
Rotterdam
W. GERMANY
Ahlen
Brussels
Lille
Düsseldorf
BELGIUM
St. Goarshausen
Paris
Luxembourg
Nantes
Stuttgart
Böblingen
FRANCE
Munic
SWITZERLAND
Lyon
Milan
Padua
San Sebastian
Toulouse
Genoa
Bologna
Marseille
Nice
Viareggio
PORTUGAL
SPAIN
Barcelona
ITAL
Rom
MOROCCO
ALGERIA
TUNISIA

European Tour
1984

Frank Zappa *guitar, vocals* **Ike Willis** *guitar, vocals* **Ray White** *guitar, vocals*
Robert Martin *keyboards, tenor saxophone, French horn, vocals*
Allan Zavod *keyboards* **Scott Thunes** *bass* **Chad Wackerman** *drums*

Sep 07	Brussels	Belgium	Vorst Nationaal
Sep 08	Ahlen	Germany	Motorcross-Stadion am Morgenbruch
Sep 09	St. Goarshausen	Germany	Loreley-Freilichtbühne
Sep 11	Berlin	Germany	Eissporthalle
Sep 13	Drammen	Norway	Drammenshallen
Sep 14	Stockholm	Sweden	Johanneshovs Isstadion
Sep 16	Rotterdam	Netherlands	The Ahoy
Sep 17	Paris	France	Palais Omnisports de Bercy
Sep 19	Barcelona	Spain	Palacio Deportes Montjulch
Sep 20	San Sebastian	Spain	Polideportivo de Anoeta
Sep 21	Toulouse	France	Palais des Sports
Sep 22	Nantes	France	Palais de la Beaujoire
Sep 24	London	UK	Hammersmith Odeon – 2 shows
Sep 25	London	UK	Hammersmith Odeon
Sep 27	Luxembourg	Luxembourg	Ancien Hall D'Expositions
Sep 28	Düsseldorf	Germany	Philipshalle
Sep 29	Lille	France	2 shows
Sep 30	Lyon	France	Espace Tony Garnier
Oct 01	Stuttgart	Germany	Liederhalle (?)
Oct 02	Böblingen	Germany	Sporthalle
Oct 03	Munich	Germany	Circus Krone – 2 shows
Oct 04	Vienna	Austria	Stadthalle
Oct 06	Marseille	France	Le Stadium
Oct 07	Nice	France	Theatre de Verdure
Oct 08	Milan	Italy	Palazzo Dello Sport, San Siro
Oct 09	Genoa	Italy	Palasport
Oct 10	Bologna	Italy	Teatro Tenda Parco Nord
Oct 12	Viareggio	Italy	Bussoladomani
Oct 13	Padua	Italy	Palazzo dello Sport, San Lazzaro
Oct 14	Rome	Italy	Teatro Tenda Pianeta
Oct 15	Rome	Italy	Teatro Tenda Pianeta
Oct 16	Rome	Italy	Teatro Tenda Pianeta

CANADA
UNITED STATES OF AMERICA
MEXICO
Vancouver
Seattle
WA
Portland
OR
ID
MT
ND
MN
SD
WI
WY
NE
IA
Chicago
IL
NV
Salt Lake City
UT
CO
San Carlos
Fresno
CA
Universal City
KS
Kansas City
MO
St. Louis
Louisvi
Oklahoma City
Memphis
AR
OK
AZ
NM
Dallas
TX
MS
LA
Austin
Houston
San Antonio
New Orleans

2nd North American Tour
1984

Frank Zappa guitar, vocals **Ike Willis** guitar, vocals **Ray White** guitar, vocals
Robert Martin keyboards, tenor sax, French horn, vocal **Allan Zavod** keyboards
Scott Thunes bass **Chad Wackerman** drums

Date	City	State	Venue
Oct 25	Worcester	MA	E. M. Loew's Center – 2 shows
Oct 26	Providence	RI	Civic Center
Oct 27	New Haven	CT	Coliseum
Oct 28	Amherst	MA	Fine Arts Center Concert Hall, UMass – 2 shows feat. **Archie Shepp** (late show)
Oct 30	Syracuse	NY	Manley Field House, Syracuse University
Oct 31	New York	NY	Felt Forum – 2 shows
Nov 02	Montreal	Canada	Forum
Nov 03	Stony Brook	NY	Gym, SUNY – 2 shows
Nov 06	Halifax	Canada	Halifax Metro Centre
Nov 08	Quebec	Canada	Le Colisee de Quebec
Nov 09	Boston	MA	Orpheum Theater
Nov 10	Upper Darby	PA	Tower Theatre – 2 shows
Nov 11	Norfolk	VA	Chrysler Hall, Scope Plaza
Nov 13	Washington	DC	D.A.R. Constitution Hall
Nov 14	Cleveland	OH	Front Row Theatre
Nov 16	Buffalo	NY	Alumni Arena, SUNY
Nov 17	Pittsburgh	PA	Syria Mosque
Nov 18	Columbus	OH	Newport Music Hall – 2 shows
Nov 20	Louisville	KY	The Louisville Palace
Nov 21	Royal Oak	MI	Royal Oak Music Theatre – 2 shows
Nov 23	Chicago	IL	Bismarck Theatre – 2 shows
Nov 24	St. Louis	MO	Kiel Opera House
Nov 25	Atlanta	GA	Civic Center
Nov 29	Orlando	FL	Orange County Civic Center
Nov 30	Sunrise	FL	Sunrise Musical Theatre – 2 shows
Dec 01	St. Petersburg	FL	Bayfront Center
Dec 03	New Orleans	LA	McAlister Auditorium, Tulane Univ. – 2 shows
Dec 04	Memphis	TN	Orpheum Theater
Dec 06	Oklahoma City	OK	Civic Center Music Hall
Dec 08	Kansas City	MO	Uptown Theater – 2 shows
Dec 10	San Antonio	TX	Majestic Performing Arts Center
Dec 11	Austin	TX	Palmer Auditorium
Dec 12	Houston	TX	Sam Houston Coliseum
Dec 13	Dallas	TX	Fair Park Coliseum
Dec 15	Salt Lake City	UT	Abravenel Hall
Dec 17	Seattle	WA	Paramount Theatre – 2 shows
Dec 18	Vancouver	Canada	Queen Elizabeth Theatre – 2 shows
Dec 20	Portland	OR	Arlene Schnitzer Concert Hall
Dec 21	San Carlos	CA	Circle Star Theatre
Dec 22	Fresno	CA	*questionable*
Dec 23	Universal City	CA	Universal Amphitheater feat. **Dweezil Zappa**

CANADA

UNITED STATES OF AMERICA

WA, OR, ID, MT, ND, MN, WI, Muskegon, Chicago, SD, WY, NE, IA, IL, NV, UT, CO, MO, CA, KS, AZ, NM, OK, AR, MS, TX, LA

MEXICO

North American Tour
1988

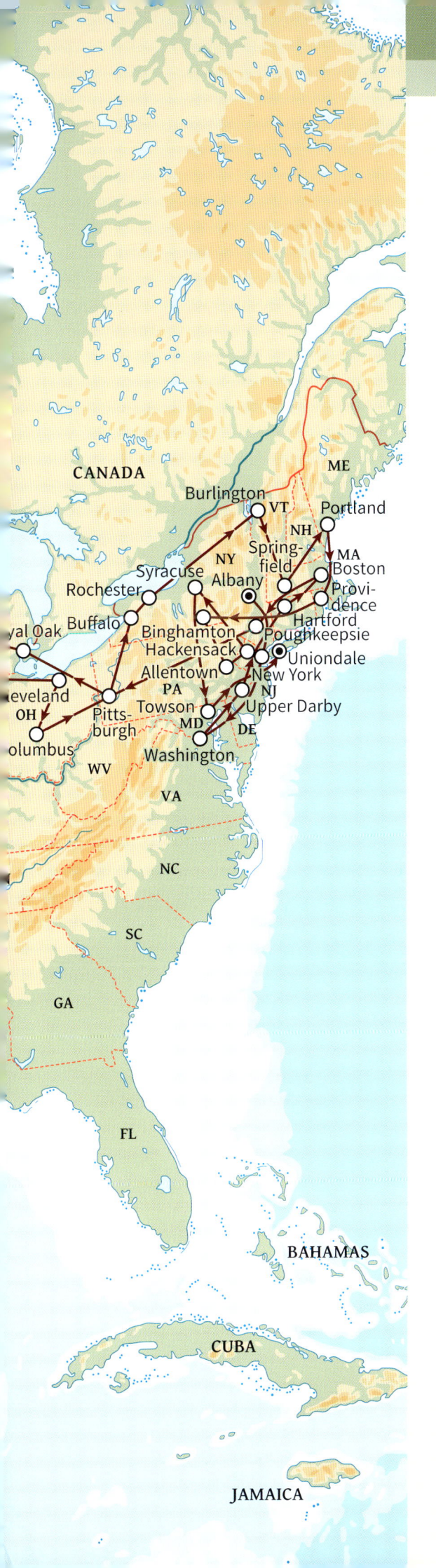

Frank Zappa guitar, synclavier, vocals **Ike Willis** rhythm guitar, vocals **Mike Keneally** stunt guitar, keyboards, vocals **Robert Martin** keyboards, synclavier, vocals **Walt Fowler** trumpet, flugelhorn, synclavier **Bruce Fowler** trombone **Paul Carman** alto sax, soprano sax **Albert Wing** tenor sax **Kurt McGettrick** baritone sax **Scott Thunes** bass, mini-moog **Ed Mann** percussion, synclavier, vocals **Chad Wackerman** drums, electronic percussion

Date	City	State	Venue
Feb 02	Albany	NY	Palace Theater
Feb 04	New York	NY	Beacon Theatre
Feb 05	New York	NY	Beacon Theater
Feb 06	New York	NY	Beacon Theater feat. **Moon, Dweezil, Ahmet** and **Diva Zappa**
Feb 08	Washington	DC	Warner Theatre
Feb 09	Washington	DC	Warner Theatre feat. **Greg Bolognese**
Feb 10	Washington	DC	Warner Theatre feat. **Daniel Schorr**
Feb 12	Upper Darby	PA	Tower Theater
Feb 13	Upper Darby	PA	Tower Theater feat. **Dweezil** and **Diva Zappa**
Feb 14	Upper Darby	PA	Tower Theater feat. **Brother A. West**
Feb 16	Hartford	CT	Bushnell Memorial Hall
Feb 17	Hartford	CT	Bushnell Memorial Hall
Feb 19	Boston	MA	Orpheum Theatre
Feb 20	Boston	MA	Orpheum Theatre
Feb 23	Poughkeepsie	NY	Mid-Hudson Civic Center
Feb 25	Pittsburgh	PA	Syria Mosque
Feb 26	Royal Oak	MI	Royal Oak Music Theatre
Feb 27	Royal Oak	MI	Royal Oak Music Theatre
Feb 28	Royal Oak	MI	Royal Oak Music Theatre
Mar 01	Muskegon	MI	Frauenthal Theater
Mar 03	Chicago	IL	Auditorium Theatre feat. **Mr. Sting**
Mar 04	Chicago	IL	Auditorium Theatre
Mar 05	Cleveland	OH	Music Hall
Mar 06	Columbus	OH	Veterans Memorial Auditorium
Mar 08	Pittsburgh	PA	Syria Mosque
Mar 09	Buffalo	NY	Shea's Theater
Mar 11	Rochester	NY	War Memorial Auditorium
Mar 12	Burlington	VT	Memorial Auditorium
Mar 13	Springfield	MA	Civic Center
Mar 15	Portland	ME	Cumberland County Civic Center
Mar 16	Providence	RI	Providence Civic Center
Mar 17	Binghamton	NY	Broome County Veterans Memorial Arena
Mar 19	Allentown	PA	Memorial Hall, Muhlenberg College
Mar 20	Hackensack	NJ	Rothman Center, Fairleigh Dickinson Univ.
Mar 21	Syracuse	NY	Landmark Theatre
Mar 23	Towson	MD	Towson Center
Mar 25	Uniondale	NY	Nassau Coliseum feat. **Dweezil Zappa, Eric Buxton** and **Brother A. West**

NORWAY
Lillestrø
IRELAND
UNITED KINGDOM
DENMARK
Birmingham
NETHERLANDS
Bremen
London
Rotterdam
W. GERMANY
Brighton
Ghent
Cologne
Dortmund
BELGIUM
Offenbach
Paris
Würzburg
Mannheim
Fürth
Strasbourg
Stuttgart
FRANCE
Munich
Bourges
Zurich
SWITZERLAND
Grenoble
Milan
Padua
Bilbao
Turin
Montpellier
Modena
Genoa
PORTUGAL
Florence
SPAIN
Madrid
ITALY
Barcelona
Seville
MOROCCO
ALGERIA
TUNISIA

European Tour
1988

Frank Zappa guitar, synclavier, vocals **Ike Willis** rhythm guitar, vocals **Mike Keneally** stunt guitar, keyboards, vocals **Robert Martin** keyboards, synclavier, vocals **Walt Fowler** trumpet, flugelhorn, synclavier **Bruce Fowler** trombone **Paul Carman** alto sax, soprano sax **Albert Wing** tenor sax **Kurt McGettrick** baritone sax **Scott Thunes** bass, mini-moog **Ed Mann** percussion, synclavier, vocals **Chad Wackerman** drums, electronic percussion

Apr 09	Bourges	France	Le Stadium
Apr 10	Ghent	Belgium	Sportpaleis
Apr 12	Berlin	Germany	Deutschlandhalle
Apr 13	Offenbach	Germany	Stadthalle
Apr 14	Cologne	Germany	Sporthalle
Apr 16	Brighton	UK	Brighton Centre
Apr 18	London	UK	Wembley Arena
Apr 19	London	UK	Wembley Arena feat. **Dweezil Zappa**
Apr 20	Birmingham	UK	National Exhibition Centre
Apr 22	Würzburg	Germany	Carl-Diem-Halle
Apr 24	Bremen	Germany	Stadthalle 4
Apr 25	Copenhagen	Denmark	Falkoner Teatret
Apr 26	Lund	Sweden	Olympen
Apr 27	Lillestrøm	Norway	Skedsmohallen
Apr 29	Helsinki	Finland	Jäähalli
May 01	Stockholm	Sweden	Johanneshovs Isstadion feat. **Dweezil Zappa, Mats Öberg** and **Morgan Ågren**
May 03	Rotterdam	Netherlands	The Ahoy
May 04	Rotterdam	Netherlands	The Ahoy
May 05	Dortmund	Germany	Westfalenhalle
May 06	Hamburg	Germany	Congress Centrum Hamburg
May 08	Vienna	Austria	Stadthalle
May 09	Munich	Germany	Rudi-Sedlmayer-Halle feat. **Dweezil Zappa**
May 11	Zurich	Switzerland	Hallenstadion
May 13	Bilbao	Spain	Velódromo
May 14	Madrid	Spain	Auditorio de la Casa de Campo
May 15	Seville	Spain	Auditorio Municipal del Prado de San Sebastián
May 17	Barcelona	Spain	Palacio de los Deportes
May 18	Montpellier	France	Le Zénith
May 19	Grenoble	France	Le Summum
May 20	Paris	France	Zénith Sud
May 23	Strasbourg	France	Hall Tivoli
May 24	Stuttgart	Germany	Liederhalle, Beethoven-Saal
May 25	Mannheim	Germany	Rosengarten, Mozartsaal
May 26	Fürth	Germany	Stadthalle
May 28	Linz	Austria	Sporthalle
May 29	Graz	Austria	Eishalle Liebenau
May 30	Udine	Italy	Palasport Primo Carnera
Jun 01	Padua	Italy	Palasport
Jun 02	Milan	Italy	Palatrussardi feat. **Fabio Treves**
Jun 03	Turin	Italy	Palasport
Jun 05	Modena	Italy	Palasport
Jun 06	Florence	Italy	Palasport
Jun 07	Rome	Italy	PalaEUR
Jun 09	Genoa	Italy	Palasport feat. **Fabio Treves**

NORWAY

IRELAND

UNITED KINGDOM

DENMA[RK]

NV
UNITED STATES OF AMERICA
CA
Los Angeles
AZ
MEXICO

NETHERLANDS

BELGIUM

GERMANY
Frankfurt

FRANCE

SWITZERLAND
A[USTRIA]

PORTUGAL

SPAIN

ITALY

MOROCCO

ALGERIA

TUNISIA

Zappa's Last Leg
1989–1993

1989

May 23	Los Angeles	CA	Schoenberg Hall – Lecture with **FZ** and **Pierre Boulez**
Nov 12	Los Angeles	CA	Rancho Park – **FZ** speech at pro-choice rally

1990

Jan	Prague	Czechoslovakia	**FZ** meets **Václav Havel**, president of Czechoslovakia
Jan 20	Prague	Czechoslovakia	Krivan Hotel – **FZ** was a special guest with Czechoslovakian bands **Garáz (Garage)** and **Milan Hlavsa's Pulnoc**
Jan 21	Prague	Czechoslovakia	**FZ** sang with **The Plastic People Of The Universe** at a party

1991

Jun 24	Prague	Czechoslovakia	Sportovní Hala – **FZ** jammed with **Michael Kocáb's** band **Prazsky Vyber**
Jun 30	Budapest	Hungary	Bucse Festival, Tabán Színpad – **FZ**'s last public performance (with a Hungarian gypsy jazz quartet "My Gypsy Friends")

1992
Ensemble Modern – "The Yellow Shark"

Peter Rundel conductor, violin **Dietmar Wiesner** flute **Catherine Milliken** oboe, english horn, didgeridoo **Roland Diry** clarinet **Wolfgang Stryi** bass clarinet, contrabass clarinet, tenor sax **Veit Scholz** bassoon, contrabassoon **Franck Ollu** horn **Stefan Dohr** horn **William Forman** trumpet, fluegelhorn, piccolo trumpet, cornet **Michael Gross** trumpet, fluegelhorn, piccolo trumpet, cornet **Uwe Dierksen** trombone, soprano trombone **Michael Svoboda** trombone, euphonium, didgeridoo, alphorn **Daryl Smith** tuba **Hermann Kretzschmar** piano, harpsichord, celeste, dramatic reading **Ueli Wiget** piano, harpsichord, celeste, harp **Rainer Römer** percussion **Rumi Ogawa-Helferich** percussion, cymbalom **Andreas Böttger** percussion **Detlef Tewes** mandolin **Jürgen Ruck** guitar, banjo **Ellen Wegner** harp **Mathias Tacke** violin **Claudia Sack** violin **Hilary Sturt** viola, dramatic reading **Friedemann Dähn** violincello **Thomas Fichter** contrabass, electrocontrabass

Sep 17	Frankfurt	Germany	Alte Oper*
Sep 18	Frankfurt	Germany	Alte Oper
Sep 19	Frankfurt	Germany	Alte Oper*
Sep 22	Berlin	Germany	Philharmonie
Sep 23	Berlin	Germany	Philharmonie
Sep 26	Vienna	Austria	Konzerthaus
Sep 27	Vienna	Austria	Konzerthaus
Sep 28	Vienna	Austria	Konzerthaus

* **FZ** appeared at two shows in Frankfurt and conducted "Overture", "Food Gathering In Post-Industrial America, 1992", "Welcome To The United States" and "G-Spot Tornado". He left from Frankfurt to Los Angeles and missed the other performances due to health problems.

1993

Jan 08	Los Angeles	CA	UMRK – **FZ** jam session at his house with **The Chieftains, L. Shankar, Johnny "Guitar" Watson** and **Tuvan throat singers**

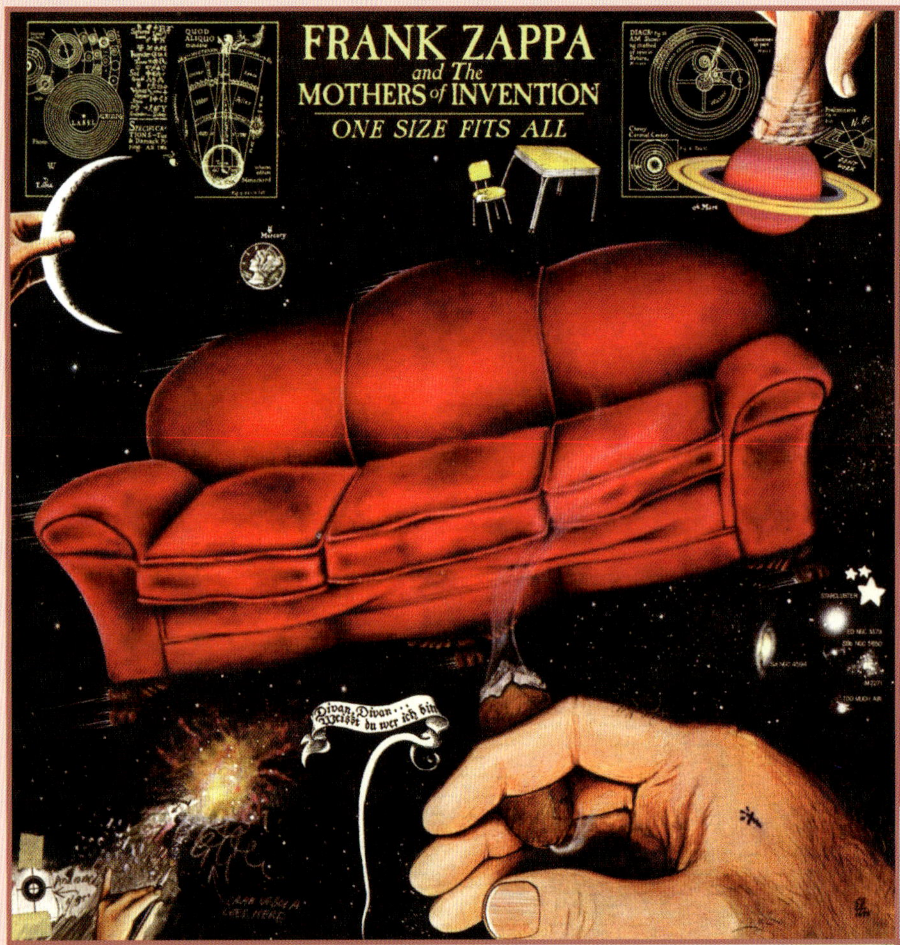
FRANK ZAPPA
and The
MOTHERS of INVENTION
ONE SIZE FITS ALL

FRAN
HOT

STEREO
Uncle Meat
(MOST OF THE MUSIC FROM THE MOTHER'S MOVIE OF THE SAME NAME WHICH WE HAVEN'T GOT ENOUGH MONEY TO FINISH YET)

F R A N
Civilizat

DA DISCZ

#	Date	Title
#1	6.66	**Freak Out!**
#2	5.67	**Absolutely Free**
#3	5.68	**Lumpy Gravy**
#4	3.68	**We're Only In It For The Money**
#5	12.68	**Cruising With Ruben & The Jets**
#6	4.69	**Uncle Meat**
#7	3.69	**Mothermania**
#8	10.69	**Hot Rats**
#9	2.70	**Burnt Weeny Sandwich**
#10	8.70	**Weasels Ripped My Flesh**
#11	10.70	**Chunga's Revenge**
#12	8.71	**Fillmore East, June 1971**
#13	10.71	**200 Motels**
#14	3.72	**Just Another Band From L.A.**
#15	7.72	**Waka/Jawaka**
#16	11.72	**The Grand Wazoo**
#17	9.73	**Over-Nite Sensation**
#18	3.74	**Apostrophe (')**
#19	9.74	**Roxy & Elsewhere**
#20	6.75	**One Size Fits All**
#21	10.75	**Bongo Fury**
#22	10.76	**Zoot Allures**
#23	3.78	**Zappa In New York**
#24	9.78	**Studio Tan**
#25	1.79	**Sleep Dirt**
#26	3.79	**Sheik Yerbouti**
#27	5.79	**Orchestral Favorites**
#28	9.79	**Joe's Garage Act I**
#29	11.79	**Joe's Garage Acts II & III**
#30	5.81	**Tinseltown Rebellion**
#31	5.81	**Shut Up 'N Play Yer Guitar**
#32	5.81	**Shut Up 'N Play Yer Guitar Some More**
#33	5.81	**Return Of The Son Of Shut Up 'N Play Yer Guitar**
#34	9.81	**You Are What You Is**
#35	5.82	**Ship Arriving Too Late To Save A Drowning Witch**
#36	3.83	**The Man From Utopia**
#37	3.83	**Baby Snakes**
#38	6.83	**London Symphony Orchestra, Vol. I**
#39	8.84	**The Perfect Stranger**
#40	10.84	**Them Or Us**
#41	12.84	**Thing-Fish**
#42	11.84	**Francesco Zappa**
#43	1.85	**The Old Masters, Box I**
#44	11.85	**Frank Zappa Meets The Mothers Of Prevention**
#45	1.86	**Does Humor Belong In Music?**
#46	11.86	**The Old Masters, Box II**
#47	11.86	**Jazz From Hell**
#48	9.87	**London Symphony Orchestra, Vol. II**
#49	12.87	**The Old Masters, Box III**
#50	4.88	**Guitar**
#51	5.88	**You Can't Do That On Stage Anymore, Vol. 1**
#52	10.88	**You Can't Do That On Stage Anymore, Vol. 2 – The Helsinki Concert**
#53	10.88	**Broadway The Hard Way**
#54	11.89	**You Can't Do That On Stage Anymore, Vol. 3**
#55	4.91	**The Best Band You Never Heard In Your Life**
#56	6.91	**You Can't Do That On Stage Anymore, Vol. 4**
#57	6.91	**Make A Jazz Noise Here**
#58	7.92	**You Can't Do That On Stage Anymore, Vol. 5**
#59	7.92	**You Can't Do That On Stage Anymore, Vol. 6**
#60	10.92	**Playground Psychotics**
#61	3.93	**Ahead Of Their Time**
#62	11.93	**The Yellow Shark**
#63	12.94	**Civilisation Phaze III**
#64	2.96	**The Lost Episodes**
#65	9.96	**Läther**
#66	10.96	**Frank Zappa Plays The Music Of Frank Zappa: A Memorial Tribute**
#67	4.97	**Have I Offended Someone?**
#68	9.98	**Mystery Disc**
#69	12.99	**EIHN – Everything Is Healing Nicely**
#70	8.02	**FZ : OZ**
#71	2.03	**Halloween**
#72	5.04	**Joe's Corsage**
#73	10.04	**Joe's Domage**
#74	9.04	**QuAUDIOPHILIAc**
#75	12.05	**Joe's XMASage**

The Official Frank Zappa Discography

#	Date	Title
#76	1.06	**Imaginary Diseases**
#77	12.06	**The MOFO Project/Object**
#78	12.06	**The MOFO Project/Object (Fazedooh)**
#79	11.06	**Trance-Fusion**
#80	4.07	**Buffalo**
#81	8.07	**The Dub Room Special!**
#82	10.07	**Wazoo**
#83	6.08	**One Shot Deal**
#84	9.08	**Joe's Menage**
#85	1.09	**The LUMPY MONEY Project/Object**
#86	12.09	**Philly '76**
#87	4.10	**Greasy Love Songs**
#88	9.10	**"Congress Shall Make No Law …"**
#89	11.10	**Hammersmith Odeon**
#90	9.11	**Feeding The Monkies At Ma Maison**
#91	10.11	**Carnegie Hall**
#92	10.12	**Road Tapes, Venue #1**
#93	10.12	**Understanding America**
#94	12.12	**Finer Moments**
#95	12.12	**Baby Snakes – The Compleat Soundtrack**
#96	10.13	**Road Tapes, Venue #2**
#97	11.13	**A Token Of His Extreme (Soundtrack)**
#98	1.14	**Joe's Camouflage**
#99	3.14	**Roxy By Proxy**
#100	6.15	**Dance Me This**
#101	11.15	**Frank Zappa: 200 Motels – The Suites**
#102	10.15	**Roxy – The Movie (Soundtrack)**
#103	5.16	**Road Tapes, Venue #3**
#104	7.16	**The Crux Of The Biscuit**
#105	7.16	**Frank Zappa For President**
#106	9.16	**ZAPPAtite – Frank Zappa's Tastlest Tracks**
#107	11.16	**Meat Light – The Uncle Meat Project/Object Audio Documentary**
#108	11.16	**Chicago '78**
#109	11.16	**Little Dots**
#110	10.17	**Halloween 77 (Box Set)**
#110K	10.17	**Halloween 77 (3 CD)**
#111	2.18	**The Roxy Performances**

Preamble

What better way to conclude this book than with a whistle-stop tour through Zappa's Official Discography?

Your guide is Andrew Greenaway – webmaster at idiotbastard.com, author of the books Zappa The Hard Way (Wymer UK, 2010) and Frank Talk: The Inside Stories Of Zappa's Other People (Wymer UK, 2017), and co-organizer of Festival Moo-ah. Andrew decided, for reasons unknown, to pen 150 untweetable words – no more, no less – on each album.

Given this constraint, Andrew has very little time to dwell on each release (though his words are supplemented by salient quotes from some very special highly evolved individuals). He does however pluck out numerous interesting nuggets of information to keep hard core fans entertained (even those who've read Charles Ulrich's excellent The Big Note!), while helping those who are not fully au fait with Frank's output have a better understanding of what happened and when.

Now brace yo'seffs, folks – this is Zappa … *THE EASY WAY!*

Freak Out!
1966

FZ / The Mothers Of Invention

Official Release #1

Originally Released: June 27, 1966

Recording data: March 9–12, 1966 at T.T.G. Studios (L.A.)

Producer: Tom Wilson

Engineers: Val Valentin, Ami Hadani, Tom Hidley

Tracks:
Hungry Freaks, Daddy (3:27)
I Ain't Got No Heart (2:33)
Who Are The Brain Police? (3:33)
Go Cry On Somebody Else's Shoulder (3:39)
Motherly Love (2:43)
How Could I Be Such A Fool (2:11)
Wowie Zowie (2:51)
You Didn't Try To Call Me (3:16)
Any Way The Wind Blows (2:54)
I'm Not Satisfied (2:38)
You're Probably Wondering Why I'm Here (3:38)
Trouble Every Day (5:49)
Help, I'm A Rock (4:43)
It Can't Happen Here (3:55)
The Return Of The Son Of Monster Magnet (12:16)

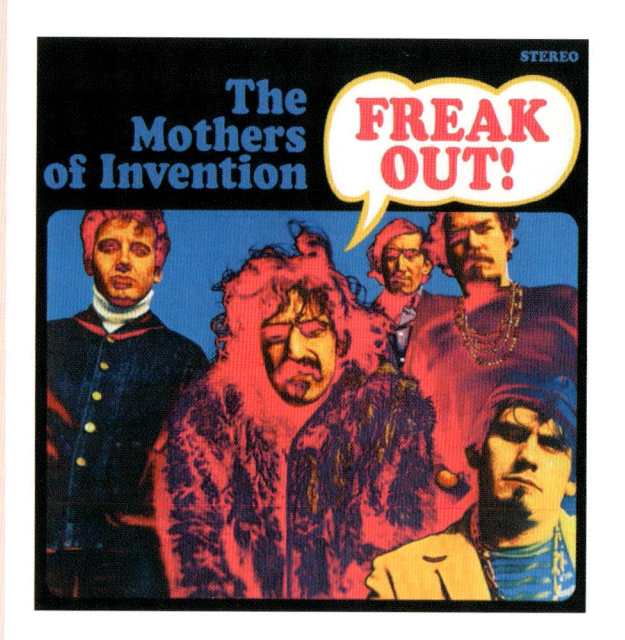

"Frank told us, 'If you will play our music, I will make you rich and famous.' He relocated us from Pomona and took us about 27 miles west to Hollywood to get us signed. I quit several times. Four times, I think. But it's an interesting album. 'Trouble Every Day' is about the Watts riots being presented on TV as a sports show. 'Help, I'm A Rock' is dedicated to Elvis Presley. 'Who Are The Brain Police?' is about mind control. Nobody heard anything like that when it came out."

Ray Collins

One of rock's first concept albums, and also one of the first double elpees (though in Germany and the UK, it was issued in abridged form as a single LP). Lyrically, the album satirises American pop culture. Musically, it's an album of two halves: the first comprising fairly conventional 2–3 minute songs; the second (starting with Trouble Every Day, an angry protest song atop a white blues backing) gets increasingly experimental – culminating in a recording made in the wee small hours after Zappa invited a bunch of freaks into the studio to play on "$500 worth of rented percussion equipment".

Zappa's extensive liner notes included a list of 179 people who had influenced him, including Edgar Varèse, Eric Dolphy, Igor Stravinsky and Guitar Slim. It is said that in turn, Freak Out! was a huge influence on The Beatles and Sgt. Pepper's Lonely Hearts Club Band, released the following year.

Absolutely Free
1967

FZ / The Mothers Of Invention

Official Release #2

Originally Released: May 26, 1967

Recording data: November 15-18, 1966 at T.T.G. Studios (L.A.)

Producer: Tom Wilson

Engineers: Val Valentin, Ami Hadani

Tracks:
Plastic People (3:42)
The Duke Of Prunes (2:13)
Amnesia Vivace (1:01)
The Duke Regains His Chops (1:50)
Call Any Vegetable (2:20)
Invocation And Ritual Dance Of The Young Pumpkin (7:00)
Soft-Sell Conclusion (1:40)
American Drinks (1:53)
Status Back Baby (2:54)
Uncle Bernie's Farm (2:11)
Son Of Suzy Creamcheese (1:34)
Brown Shoes Don't Make It (7:30)
America Drinks & Goes Home (2:46)

Additional tracks on CD:
Big Leg Emma (2:32)
Why Don'tcha Do Me Right? (2:37)

Additional tracks on 50th Anniversary Expanded 2 LP Edition:
Absolutely Free Radio Ad #1 (1:01)
Why Don'tcha Do Me Right (2:39)
Big Leg Emma (2:32)
Absolutely Free Radio Ad #2 (1:01)
"Glutton For Punishment …" (0:24)
America Drinks – 1969 Re-Mix (1:55)
Brown Shoes Don't Make It – 1969 Re-Mix (7:27)
America Drinks & Goes Home – 1969 Re-Mix (2:42)

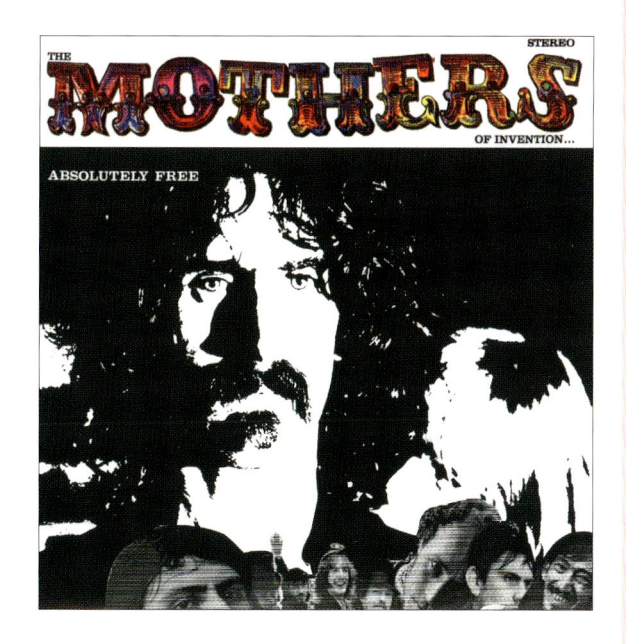

"We found a little rehearsal room just by Santa Monica Boulevard and that's where we rehearsed the material for Absolutely Free. 'Brown Shoes Don't Make It' took a lot of work because we had to learn it in sections. Frank would say, 'Do a Beach Boys thing here.' and then we'd move on to another section. We also worked on 'Call Any Vegetable' and 'The Duke Of Prunes' and a thing called 'No Regrets'. That became our ending song every night and Ray used to ad-lib around it. It was a great comedy piece that evolved into 'America Drinks & Goes Home'."

Jimmy Carl Black

Each side of the original long player were described as 'Underground Oratorios' (titled "Absolutely Free" and "The M.O.I. American Pageant" respectively). These mini-suites are separated on the CD release by a contemporaneous smash/flop single. Notable additions to the Mothers' line-up for this album are woodwinds player Bunk Gardner and keyboardist Don Preston – now octogenarians, who finally stopped touring with the GrandMothers Of Invention in 2018. Original Mothers Collins and Black cite this as their favourite album, with Brown Shoes … being the stand-out track for many – a song informing young America that, "dirty old men have no business running your country."

The album borrows from sources as diverse as 1950s blues artists and late 19th century experimental composers – eg. Lightnin' Slim (Have Your Way) and Cheltonian Gustav Holst (The Planets) – as well as quoting Richard Berry's Louie Louie. These were all things Zappa would do for the rest of his career.

Lumpy Gravy
1968

FZ / Abnuceals Emuukha Electric Symphony Orchestra & Chorus ("with maybe even some members of The Mothers of Invention")

Official Release #3

Originally Released: May 13, 1968

Recording data: January 1961 to October 1967 at Pal Recording Studio (Cucamonga), Fillmore Auditorium (San Francisco), Capitol Studios (Hollywood) and Apostolic Studios (NYC)

Producer: FZ

Engineers: Paul Buff, Joe, Rex, Pete, Jim, Bob, Gary, Dick Kunc

Indexes:
The Way I See It, Barry (0:06)
Duodenum (1:32)
Oh No (2:03)
Bit Of Nostalgia (1:35)
It's From Kansas (0:30)
Bored Out 90 Over (0:31)
Almost Chinese (0:25)
Switching Girls (0:29)
Oh No Again (1:13)
At The Gas Station (2:41)
Another Pickup (0:54)
I Don't Know If I Can Go Through This Again (3:49)
Very Distraughtening (1:33)
White Ugliness (2:22)
Amen (1:33)
Just One More Time (0:58)
A Vicious Circle (1:12)
King Kong (0:43)
Drums Are Too Noisy (0:58)
Kangaroos (0:57)
Envelops The Bath Tub (3:42)
Take Your Clothes Off (1:53)

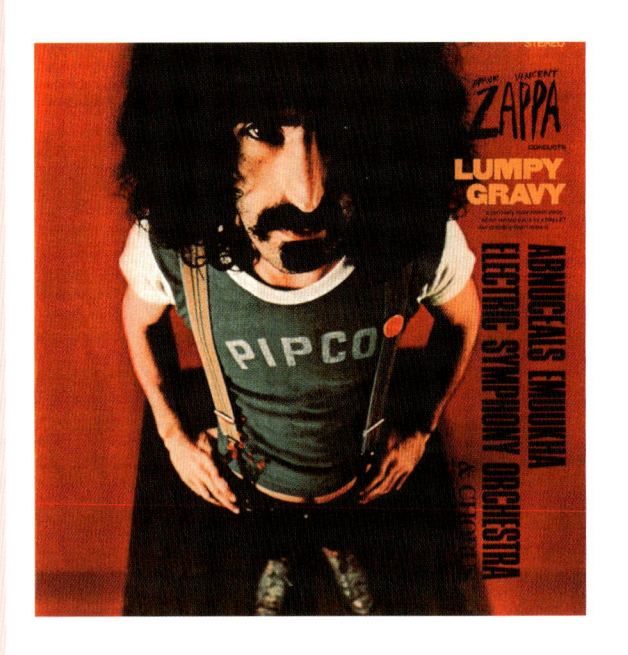

"It's from a commercial for Aloma Linda Gravy Quick, that's where the name came from. I was offered a chance to write for a 40 piece orchestra by a producer, Nick Venet, who was with Capitol Records at the time. It was the first chance I had to get a professional recording of my stuff with an orchestra, and we did it. Then there was a thirteen month litigation that held up the release."

Frank Zappa

This was issued after Official Release #4, but was largely completed beforehand; indeed, an all-orchestral version was released by Capitol Records in August 1967 but was quickly withdrawn after MGM said it violated Zappa's contract with them. The composer re-edited the material, adding Cucamongan surf music and new dialogue taped after his discovery that the strings of the Apostolic's grand piano would vibrate when a person spoke near them.

The record is dedicated to daughter Moon Unit, who was conceived prior to the orchestral recordings and born the month before the chorus of piano people were captured

If pressed, Zappa would cite this concrete mix as the favourite of all his albums.

On the back cover, he asks "Is this Phase 2 of We're Only In It For The Money?" and maintained that the material on this and his next three releases were organically related – in effect, "all one album".

We're Only In It For The Money
1968

FZ / The Mothers Of Invention

Official Release #4

Originally Released: March 04, 1968

Recording data: February to October 1967 at Capitol Studios (Hollywood), Mayfair Studios (NYC) and Apostolic Studios (NYC)

Producer: FZ

Executive Producer: Tom Wilson

Engineers: Gary Kellgren, Dick Kunc

Tracks:
Are You Hung Up? (1:24)
Who Needs The Peace Corps? (2:34)
Concentration Moon (2:22)
Mom & Dad (2:16)
Telephone Conversation (0:48)
Bow Tie Daddy (0:33)
Harry, You're A Beast (1:21)
What's The Ugliest Part Of Your Body? (1:03)
Absolutely Free (3:24)
Flower Punk (3:03)
Hot Poop (0:26)
Nasal Retentive Calliope Music (2:02)
Let's Make The Water Turn Black (2:01)
The Idiot Bastard Son (3:18)
Lonely Little Girl (1:09)
Take Your Clothes Off When You Dance (1:32)
What's The Ugliest Part Of Your Body? (Reprise) (1:02)
Mother People (2:26)
The Chrome Plated Megaphone Of Destiny (6:25)

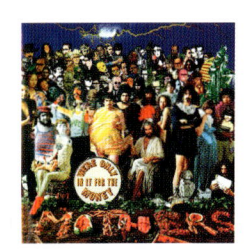

"I joined the band in August 1967, while they were based in New York. I'd never heard of Zappa, but as soon as I saw his band I knew I wanted to be a part of it. They were playing a residency at the Garrick, a tiny downstairs venue in the West Village which held maybe 150 people. The spirit of those chaotic shows spilled over into the LP. He started recording it at the Apostolic Studios in the Village, at the same time as recording Uncle Meat. The band were 'playing musicians' as opposed to trained, sight-reading musicians. I guess Frank was frustrated that he couldn't write out parts for them, but he used their characters creatively."

Ian Underwood

Both the sleeve and, in part, the music are a parody of the Beatles' Sgt. Pepper's Lonely Hearts Club Band. Fearing a lawsuit, the record label reversed the artwork; on the back, Zappa asks "Is this Phase One of Lumpy Gravy?"

Lyrically We're Only In It For The Money is heavy on political satire, taking a swing at the then happening hippie subculture which was starting to embrace the band (Jimi Hendrix is pictured on the sleeve, and Eric Clapton speaks on the record). Musically, it comprises rock and experimental music, as well as leftover orchestral segments from Lumpy Gravy.

Despite eight Mothers in dresses on the cover, plus the drummer's repeated catchphrase of "Hi, boys and girls. I'm Jimmy Carl Black and I'm the Indian of the group!", Gail Zappa would later claim that the only players on the record were FZ, Ian Underwood, Roy Estrada and Billy Mundi.

Cruising With Ruben & The Jets
1968

FZ / The Mothers Of Invention

Official Release #5

Originally Released: December 02, 1968

Recording data: 1967 to 1968 at Apostolic Studios (NYC)

Producer: FZ

Engineer: Dick Kunc

Tracks:
Cheap Thrills (2:20)
Love Of My Life (3:17)
How Could I Be Such A Fool (3:33)
Deseri (2:04)
I'm Not Satisfied (3:59)
Jelly Roll Gum Drop (2:17)
Anything (3:00)
Later That Night (3:04)
You Didn't Try To Call Me (3:53)
Fountain Of Love (2:57)
"No. No. No." (2:27)
Anyway The Wind Blows (2:56)
Stuff Up The Cracks (4:29)

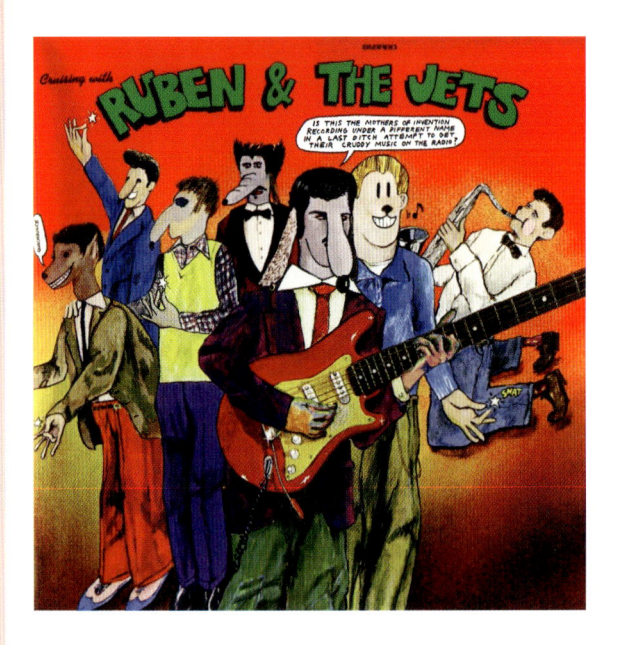

"There was a lot of nonsense in the press when Cruising With Ruben & The Jets came out, about how it 'fooled people'. The fact is, everybody knew it is the Mothers Of Invention because it said so on the cover. I conceived that album along the same lines as the compositions in Stravinsky's neo-classical period. If he could take the forms and clichés of classical era and pervert them, why not do the same with rules and regulations applied to doo-wop in the fifties?"

Frank Zappa

An album of "greasy love songs and cretin simplicity" that is Zappa's perverted paean to the 50s doo-wop music he loved. By the time of Zappa's wah-wah guitar solo on the final track, the band's cover is completely blown – yet reputedly some disc jockeys were taken in by this uncharacteristic Mothers' album.

Sharing Zappa's passion for doo-wop – and having the perfect high falsetto for the job – singer Ray Collins wrote (or co-wrote) four of the songs: unusual for a Zappa album.

Singer/songwriter Ruben Guevara later told Zappa of his fondness for the album and the style of music it pastiched, and in 1973 Zappa produced For Real!, an album by Ruben's group (now renamed Ruben And The Jets), bolstered by "Motorhead" Sherwood of the Mothers on sax. The Jets also included Tony Duran on slide guitar, who would tour and record with Zappa during the Grand (and 'Petit') Wazoo years.

Uncle Meat
1969

FZ / The Mothers Of Invention

Official Release #6

Originally Released: *April 21, 1969*

Recording data: *1967 to September 1982 at Apostolic Studios (NYC), Royal Albert Hall (London), Falkoner Teatret (Copenhagen), Gulfstream Park, Hallandale (FL), Whisky à Go-Go (LA), Sunset Sound (LA), Stadio Communale La Favorita (Palermo) and UMRK (LA)*

Producer: *FZ*

Engineers: *Dick Kunc, Jerry Hansen, Wally Heider*

Tracks:
Uncle Meat: Main Title Theme (1:55)
The Voice Of Cheese (0:26)
Nine Types Of Industrial Pollution (6:00)
Zolar Czakl (0:54)
Dog Breath, In The Year Of The Plague (3:59)
The Legend Of The Golden Arches (3:27)
Louie Louie (At the Royal Albert Hall in London) (2:18)
The Dog Breath Variations (1:48)
Sleeping In A Jar (0:50)
Our Bizarre Relationship (1:05)
The Uncle Meat Variations (4:46)
Electric Aunt Jemima (1:46)
Prelude To King Kong (3:38)
God Bless America (Live at the Whisky A Go Go) (1:10)
A Pound For A Brown On The Bus (1:29)
Ian Underwood Whips It Out (Live in Copenhagen) (5:05)
Mr. Green Genes (3:14)
We Can Shoot You (2:03)
"If We'd All Been Living In California …" (1:14)
The Air (2:57)
Project X (4:48)
Cruising For Burgers (2:18)
King Kong Itself (as played by the Mothers in a studio) (0:51)
King Kong (its magnificence as interpreted by Dom DeWild) (1:19)
King Kong (as Motorhead explains it) (1:45)
King Kong (the Gardner Varieties) (6:17)
King Kong (as played by 3 deranged Good Humor Trucks) (0:33)
King Kong (live on a flat bed diesel in the middle of a race track at a Miami Pop Festival … the Underwood ramifications) (7:25)

Additional tracks on CD:
Uncle Meat Film Excerpt Part I (37:34)
Tengo Na Minchia Tanta (3:46)
Uncle Meat Film Excerpt Part II (3:51)

"It has a piece where Jimmy Carl Black, the Indian in the group, is bitching because we are not making any money and it's taking too long for the band to make it. Two songs about El Monte Legion Stadium. A song about fake IDs. Another song about teats. A surrealistic R&B song called 'The Air Escaping From Your Mouth'. Two other surrealistic things: 'Mr Green Genes' and 'Electric Aunt Jemima'. Lots of instrumentals. On one song we used 40 tracks and the tune lasts 90 seconds. That one took us four days to put together."
Frank Zappa

Zappa introduced this as the soundtrack to a film "you will probably never get to see", though a straight-to-video 'making of' documentary of the same name was released 18 years later.

On this album, Zappa not only demonstrates what he's learnt in the studio thus far but develops things further still with an innovative approach to recording: experimenting with tape speeds, using instruments not normally associated with rock music, a larger ensemble, extensive overdubbing and razor-sharp editing.

Uncle Meat contains a mad variety of delicious jazz, doo-wop, spoken word segments and baroque & roll that prepare us for the thrilling denouement that is King Kong – a snippet of which appeared on Lumpy Gravy, and a piece that would become a staple of live shows up until Zappa's final tour.

This is the first Mothers' album to focus on the music rather than the politically conscious lyrics of their previous albums.

Mothermania
1969

FZ / The Mothers Of Invention

Official Release #7

Originally Released: *March 24, 1969*

Recording Data: *March 09, 1966 to October 1967 at T.T.G. Studios (LA) and Mayfair & Apostolic Studios (NYC).*

Producers: *Tom Wilson, FZ*

Engineers: *Val Valentin, Ami Hadani, Tom Hidley, Gary Kellgren, Dick Kunc*

Tracks:
Brown Shoes Don't Make It (7:26)
Mother People (1:41)
Duke Of Prunes (5:09)
Call Any Vegetable (4:31)
The Idiot Bastard Son (2:26)
It Can't Happen Here (3:13)
You're Probably Wondering Why I'm Here (3:37)
Who Are The Brain Police? (3:22)
Plastic People (3:40)
Hungry Freaks, Daddy (3:27)
America Drinks And Goes Home (2:43)

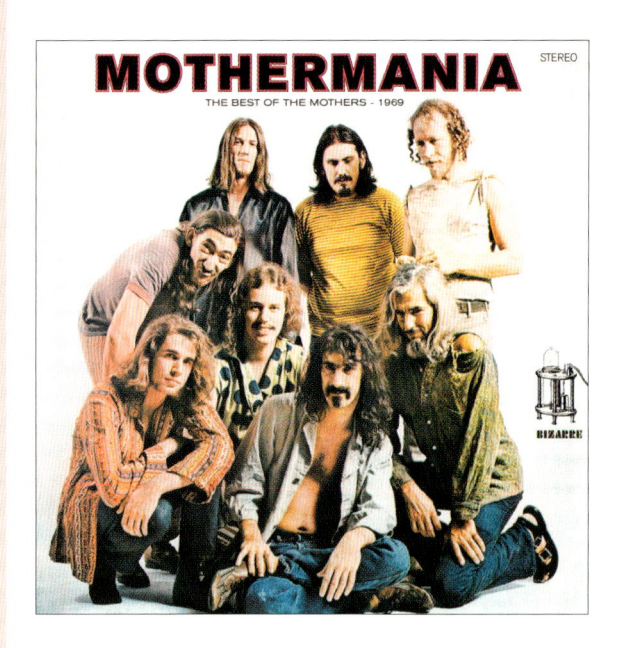

"I put Mothermania together. Instead of sending them a final master tape, I sent them lacquers. You can't play back a lacquer. They couldn't listen to it, but they released it anyway."

Frank Zappa

The sole 'best of' album compiled and released by Zappa during his lifetime saw him pull the wool over Verve's eyes by including an uncensored version of Mother People and different mixes of other songs.

Later in 1969, Zappa would break up the band, complaining "Maybe in two or three years people will be able to look back and assess what the Mothers accomplished; maybe they'll be able to catch up with the music." This album though was prepared in order to recoup some of the money the record label felt it lost funding the first three Mothers albums.

Percussionist Art Tripp appears with the band on the album's front cover, but all of the material included was recorded before he became a Mother.

Mothermania was unavailable for many years, until its release as a digital download (via Zappa.com) in 2009, and then UMe reissued it (on CD) in 2012.

Hot Rats
1969

FZ

Official Release #8

Originally Released: October 10, 1969

Recording data: July to August 1969 at T.T.G. (LA), Sunset Sound (LA) and Whitney Studios (Glendale)

Producer: FZ

Engineers: Dick Kunc, Jack Hunt, Cliff Goldstein, Brian Ingoldsby

Tracks:
Peaches En Regalia (3:37)
Willie The Pimp (9:16)
Son Of Mr. Green Genes (8:58)
Little Umbrellas (3:03)
The Gumbo Variations (16:57)
It Must Be A Camel (5:16)

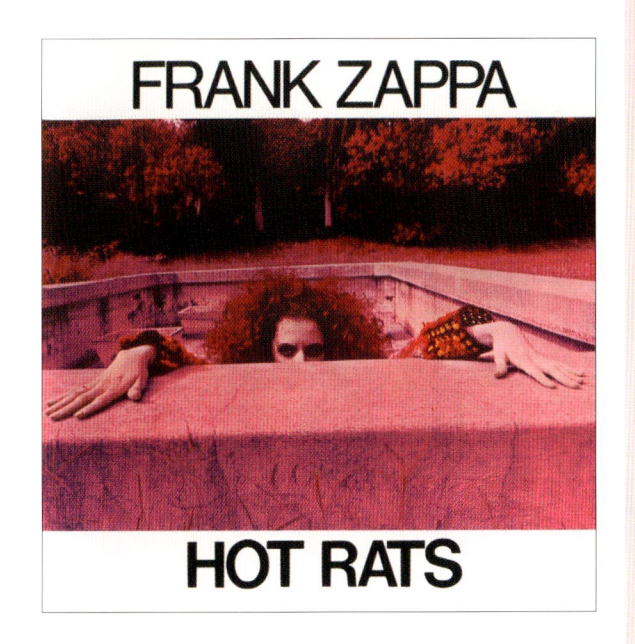

"This was a big change in direction for Frank. What attracted me to the band when I joined was a mixture of all the things I liked – a combination of Stockhausen, Ornette Coleman, corny jokes, blues, Stravinsky and so on. That's what I liked – complex music with bizarre humour. By the time we got to Hot Rats, the standard line is that Frank didn't want to be stereotyped as just a comedy rock performer, so he ditched the jokey lyrics and the experimental stuff for this album of instrumentals. That's not quite the case. I think he was keen to record an album of instrumentals, and he wanted to work with very technically adept players who could play anything he put in front of them. The album was kind of a turn from the way the earlier band had been. It was a chance to use a few studio musicians and try other routines out."

Ian Underwood

Having split-up the Mothers, Zappa set about making a second solo album that appealed to a wider audience – notably in the UK and Holland. The jazz-flavoured Hot Rats is one of the first rock albums to be recorded using 16-track equipment. To help fully utilise this new technology, he retained the services of Underwood, who overdubbed a dazzling array of wind instruments and keyboards – including the 'organus maximus', which was the pipe organ at Whitney Studios.

Only Willie The Pimp included vocals – those of old schoolfriend Don Van Vliet (a.k.a. Captain Beefheart). But all featured top-notch musicians, such as the drummers Ron Selico and John Guerin, bassist Max Bennett, and violinists Jean-Luc Ponty and Don 'Sugarcane' Harris (who Zappa helped get out of jail to play on this "movie for your ears").

The iconic cover depicts Christine Frka of the GTOs peering out from an abandoned Beverly Hills lily pond.

Burnt Weeny Sandwich
1970

FZ / Mothers Of Invention

Official Release #9

Originally Released: February 09, 1970

Recording data: July 1967 to July 24, 1969 at Mayfair & Apostolic Studios (NYC), The Ark, Boston (MA), Royal Albert Hall (London), A&R Studios (NYC) and T.T.G. Studios (LA)

Producer: FZ

Engineers: Dick Kunc, et al.

Tracks:
WPLJ (2:52)
Igor's Boogie, Phase One (0:37)
Overture To A Holiday In Berlin (1:27)
Theme From Burnt Weeny Sandwich (4:32)
Igor's Boogie, Phase Two (0:37)
Holiday In Berlin, Full-Blown (6:23)
Aybe Sea (2:46)
The Little House I Used To Live In (18:42)
Valarie (3:14)

"Frank gave us the music to a piece that was called 'The Hunchback Duke' which later became known as 'Little House I Used To Live In'. He had been writing a lot of new music on the road. We rehearsed it every day before the show. As with lots of the pieces he was writing, we would learn them in sections."

Jimmy Carl Black

The first of two 'posthumous' Mothers releases features live and studio recordings of the band sandwiched between doo-wop covers.

WPLJ was originally recorded by The 4 Deuces in 1955; its b-side was Here Lies Love, which the Mothers also performed (see You Can't Do That On Stage Anymore, Vol. 5).

The original material is all instrumental and belatedly demonstrates, in the wake of Hot Rats' success, that the Mothers had contained great players all along.

The Little House I Used To Live In is edited together from a number of performances and improvisations to form one cohesive piece that takes up the bulk of side two. Tagged onto the end is Zappa's response to a heckler at London's Royal Albert Hall in June 1969.

Burnt Weeny Sandwich is also the title of "an 18 minute fantasy film" directed by Zappa that confusingly contained mostly music from the Uncle Meat record.

Weasels Ripped My Flesh
1970

FZ / Mothers Of Invention

Official Release #10

Originally Released: *August 10, 1970*

Recording data: *1967 to September 1969 at Apostolic Studios (NYC), Royal Festival Hall (London), Thee Image, Miami (FL), Criteria Studios, Miami (FL), The Factory (The Bronx), Philadelphia Arena (PA), Town Hall (Birmingham, UK), A&R Studios (NYC), T.T.G. Studios (LA), Whitney Studios (Glendale)*

Producer: *FZ*

Engineers: *Dick Kunc, et al.*

Tracks:
Didja Get Any Onya? (6:51)
Directly From My Heart To You (Penniman) (5:16)
Prelude to the Afternoon of a Sexually Aroused Gas Mask (3:48)
Toads of the Short Forest (4:48)
Get a Little (2:31)
The Eric Dolphy Memorial Barbecue (6:52)
Dwarf Nebula Processional March & Dwarf Nebula (2:12)
My Guitar Wants To Kill Your Mama (3:32)
Oh No (1:45)
The Orange County Lumber Truck (3:21)
Weasels Ripped My Flesh (2:08)

"... it was one of those men's magazines like Saga. The cover story was 'Weasels Ripped My Flesh' and it was the adventure of a guy, naked to the waist, who was in water. The water was swarming with weasels, and they were all kind of climbing on him and biting him. So Frank said, 'This is it. What can you do that's worse than this?' And the rest is history."

Neon Park

With a tribute to jazz multi-instrumentalist Eric Dolphy, a preponderance of improvised live cuts, dazzling edits, a cover of a Little Richard's Directly From My Heart To You (featuring stupendous vox and violin from "Sugarcane" Harris), the second posthumous Mothers album is different from the first, though equally compelling.

The opening track on the Rykodisc CD reissue interpolates a live performance of a piece called Charles Ives (another listee in Freak Out's liners), a studio recording of which was used as the backing for The Blimp on the Zappa-produced Beefheart album, Trout Mask Replica.

The track also features Lowell George, affecting a German accent to talk about childhood experiences.

The album's striking cover art is by Neon Park, whose work would adorn several albums by Little Feat, the band George later formed with Estrada.

Zappa would work again with Preston, Estrada and Black, but never all at the same time.

Chunga's Revenge
1970

FZ

Official Release #11

Originally Released: October 23, 1970

Recording data: July 1969 to August 29, 1970 at T.T.G. (LA), The Record Plant (LA), Trident Studios, London (UK), Tyrone Guthrie Theater (Minneapolis) and Whitney Studios (Glendale)

Producer: FZ

Engineers: Dick Kunc, Stan Agol, Roy Baker, Bruce Margolis

Tracks:
Transylvania Boogie (5:01)
Road Ladies (4:10)
Twenty Small Cigars (2:17)
The Nancy & Mary Music (9:27)
part 1 (2:42)
part 2 (4:11)
part 3 (2:37)
Tell Me You Love Me (2:33)
Would You Go All The Way? (2:29)
Chunga's Revenge (6:15)
The Clap (1:23)
Rudy Wants To Buy Yez A Drink (2:44)
Sharleena (4:03)

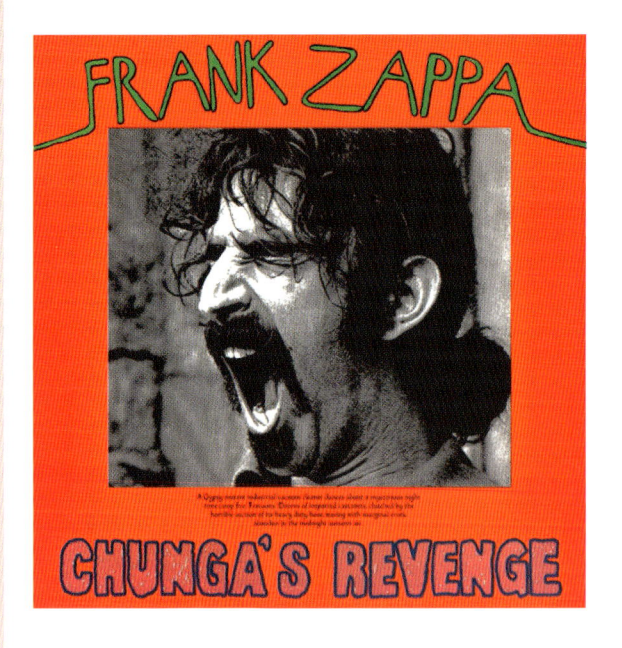

"This was my first LP with Frank, and it was a steep learning curve for me – I was the strait-laced jazz musician in a rock'n'roll band. Most jazz guys would consider themselves too heavy to do the kind of stupid things Frank had us doing. But I dug it. You had guys like Aynsley Dunbar, who was pure rock'n'roll. Ian Underwood was still in the band. There was always a lot of multi-tasking with Frank. He liked musicians who could double up on tour. That helped to keep costs down! But you can hear that we're adept at blues ('Road Ladies'), heavy rock ('Tell Me You Love Me') and even vaudeville ('Rudy Wants To Buy Yez A Drink')."

George Duke

Following the success of Hot Rats and the disbandment of the original band, Zappa was now better placed to pick musicians he wanted to work with, and so this album introduces the sophomore Mothers. Fronted by former Turtles vocalists Mark Volman and Howard Kaylan (due to contractual complications, here re-named The Phlorescent Leech and Eddie), with keyboard whiz George Duke and ex-Bluesbreakers' drummer Aynsley Dunbar, the new band is musically more adept as well as being fairly accessible to mainstream rock audiences.

The Nancy & Mary Music is the sole 'in concert' recording here, and Twenty Small Cigars (a song from Studio Z days, and originally titled Transition) was recorded during the Hot Rats sessions.

Lyrically, Zappa was becoming quite brazen – doubtless egged-on by Flo & Eddie, whose vocal prowess shone on tracks like Tell Me You Love Me and Sharleena.

The opening and title tracks are both stand-out instrumentals.

Fillmore East, June 1971
1971

FZ / The Mothers

Official Release #12

Originally Released: August 02, 1971

Recording data: June 05-06, 1971 at Fillmore East (NYC)

Producer: FZ

Engineer: Barry Keene

Tracks:
Little House I Used To Live In (4:41)
The Mud Shark (5:22)
What Kind Of Girl Do You Think We Are? (4:17)
Bwana Dik (2:21)
Latex Solar Beef (2:38)
Willie The Pimp Part One (4:03)
Willie The Pimp Part Two (1:54)
Do You Like My New Car? (7:08)
Happy Together (2:57)
Lonesome Electric Turkey (2:32)
Peaches En Regalia (3:22)
Tears Began To Fall (2:46)

"I am pleased with the way it came out. We did it on 16 tracks and Barry Keene engineered it. The better cuts on the album were 'Willie The Pimp' and 'Peaches En Regalia'. It turned out very well."

Frank Zappa

After issuing a number of tracks recorded in concert, this is the first fully live Zappa long player – sometimes known as the 'penzil front' album.

1971 was the year that the right to vote in the United States was extended to all citizens aged eighteen and older, Zappa added to Cal Schenkel's handwritten liner notes, "Don't forget to register to vote" – something he would continue to urge America to do for the rest of his life, arguing that "Democracy doesn't work unless you participate."

Utilising the comedic talents of the former Turtles vocalists, the album contains a number of groupie routines that start with the story of a girl, a mud shark and members of the Vanilla Fudge, and culminate with Volman demanding that Kaylan play his "big hit record" before they'll agree to fulfil his wildest dreams. This is a cue for a rousing rendition of Happy Together.

200 Motels
1971

FZ

Official Release #13

Originally Released: October 04, 1971

Recording data: January 28 to Summer 1971 at Pinewood Studios (London) and Whitney Studios (LA)

Producer: FZ

Engineers: Bob Auger, Barry Keene

Tracks:
Semi-Fraudulent/Direct-From-Hollywood Overture (1:59)
Mystery Roach (2:32)
Dance Of The Rock & Roll Interviewers (0:48)
This Town Is A Sealed Tuna Sandwich (prologue) (0:55)
Tuna Fish Promenade (2:29)
Dance Of The Just Plain Folks (4:40)
This Town Is A Sealed Tuna Sandwich (reprise) (0:58)
The Sealed Tuna Bolero (1:40)
Lonesome Cowboy Burt (3:59)
Touring Can Make You Crazy (2:52)
Would You Like A Snack? (1:23)
Redneck Eats (3:02)
Centerville (2:31)
She Painted Up Her Face (1:41)
Janet's Big Dance Number (1:18)
Half A Dozen Provocative Squats (1:57)
Mysterioso (0:48)
Shove It Right In (2:32)
Lucy's Seduction of A Bored Violinist & Postlude (4:01)
I'm Stealing The Towels (2:14)
Dental Hygiene Dilemma (5:11)
Does This Kind of Life Look Interesting To You? (2:59)
Daddy, Daddy, Daddy (3:11)
Penis Dimension (4:37)
What Will This Evening Bring Me This Morning (3:32)
A Nun Suit Painted On Some Old Boxes (1:08)
Magic Fingers (3:53)
Motorhead's Midnight Ranch (1:28)
Dew On The Newts We Got (1:09)
The Lad Searches The Night For His Newts (0:41)
The Girl Wants To Fix Him Some Broth (1:10)
The Girl's Dream (0:54)
Little Green Scratchy Sweaters & Courduroy Ponce (1:00)
Strictly Genteel (the finale) (11:10)

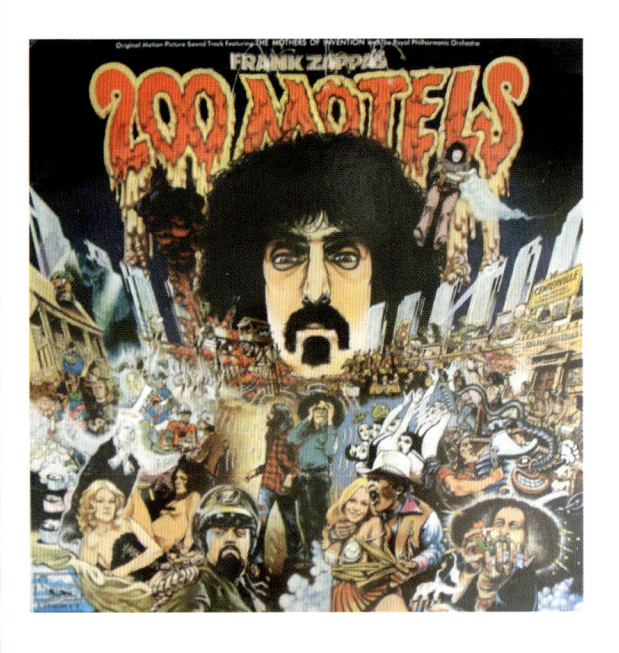

"This music is not in the same order as in the movie. Some of this music is not in the movie. Some of the music that's in the movie is not in the album. Some of the music that was written for the movie or the album. All of this music was written for the movie over a period of four years."

Frank Zappa

Intent on proving 'touring can make you crazy', but with no real script as such, the overly ambitious Zappa somehow persuaded United Artists to let him make a film in the UK that would feature Ringo Starr (dressed as Zappa, playing Larry the Dwarf), The Who's Keith Moon (as a hot nun), actor/folk singer Theodore Bikel (as the narrator), and to have his music performed by the Royal Philharmonic Orchestra conducted by Elgar Howarth.

Zappa also managed to lure back for cameo appearances, spurned Mothers Black (as Lonesome Cowboy Burt) and Preston.

Bassist Jeff Simmons walked out during filming to be replaced on screen by Ringo's driver, Martin Lickert, whose bass playing was largely overdubbed by Zappa later.

This soundtrack album features music by The Mothers and the RPO, as well as a classical guitar ensemble supervised by John Williams, later of Sky and Theme from The Deer Hunter fame.

Just Another Band From L.A.
1972

FZ / The Mothers

Official Release #14

Originally Released: March 26, 1972

Recording data: August 07, 1971 at Pauley Pavilion, UCLA (CA)

Producer: FZ

Engineer: Barry Keene

Tracks:
Billy The Mountain (24:47)
Call Any Vegetable (7:22)
Eddie, Are You Kidding? (3:09)
Magdalena (6:24)
Dog Breath (3:38)

"Frank used to give Howard and I the job of going into every town we went to and researching things like the hip places to go and what the kids would laugh at. If we played a university, it'd be our responsibility to find out the people to use in the show to make fun of, and that was Frank's way of keeping the show alive. Every time we played it, 'Billy The Mountain' had little idiosyncrasies about the town, all the psychedelic dungeons, the places you'd go to eat, the hip pseudo-intellectual spots where pot was smoked, the professors who were in trouble because they messed around with girls in class. Whatever it was, we'd use these things, and it was a very clever way of taking the show to the next level. It made the show very three-dimensional, because it wasn't just us performing, we were using places that the audience would recognise in the show, to show how important they were as well. It brought you into the show."

Mark Volman

Dominated by the side-long tale of Billy The Mountain (and his stunning wife Ethell, a tree), Just Another Band From L.A. marks the end of the second incarnation of the Mothers.

Edited while recovering from his annus horribilis (a planned 200 Motels show at the Albert Hall got cancelled, the band lost all of its equipment in a fire in Montreux, and Zappa was pushed from the stage of London's Rainbow Theatre), it makes a perfect companion to the Fillmore East album, recorded two months earlier.

As well as listing himself, Kaylan and Volman as co-composers of Eddie, Are You Kidding? (about a Wilshire Boulevard clothing store owner who made cheesy TV commercials in the 70s), Zappa also bequeathed a credit to Turtles drummer John Seiter. Kaylan penned the troublesome words to Magdalena (about a father lusting after his teenage daughter). Much better are the two 'oldies' on side two.

Waka / Jawaka
1972

FZ / Hot Rats

Official Release #15

Originally Released: July 05, 1972

Recording data: April to May 1972 at Paramount Studios (LA)

Producer: FZ

Engineer: Kerry McNabb

Tracks:
Big Swifty (17:22)
Your Mouth (3:12)
It Just Might Be A One-Shot Deal (4:16)
Waka/Jawaka (11:19)

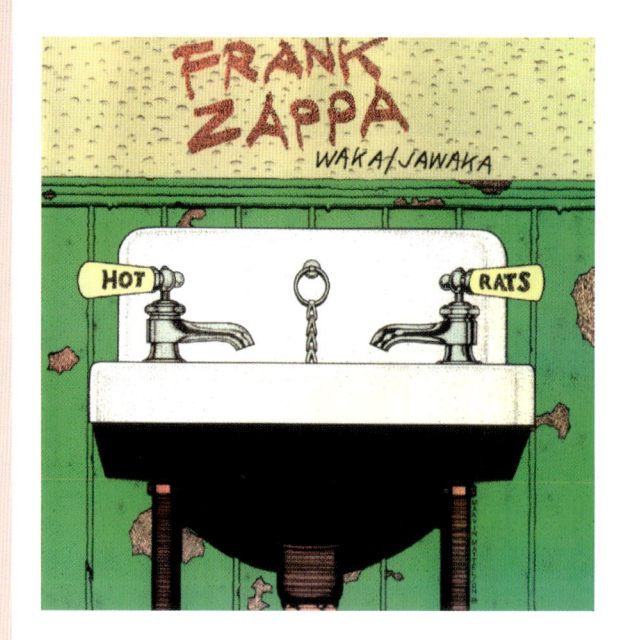

"It was a pleasure to work with Frank. He let things flow. I just sat back and wrote down his licks while he played them, which I suspect he was very impressed with. On the Waka/Jawaka and Grand Wazoo albums I ended up writing and arranging all the horn parts and giving him ideas – and he was very accepting. We had a good chemistry, maybe because we shared the same birthday."

Sal Marquez

Now confined to a wheelchair, Zappa pursued the jazz-fusion avenues explored on Hot Rats, recruiting notable horn players like trumpeter Sal Marquez and bringing back former Mothers Duke, Dunbar and Preston (whose mini-moog solo on Waka/Jawaka deserves special mention).

Big Swifty is a side-long instrumental (interestingly, Miles Davis, Return To Forever, Yes, Genesis and Jethro Tull released similarly epic pieces in 1972) that, like the title track, features multi-tracked brass to create a big band sound.

The two short songs in-between are not typical Zappa pieces, though at this point nobody could second-guess what he might come out with next – especially having Flying Burrito Brother "Sneaky Pete" Kleinow provide a thrilling pedal steel solo on It Just Might Be A One-Shot Deal, which also features Zappa on electric bed springs and Simmons on Hawaiian guitar.

Zappa said that the album's title was "something that showed up on a ouija board."

The Grand Wazoo
1972

FZ

Official Release #16

Originally Released: November 27, 1972

Recording data: April to May 1972 at Paramount Studios (LA)

Producer: FZ

Engineer: Kerry McNabb

Tracks:
The Grand Wazoo (13:20)
For Calvin (And His Next Two Hitch-Hikers) (6:06)
Cletus Awreetus-Awrightus (2:57)
Eat That Question (6:42)
Blessed Relief (8:00)

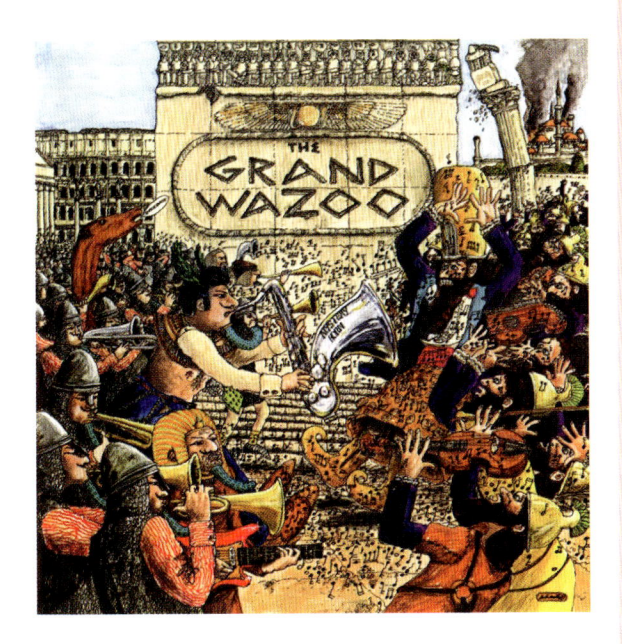

"Waka/Jawaka and The Grand Wazoo were jazz records, but Frank wouldn't admit it. I'd say, 'Frank, you're playing jazz.' He'd say, 'No I'm not.' That whole thing led to his well-known saying, 'Jazz isn't dead, it just smells funny.' One reason I went back with Frank from Cannonball was because he'd hired a bunch of jazz guys that I'd worked with – like Sal Marquez, who's a great trumpet player."

George Duke

Recorded in tandem with Waka/Jawaka, but featuring many more woodwind and brass players, The Grand Wazoo is again largely instrumental and came with a story poking fun at the music business (vividly brought to life in Cal Schenkel's cover art).

On release, the album opened with For Calvin, about a hippie couple who jumped uninvited into the backseat of Schenkel's car ("I figured they were on acid or something. I just couldn't communicate with them.")

The title track (which became Think It Over when Zappa added lyrics for a proposed science fiction musical) is a lengthy blues/jazz shuffle that gives ample opportunity for extended soloing from the ensemble. Eat That Question starts with delightful electric piano playing from Duke, and ends with some roof-raising horn blowing.

Blessed Release provides a lovely, melodic ending, and should become a jazz standard. The Grand Wazoo was the final release on Zappa's Bizarre label.

Over-Nite Sensation
1973

FZ / The Mothers

Official Release #17

Originally Released: September 07, 1973

Recording data: March to June 1973 at Bolic Sound (Inglewood), Whitney (Glendale) and Paramount Studios (LA)

Producer: FZ

Engineers: Barry Keene, Terry Dunavan, Fred Borkgren, Steve Desper, Kerry McNabb

Tracks:
Camarillo Brillo (3:59)
I'm The Slime (3:34)
Dirty Love (2:58)
Fifty-Fifty (6:10)
Zomby Woof (5:10)
Dinah-Moe Humm (6:02)
Montana (6:33)

Bonus track on 2012 iTunes download:
I'm The Slime (single version)

"Bruce called me up and I auditioned for Frank and somehow I got the gig. I hadn't even been playing bass, but I guess he got sick of looking for a bass player. This was in 1973. The audition was very simple. He had me play a couple of odd muted things and groove for a while, and then he said 'OK, you're it'. That was a really good band."
Tom Fowler

Between the release of Waka/Jawaka and The Grand Wazoo, Zappa hit the road with the 20-piece Mothers/Hot Rats/Grand Wazoo electric orchestra.

Following these big band forays, he now started to piece together a tight-knit rocking combo.

For the recording of Over-Nite Sensation (and the solo album that followed), Zappa retained Marquez and Duke, brought back Ponty and Ian & Ruth Underwood (who had played marimba on Uncle Meat), and added Fowler brothers Bruce (trombone) and Tom (bass). He also came up with a batch of lyrics that would have an enduring appeal, some of which he would pay Tina Turner and the Ikettes to sing, though most he would sing himself in his new, lower voice (thanks to a crushed larynx).

Camarillo Brillo, Dirty Love and Dinah-Moe Humm detail tales of a sexual nature, I'm The Slime mocks TV, while Montana is a sing-along yarn of a dental floss farmer.

Apostrophe (')
1974

FZ

Official Release #18

Originally Released: March 22, 1974

Recording data: August 1969 to early 1974 at Electric Lady (NYC), Bolic Sound (Inglewood), Paramount Studios (Hollywood), et al.

Producer: FZ

Engineers: Steve Desper, Terry Dunavan, Barry Keene, Bob Hughes, Kerry McNabb

Tracks:
Don't Eat The Yellow Snow (2:07)
Nanook Rubs It (4:37)
St. Alfonzo's Pancake Breakfast (1:51)
Father O'Blivion (2:18)
Cosmik Debris (4:13)
Excentrifugal Forz (1:33)
Apostrophe' (5:50)
Uncle Remus (2:44)
Stink-Foot (6:34)

"This was my first album with Frank. On most of his records he'd featured guest singers on a lot of tracks – guys like Ray Collins, Roy Estrada, Jimmy Carl Black. But on this he wanted to feature himself, to use the unique oddness of his voice. The backing vocals were done by myself, George Duke, Tina Turner and the Ikettes. People often say his music is virtuosic – musicians trying to play as many notes as they can – but it's the very opposite of that. Sure, he needed virtuosos like myself to play the music he wrote. But his music was trying to connect to people in a unique fashion. It's close to stand-up comedy in places. 'Don't Eat The Yellow Snow' and 'Stink-Foot' are both hilarious."

Napoleon Murphy Brock

The bulk of this album was recorded during the summer of 1973, but as became the norm as his career progressed, Zappa would use bits and pieces from many different eras to achieve whatever was in his head at the time – hence some basic tracks recorded over three years earlier.

This album was originally issued in both stereo and quadraphonic formats, and an edited version of the opening song became Zappa's first chart single – albeit somewhat of a novelty hit. The first four tracks, often referred to as the 'Yellow Snow Suite', are based on a dream about an Eskimo named Nanook.

The title track is an instrumental jam featuring legendary Cream bassist Jack Bruce and drummer Jim Gordon.

The final cut, which would become a staple of his live shows, is partly inspired by a Dr. Scholl's TV advert featuring a dog that faints when confronted with smelly feet.

Roxy & Elsewhere
1974

FZ / Mothers

Official Release #19

Originally Released: September 10, 1974

Recording data: December 08 to May 11, 1974 at The Roxy (LA), Edinboro State College (PA) and Auditorium Theater (Chicago) with overdubs at Bolic & Paramount Studios (Hollywood)

Producer: FZ

Engineers: Wally Heider, Kerry McNabb, Bill Hennigh

Tracks:
Penguin In Bondage (6:48)
Pygmy Twylyte (2:12)
Dummy Up (6:03)
Village Of The Sun (4:17)
Echidna's Arf (Of You) (3:53)
Don't You Ever Wash That Thing? (9:40)
Cheepnis (6:31)
Son Of Orange County (5:53)
More Trouble Every Day (6:00)
Be-Bop Tango (Of The Old Jazzmen's Church) (16:41)

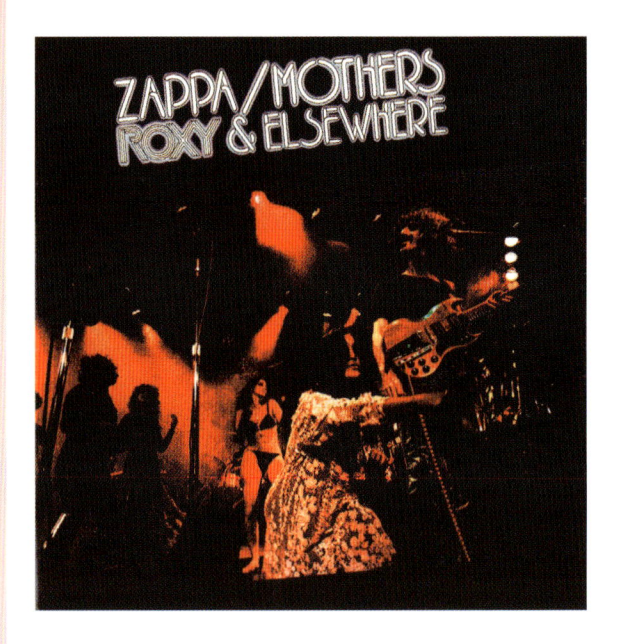

"Back in 1973, he had Ruth and George who could play that super-fast stuff faster than me. The trombone is just too hard; it's impossible to play as fast as a marimba or a piano. We did things like 'The Be-Bop Tango' and 'Echidna's Arf' pretty well, but then they got so fast that I could only just play them."

Bruce Fowler

Mostly recorded at the Roxy Theatre on Sunset Strip, this album captures the brief but exciting overlapping tenure of drummers Ralph Humphrey and Chester Thompson. The musicianship is on another level, and many fans regard this era as the Mothers' finest. Listen to the breathtaking Village/Echidna's/Wash That segue (side two of the original vinyl), and it's hard to argue.

Zappa's droll preambles to a number of the songs were originally listed as separate tracks.

Penguin In Bondage deals with consensual sexual deviation; Dummy Up has Brock verbally sparring with special guest Simmons (their improvisation belatedly earning them a writing credit); Cheepnis is about cheesy monster movies; and Be-Bop Tango acts as both a vehicle for audience participation and for Zappa to mock jazz.

It would be over 40 years later – with the release of Roxy – The Movie – that the world could witness exactly what was happening up there on stage.

One Size Fits All
1975

FZ / The Mothers Of Invention

Official Release #20

Originally Released: June 25, 1975

Recording data: August 27, 1974 to April 1975 at KCET (LA), Kulttuuritalo (Helsinki), Caribou Ranch (Nederland), The Record Plant (LA) and Paramount Studios (LA)

Producer: FZ

Engineers: Kerry McNabb, Gary O, Jukka, Michael Braunstein

Tracks:
Inca Roads (8:45)
Can't Afford No Shoes (2:38)
Sofa No. 1 (2:39)
Po-Jama People (7:39)
Florentine Pogen (5:27)
Evelyn, A Modified Dog (1:04)
San Ber'dino (5:57)
Andy (6:04)
Sofa No. 2 (2:42)

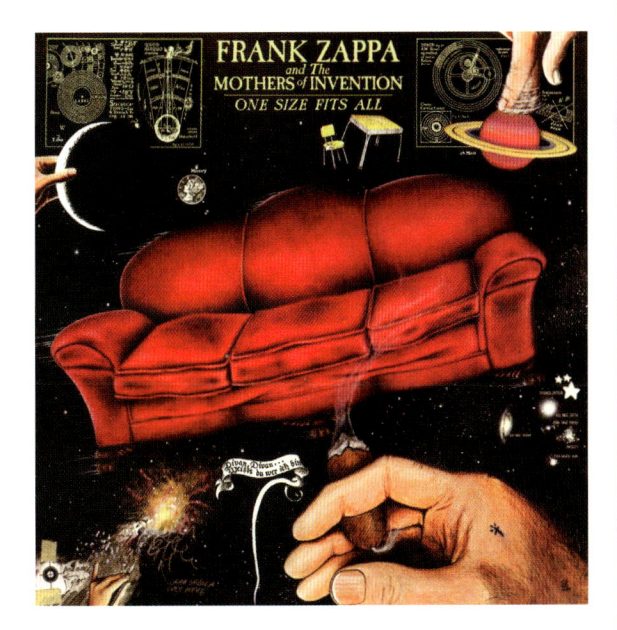

"For me, this was Frank's best line-up: me, George Duke on keyboards, Ruth Underwood on vibes and marimba, Chester Thompson on drums, Tom Fowler on bass. Everyone is brilliant. And we had gotten used to working with each other, so it was like a family. We listened to each other. We had conscious awareness of each other's playing. Frank had found a combination of six people who could play anything he wrote, but make it sound like we were improvising. He'd also started writing for our characters. He wrote 'Inca Roads' for George's voice. Same with 'Florentine Pogen', which he wrote for me. And he wrote two great songs for Johnny 'Guitar' Watson, 'San Ber'dino' and 'Andy', which really use Johnny's lovely, creamy voice. You look at the later line-ups, and there are some great musicians there, but there wasn't the same camaraderie. Frank was working with yes-men, people who just wanted to kiss his ass. We were different. We pushed Frank as much as he pushed us."

Napoleon Murphy Brock

In his sleeve notes, Zappa pronounced himself "ready to go back on the road" though he would do so without Chester Thompson and Ruth Underwood. In 1975, he threw a lifeline to his teenage pal Captain Beefheart (who guests here under the pseudonym Bloodshot Rollin' Red): despite still having the Fowler brothers, Brock and Duke onboard, the new incarnation of the Mothers would not be as enduring or memorable.

But we're jumping ahead: One Size Fits All was the Roxy band's sublime swansong.

The majestic Inca Roads was inspired by Erich von Däniken's book, Chariots Of The Gods? and, like Florentine Pogen and Andy, would subsequently become a staple of every tribute band's live set – including Zappa Plays Zappa, who in fact performed the album in its entirety on its 2015 tour.

Sofa was first performed by the Flo & Eddie line-up and appears here with and without lyrics.

Bongo Fury
1975

FZ / Beefheart

Official Release #21

Originally Released: October 02, 1975

Recording data: January 08 to May 21, 1975 at The Record Plant (LA) and Armadillo World Headquarters (Austin)

Producer: FZ

Engineers: Kerry McNabb, Mike Braunstein, Kelly Kotera, Mike Stone, Davey Moire, Frank Hubach

Tracks:
Debra Kadabra (3:54)
Carolina Hard-core Ecstasy (5:59)
Sam With The Showing Scalp Flat Top (2:51)
Poofter's Froth Wyoming Plans Ahead (3:03)
200 Years Old (4:32)
Cucamonga (2:24)
Advance Romance (11:17)
Man With The Woman Head (1:28)
Muffin Man (5:32)

"This is his most compelling live album. You've got the vestige of that tight jazz band that he developed – myself, Napi, Chester Thompson and the Fowler brothers, Tom on bass and Bruce on trombone – but it sure as hell ain't jazz we're playing. It's heavy blues rock, very dense. On the live tracks, you had this young, brash drummer, Terry Bozzio, giving us this rockier edge. And Beefheart is incredible on this. My memories are of that '75 tour. What a trip! Sitting on the bus with all these crazy people. Beefheart never slept. He'd always be drawing, and he'd carry shopping bags filled with poems. He'd be pacing hotel hallways, muttering to himself. Beefheart couldn't remember lyrics, so the words would be scribbled on bits of paper on the floor. Onstage, Frank would always place Beefheart in front of Frank's guitar amp. He knew that, whenever he hit this one particular chord, real loud, Beefheart would do something funny. It was hilarious, every night. But Frank got a kick out of it. He loved to push people's buttons!"
George Duke

Almost totally live, this album marks the US Bicentennial through 200 Years Old (one of two full studio recordings) and Poofter's Froth. It also introduces slide guitarist Denny Walley, who would join Beefheart's Magic Band later that year, and the talents of young drummer Terry Bozzio.

Debra Kadabra is loaded with private jokes and was custom-made for Beefheart, who gets to recite his own Sam With The Showing Scalp Flat Top and Man With The Woman Head.

Like the curiously sentimental Village Of The Sun before, Cucamonga harks back to Zappa's early years. Muffin Man starts with studio-recorded silliness that segues into a memorable riff and blistering guitar solo from Zappa.

Due to contractual issues between Beefheart and Virgin, the album was available only on import in the UK until its CD release in 1989, the year Václav Havel became President of Czechoslovakia. Bongo Fury was Havel's favourite Zappa album.

Zoot Allures
1976

FZ

Official Release #22

Originally Released: October 20, 1976

Recording data: 1972 to June 1976 at Bolic Sound (Inglewood), Hofstra University (Hempstead), Kosei Nenkin Kaikan (Osaka) and The Record Plant (LA)

Producer: FZ

Engineers: Michael Braunstein, Davey Moire, FZ

Tracks:
Wind Up Workin' In A Gas Station (2:30)
Black Napkins (4:15)
The Torture Never Stops (9:45)
Ms. Pinky (3:40)
Find Her Finer (4:07)
Friendly Little Finger (4:17)
Wonderful Wino (3:38)
Zoot Allures (4:12)
Disco Boy (5:10)

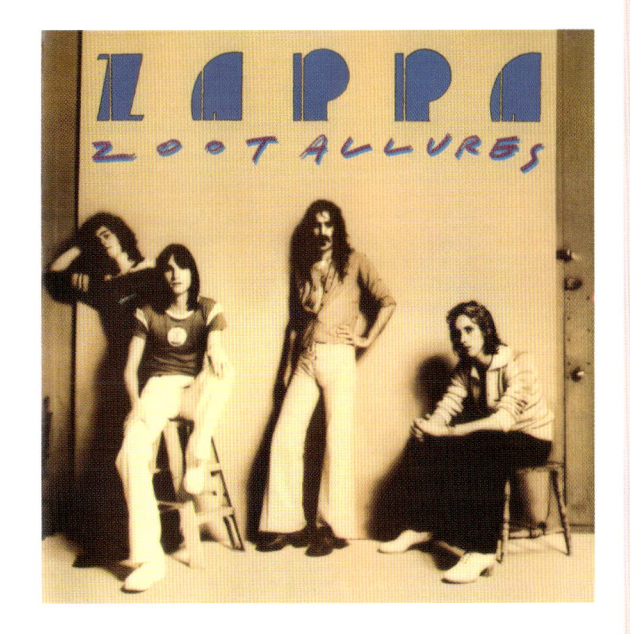

"The sound effects to 'The Torture Never Stops' were an evening's work. We did most of it in the bedroom of my house. There were two chicks there – one was my wife – plus myself. I think they enjoyed it very much. We got four hours on tape and then cut it down to just under ten minutes. My friend opens up with the first grunt and it carries on from there."

Frank Zappa

Hot Rats was essentially a team effort by Zappa and Underwood, and so too is Zoot Allures something of a collaboration – this time with Bozzio. Beefheart is again one of the 'guest' musicians, playing harmonica on Ms. Pinky (a 'lonely person device') and Find Her Finer.

Friendly Little Finger is an early example of Xenochrony, where tracks from unrelated sources are synchronized, creating a brand new composition.

Zoot Allures features two of Zappa's 'signature' guitar pieces: Black Napkins (recorded on the Pacific tour at the start of 1976) and the titular tune.

Wonderful Wino started life as an instrumental by Simmons for his Lucille Has Messed My Mind Up album, for which producer Zappa penned some words. The song would be played by the 1970 Mothers, and was re-recorded for this elpee.

Gas Station (an ode to higher education) and Disco Boy feature the hilarious high-pitched vocals of engineer Moire.

Zappa In New York
1978

FZ

Official Release #23

Originally Released: March 03, 1978

Recording data: December 26-29, 1976 to April 1977 at The Palladium (NYC) and The Record Plant (LA)

Producer: FZ

Engineers: Bob Liftin, Rick Smith, Davey Moire, FZ

Tracks:
Titties & Beer (7:36)
I Promise Not To Come In Your Mouth (3:31)
Punky's Whips (10:50)
Honey, Don't You Want A Man Like Me? (4:11)
The Illinois Enema Bandit (12:41)
Manx Needs Women (1:50)
The Black Page Drum Solo-Black Page #1 (3:50)
Big Leg Emma (2:17)
Sofa (2:56)
Black Page #2 (5:36)
The Purple Lagoon – Approximate (16:40)

Additional tracks on CD:
Cruisin' For Burgers (9:12)
I'm The Slime (4:24)
Pound For A Brown (3:41)
The Torture Never Stops (12:34)

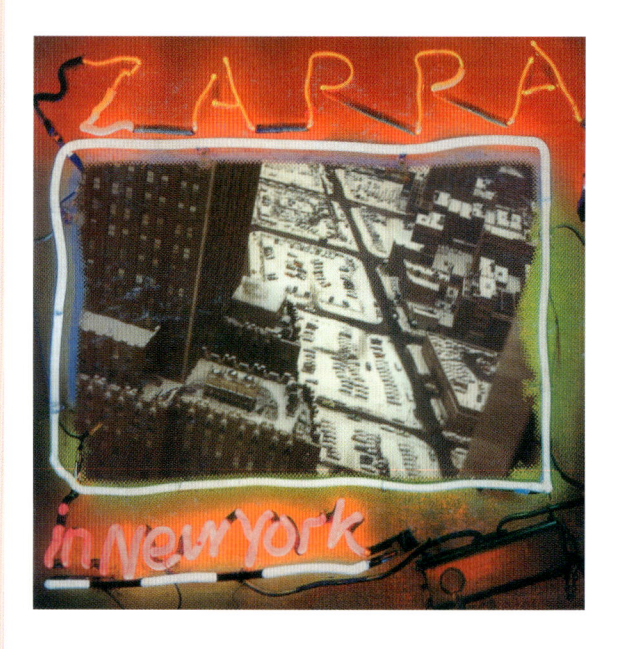

"He was always hearing the studio musicians in LA talking about the fear of going into sessions some morning and being faced with 'the black page'. So he decided to write his 'Black Page'. Then he gave it to me, and I could play parts of it right away. But it wasn't a pressure thing, it just sat on my music stand and for about 15 minutes every day for two weeks before we would rehearse I would work on it. And after two weeks I had it together and I played it for him. And he said, "Great!" took it home, wrote the melody and the chord changes, brought it back in. And we all started playing it."

Terry Bozzio

Shortly after issuing this double-album, Warners became concerned that Punky Meadows (guitar player with glam-rockers Angel, whose pout and hair Zappa mocks on Punky's Whips) might take legal action, and removed the offending track from subsequent pressings. An enraged Zappa would sue the company, while Meadows would claim to be flattered.

Zappa appeared on the late-night TV sketch show, Saturday Night Live, on 11 December 1976 and borrowed some of the house band's horn section – as well as Don Pardo, the show's announcer – for these festive season recordings.

Zappa's band proper now included Zoot Allures' cover stars Eddie Jobson (ex-Roxy Music on keyboards/violin) and Patrick O'Hearn (bass). And Ray White, whose soulful vocals on Enema Bandit are a delight.

Titties & Beer features Bozzio as the devil trying to attain Zappa's soul in exchange for the titular t'ings. With The Black Page the album's showpiece, the drummer's future was assured.

Studio Tan
1978

FZ

Official Release #24

Originally Released: *September 15, 1978*

Recording data: *August 1969 to 1976 at Caribou Ranch (Nederland), The Record Plant (LA), Royce Hall (LA), et al.*

Producer: *FZ*

Engineers: *Unknown*

Tracks:
The Adventures Of Greggery Peccary (20:34)
Revised Music For Guitar And Low-Budget Orchestra (7:36)
Lemme Take You To The Beach (2:44)
RDNZL (8:13)

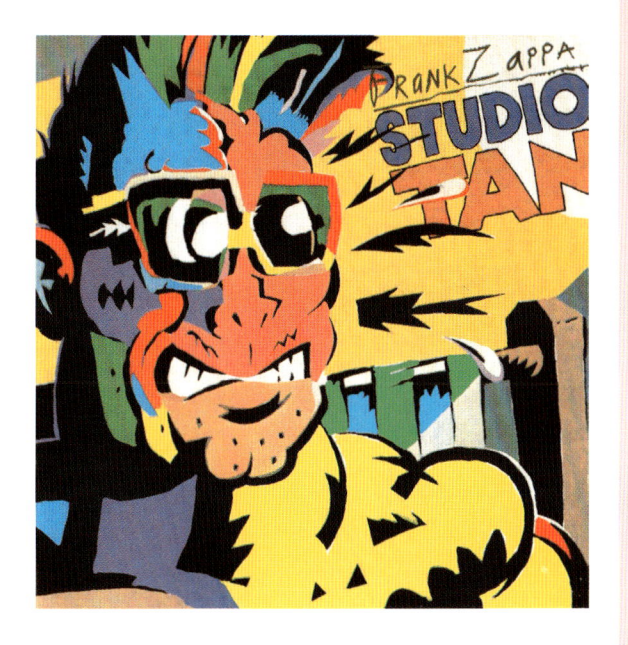

"'Revised Music for Guitar And Low-Budget Symphony Orchestra' is a short chamber orchestra piece originally composed as a vehicle for violinist Jean-Luc Ponty, re-orchestrated here as a solo vehicle for guitar. One segment began as an improvised solo, played in the studio to the existing track. Bruce Fowler transcribed it and quadrupled it with trombone parts recorded at various speeds."

Frank Zappa

The first of three legal obligation albums that, to Zappa's chagrin, Warners presented in sleeves with 'unappealing' artwork by Gary Panter. For the 1991 CD release of Studio Tan, Zappa slightly amended some of the song titles – and the running order – to those shown above. But for all three albums, he retained the original cover art.

Petulant!

The first track here is a chamber orchestra piece with narration, telling the story of a little pig who invents the calendar and the problems that triggers.

Bonkers!

Revised Music is a truncated re-recording of a piece that first appeared on the King Kong: Jean-Luc Ponty Plays The Music Of Frank Zappa album in 1970.

Epic!

Lemme Take You To The Beach is a breezy little number ideal for more Moire vocals.

Riotous!

RDNZL is a showcase for Duke's keyboard prowess that had been first performed by the 1973 band with Ponty.

Righteous!

159

Sleep Dirt
1979

FZ

Official Release #25

Originally Released: *January 19, 1979*

Recording data: *December 1974 to 1984 at Caribou Ranch (Nederland), Record Plant (LA) and UMRK (LA)*

Producer: *FZ*

Engineers: *Mark Pinske, et al.*

Tracks:
Filthy Habits (7:33)
Flambay (4:54)
Spider Of Destiny (2:33)
Regyptian Strut (4:13)
Time Is Money (2:49)
Sleep Dirt (3:21)
The Ocean Is The Ultimate Solution (13:17)

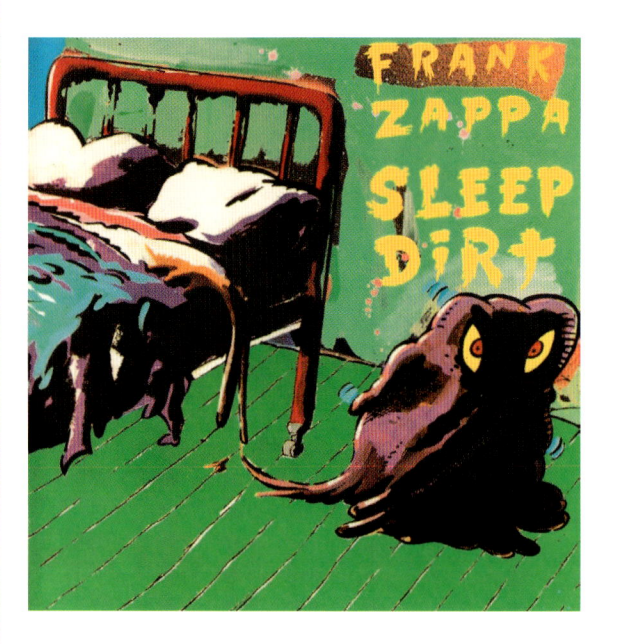

"You listen to it ['Sleep Dirt'] and you think somebody just pressed record and this is two people playing, you know my dad playing a solo and the other guy playing the accompaniment. And if that's what happens when he's improvising, it's amazing to me – his ability to spontaneously compose in that way, because it's an amazing guitar solo in every way."

Dweezil Zappa

The second legal obligation album, released in what was an annus mirabilis for fans (four more albums would follow; two of them doubles), at a time when the early records were hard to acquire legitimately, causing new admirers to have a somewhat distorted view of Zappa's output.

Presented to Warners as Hot Rats III, this album was wholly instrumental. But Zappa had written lyrics for Flambay, Spider Of Destiny and Time Is Money, which were all intended for Hunchentoot, a planned science-fiction musical. It would take Zappa several years to find a suitable singer, and it wasn't until the 1991 CD reissue that they would appear with vocals overdubbed by Thana Harris.

Filthy Habits (an aptly dirty sounding guitar excursion) and the title track (an acoustic guitar duet) were intended for an aborted two disc version of Zoot Allures.

Ocean is an edited trio-jam, featuring Zappa on 'glass-shattering' 12-string guitar.

Sheik Yerbouti
1979

FZ

Official Release #26

Originally Released: March 03, 1979

Recording data: October 31, 1977 to 1979 at The Palladium (NYC), Hammersmith Odeon (London), Deutschlandhalle (Berlin), Hemmerleinhalle (Neunkirchen am Brand) and The Village Recorders (LA)

Producer: FZ

Engineers: Peter Henderson, Davey Moire, Claus Wiedemann, Kerry McNabb, Joe Chiccarelli

Tracks:
I Have Been In You (3:34)
Flakes (6:41)
Broken Hearts Are For Assholes (3:42)
I'm So Cute (3:09)
Jones Crusher (2:49)
What Ever Happened To All The Fun In The World (0:33)
Rat Tomago (5:17)
Wait A Minute (0:31)
Bobby Brown Goes Down (2:49)
Rubber Shirt (2:43)
The Sheik Yerbouti Tango (3:58)
Baby Snakes (1:50)
Tryin' To Grow A Chin (3:32)
City Of Tiny Lites (5:31)
Dancin' Fool (3:43)
Jewish Princess (3:16)
Wild Love (4:09)
Yo' Mama (12:35)

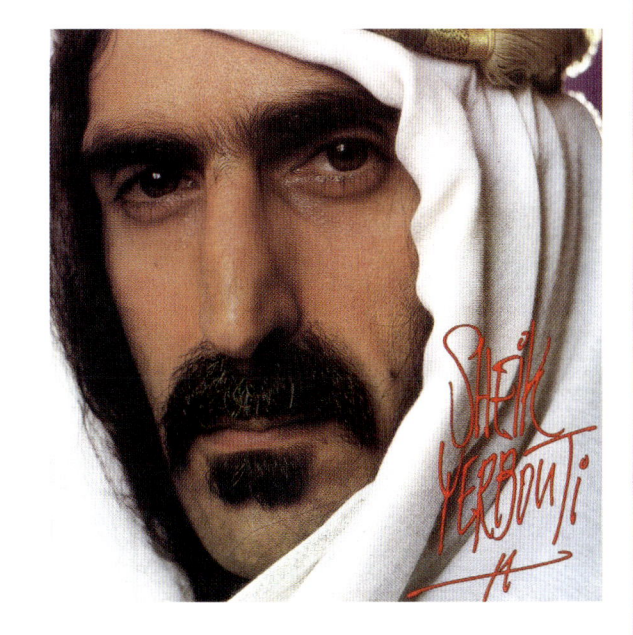

"It has three guitar solos on it. One of them is called 'The Sheik Yerbouti Tango', the other one is 'Rat Tomago' and the longest one is in a song called 'Yo' Mama', which is on side four."

Frank Zappa

The basic tracks for the majority of these songs were recorded at London's Hammersmith Odeon in early 1978. Massive studio overdubbage then ensued.

What's particularly notable is that Zappa had not released any of these songs before, so he was using the road to test and embellish material before recording it for posterity – just as the Marx Brothers had done before many of their better films. This would cause him problems, though, as bootleggers released new songs before him.

There's a whole lotta mocking going on here: the opening number pokes fun at Peter Frampton's I'm In You; the album title is a play on KC And The Sunshine Band's Shake Your Booty; Dancin' Fool sends up 70s disco culture; and Jewish Princess roused the ire of the Anti-Defamation League.

Rubber Shirt is another winning instance of Xenochrony, featuring Bozzio and O'Hearn seemingly playing together at different times and spaces.

Orchestral Favorites
1979

FZ

Official Release #27

Originally Released: May 04, 1979

Recording data: September 18-19, 1975 at Royce Hall (LA)

Producer: FZ

Engineers: Unknown

Tracks:
Strictly Genteel (7:04)
Pedro's Dowry (7:41)
Naval Aviation In Art? (1:22)
Duke Of Prunes (4:20)
Bogus Pomp (13:27)

"I really needed a vacation and even had a room reserved at a hotel. Then I decided I would do this orchestra thing, so I sat down in my basement workroom and started writing 'Pedro's Dowry'. I was really involved — 14 to 18 hours a day, for three weeks. I haven't felt that good in years! I told my wife, 'That's the best vacation I ever had!' 'Pedro's Dowry' is wonderful. It may even last as a great piece of music — and this is only the second time I've felt this way about one of my own pieces. It's got some neat things in it."

Frank Zappa

The final Warners album features some of Zappa's more serious endeavours performed by The Abnuceals Emuukha Electric Symphony Orchestra, conducted by Michael Zearott.

Strictly Genteel was the grand finale of 200 Motels and the two concerts from which these recordings are taken, yet here it kicks things off.

Naval Aviation In Art? would be played trough the PA as an intro tape to many shows during 1975/76, when keyboardist André Lewis was part of the touring band; Lewis was one of a number of guests at Royce Hall.

Side two of the original vinyl was titled The Duke Of Orchestral Prunes and slightly incongruously features Zappa on guitar. Other musicians involved in these recordings include Bozzio, Ian Underwood, Bruce Fowler and – as guests – Captain Beefheart on soprano saxophone and Tommy Morgan on harmonica, both featured on the opening cut.

Bogus Pomp is essentially comprised of passages composed for 200 Motels.

Joe's Garage Act I
1979

FZ

Official Release #28

Originally Released: September 17, 1979

Recording data: March 21 to June 1979 at Rhein-Neckar-Halle (Eppelheim) and The Village Recorders (LA)

Producer: FZ

Engineers: Joe Chiccarelli, Mick Glossop, Steve Nye

Tracks:
The Central Scrutinizer (3:28)
Joe's Garage (6:10)
Catholic Girls (4:19)
Crew Slut (6:38)
Fembot In A Wet T-Shirt (4:44)
On The Bus (4:31)
Why Does It Hurt When I Pee? (2:23)
Lucille Has Messed My Mind Up (5:42)
Scrutinizer Postlude (1:35)

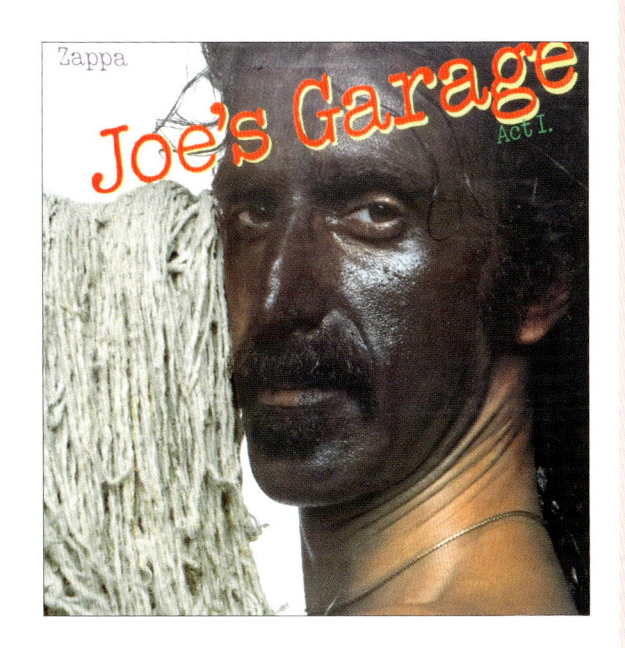

"We went into the studio to cut a single – 'Joe's Garage' on one side, and 'Catholic Girls' on the b-side. Then we started messing around while we were in there; next thing we knew, we had 17 tracks. I noticed a continuity in the text of the lyrics so I figured I'd add a few more things to give more continuity to it and make it into a story. So that's what we did. Then it turned out to be a 3-record set. And with the recession taking its effect on the economy, it looked like nobody would have the money to buy a 3-record set when they're scrambling to buy gas and hamburgers, the important things in life. So I decided to split it up, putting out one record in August and the other two in November."

Frank Zappa

The first part of Zappa's rock opera "about how the government is going to do away with music." Zappa is the story's narrator, the Central Scrutinizer, talking through a plastic megaphone at various points.

The title track tells of where Joe and his band rehearsed, and how they got noticed, signed-up and immediately disbanded.

Catholic Girls was written in response to the kerfuffle caused by Jewish Princess, Zappa ham-fistedly demonstrating that he wasn't anti-Semitic, as any group could be the target of his cynicism if he felt they merited it.

On The Bus is a guitar solo recorded live in Eppelheim, Germany in March 1979 that includes quotes from Toto's hit single Hold The Line.

Why Does It Hurt When I Pee? was the question jokingly posed by road manager deluxe Phil Kaufman on the tour bus, while Lucille was written for Jeff Simmons' 1970 album of the same name.

Joe's Garage Acts II & III
1979

FZ

Official Release #29

Originally Released: November 19, 1979

Recording data: March 23 to June 1979 at Liebenau Stadion (Graz), Rhein-Main-Halle (Wiesbaden), Rudi-Sedlmayer-Halle (Munich), Hallenstadion (Zurich) and The Village Recorders (LA)

Producer: FZ

Engineers: Joe Chiccarelli, Mick Glossop, Steve Nye

Tracks:
A Token Of My Extreme (5:29)
Stick It Out (4:34)
Sy Borg (8:55)
Dong Work For Yuda (5:03)
Keep It Greasy (8:21)
Outside Now (5:49)
He Used To Cut The Grass (8:35)
Packard Goose (11:31)
Watermelon In Easter Hay (9:05)
A Little Green Rosetta (8:14)

"It's based on the theme that the government likes to have things running smoothly. The more people are the same, the easier it is for governments, businesses, and so on, to control them. Down through history people have grappled with the problem. In the future, where our story takes place, they've come up with this idea of total criminalization. They figure that when everybody is a crook, we'll all be the same. The minute you commit a crime, you become the same as the President, the same as the heads of all the major corporations, the same as all the religious people. We'll all be the same when we are all criminals."

Frank Zappa

To flesh-out his opus, Zappa Xenochronised lengthy guitar solos culled from live performances with studio backing (by and large, by bassist Arthur Barrow and ace drummer Vinnie Colaiuta) for Keep It Greasy, Outside Now, He Used To Cut The Grass and Packard Goose. He also recorded the bespoke track that Zappa himself described as the best song on the album: his third signature guitar piece, Watermelon In Easter Hay.

Rather than end on a serious note, Joe's Garage concludes with the rowdy sort-of sequel to Muffin Man that also alludes to the Utility Muffin Research Kitchen, the recording studio then being built in Zappa's house where his records would be concocted from hereon in.

Despite the release of so many albums, Zappa didn't play a single gig on US soil in 1979. Fans would now have to wait until the second year of the next decade for any new recordings.

Tinseltown Rebellion
1981

FZ

Official Release #30

Originally Released: May 11, 1981

Recording data: *October 27, 1978 to 1981 at The Palladium (NYC), Hammersmith Odeon (London), Tower Theater, Upper Darby (PA), Dallas Convention Center (Texas), Southern Illinois University (Carbondale), Berkeley Community Theater (CA), Santa Monica Civic Auditorium (CA) and UMRK (LA)*

Producer: *FZ*

Engineers: *Mark Pinske, George Douglas, Joe Chiccarelli, Allen Sides, Tom Flye, Bob Stone*

Tracks:
Fine Girl (3:31)
Easy Meat (9:19)
For The Young Sophisticate (2:48)
Love Of My Life (2:15)
I Ain't Got No Heart (1:59)
Panty Rap (4:35)
Tell Me You Love Me (2:07)
Now You See It–Now You Don't (4:54)
Dance Contest (2:58)
The Blue Light (5:27)
Tinsel Town Rebellion (4:35)
Pick Me, I'm Clean (5:07)
Bamboozled By Love (5:46)
Brown Shoes Don't Make It (7:14)
Peaches III (5:03)

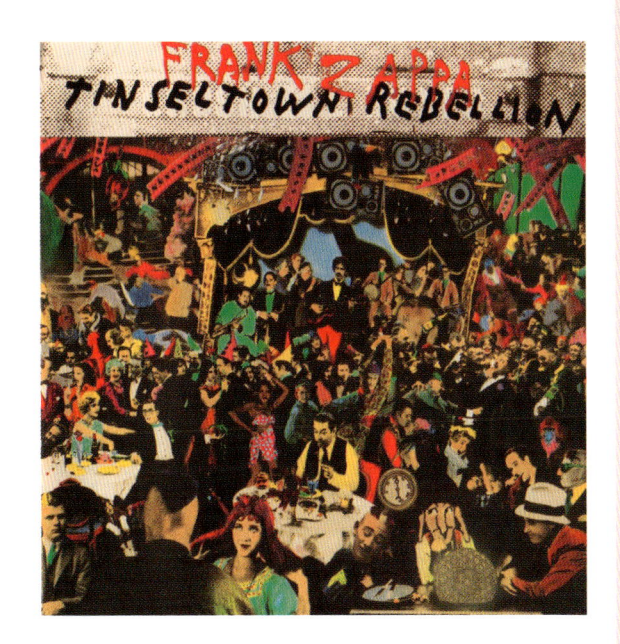

"The first cut on side one is a very nice little tune called 'Fine Girl', which may disturb some people. And then the next cut is 'Easy Meat', and the first part of that has a mass of keyboard overdubs done by Tommy Mars on this classical section and then after that, all the rest of the album is totally live including the vocals. Everything is just as it actually happened and the concerts that are recorded are from London, Berkeley, Los Angeles, Illinois, Dallas and one other place ... Philadelphia."

Frank Zappa

This was the first release on Zappa's Barking Pumpkin mail order record label, founded following Phonogram's refusal to distribute his I Don't Wanna Get Drafted single (which criticised President Jimmy Carter's reintroduction of the Selective Service System). Both single and album saw the welcome return of Cal Schenkel cover art.

Borne out of two abandoned album projects – Warts And All and Crush All Boxes – Tinseltown Rebellion is a mix of in-concert recreations of early 'classics' and some more contemporary pieces, plus the studio-recorded appetizer Fine Girl (included so that "conservative radio stations can play something on the air").

Easy Meat and Bamboozled By Love show Zappa at his misogynistic best, while in Panty Rap he endearingly collects feminine underclothing from the audience and details their contents. (Zappa would collect enough of these to have them fashioned into a quilt and proudly displayed at the Hard Rock Cafe in Biloxi, Mississippi.)

Shut Up 'N Play Yer Guitar
1981

FZ

Official Release #31

Originally Released: May 11, 1981

Recording data: February 17, 1979 to December 11, 1980 at Hammersmith Odeon (London), The Village Recorders (LA), Brady Theater (Tulsa), Berkeley Community Theater (CA) and Santa Monica Civic Auditorium (CA)

Producer: FZ

Engineers: Mick Glossop, George Douglas, Joe Chiccarelli, Tom Flye, Bob Stone

Tracks:
five-five-FIVE (2:35)
Hog Heaven (2:49)
Shut Up 'N Play Yer Guitar (5:38)
While You Were Out (6:00)
Treacherous Cretins (5:34)
Heavy Duty Judy (4:42)
Soup 'N Old Clothes (7:53)

"I'm putting together an album for mail order called Shut Up 'N Play Yer Guitar, and all it is is guitar solos, one after another. No songs, no words, no head, no ending. Just guitar solos. Most of them live, and when the solo's over there's a little noise and it goes on to the next one. This is for guitar fetishists. There's a lot of people who've never paid any attention to what I play. They might have read about it or watched somebody's clothes while I was playing, but if they actually want to hear what I was doing this'll be a chance for them to hear it."
Frank Zappa

The first of three albums issued simultaneously consisting only of guitar solos, punctuated by vocal asides from the likes of Bozzio and O'Hearn. The tracks on this first disc were taken from concert recordings, with the exception of the studio jammed guitars on While You Were Out (Warren Cuccurullo, later of Duran Duran, plays rhythm to Frank's lead over a discrete drum track by Colaiuta), recorded during the same session that produced Stucco Homes on the third disc.

Although some tracks are bona fide through-composed pieces that would be performed again in similar style, a few are unique in-the-moment solos culled from other songs: like five-five-FIVE from the yet to be released Conehead, the title track from Inca Roads, and Soup 'N Old Clothes from The Illinois Enema Bandit.

Heavy Duty Judy would be performed and recorded again in blistering brass enhanced form on the Broadway The Hard Way tour.

Shut Up 'N Play Yer Guitar Some More 1981

FZ

Official Release #32

Originally Released: May 11, 1981

Recording data: February 03, 1976 to December 11, 1980 at Kosei Nenkin Kaikan (Osaka), Hammersmith Odeon (London), The Village Recorders (LA) and Santa Monica Civic Auditorium (CA)

Producer: *FZ*

Engineers: *George Douglas, Mick Glossop, Joe Chiccarelli, Alan P., Bob Stone*

Tracks:
Variations On The Carlos Santana Secret Chord Progression (3:58)
Gee, I Like Your Pants (2:35)
Canarsie (6:05)
Ship Ahoy (5:20)
The Deathless Horsie (6:20)
Shut Up 'N Play Yer Guitar Some More (6:53)
Pink Napkins (4:38)

"On the guitar album you can hear the [Bulgarian bagpipe] technique on 'Gee, I Like Your Pants' and 'Variations On The Carlos Santana Secret Chord Progression'. With your left hand you're fretting the notes and with your right hand you're also fretting the notes with a pick. Instead of plucking the string you're fretting the string, you hit the string and then that presses it against the fret so it actuates the string and also determines the pitch, and you can move back and forth real fast that way ... just aiming it straight down at the string. I learned it from Jim Gordon, who is a drummer, and he picked it up from some other guitar player. He showed it to me in 1972. That's when I first saw anybody do it, and the first time I ever used it in concert was in Vienna in 1972 or 73. I decided I would try it, and I've done it ever since."

Frank Zappa

The second of three albums issued simultaneously consisting solely of Zappa's improvised guitar solos. Those on this second disc are exclusively from concert recordings, with most being spontaneous six-string air sculptures culled from other compositions: Variations On The Carlos Santana Secret Chord Progression is from a performance of City Of Tiny Lites, Gee, I Like Your Pants and the title track come from Inca Roads, Ship Ahoy was the coda from Zoot Allures recorded in Japan in 1976, and Pink Napkins comes unsurprisingly from Black Napkins.

"Gee, I like your pants" is a line Zappa would later add to Dead Girls Of London, which he co-wrote with L. Shankar and produced for the violinist's 1979 Touch Me There album.

Dweezil recorded a version of The Deathless Horsie with Zappa Plays Zappa that was nominated for a Grammy for Best Rock Instrumental Performance in 2011; it lost to Jeff Beck's Hammerhead.

Return Of The Son Of Shut Up 'N Play Yer Guitar   1981

FZ

Official Release #33

Originally Released: May 11, 1981

Recording data: October 1967 to December 05, 1980 at Apostolic Studios (NYC), Paramount Recording Studios (LA), Hammersmith Odeon (London), The Village Recorders (LA), UMRK (LA), The Palladium (NYC) and Berkeley Community Theater (CA)

Producer: FZ

Engineers: George Douglas, Mick Glossop, Tom Flye, Joe Chiccarelli, Steve Nye, Kerry McNabb, Bob Stone

Tracks:
Beat It With Your Fist (1:58)
Return Of The Son Of Shut Up 'N Play Yer Guitar (8:30)
Pinocchio's Furniture (2:05)
Why Johnny Can't Read (4:15)
Stucco Homes (9:08)
Canard Du Jour (9:57)

"Here's a flashback to the beginning. An overnight basement (pre-UMRK) studio session with Frank and engineer Steve Nye led to this beautiful recording ['Stucco Homes']. Initially I was playing over the solo vamp of 'Inca Roads'. Frank took the guitar track I recorded and laid it over a track of Vinnie's from another tune. (Can't recall which one, but all of the basic tracks were from live mobile recordings from the '79 European tour). Frank improvised sitting at the desk, playing an acoustic (brand) 'black widow' guitar. I'd never seen or heard of one before. I was playing an unusual guitar as well: Frank's Vox Winchester, which he decided should be my payment for the session because it was the perfect size for me and he said it looked like it should be sewn right into my jacket! Anyway, Frank blew this down in one take, no punches. What a night! Frank Zappa is the greatest thing that ever happened to music! Period!"

Warren Cuccurullo

The final of the three guitar albums issued on the day Bob Marley died comprises all concert recordings, with the exception of Canard Du Jour (a studio duet from 1972 with Jean-Luc Ponty on baritone violin and Zappa on bouzouki) and Stucco Homes.

Tracks extracted from other songs this time are Beat It With Your Fist (from The Torture Never Stops), the title track (from Inca Roads), Pinocchio's Furniture (from Chunga's Revenge) and Why Johnny Can't Read (from A Pound For A Brown).

Why Johnny Can't Read is a 1955 book by Austrian-born author Rudolf Flesch. He published a sequel in 1981, and in 1982 Johnny Can't Read would be the first solo single by Eagle Don Henley.

After two weeks of selling the Shut Up albums via mail-order, Zappa recouped his manufacturing costs.

The following year, the three albums were boxed together and sold more conventionally via CBS Records.

You Are What You Is
1981

FZ

Official Release #34

Originally Released: September 23, 1981

Recording data: October 27, 1978 to September 1980 at The Palladium (NYC), Tower Theater, Upper Darby (PA) and UMRK (LA)

Producer: FZ

Engineers: Mark Pinske, Allen Sides, George Douglas, David Gray, Bob Stone

Tracks:
Teen-age Wind (3:02)
Harder Than Your Husband (2:28)
Doreen (4:44)
Goblin Girl (4:06)
Theme From The 3rd Movement Of Sinister Footwear (3:31)
Society Pages (2:26)
I'm A Beautiful Guy (1:56)
Beauty Knows No Pain (3:01)
Charlie's Enormous Mouth (3:36)
Any Downers? (2:08)
Conehead (4:18)
You Are What You Is (4:23)
Mudd Club (3:11)
The Meek Shall Inherit Nothing (3:10)
Dumb All Over (4:03)
Heavenly Bank Account (3:44)
Suicide Chump (2:49)
Jumbo Go Away (3:43)
If Only She Woulda (3:47)
Drafted Again (3:07)

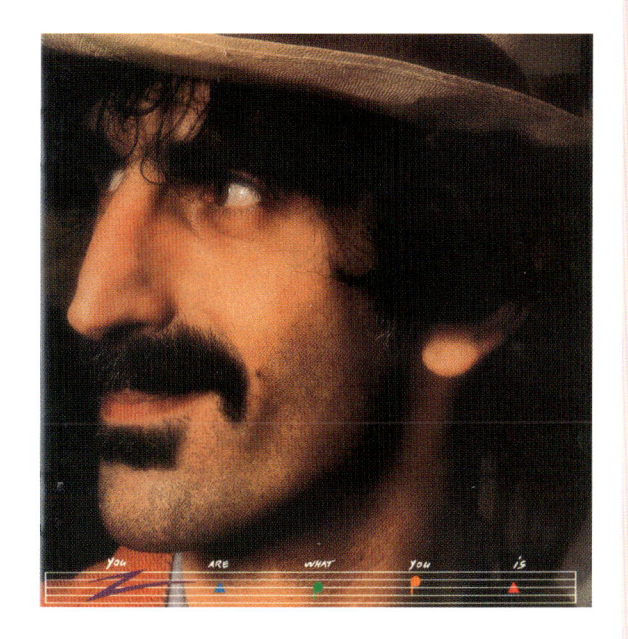

"Thomas Nordegg gave me a tape of Frank singing the song 'Harder Than Your Husband' and a copy of just the backing. He also gave me a tape recorder, so I practiced in my hotel room on the first evening. The next day, at six in the afternoon, Thomas came to pick me up in Frank's brand new Rolls Royce. He drove me up to the house, where Frank had just built a big new studio. We recorded the song that night and Frank loved it. I thought that that was it and I'd be flying out the next day but he said, 'I want you to stay for another day or so because I've got some other songs that I'd like you to sing on.'"

Jimmy Carl Black

With the UMRK now complete, Zappa recorded the vast majority of this record at home with his mid-1980 touring band, plus a few special guests (as well as guest vocalist Jimmy Carl Black, Motorhead Sherwood also returned to contribute tenor sax and snorks).

By the middle of the decade, Zappa would largely eschew other musicians and produce albums on his own, but for now he was enjoying the more conventional studio recording process without the restrictions imposed by commercial facilities.

During the Spring 1980 tour, he announced that much of this album was an extension of Joe's Garage, with the songs revealing what Joe got up after quitting the day shift.

Although not a full concept album, many of the songs run together and were often performed that way live.

Teen-age Wind was a pastiche of Ride Like The Wind, a 1980 hit for bass player Barrow's friend Christopher Cross.

Ship Arriving Too Late To Save A Drowning Witch   1982

FZ

Official Release #35

Originally Released: May 03, 1982

Recording data: Summer 1981 to 1982 at The Ritz (NYC), Uptown Theatre (Chicago), Santa Monica Civic Auditorium (CA), UMRK (LA)

Producer: FZ

Engineers: Mark Pinske, Bob Stone

Tracks:
No Not Now (5:50)
Valley Girl (4:50)
I Come From Nowhere (6:09)
Drowning Witch (12:03)
Envelopes (2:45)
Teen-age Prostitute (2:41)

Ship arriving too late to save a drowning witch

"Most people don't realise most of this was recorded live, at various gigs. With previous live LPs, like Roxy & Elsewhere, he'd record the entire band and then re-record everything except the bass and drums, so it had that nice live feel. But, by the 80s, he felt he didn't need to do that. Some tracks were so difficult to get right. 'Drowning Witch', inspired by Stravinsky, is so hard to play that Frank said he needed 17 cities worth of recordings to get a useful version! The only studio track was 'Valley Girl'. It started out as a guitar riff in some crazy metre. Frank was into 'My Sharona' at this time, you can hear it in the rhythm and the melody. Then he woke up his daughter, Moon Unit, at 3 am to sing the lead!"

Scott Thunes

When Zappa was 13, American humorist Roger Price invented Droodles, "a borkley-looking sort of drawing that doesn't make any sense until you know the correct title." One of these adorned this album's cover, giving it its title.

Valley Girl gave Zappa his only US top 40 single, lost out on a Grammy to Survivor's Eye Of The Tiger, spawned a cash-in movie of the same name (starring a teenage Nicholas Cage) which Zappa failed to stop, and provided a fleeting fascination with the San Fernando Valley patois amusingly mimicked by Moon.

Elsewhere, over-the-top lead vocals are supplied by Roy Estrada and the classically trained Lisa Popeil.

In the UK, the album included a 'free' live 7" EP comprising Shut Up 'N Play Yer Guitar, Variations On The Carlos Santana Secret Chord Progression and Why Johnny Can't Read.

Gail would subsequently have engineer Pinske's name removed from the credits for noncompliance.

The Man From Utopia
1983

FZ

Official Release #36

Originally Released: March 28, 1983

Recording data: October 16, 1980 to 1982 at Armadillo World Headquarters (Austin), Southern Illinois University (Carbondale), Uptown Theatre (Chicago), Santa Monica Civic Auditorium (CA) and UMRK (LA)

Producer: FZ

Engineers: Bob Stone, Mark Pinske, Dave Jerdan

Tracks:
Cocaine Decisions (3:54)
SEX (3:43)
Tink Walks Amok (3:38)
The Radio Is Broken (5:51)
We Are Not Alone (3:18)
The Dangerous Kitchen (2:51)
The Man From Utopia Meets Mary Lou (3:22)
Stick Together (3:13)
The Jazz Discharge Party Hats (4:28)
Moggio (2:36)

Additional track on CD:
Luigi & The Wise Guys (3:24)

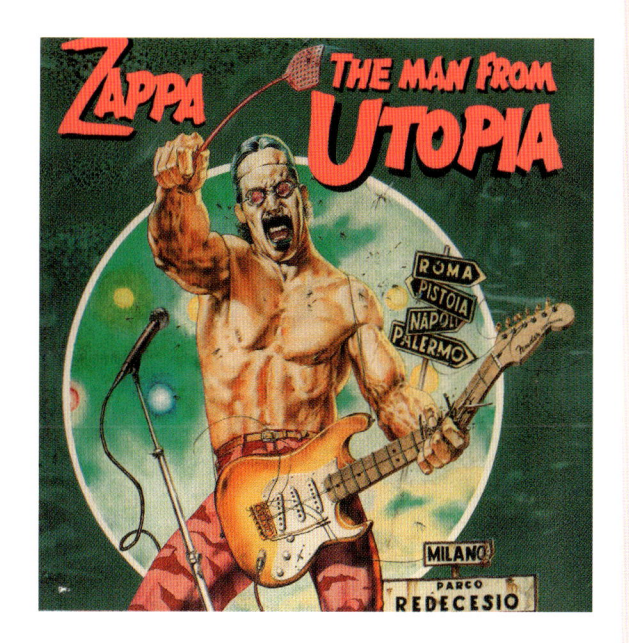

"The credits on The Man From Utopia are vague, so for the record, I am playing piano and guitar on 'The Radio Is Broken', and I came up with the idea to use the chord progression from the Doors' 'Love Street' in that song, too. I recorded multiple bass tracks on 'Tink Walks Amok' of course, and I'm pretty sure that's me playing bass on 'We Are Not Alone', too."

Arthur Barrow

This is a great summation of Zappa, with songs covering two of his bugbears: drugs (Cocaine Decisions) and unions (Stick Together); and a few of his preoccupations: cheap monster movies (The Radio Is Broken), doo-wop and R&B (Luigi & The Wise Guys and The Man From Utopia Meets Mary Lou) and sex (SEX).

Zappa was especially pleased with The Radio Is Broken, a bonkers duet with Estrada that references a number of 50s sci-fi films.

The album also embraces Sprechgesang on The Dangerous Kitchen and The Jazz Discharge Party Hats, both live 'meltdown' recordings with studio overdubs by stunt guitarist Steve Vai that follow Zappa's every vocal nuance.

Tink Walks Amok, We Are Not Alone and Moggio are all stonking instrumentals, but the album is not generally regarded as a high point of Zappa's career.

The cover art by Italian comic illustrator Tanino Liberatore, depicts Zappa as the character RanXerox.

Baby Snakes
1983

FZ

Official Release #37

Originally Released: March 28, 1983

Recording data: October 28-31, 1977 at The Palladium (NYC)

Producer: FZ

Engineers: Kerry McNabb, Mark Pinske

Tracks:
Baby Snakes (1:45)
Titties & Beer (6:13)
The Black Page #2 (2:50)
Jones Crusher (2:53)
Disco Boy (3:51)
Dinah-Moe Humm (6:37)
Punky's Whips (11:29)

Additional track on CD:
Intro Rap (0:36)

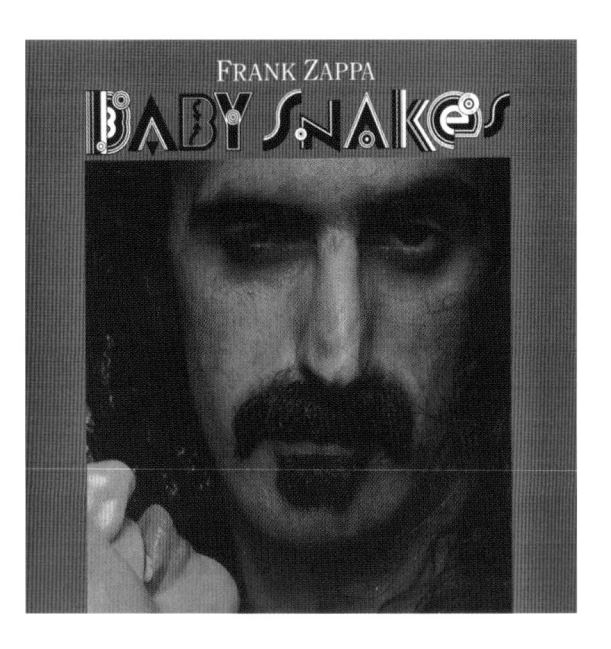

"I started another movie. A bunch of really famous people are in it. You have these baby snakes, see, and you have the universe. And they relate to each other."

Frank Zappa

Failing to secure a distributor for his three hour plus movie (which revolves around his 1977 Halloween concerts), Zappa released the film independently on 21 December 1979. While its run at New York's Victoria Theater made a profit, the film failed to garner a single Academy Award nomination – though Bruce Bickford's claymation sequences received first prize at a French film competition.

This soundtrack album was released as a picture disc (all the rage then), and two years later a 90 minute edit of the film was unleashed on video.

The title track is the studio recording from Sheik Yerbouti (slightly truncated), while the rest of the songs are unique live recordings (albeit some not massively dissimilar to those on the … In New York album).

In 1988, the CD version added an excerpt from the film at the start in which Zappa urges future band member Cuccurullo to sing Baby Snakes.

London Symphony Orchestra
Vol. I 1983

FZ

Official Release #38

Originally Released: June 09, 1983

Recording data: January 12-14, 1983 at Twickenham Film Studio (London)

Producer: FZ

Engineer: Mark Pinske

Tracks:
Sad Jane (9:51)
Mo 'N Herb's Vacation I (4:50)
Mo 'N Herb's Vacation II (10:04)
Mo 'N Herb's Vacation III (12:52)
Bogus Pomp (24:31)

Additional tracks on original US vinyl release:
Pedro's Dowry (large orchestra version) (10:26)
Envelopes (04:11).

Bogus Pomp was not on the original vinyl release, but was included later on a 1986 CD called simply The London Symphony Orchestra.

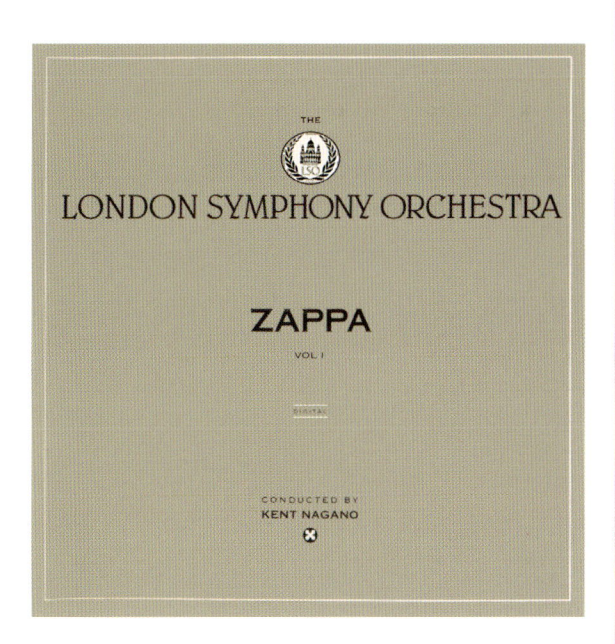

"First of all, we performed in the London Symphony Orchestra's new permanent hall, the Barbican – a huge, gigantic, multi-million dollar cultural complex, English style. A real shitty hall. The acoustics are not great, and they vary drastically from seat to seat. The stage is too small for a major production. It was so tight for our set-up, in fact, that we had to leave two violas out of the orchestra because there was no place to sit them. So I wouldn't have wanted to record it in there anyway. The two halls in London where orchestras ordinarily record, with good acoustics, were both booked, so we wound up recording at a place called Twickenham Studios Stage One, which is a movie sound stage. Very dead acoustics – which at first I thought was going to be a disaster. But after getting the tape back and finding out what I can do with different types of reverberation added to different sections, it's better than having done it in a live hall where you have no control over it. So we miked it with PZMs, 90% of the orchestra, plus we had an Edcor Calrec over the conductor's head."

Frank Zappa

Always keen to embrace new technology and break new ground, this was the first digital multitrack recording of an orchestra. Ever. The origins of all of the pieces date back several years: the last movement of Sad Jane coming from a guitar solo from a 1968 concert at LA's Shrine Exposition Hall (transcribed by Ian Underwood); the opening phrase of Mo 'N Herb's Vacation from another solo (recorded at New York's Palladium in 1976); Bogus Pomp deriving from themes performed by the BBC Symphony Orchestra in 1968 (later issued on the Ahead Of Their Time album); Envelopes being written in 1968 for "two amplified keyboard instruments with rhythm section accompaniment"; and Pedro's Dowry penned while on vacation in 1975.

Zappa chose Kent Nagano to conduct the LSO, giving the lad his first real break. Nagano would go on to become principal conductor of the Hallé Orchestra and Deutsches Symphonie-Orchester Berlin.

The Perfect Stranger
1984

Boulez / FZ

Official Release #39

Originally Released: August 23, 1984

Recording data: January 10 to April 1984 at IRCAM (Paris) and UMRK (LA)

Producer: FZ

Engineers: Didier Arditi, Bob Stone, David Ocker, Steve De Furia

Tracks:
The Perfect Stranger (12:44)
Naval Aviation In Art? (2:45)
The Girl In The Magnesium Dress (3:13)
Dupree's Paradise (7:54)
Love Story (0:59)
Outside Now Again (4:06)
Jonestown (5:27)

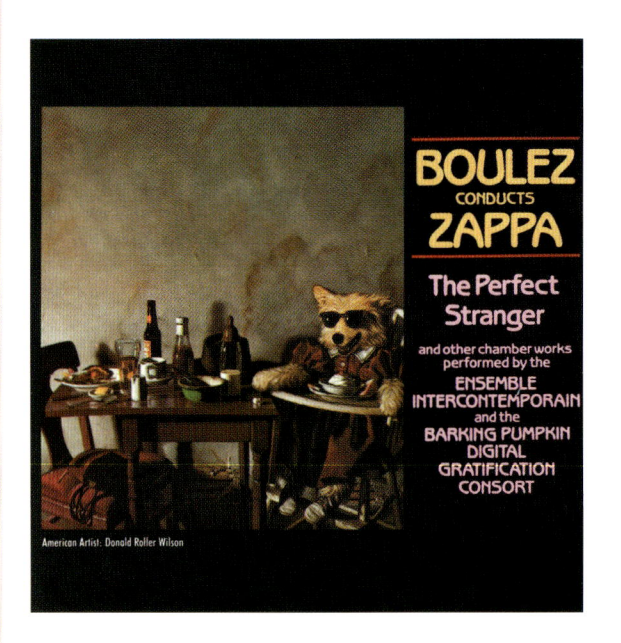

"I was visiting IRCAM in Paris – some of my friends worked there under the patronage of Pierre Boulez – and I saw the list of the various pieces that were to be performed in the future. Included on that list were some pieces by Frank Zappa. I was really surprised, and I said, 'Why are you doing Frank Zappa's music?' My friend said, 'Well, it seems he's written a number of serious compositions and he wanted the Ensemble to perform it, and Pierre Boulez has agreed to conduct it'."

Kent Nagano

Having worked with the Royal Philharmonic and London Symphony Orchestras, Zappa now demonstrated he meant business as an orchestral composer by hooking up with highly respected French conductor Pierre Boulez and his rocking teenage combo, Ensemble InterContemporain.

Together they perform three of the pieces here: the newly composed title track (which starts where Pedro's Dowry ends) and the older Naval Aviation In Art? and Dupree's Paradise (the latter a staple of the Roxy-era band).

The remaining tracks are all performed by The Barking Pumpkin Digital Gratification Consort – that is, Zappa's new machine the Synclavier.

When originally issued, the track order was slightly different, and The Girl In The Magnesium Dress featured synthesized percussion that would be replaced by sampled marimba on the remixed CD in 1992.

The final track is named after the Peoples Temple, an American religious organisation formed by Jim Jones, where over 900 people simultaneously committed suicide.

Them Or Us
1984

FZ

Official Release #40

Originally Released: October 18, 1984

Recording data: December 1974 to 1984 at Caribou Ranch (Nederland), Record Plant (LA), Painter's Mill Music Fair, Owings Mills (Maryland), The Ritz (NYC), Northrop Auditorium (Minneapolis), Santa Monica Civic Auditorium (CA), Fox Theater (San Diego), Alte Oper (Frankfurt), Hammersmith Odeon (London), Sporthalle (Böblingen), Olympiahalle (Munich), Stadio Communale (Bolzano) and UMRK (LA)

Producer: FZ

Engineers: Mark Pinske, Bob Stone

Tracks:
The Closer You Are (2:58)
In France (3:30)
Ya Hozna (6:26)
Sharleena (4:33)
Sinister Footwear II (8:40)
Truck Driver Divorce (9:03)
Stevie's Spanking (5:24)
Baby, Take Your Teeth Out (1:24)
Marque-son's Chicken (7:34)
Planet Of My Dreams (1:40)
Be In My Video (3:39)
Them Or Us (5:08)
Frogs With Dirty Little Lips (2:46)
Whipping Post (7:32)

"Whenever anyone asks what Zappa album they should listen to, I suggest Them Or Us. This is one of the best records that I have ever recorded and it also was probably the peak point of Frank's creative genius. We experimented and tried more new things in the recording process and the tracking and mixing of this record than at any other time."

Mark Pinske

Like The Perfect Stranger before, this album sports front cover art by Donald Roller Wilson, depicting Patricia the dog with her red dress on. And like Burnt Weeny, Zappa's songs are sandwiched between a couple of old covers.

Johnny 'Guitar' Watson sings In France, a piece inspired both by Gary Numan's Cars and a miserable time on the 1979 European tour. Ya Hozna is a backward mash-up of Sofa No. 2, Lonely Little Girl and some of Moon's Valley Girl outtakes.

A full orchestral version of Sinister Footwear was performed under the baton of Nagano in June 1984; the second movement here is a part live/part studio rock band rendition.

Planet Of My Dreams is another Hunchentoot song, sung by Thana Harris' husband Bob.

A fan amusingly requested Gregg Allman's Whipping Post at a concert in 1973, which years later Zappa began to perform to showcase Robert Martin's vocal prowess.

Thing-Fish
1984

FZ

Official Release #41

Originally Released: December 21, 1984

Recording data: 1976 to 1984 at Record Plant (LA), Berkeley Community Theater (CA), Santa Monica Civic Auditorium (CA), The Ritz (NYC), Stadthalle (Vienna), Stadio Ferraris (Genoa) and UMRK (LA)

Producer: FZ

Engineers: Mark Pinske, Bob Stone

Tracks:
Prologue (2:56)
The Mammy Nuns (3:31)
Harry & Rhonda (3:36)
Galoot Up-Date (5:27)
The 'Torchum' Never Stops (10:33)
That Evil Prince (1:17)
You Are What You Is (4:31)
Mudd Club (3:17)
The Meek Shall Inherit Nothing (3:14)
Clowns On Velvet (1:51)
Harry-As-A-Boy (2:34)
He's So Gay (2:45)
The Massive Improve'lence (5:08)
Artificial Rhonda (3:29)
The Crab-Grass Baby (3:47)
The White Boy Troubles (3:34)
No Not Now (5:49)
Briefcase Boogie (4:10)
Brown Moses (3:00)
Wistful Wit A Fist-Full (4:00)
Drop Dead (7:56)
Won Ton On (4:18)

"There was a lot of work involved and a lot of changes because the script would change every day and we'd have to go back and do things over, not because they were wrong but because we had more ideas. The ideas kept on coming and we would just change things around a lot. The fact that we were doing that and working with the Synclavier, which had just come out ... I worked the hardest on that."
Ike Willis

On paper, this should be wonderful: Zappa reworks a few familiar songs into a lengthy concept album assisted by a dazzling array of his past and present musicians.

The reality depends on your reaction to Ike Willis as the eponymous potato-headed whatchamacallit (whose moniker is inspired by a character from US sitcom Amos 'N' Andy) – speaking in Paul Laurence Dunbar-influenced African-American dialect. And whether you subscribe to theories that Governments like to manufacture diseases.

Certainly only Zappa seems to see this as ideal material for a Broadway musical, and bringing back drummer Terry Bozzio for a speaking only role is baffling.

An alternate 'demo' version circulates, and Zappa officially issued a 12-inch maxi-single featuring a different rendering of the final track with 'Guitar' Watson's voiceover (on later CD editions only) from He's So Gay bolted on.

If he'd tinkered some more, we may have got a definitive – and superior – album.

Francesco Zappa
1984

FZ / The Barking Pumpkin Digital Gratification Consort

Official Release #42

Originally Released: November 21, 1984

Recording data: February to April 1984 at the Utility Muffin Research Kitchen (Hollywood)

Producer: FZ

Engineers: Bob Stone, Mark Pinske

Tracks:
OPUS I –
No. 1 1st Movement Andante (3:28)
2nd Movement Allegro Con Brio (1:27)
No. 2 1st Movement Andantino (2:14)
2nd Movement Minuetto Grazioso (2:02)
No. 3 1st Movement Andantino (1:52)
2nd Movement Presto (1:50)
No. 4 1st Movement Andante (2:20)
2nd Movement Allegro (3:02)
No. 5 2nd Movement Minuetto Grazioso (2:26)
No. 6 1st Movement Largo (2:05)
2nd Movement Minuet (2:01)
OPUS IV –
No. 1 1st Movement Andantino (2:42)
2nd Movement Allegro Assai (1:58)
No. 2+ 2nd Movement Allegro Assai (1:17)
No. 3 1st Movement Andante (2:22)
2nd Movement Tempo Di Minuetto (1:58)
No. 4 1st Movement Minuetto (2:07)

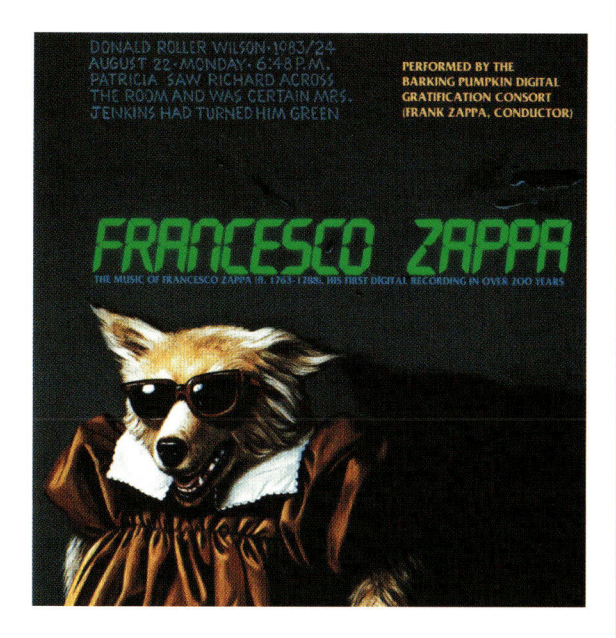

"I doubt there is a stranger coincidence among musicians' names than that of Francesco Zappa and Frank Zappa. Francesco was an 18th century Italian cellist and composer who gathered just enough mentions in history books and left behind just enough manuscripts to avoid being completely forgotten. The dates of Francesco's birth and death were never recorded. We only know that he 'flourished' between 1763 and 1788 and lived for a long time in the Netherlands. Frank Zappa was a 20th century guitarist and composer who flourished almost exactly two hundred years later – give or take a few. According to Frank, the two were not related."

David Ocker

After introducing us to his Synclavier earlier in the year, Zappa decided to follow-up 'that difficult 41st album' with a collection of chamber works composed by a long-dead namesake, totally realised on his new toy.

Zappa's music copyist and Synclavier programmer, David Ocker, had managed to obtain the scores for some of Francesco's trio sonatas and entered them into the machine. Zappa's sole input was picking which sounds would go with which musical lines.

The results were quickly put together.

While not as appealing as Walter Carlos' Switched-On Bach, listening to tracks in isolation does minimise that monotonous Metal Machine Music effect. And, thanks to this album, orchestras would go on to perform and record Francesco's music as he originally intended.

While sticking a picture of Donald Roller Wilson's Patricia on the cover does not necessarily a Frank Zappa album make, this remains a legitimate part of the official catalogue.

The Old Masters, Box I
1984

FZ

Official Release #43

Originally Released: April 01, 1985

Recording data: January 1961 to November 1968

Producer: FZ

Engineers: Bob Stone, Mark Pinske, Tom Ehle

Contains the albums:
FREAK OUT!
ABSOLUTELY FREE
WE'RE ONLY IN IT FOR THE MONEY
LUMPY GRAVY
CRUISING WITH RUBEN & THE JETS

Plus:
MYSTERY DISC

Tracks:
Theme From "Run Home Slow" (1:23)
Original Duke Of Prunes (1:17)
Opening Night At "Studio Z" (Collage) (1:34)
The Village Inn (1:17)
Steal Away (3:43)
I Was A Teen-Age Malt Shop (1:10)
The Birth Of Captain Beefheart (0:18)
Metal Man Has Won His Wings (3:06)
Power Trio From The Saints 'N Sinners (0:34)
Bossa Nova Pervertamento (2:15)
Excerpt From The Uncle Frankie Show (0:40)
Charva (2:01)
Speed-Freak Boogie (4:14)
Original Mothers At The Broadside (Pomona) (0:55)
Party Scene From "Mondo Hollywood" (1:54)
Original Mothers Rehearsal (0:22)
How Could I Be Such A Fool? (1:49)
Band Introductions At The Fillmore West (1:10)
Plastic People (1:58)
Original Mothers At Fillmore East (0:50)
Why Don'tcha Do Me Right? (2:37)
Big Leg Emma (2:32)

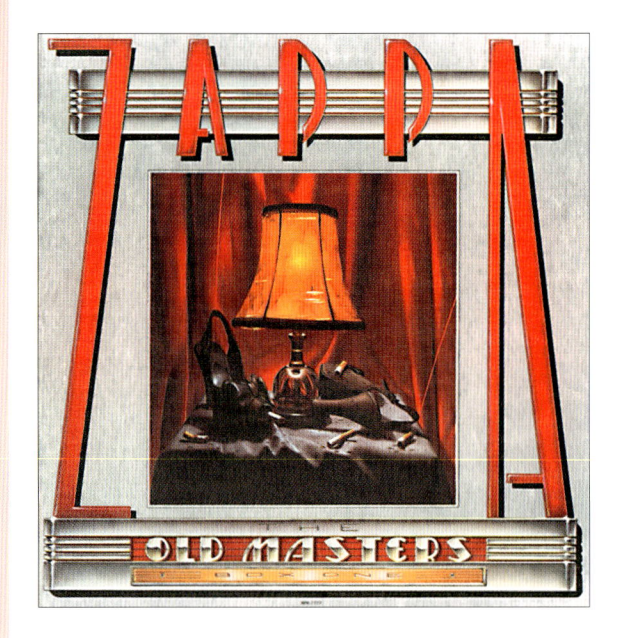

"Frank has this great new UMRK studio and he's spent days, maybe weeks fine tuning what he believes to be a fabulous state of the art drum sound. At the same time, after a long fight, he finally gets posession of his old tapes. He listens to the tracks, and finds the drum sound to be bad in his opinion. He was probably never happy with the original drums in the first place. He puts two and two together and comes up with this 'great idea' to replace the drums. And while he's at it, why not do the bass as well. 'Arthur knows all these tunes, right?'"

Arthur Barrow

Because the early albums were hard to come by, and because he'd just acquired the rights to them all, Zappa digitally refurbished and, here, reissued the first five on vinyl, adding a bonus disc of mostly unreleased material dating back to 1963.

He stated that the original master tapes were in a 'wretched condition' and, for Money and Ruben, he'd had to re-record new drum and bass tracks. This turned out to be phooey, and the purists were outraged.

He'd also had drummer Chad Wackerman and bassist Barrow – and vocalist Willis – overdub parts for a Lumpy Gravy remix, but this would not be released during his lifetime (though a three minute excerpt was included on a promo-only sampler for this box set).

Over the next few years, Zappa would reissue the majority of his back catalogue on Compact Disc, altering them here and there, but never to the same extent.

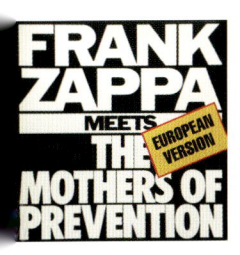

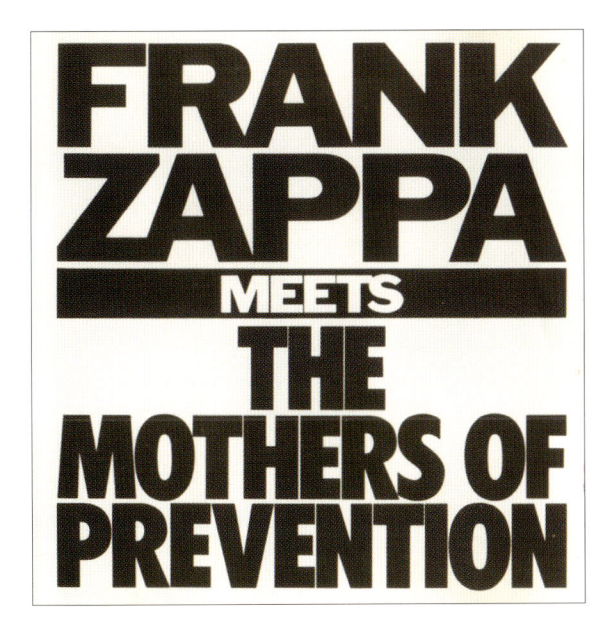

Frank Zappa Meets The Mothers Of Prevention   1985

FZ

Official Release #44

Originally Released: November 21, 1985

Recording data: October 1967 to 1985 at Apostolic Studios (NYC), Santa Monica Civic Auditorium (CA), Painter's Mill Music Fair, Owings Mills (Maryland), Assembly Hall, University Of Illinois (Champaign), Community Theater, Berkeley (CA), Committee on Commerce, Science and Transportation and UMRK (LA)

Producer: FZ

Engineers: Bob Stone, Mark Pinske, Bob Rice, Arthur 'Midget' Sloatman

Tracks:
I Don't Even Care (4:39)
One Man, One Vote (2:35)
Little Beige Sambo (3:02)
Aerobics In Bondage (3:16)
We're Turning Again (4:55)
Alien Orifice (4:10)
Yo Cats (3:33)
What's New In Baltimore? (5:20)
Porn Wars (12:05)
H.R. 2911 (3:35)

"I'm lucky I got a couple of co-writing credits, like on 'Yo Cats'. No-one ever really got that, especially in the later days. The beauty to me when we finally had the song constructed and went on the road with it, played it so that it was part of our daily routine, was to go back and finally record the song. To me there's nothing like that. Many times you go in to do a session and it's the first and last time you ever get to hear the song. When you really know a song intimately and it becomes your friend because you live with it, when you finally do record it, the intimacy you have with it as an artist and a performer makes it so much deeper."

Tommy Mars

The title was an amusing reference to the Parents Music Resource Center lobby group who successfully campaigned for albums to have 'Parental Guidance: Explicit Lyrics' stickers slapped on them. Zappa vociferously challenged the 'Washington wives', testifying before the US Senate in September 1985. Parts of this testimony, and comments from various Senators, are included on the album's centrepiece, Porn Wars.

This track was omitted from European versions of the album – Zappa deeming it too parochial – and replaced it with I Don't Even Care (a song he co-wrote with Johnny "Guitar" Watson) and two Synclavier instrumentals (One Man, One Vote and H.R. 2911).

Little Beige Sambo and Aerobics In Bondage are fairly forgettable Synclavier pieces, especially when placed alongside band performed instrumentals like Alien Orifice and What's New In Baltimore?

We're Turning Again is an almost sentimental reflection on the demise of the sixties, name-checking old 'friends' Hendrix, Moon and Joplin.

Does Humor Belong In Music?
1986

FZ

Official Release #45

Originally Released: January 27, 1986

Recording data: September 25 to December 23, 1984 at Hammersmith Odeon (London), Civic Center (Providence), Fine Arts Center Concert Hall, Amherst (MA), Tower Theater, Upper Darby (PA), Bismarck Theater (Chicago), Bayfront Center, St. Petersburg (FL), Queen Elizabeth Theater (Vancouver), Universal Amphitheater, Universal City (CA)

Producer: FZ

Engineers: Mark Pinske, Thom Ehle, Bob Stone

Tracks:
Zoot Allures (5:26)
Tinsel-Town Rebellion (4:43)
Trouble Every Day (5:31)
Penguin In Bondage (6:44)
Hot-Plate Heaven At The Green Hotel (6:42)
What's New In Baltimore? (4:47)
Cock-Suckers' Ball (1:05)
WPLJ (1:30)
Let's Move To Cleveland (16:43)
Whippin' Post (8:23)

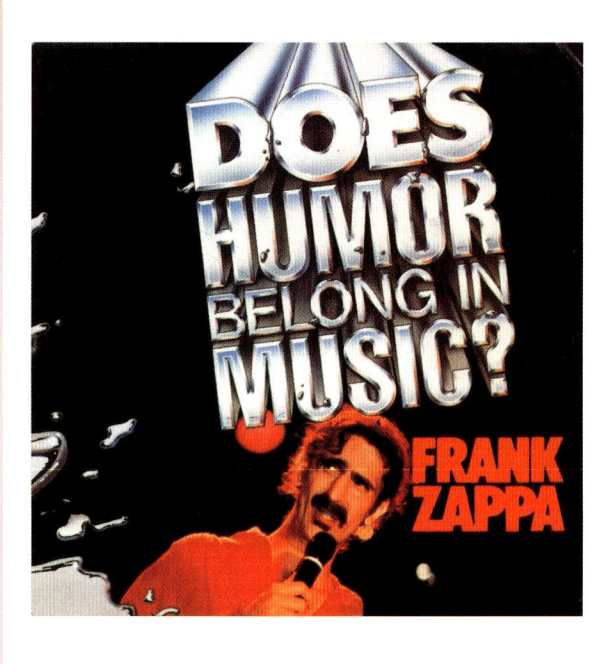

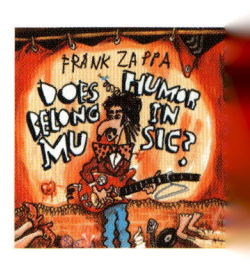

"Every night was a different program, but every night we always played Cleveland, never missed a night. He was a great leader. He had to keep everybody happy in the band. The way you make them happy is you played a big solo every night, but made it different. He didn't say it but we made it different every night. I never played the same solo twice. I played it a hundred and fifty times but I never repeated the same solo, and him, too, always new. So it was always a new adventure every night. The only thing is we always played that one piece every night, every concert, but it was always different, so that's why he played it every night. Then he was inspired and he inspired me and I inspired him."

Allan Zavod

Also the title of a live DVD, filmed at New York's The Pier. EMI wanted a companion album recorded at London's Hammersmith Odeon, but Zappa put this together from various shows on his 1984 tour, culminating in what Zappa thought might be the last time he'd pick up the guitar at California's Universal Amphitheater for a blinding duel with his son Dweezil on the Allman Brothers' At Fillmore East closer.

Those who think Zappa's lyrics could be a little suspect will be appalled by his decision to cover The Clovers' Rotten Cock-Suckers' Ball (a 1954 doo-wop parody of the jazz standard Darktown Strutters' Ball). For the rest of us, it merely answers the question posed by the album's title.

Hot-Plate Heaven is the only true new song, as Let's Move To Cleveland evolved from something Zappa wrote for violin and piano in 1968 and first performed live in 1975.

The Old Masters, Box II
1986

FZ

Official Release #46

Originally Released: *November 01, 1986*

Recording data: *1968 to August 07, 1971*

Producer: *FZ*

Engineers: *Bob Stone, Mark Pinske*

Contains the albums:
UNCLE MEAT
HOT RATS
BURNT WEENY SANDWICH
WEASELS RIPPED MY FLESH
CHUNGA'S REVENGE
FILLMORE EAST, JUNE 1971
JUST ANOTHER BAND FROM L.A.

Plus:
MYSTERY DISC

Tracks:
Harry, You're A Beast (0:30)
Don Interrupts (4:39)
Piece One (2:26)
Jim/Roy (4:04)
Piece Two (6:59)
Agency Man (3:25)
Agency Man (Studio Version) (3:27)
Lecture From Festival Hall Show (0:21)
Wedding Dress Song-The Handsome Cabin Boy (2:36)
Skweezit Skweezit Skweezit (2:57)
The Story Of Willie The Pimp (1:33)
Black Beauty (5:23)
Chucha (2:47)
Mothers at KPFK (3:26)
Harmonica Fun (0:41)

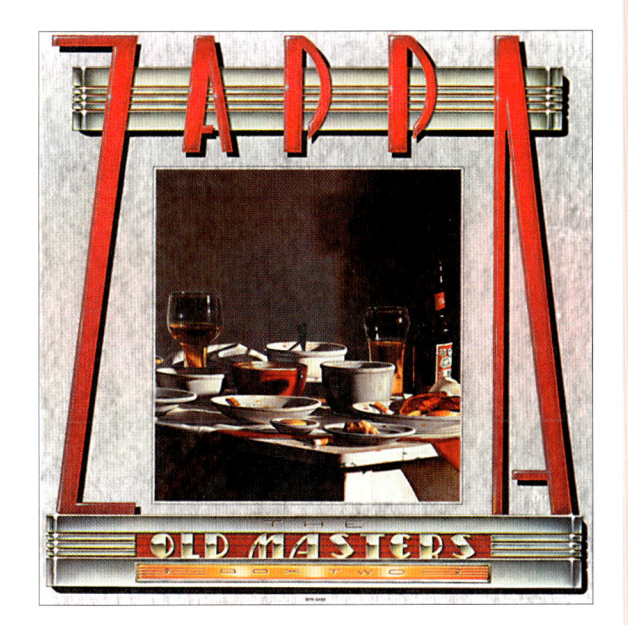

"The Mystery Disc in Box 2 is really fantastic. It's got one side, about 22 minutes, of an unreleased, never before heard, live concert with the original Mothers of Invention and the members of the BBC Orchestra recorded in London in 1968. The members of the band are doing a play, and the orchestra is backing them up. And the play is about why everybody wants to quit the group. It's really funny. On the other side there are odd little things like the origin of the story of 'Willie The Pimp'. There's a cassette recording of an interview that I did with these girls from Coney Island; they're talking about one of the girls' father, calling him Willie the Pimp, from the Lido Hotel. You can see where the song came from."

Frank Zappa

Less controversial than Box One, with each of the old albums (straddling the period that saw the disbandment of the 'original' Mothers and the rise and fall of the 'Vaudeville' band) being 'digitally re-tweezed'. Burnt Weeny, Chunga's Revenge, Fillmore East and Just Another Band noticeably have 'eighties-sounding' reverb added, which Zappa would deploy on many of the other titles he was then readying for individual CD release.

All of the material on this Mystery Disc was either recorded in 1968 or 1969, with much of it coming from the Mothers' Royal Festival Hall show that would appear in expanded form on Ahead Of Their Time.

The albums are encased in a silver box adorned with artwork by Donald Roller Wilson. Box Two sports a typical Roller painting of a table replete with Budweiser, a leftover meal and some dog-ends. But Patricia ("the Seeing Eye Dog of Houston") is sadly absent.

Jazz From Hell
1986

FZ

Official Release #47

Originally Released: November 15, 1986

Recording data: May 28, 1982 to 1986 at Palais des Sports (St. Etienne) and UMRK (LA)

Producer: FZ

Engineers: Bob Rice, Bob Stone, Mark Pinske

Tracks:
Night School (4:50)
The Beltway Bandits (3:26)
While You Were Art II (7:18)
Jazz From Hell (3:00)
G-Spot Tornado (3:17)
Damp Ankles (3:45)
St. Etienne (6:26)
Massaggio Galore (2:31)

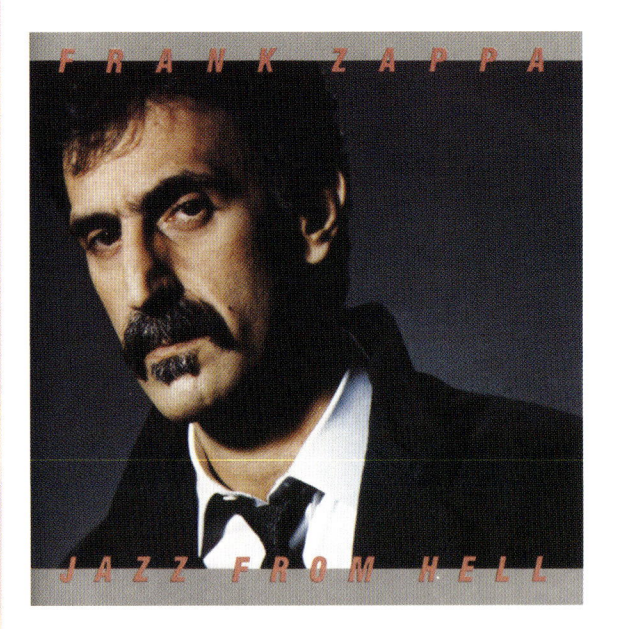

"'While You Were Art' began as a guitar solo on a song called 'While You Were Out' on an album released in 1981. A chamber group from Cal Arts commissioned me to write an arrangement of that guitar solo for their ensemble – cello, clarinet, two percussion, two keyboards. There might have been a flute, too. No guitar. The solo on the LP had been transcribed by Steve Vai and was available in this guitar book of solos, so Bob Rice typed into the Synclavier the original rhythms which were all real complicated, and then taking that basic material I put it through a bunch of permutations and came out with this piece. They came over to pick up the parts and they looked at it and said, 'Oh, this is real hard. We don't have enough time to rehearse it. What are we going to do?' I said, 'No Problem. I'll have the machine play it for you and we'll make this tape and you guys will go on stage and you'll lip-sync it and nobody will know.' And nobody knew. When I got the polyphonic sampling system I took the thing they had played, put some samples on it, tweaked it again and that's the version on the record."

Frank Zappa

Despite noodling on the machine for the last eight or so years of his life, Zappa was never convinced that the public could handle a whole album of his compositions executed on the Synclavier. This is the nearest we got to one in his lifetime.

Damp Ankles got its name from the art director of Larry Flynt's wank mag, Hustler, who once worked in a mental institution where the inmates showed their appreciation by licking his talocrural region.

St. Etienne is the one piece not executed on the Synclavier and was included "because I felt it might be nice to have a contrast with something that sounded like a real live band in the middle of all the mechanical stuff." It's Zappa's solo from a performance of Drowning Witch recorded in 1982.

The title track won the Grammy Award for Best Rock Instrumental Performance (Orchestra, Group or Soloist) in 1988.

London Symphony Orchestra
Vol. II 1987

FZ

Official Release #48

Originally Released: September 17, 1987

Recording data: January 12-14, 1983 at Twickenham Film Studio (London)

Producer: FZ

Engineer: Mark Pinske

Tracks:
Bogus Pomp (24:35)
Bob In Dacron (12:11)
Strictly Genteel (6:56)

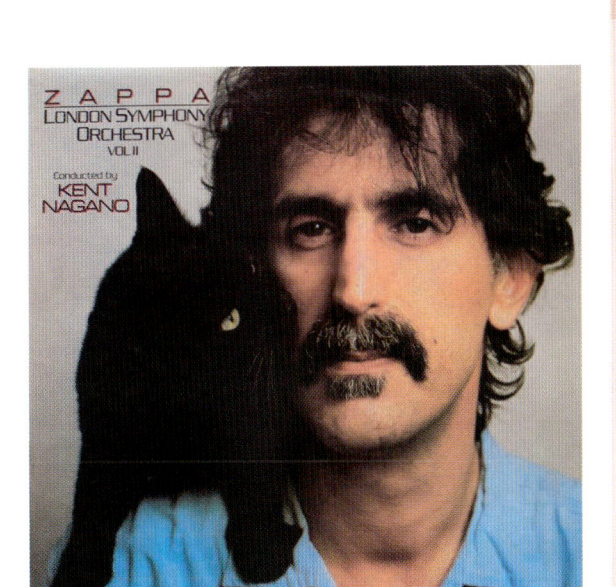

"I was standing about five feet from the trumpet players when they finally did return from lunch and watched the LSO personnel manager ask one for some change for the payphone so he 'could call some new trumpet players' – it seemed to be a subtle joke as if to say that he had noticed which players had screwed up. He certainly didn't say 'You'll never work in this town again.' Were the trumpeters late? Yes. Had they been drinking? Probably. Were they drunk? Not that I could tell. Was their playing worse after lunch? Probably. I'd believe Frank, and he thought so."

David Ocker

So this is where things start to get really screwy.

Around this time, a complete version of Joe's Garage – comprising all three acts in one set – was issued on vinyl and CD.

But that's not a part of the Official Discography.

The version of Bogus Pomp that kicks this set off had previously appeared on CD ('London Symphony Orchestra', neither Volume I nor II), but is officially listed as part of Vol. I.

Confusing, right?

Anyway, this first piece here is a parody of movie music clichés, whose themes were developed in the 200 Motels film.

Zappa started writing Bob In Dacron in 1971, developed it over the next few years, and finally decreed this the definitive version ("unless I decide to change it again!")

Zappa claimed that the LSO's recording of Strictly Genteel (the finale from 200 Motels) required around 50 edits to correct the orchestra's mistakes.

The Old Masters, Box III
1987

FZ

Official Release #49

Originally Released: December 01, 1987

Recording data: August 1969 to June 1976

Producer: FZ

Engineers: Bob Stone, Mark Pinske

Contains the albums:
WAKA/JAWAKA
THE GRAND WAZOO
OVER-NITE SENSATION
APOSTROPHE (')
ROXY & ELSEWHERE
ONE SIZE FITS ALL
BONGO FURY
ZOOT ALLURES

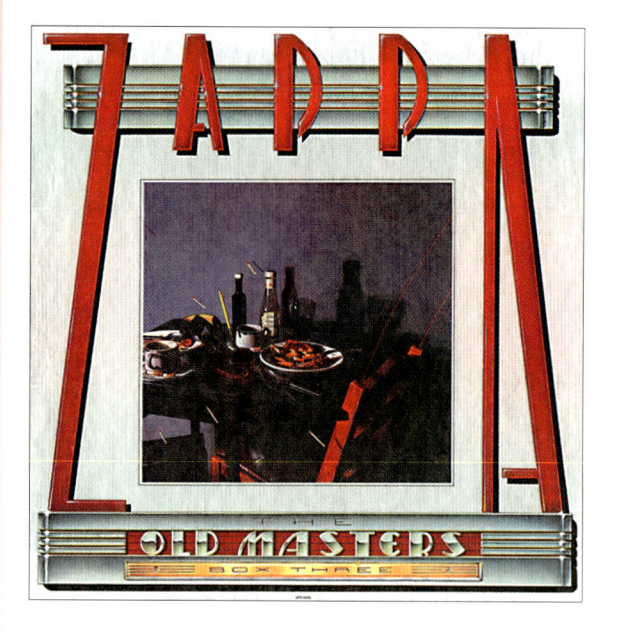

"He gets off on the sexual, the cheap (cheapness is one of Frank's main pleasures in life it would seem, eg. the giant genetically awry spider with nylon strings which only just and only occasionally catch the gleam of the lighting crew's eerie twilight, as the archaeologist's daughter screams out 'Scotty! no! Don't go into the Cave of Danger!'), assorted musics, rhythm n blues singers '55-'58 (well some) and their lyrics, artwork by his cover-designer Cal Shenkel, hoops, lewdicrous, and all things 'hot' and 'classical'."

Jen Jewel Brown

Like the first two boxes, copies of Box III were individually numbered and purchasers could send away for an "owner's certificate". While the individual album covers replicated the originals, the dedication on the reverse of Waka/Jawaka had been scrawled through and amended to say 'was' dedicated to technician Paul Hof and engineer Keene.

Since issuing Box I, Rykodisc had started to release the Old Masters albums on compact disc. Although a fourth box set was planned, the writing was on the wall for the series. No Mystery Disc was included this time, and Zappa fully succumbed to the CD revolution.

Does Humor Belong ... had been his first CD-only album, and all subsequent releases would now be issued in that format.

This was also the last time he'd utilise a Donald Roller Wilson painting: the one on this box features another leftover meal, a bottle of Heinz ketchup and flying matches.

Guitar
1988

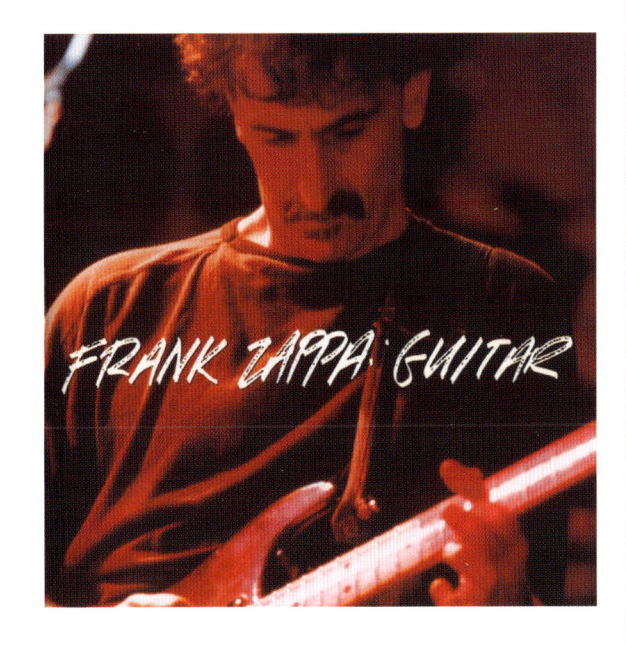

"In assembling the wild card CDs for Rykodisc, I found some real neat guitar solos. It hasn't been edited to a format yet, but I probably have enough for at least a CDs worth ..."

Frank Zappa

Devoid of 'audio grouts', acoustic studio performances and a wide timespan, this album is perhaps a more onerous listen than Shut Up 'N Play Yer Guitar. The inclusion of a Synclavier piece (the converse of Jazz From Hell) might have leavened things: far too many of the solos are taken from performances of Drowning Witch, City Of Tiny Lites or Let's Move To Cleveland.

Sexual Harassment In The Workplace is one of two compositions not extracted from another, and was a great occasional set opener.

In-A-Gadda-Stravinsky derives its name from Zappa referencing the The Rite Of Spring while bassist Thunes plays the vamp from the Iron Butterfly epic.

But Who Was Fulcanelli? and For Duane are edited versions of A Solo From Cologne and A Solo From Atlanta from The Guitar World According To Frank Zappa; a shorter version of Things That Look Like Meat also appears on said cassette.

FZ

Official Release #50

Originally Released: April 26, 1988

Recording data: March 27, 1979 to December 20, 1984 at Rhein-Main-Halle (Wiesbaden), Rudi-Sedlmayer-Halle (Munich), Terrace Ballroom (Salt Lake City), Berkeley Community Theatre (Berkeley), Fox Theater (San Diego), Brondbyhallen (Copenhagen), Sporthalle (Cologne), Philipshalle (Düsseldorf), La Patinoire (Bordeaux), Alte Oper (Frankfurt), Hammersmith Odeon (London), Hallenstadion (Zurich), Olympiahalle (Munich), Parco Redecesio (Milan), Stadio Communale (Pistoia), Oscar Mayer Theater (Madison), Jones Beach Theater (Wantagh), Bismarck Theater (Chicago), Civic Center (Atlanta), Sunrise Musical Theatre (Florida), Orpheum Theater (Memphis), Majestic Performing Arts Center (San Antonio), Queen Elizabeth Theatre (Vancouver) and Arlene Schnitzer Concert Hall (Portland)

Producer: FZ

Engineers: Mark Pinske, Claus Wiedemann, Bob Stone

Tracks:
Sexual Harassment In The Workplace (3:42)
Republicans (5:07)
Do Not Pass Go (3:36)
That's Not Really Reggae (3:17)
When No One Was No One (4:48)
Once Again, Without The Net (3:43)
Outside Now (Original Solo) (5:28)
Jim & Tammy's Upper Room (3:11)
Were We Ever Really Safe In San Antonio? (2:49)
That Ol' G Minor Thing Again (5:02)
Move It Or Park It (5:43)
Sunrise Redeemer (3:58)
But Who Was Fulcanelli? (2:48)
For Duane (3:24)
GOA (4:51)
Winos Do Not March (3:14)
Systems Of Edges (5:32)
Things That Look Like Meat (6:57)
Watermelon In Easter Hay (4:02)

Additional tracks on CD:
Which One Is It? (3:04)
Chalk Pie (4:51)
In-A-Gadda-Stravinsky (2:50)
Hotel Atlanta Incidentals (2:44)
That's Not Really A Shuffle (4:23)
Variations On Sinister #3 (5:15)
Orrin Hatch On Skis (2:12)
Swans? What Swans? (4:23)
Too Ugly For Show Business (4:20)
Do Not Try This At Home (3:46)
Canadian Customs (3:34)
Is That All There Is? (4:09)
It Ain't Necessarily The Saint James Infirmary (5:15)

You Can't Do That On Stage Anymore, Vol. 1   1988

FZ

Official Release #51

Originally Released: May 16, 1988

Recording data: February 16, 1969 to August 26, 1984 at The Ballroom, Stratford (CT), The Factory, The Bronx (NYC), an airport in Florida, Pauley Pavillion, UCLA (CA), Rainbow Theatre (London), The Roxy (LA), Capitol Theatre, Passaic (NJ), Hemmerleinhalle (Neunkirchen am Brand), Hammersmith Odeon (London), Olympiahalle (Munich), The Palladium (NYC), Le Patinoire des Vernets (Geneva), Parco Redecesio (Milan), Stadio Communale (Pistoia), Ex Mattatoio do Testaccio (Rome), Stadio Communale (Palermo) and The Pier (NYC)

Producer: FZ

Engineers: FZ, Mark Pinske, Mick Glossop, Dick Kunc, Barry Keene, Brian Krokus, Kerry McNabb, Davey Moire, Bob Stone, Mick Glossop

Tracks:
The Florida Airport Tape (1:03)
Once Upon A Time (4:37)
Sofa #1 (2:53)
The Mammy Anthem (5:41)
You Didn't Try To Call Me (3:39)
Diseases Of The Band (2:22)
Tryin' To Grow A Chin (3:44)
Let's Make The Water Turn Black / Harry, You're A Beast / The Orange County Lumber Truck (3:28)
The Groupie Routine (5:41)
Ruthie-Ruthie (2:57)
Babbette (3:35)
I'm The Slime (3:13)
Big Swifty (8:47)
Don't Eat The Yellow Snow (20:16)
Plastic People (4:38)
The Torture Never Stops (15:48)
Fine Girl (2:55)
Zomby Woof (5:39)
Sweet Leilani (2:39)
Oh No (4:34)
Be In My Video (3:29)
The Deathless Horsie (5:29)
The Dangerous Kitchen (1:49)
Dumb All Over (4:20)
Heavenly Bank Account (4:05)
Suicide Chump (4:56)
Tell Me You Love Me (2:09)
Sofa #2 (3:01)

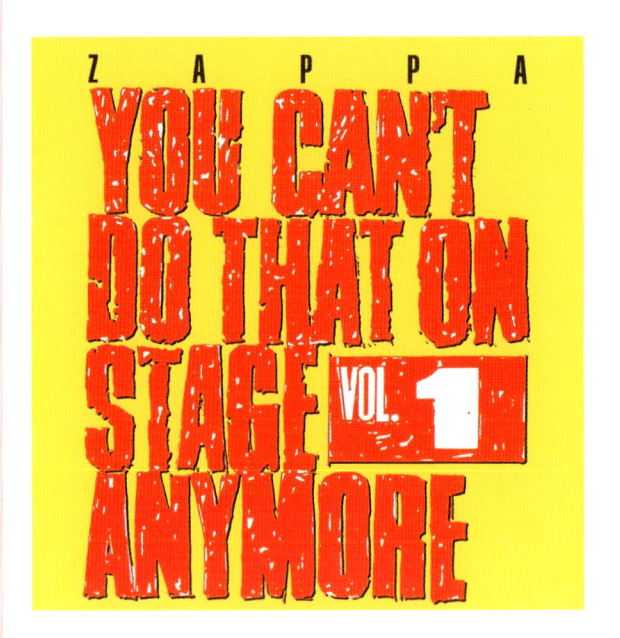

"As well as chronicling the exploits of various bands, it will be a living history of what has happened to recording technology in the last two decades, since the mediums in which the music was recorded range all the way from tape made with two microphones to 24-track digital."
Frank Zappa

The first 'wild card' album for Ryko, and the first of six volumes of unreleased live recordings – all double CD sets.

This one non-sequentially spans the period 1969 to 1984.

A sampler double album issued around the same time contains material from the first four volumes: the series would go on to include tracks that hadn't been recorded when this volume appeared.

Starting with Volman asking "Did anybody see me puke on stage?" we segue into an extract from the fateful Rainbow concert, culminating with Sofa #1. From there, we bounce from decade to decade with different line-ups, and it works incredibly well.

Yellow Snow and The Torture … are obvious highlights, but there are many gems here.

Zappa was keen to beat the bootleggers, and for those who had been trading tapes, there were few surprises here. But no one had heard this material in such great sound quality before.

You Can't Do That On Stage Anymore, Vol. 2 – The Helsinki Concert 1988

FZ

Official Release #52

Originally Released: October 25, 1988

Recording data: September 22-23, 1974 at the Kulttuuritalo (Helsinki)

Producer: FZ

Engineers: Jukka Teittinen, Bob Stone

Tracks:
Tush Tush Tush (A Token Of My Extreme) (2:48)
Stinkfoot (4:18)
Inca Roads (10:54)
RDNZL (8:43)
Village Of The Sun (4:33)
Echidna's Arf (Of You) (3:30)
Don't You Ever Wash That Thing? (4:56)
Pygmy Twylyte (8:22)
Room Service (6:22)
The Idiot Bastard Son (2:39)
Cheepnis (4:29)
Approximate (8:11)
Dupree's Paradise (23:59)
Satumaa (Finnish Tango) (3:51)
T'Mershi Duween (1:31)
The Dog Breath Variations (1:38)
Uncle Meat (2:28)
Building A Girl (1:00)
Montana (Whipping Floss) (10:15)
Big Swifty (2:17)

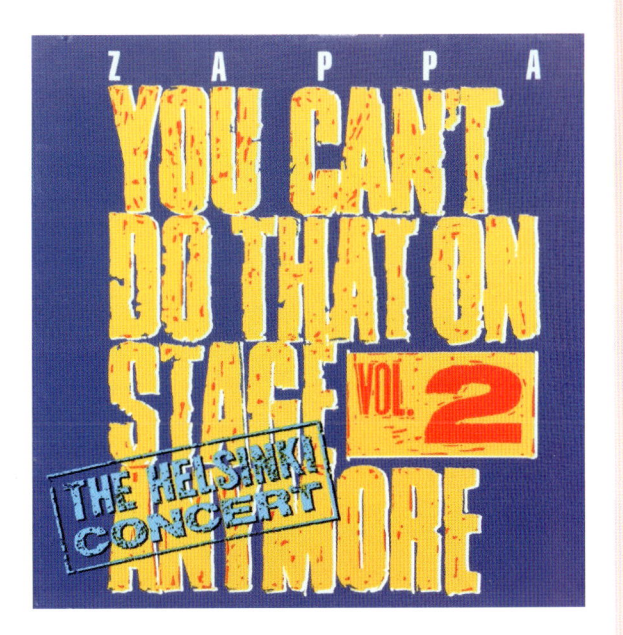

"About twelve years ago, some guy in the audience at a concert in Helsinki, Finland, yelled out 'Whipping Post!' in broken English. I have it on tape. And I said, 'Excuse me?' I could just barely make it out. We didn't know it, and I felt kind of bad that we couldn't just play it and blow the guy's socks off. So when Bobby Martin joined the band, and I found out that he knew how to sing that song, I said, 'We're definitely going to be prepared for the next time somebody wants 'Whipping Post' – in fact we're going to play it before somebody even asks for it.'"

Frank Zappa

Unlike the other volumes in the series, this was entirely recorded at the same venue (over three separate performances on consecutive days) and was the only one issued on vinyl. In the liner notes of the 1987 cassette The Guitar World According To Frank Zappa, we are told we will soon be getting a 3-record set called The Helsinki Tapes 1974, which would have been a more accurate sub-title.

Room Service affords Zappa and Brock an opportunity to natter about life on the road, with Building A Girl a semi-improvised transition piece.

Zappa's excellent solo during Inca Roads is the one used on the One Size Fits All album, but edited slightly differently.

This was the first time the short bongo number T'Mershi Duween had appeared on record.

By this time, the so-called Roxy band knew the material inside and out, and the tempo of these songs has noticeably accelerated.

Broadway The Hard Way
1988

FZ

Official Release #53

Originally Released: October 14, 1988

Recording data: February 09 to June 09, 1988 at Warner Theatre, Washington (DC), Tower Theater, Upper Darby (PA), Bushnell Memorial Hall, Hartford (CT), Syria Mosque, Pittsburgh (PA), Royal Oak Music Theatre, Detroit (MI), Frauenthal Auditorium, Muskegon (MI), Auditorium Theatre, Chicago (IL), Music Hall, Cleveland (OH), Shea's Theater, Buffalo (NY), War Memorial Auditorium, Rochester (NY), Cumberland County Civic Center, Portland (ME), Civic Center, Providence (RI), Broome County Arena, Binghamton (NY), Memorial Hall, Muhlenburg College, Allentown (PA), Rothman Center, Teaneck (NJ), Nassau Coliseum, Uniondale (NY), Wembley Arena (London), Falkoner Teatret (Copenhagen), Olympen (Lund), Stadthalle (Vienna), Rudi-Sedlmayer-Halle (Munich), Hall Tivoli (Strasbourg), Beethovensaal, Liederhalle (Stuttgart) and Palasport (Genoa)

Producer: FZ

Engineers: Bob Stone, Harry Andronis

Tracks:
Elvis Has Just Left The Building (2:24)
Planet Of The Baritone Women (2:48)
Any Kind Of Pain (5:42)
Jesus Thinks You're A Jerk (9:16)
Dickie's Such An Asshole (5:45)
When The Lie's So Big (3:38)
Rhymin' Man (3:50)
Promiscuous (2:02)
The Untouchables (2:26)

Additional tracks on CD:
Why Don't You Like Me? (2:57)
Bacon Fat (1:29)
Stolen Moments (2:58)
Murder By Numbers (5:37)
Jezebel Boy (2:27)
Outside Now (7:49)
Hot Plate Heaven At The Green Hotel (6:40)
What Kind Of Girl? (3:16)

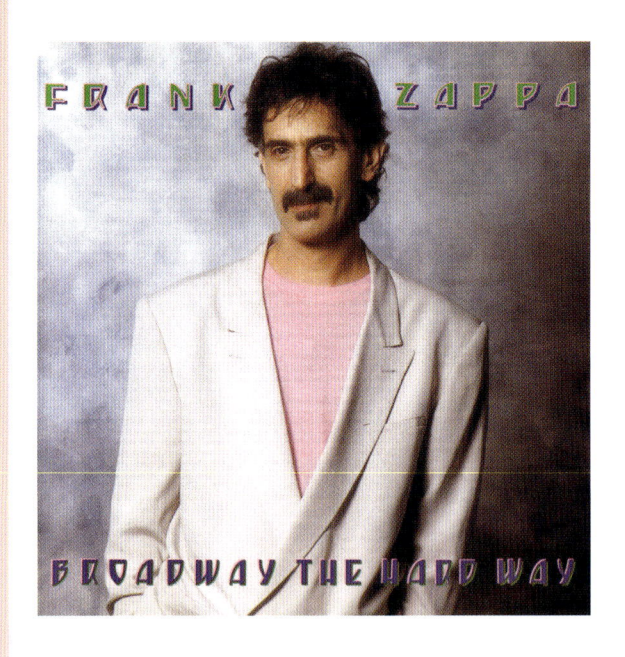

"For 'Promiscuous', Frank said, 'Do a rap rhythm.' Technically, rap songs don't have any 'music'. So what's the bass to do? I wrote the bass part. Frank never told me what to do on that song. That's my bass line, one hundred percent. I never considered it until Keneally pointed it out. And he's Mr Nice Guy. He's not doing anything to make anybody annoyed. He just said. 'Did you ever think about that?' I said, 'No.' I don't give a shit about it enough to cause a stink. I'm not gonna tell Frank about it, or ask for any fuckin' profits, or anything. That's not gonna do any good at all. Frank doesn't have time to take care of everything. There's no need with a piece of music like that anyway."
Scott Thunes

Zappa quickly compiled the first official release from his final world tour, featuring all of the tour's new songs. Broadway The Hard Way was initially released as a mail order nine-track vinyl album, a week before the US elections. By including the 'Republican Retrospective' songs and Rhymin' Man, it was intended to help the undecided voter make up their minds on how to vote. Because of its US centric nature, Zappa was in no hurry for the album to be made readily available overseas.

Seven months later, an expanded CD version was issued in the US and Europe. While this added eight songs – including his King Of Pop-taunting re-write of Tell Me You Love Me (Why Don't You Like Me?) and an uncredited guest appearance by Mr Sting on The Police's Murder By Numbers – for some reason it excised the confinement loaf rap intro to Dickie's Such An Asshole.

You Can't Do That On Stage Anymore, Vol. 3   1989

FZ

Official Release #54

Originally Released: November 13, 1989

Recording data: December 10, 1971 to December 23, 1984 at Rainbow Theatre (London), The Roxy (LA), Kosei Nenkin Kaikan (Osaka), The Palladium (NYC), Hammersmith Odeon (London), Les Arenes (Cap d'Agde), Palais des Sports (Dijon), Parc Des Expositions (Metz), Stadio Communale (Bolzano), Stadio Communale (Palermo), The Pier (NYC), Forum, Montreal (Quebec), Bismarck Theater (Chicago), Bayfront Center Arena, St. Petersburg (FL), Paramount Theatre (Seattle), Queen Elizabeth Theatre (Vancouver) and Universal Amphitheater (Universal City)

Producer: FZ

Engineers: Mark Pinske, Kerry McNabb, Bob Stone

Tracks:
Sharleena (8:53)
Bamboozled By Love-Owner Of A Lonely Heart (6:06)
Lucille Has Messed My Mind Up (2:52)
Advance Romance (1984) (6:58)
Bobby Brown Goes Down (2:44)
Keep It Greasy (3:30)
Honey, Don't You Want A Man Like Me? (4:16)
In France (3:01)
Drowning Witch (9:22)
Ride My Face To Chicago (4:22)
Carol, You Fool (4:06)
Chana In De Bushwop (4:52)
Joe's Garage (2:20)
Why Does It Hurt When I Pee? (3:06)
Dickie's Such An Asshole (10:08)
Hands With A Hammer (3:18)
Zoot Allures (6:09)
Society Pages (2:32)
I'm A Beautiful Guy (1:54)
Beauty Knows No Pain (2:55)
Charlie's Enormous Mouth (3:39)
Cocaine Decisions (3:14)
Nig Biz (4:58)
King Kong (24:32)
Cosmik Debris (5:13)

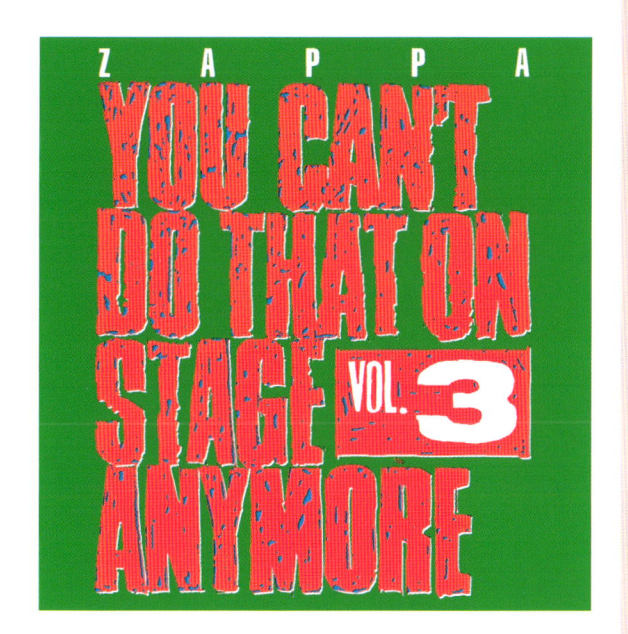

"I stopped listening to Yes once I started listening to Devo, but I always went back to Yessongs for some much-needed nostalgia and generation-of-those-feelings. I even got to BE Chris Squire for a few minutes most nights with Frank as he decided that 'Owner Of A Lonely Heart' was a great groove to solo over after the 1984 tour, so even though I didn't really enjoy playing 'Bamboozled By Love', I enjoyed thoroughly the 'Owner Of A Lonely Heart' line and made it 'mine', as I generally do to most lines handed to me by the greats."
                                                                    Scott Thunes

The bulk of the first disc is taken from the 1984 tour, which had already been well represented on Does Humor Belong In Music?, Guitar and Volume 1 (and would some more on Volume 4).

Sharleena documents the first time Zappa and son Dweezil played together live.

Dickie's Such An Asshole dates back to the 1973 Roxy shows when Nixon was still US President and Zappa obviously felt he couldn't release it. This segues (via an apt excerpt from the Baby Snakes movie) into a Terry Bozzio drum solo from Osaka, Japan in 1976. Zoot Allures contains a brilliant edit, jumping from the same 1976 show to one in 1982.

Similarly, King Kong flits between the infamous 1971 Rainbow performance (moments before Zappa was pushed off the stage – "the tape ran out before my crash-landing, otherwise I would have included it here", he said) and shows from the 1982 European tour.

The Best Band You Never Heard In Your Life   1991

FZ

Official Release #55

Originally Released: April 16, 1991

Recording data: February 14 to 06 June, 1988 at Tower Theater, Upper Darby (PA), Mid Hudson Civic Center, Poughkeepsie (NY), Syria Mosque, Pittsburgh (PA), Royal Oak Music Theatre, Detroit (MI), Broome County Arena, Binghamton (NY), Memorial Hall, Allentown (PA), Rothman Center, Teaneck (NJ), Landmark Theater, Syracuse (NY), Brighton Centre (Brighton), Wembley Arena (London), Carl-Diem-Halle (Würzburg), The Ahoy (Rotterdam), Stadthalle (Vienna), Rudi-Sedlmayer-Halle (Munich), Le Zenith (Montpellier), Hall Tivoli (Strasbourg), Beethovensaal, Liederhalle (Stuttgart), Stadthalle (Fürth), Sporthalle (Linz), Palasport (Modena) and Palasport (Florence)

Producer: FZ

Engineer: Bob Stone

Tracks:
Heavy Duty Judy (6:04)
Ring Of Fire (2:00)
Cosmik Debris (4:32)
Find Her Finer (2:42)
Who Needs The Peace Corps? (2:40)
I Left My Heart In San Francisco (0:36)
Zomby Woof (5:41)
Bolero (5:19)
Zoot Allures (7:07)
Mr. Green Genes (3:40)
Florentine Pogen (7:11)
Andy (5:51)
Inca Roads (8:19)
Sofa #1 (2:49)
Purple Haze (2:27)
Sunshine Of Your Love (2:30)
Let's Move To Cleveland (5:51)
When Irish Eyes Are Smiling (0:46)
"Godfather Part II" Theme (0:30)
A Few Moments With Brother A. West (4:01)
The Torture Never Stops Part One (5:20)
Theme From "Bonanza" (0:28)
Lonesome Cowboy Burt (Swaggart Version) (4:54)
The Torture Never Stops Part Two (10:47)
More Trouble Every Day (Swaggart Version) (5:28)
Penguin In Bondage (Swaggart Version) (5:05)
The Eric Dolphy Memorial Barbecue (9:18)
Stairway To Heaven (9:20)

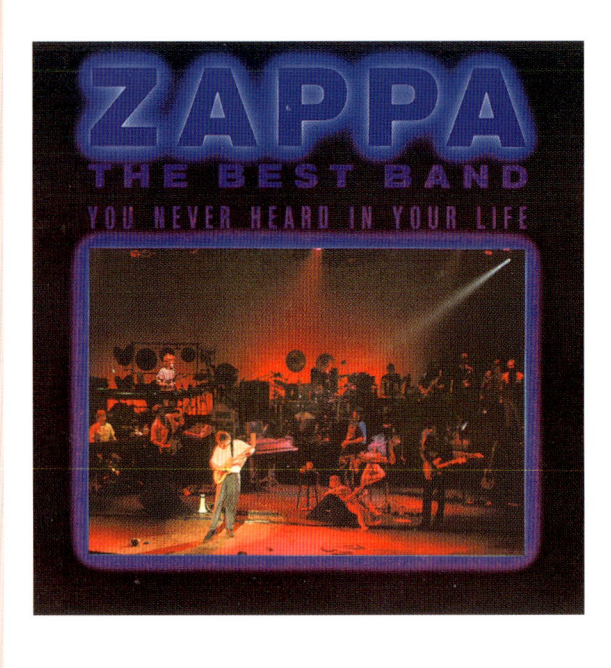

"I think every tour Frank undertook in the 80s lost money. His last one did, in particular, because it was such a huge band – 12 pieces. If we had continued touring we might have made some of it back, but he just couldn't deal with the personality conflicts anymore. That had happened before, but apparently it had never escalated to such a peak that it was starting to affect performances, including Frank's. At that point it just ceased to be fun. As far as I could tell, that was part of Frank's primary motivation – to give himself a chuckle, to write something that amused him and then see it executed properly."
Mike Keneally

This release was preceded by a UK single comprising Led Zeppelin's Stairway To Heaven and Ravel's Bolero (later removed from European editions of the album when the composer's estate complained: it was reinstated on the 1995 worldwide reissue, which also sported new cover artwork by Cal Schenkel).

Two other classic rock songs are included: against a repetitive fake-Devo horn-punctuated background, Willis (in Thing-Fish guise) and Keneally (as the Man In Black) have fun with Hendrix's Purple Haze and Cream's Sunshine Of Your Love.

The recording locations from which each song is pieced together are listed, but these are by no means comprehensive: Inca Roads, for instance, was compiled from a number of shows allowing Zappa to squeeze in quotes from the Bee Gees' Stayin' Alive: this was another example of 'conceptual continuity', as the song had earlier been referenced during a 1982 performance of Approximate (issued on YCDTOSA Vol. 4).

You Can't Do That On Stage Anymore, Vol. 4   1991

FZ

Official Release #56

Originally Released: *June 14, 1991*

Recording data: *February 21, 1969 to May 19, 1988 at Fillmore East (NYC), The Factory, The Bronx (NYC), The Roxy (LA), Kulttuuritalo (Helsinki), Capitol Theatre, Passaic (NJ), Armadillo World Headquarters (Austin), The Palladium (NYC), Mudd Club (NYC), Alte Oper (Frankfurt), Hammersmith Odeon (London), Parc des Expositions (Metz), Olympiahalle (Munich), Stadio Communale (Pistoia), Ex Mattatorio do Testaccio (Rome), Detroit (MI), The Pier (NYC), Fine Arts Center Concert Hall, Amherst (MA), Tower Theater, Upper Darby (PA), Royal Oak Music Theatre, Royal Oak (MI), Bismarck Theater (Chicago), Bayfront Center (St. Petersburg), Paramount Theatre (Seattle), Queen Elizabeth Theatre (Vancouver), Universal Amphitheater, Universal City (CA), Pabellón de los Deportes de La Casilla (Bilbao) and Le Summum (Grenoble)*

Producer: *FZ*

Engineers: *Joe Chiccarelli, Mark Pinske, Kerry McNabb, Bob Stone, Claus Wiedemann, Dick Kunc, Davey Moire, Mick Glossop*

Tracks:
Little Rubber Girl (2:57)
Stick Together (2:04)
My Guitar Wants To Kill Your Mama (3:20)
Willie The Pimp (2:06)
Montana (5:47)
Brown Moses (2:38)
The Evil Prince (7:12)
Approximate (1:49)
Love Of My Life Mudd Club Version (1:58)
Let's Move To Cleveland Solos (1984) (7:10)
You Call that Music? (4:07)
Pound For A Brown Solos (1978) (6:29)
The Black Page (1984) (5:14)
Take Me Out To The Ball Game (3:01)
Filthy Habits (5:39)
The Torture Never Stops Original Version (9:14)
Church Chat (2:00)
Stevie's Spanking (10:51)
Outside Now (6:09)
Disco Boy (2:59)
Teen-Age Wind (1:54)
Truck Driver Divorce (4:46)
Florentine Pogen (5:09)
Tiny Sick Tears (4:29)
Smell My Beard (4:30)
The Booger Man (2:46)
Carolina Hard Core Ecstasy (6:27)
Are You Upset? (1:29)
Little Girl Of Mine (1:40)
The Closer You Are (2:05)
Johnny Darling (0:51)
No, No Cherry (1:26)
The Man From Utopia (1:15)
Mary Lou (2:14)

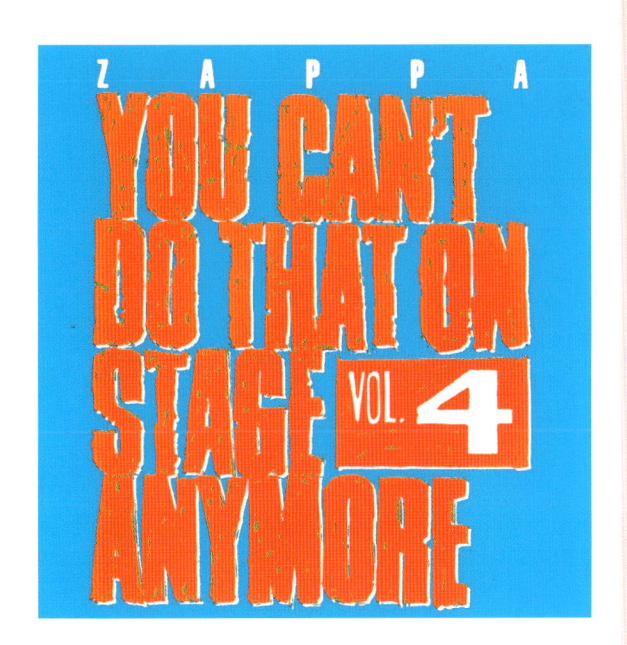

"A Booger Bear is an extremely ugly anything, and a Booger is short for Booger Bear, in the parlance of that '73 band. Marty Perellis was our road manager, and there was an occasion where he met some girl, I think it was in Memphis, who had a great Dane. Apparently, this girl liked to do things in conjunction with the great Dane, and Marty brought the girl and the dog to his room ..."

Frank Zappa

This volume starts with the introduction to Go Cry On Somebody Else's Shoulder before mutating into a paean for an inflatable doll (which were all the rage in the mid-70s, with Roxy Music, Neil Innes and The Police all having a stab); Zappa here is egged on by Denny Walley.

The Evil Prince (which formed part of The 'Torchum' Never Stops) has Ray White on lead vocals and a Zappa solo that embiggens the Thing-Fish version.

The Torture Never Stops was originally performed when Beefheart was in the band and was named Why Doesn't Somebody Get Him a Pepsi? in his honour; at this time, it owed much to Howlin' Wolf's Smokestack Lightnin'.

Like Ruthie-Ruthie and Babbette on Vol. 1, Smell My Beard and The Booger Man delve into the folklore of the Roxy band.

The album ends with a fun run of RnB covers recorded in 1982 & 1984.

Make A Jazz Noise Here
1991

FZ

Official Release #57

Originally Released: June 04, 1991

Recording data: February 09, 1988 to June 07, 1988 at Warner Theatre, Washington (DC), Tower Theater, Upper Darby (PA), Orpheum Theater, Boston (MA), Mid Hudson Civic Center, Poughkeepsie (NY), Syria Mosque, Pittsburgh (PA), Royal Oak Music Theatre, Detroit (MI), Music Hall, Cleveland (OH), Memorial Auditorium, Burlington (VT), Civic Center, Springfield (MA), Memorial Hall, Allentown (PA), Sporthalle (Cologne), Brighton Centre (Brighton), Wembley Arena (London), Stadthalle (Bremen), Olympen (Lund), The Ahoy (Rotterdam), Stadthalle (Vienna), Rudi-Sedlmayer-Halle (Munich), Pabellón de los Deportes de La Casilla (Bilbao), Prado de San Sebastián (Seville), Le Summum (Grenoble), Liederhalle, Beethoven-Saal (Stuttgart), Rosengarten, Mozartsaal (Mannheim), Sporthalle (Linz), Palasport (Modena), Palasport (Florence) and PalaEur (Rome)

Producer: FZ

Engineer: Bob Stone

Tracks:
Stinkfoot (7:39)
When Yuppies Go To Hell (13:28)
Fire And Chains (5:04)
Let's Make The Water Turn Black (1:36)
Harry, You're A Beast (0:47)
The Orange County Lumber Truck (0:41)
Oh No (4:43)
Theme From Lumpy Gravy (1:11)
Eat That Question (1:54)
Black Napkins (6:56)
Big Swifty (11:12)
King Kong (13:04)
Star Wars Won't Work (3:40)
The Black Page (New Age Version) (6:45)
T'Mershi Duween (1:42)
Dupree's Paradise (8:34)
City Of Tiny Lights (8:01)
Royal March From "L'Histoire Du Soldat" (0:59)
Theme From The Bartok Piano Concerto #3 (0:43)
Sinister Footwear 2nd mvt. (6:39)
Stevie's Spanking (4:25)
Alien Orifice (4:15)
Cruisin' For Burgers (8:27)
Advance Romance (7:43)
Strictly Genteel (6:36)

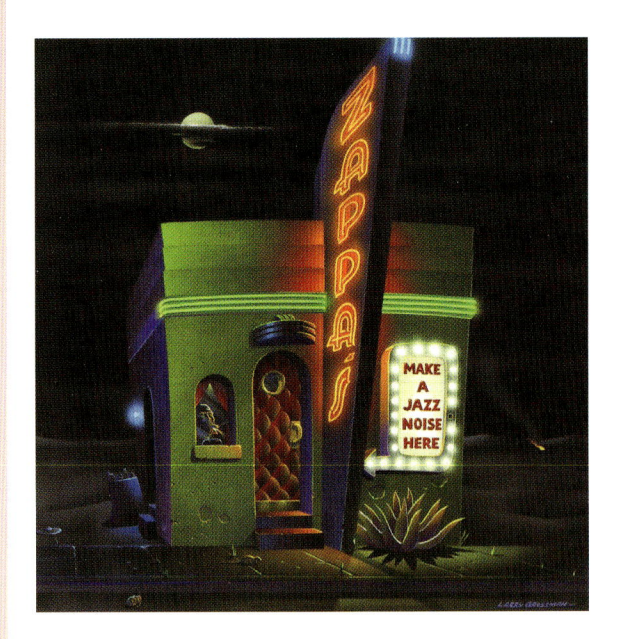

"I never knew 'Cruisin' For Burgers'. I never knew the gloriou gloriousness of playing that solo. I love that solo section. And on thi album, he cuts off the last chord. My favourite part of the song i the pay-off. And he cut it off and starts 'Advance Romance' with th ugliest guitar noise in the universe. I cannot stand listening to tha It's so absolutely painful. It's the exact wrong production decisio to make. Hit the chord, then go into 'Advance Romance'. But don' replace my favourite bit of music with my least favourite bit of music And I loved playing 'Advance Romance', but that was wrong. Tha was a really, really wrong decision."

Scott Thune

Another two-disc set from the 1988 tour. So, in quick succession Zappa gave us: a single album featuring all the new songs; double comprising the more vocal-oriented, recognisable an humorous stuff; and this, focussing on the improvised, non vocal pieces.

The album starts with Zappa announcing that the televangelis Jimmy Swaggart is finally under investigation over a sexua encounter with a prostitute; Swaggart was the subject o numerous humourous lyric changes throughout the tour.

When Yuppies Go To Hell is mostly taken from performances o a Synclavier based improvisation he had first titled Desiccated

Stravinsky's Royal March and Bartok's Piano Concerto ar edited from a discarded performance of Packard Goose, an sandwiched between two different songs.

During the Big Swifty monster mash-up, we are treated to wha was nicknamed The Reader's Digest Classical Medley: a joyou romp by this fantastic band through Wagner's Lohengrir Bizet's "Habanera" and Tchaikovsky's 1812 Overture.

You Can't Do That On Stage Anymore, Vol. 5   1992

FZ

Official Release #58

Originally Released: July 10, 1992

Recording data: June 24, 1966 to July 14, 1982 at Fillmore Auditorium, San Francisco (CA), Falkoner Teatret (Copenhagen), Whisky à Go-Go (LA), Sunset Sound Studios (Hollywood), Criteria Studios, Miami (FL), Thee Image, Miami Beach (FL), McMillin Theater, Columbia University (NYC), Fillmore East (NYC), The Factory, The Bronx (NYC), Royal Albert Hall (London), The Ark, Boston (MA), A & R Studios (NYC), Greyhound tour bus interior, dressing room (Providence), Les Arenes (Frejus), Les Arenes (Cap d'Agde), La Patinoire (Bordeaux), Grugahalle (Essen), Alte Oper (Frankfurt), Hammersmith Odeon (London), Olympiahalle (Munich), La Patinoire des Vernets (Geneva), Stadio Comunale (Bolzano), Stadio Ferraris (Genoa), Ex Mattatoio di Testaccio (Rome) and Stadio Communale La Favorita (Palermo)

Producer: FZ

Engineers: John Judnich, Dick Kunc, Steve, Wally Heider, FZ, Mark Pinske, Bob Stone, Spencer Chrislu

Tracks:
The Downtown Talent Scout (4:01)
Charles Ives (4:37)
Here Lies Love (2:44)
Piano/Drum Duet (1:57)
Mozart Ballet (4:05)
Chocolate Halvah (3:25)
JCB & Kansas On The Bus #1 (1:03)
Run Home Slow: Main Title Theme (1:16)
The Little March (1:20)
Right There (5:07)
Where Is Johnny Velvet? (0:51)
Return Of The Hunch-Back Duke (1:44)
Trouble Every Day (4:06)
Proto-Minimalism (1:39)
JCB & Kansas On The Bus #2 (1:10)
My Head? (1:21)
Meow (1:23)
Baked-Bean Boogie (3:26)
Where's Our Equipment? (2:29)
FZ/JCB Drum Duet (4:26)
No Waiting For The Peanuts To Dissolve (4:45)
A Game Of Cards (0:46)
Underground Freak-Out Music (3:51)
German Lunch (6:42)
My Guitar Wants To Kill Your Mama (2:11)
Easy Meat (7:38)
Dead Girls Of London (2:29)
Shall We Take Ourselves Seriously? (1:44)
What's New In Baltimore? (5:03)
Moggio (2:29)
Dancin' Fool (3:12)
RDNZL (7:58)
Advance Romance (7:01)
City Of Tiny Lites (10:38)
A Pound For A Brown (On The Bus) (8:38)
Doreen (1:58)
The Black Page #2 (9:59)
Geneva Farewell (1:24)

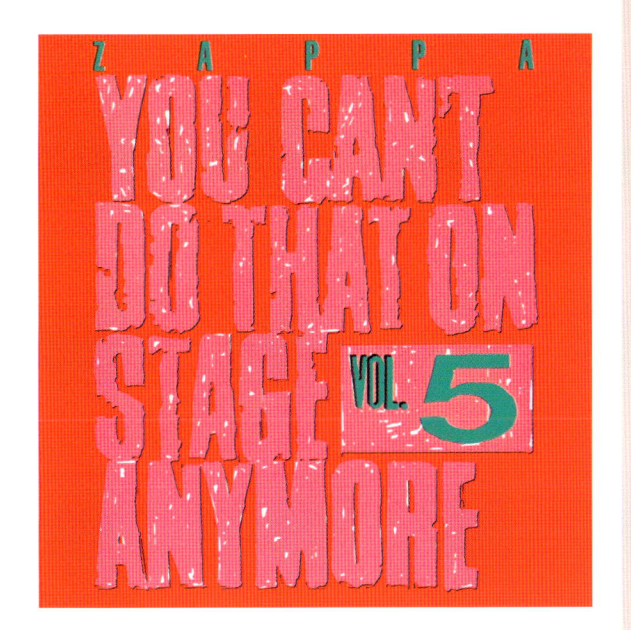

"Disc two of this set is dedicated to the 1982 band. About half of the material here comes from our ill-fated concert in Geneva, Switzerland (which ended with a small riot). The 1982 tour itself ended with a much larger riot in Palermo, Sicily a few weeks later. The 82 band could play beautifully when it wanted to. It is unfortunate that the audiences of the time didnt understand that we had no intention of posing as targets for their assorted love offerings cast onto the stage (in Milan they threw used hypodermic syringes)."

Frank Zappa

A game of two halves: disc one consists of material recorded by the 'original Mothers', mostly in 1969, including two studio recordings (German Lunch and My Guitar) and a bunch of studio, dressing room and tour bus chatter; disc the second comprises all live performances from Zappa's summer 1982 European tour.

In the notes that appear with each release in the series, Zappa refers to the "peculiar misconception" that the only good material was performed by the original Mothers – a notion he hoped to dispel. Strange then that he should devote a whole disc to that particular group.

It was a relief to see the return of Zappa's notes on some of the individual performances, as rumours about his ill health were now rife – despite Moon's statement in December 1991 that he had prostate cancer, but was fighting it successfully. There had been no such notes accompanying Volume 4.

You Can't Do That On Stage Anymore, Vol. 6   1992

FZ

Official Release #59

Originally Released: July 10, 1992

Recording data: October 09, 1970 to June 09, 1988 at Tully Gymnasium, Florida State University, Tallahassee (FL), Fillmore East (NYC), Pauley Pavilion, UCLA (CA), Hordern Pavilion (Sydney), Tivolis Koncertsal (Copenhagen), The Spectrum, Philadelphia (PA), The Palladium (NYC), Hemmerleinhalle (Neunkirchen am Brand), Hammersmith Odeon (London), Dane County Coliseum, Madison (WI), Terrace Ballroom, Salt Lake City (UT), Berkeley Community Theater (CA), Santa Monica Civic Auditorium (CA), Stadio Communale (Pistoia), The Pier (NYC), Royal Oak Music Theatre, Royal Oak (MI), Bismarck Theatre, Chicago (IL), Paramount Theatre, Seattle (WA), Universal Amphitheater, Universal City (CA), Tower Theater, Upper Darby (PA), Auditorium Theatre, Chicago (IL), Broome County Arena, Binghamton (NY), Towson Center, Towson (MD), Rosengarten, Mozartsaal (Mannheim) and Palasport (Genoa)

Producer: FZ

Engineers: FZ, Kerry McNabb, Mick Glossop, George Douglas, Bob Stone, Davey Moire, Joe Chiccarelli, Mark Pinske, Bob Liftin, Barry Keene, Spencer Chrislu

Tracks:
The M.O.I. Anti-Smut Loyalty Oath (3:01)
The Poodle Lecture (5:02)
Dirty Love (2:39)
Magic Fingers (2:21)
The Madison Panty-Sniffing Festival (2:44)
Honey, Don't You Want A Man Like Me? (4:01)
Father O'Blivion (2:21)
Is That Guy Kidding Or What? (4:02)
I'm So Cute (1:39)
White Person (2:07)
Lonely Person Devices (3:13)
Ms. Pinky (2:00)
Shove It Right In (6:45)
Wind Up Working In A Gas Station (2:32)
Make A Sex Noise (3:09)
Tracy Is A Snob (3:54)
I Have Been In You (5:04)
Emperor Of Ohio (1:31)
Dinah-Moe Humm (3:16)
He's So Gay (2:34)
Camarillo Brillo (3:09)
Muffin Man (2:25)
NYC Halloween Audience-The Illinois Enema Bandit (8:49)
Thirteen (6:10)
Lobster Girl (2:20)
Black Napkins (5:21)
We're Turning Again (4:56)
Alien Orifice (4:16)
Catholic Girls (4:04)
Crew Slut (5:33)
Tryin' To Grow A Chin (3:33)
Take Your Clothes Off When You Dance (3:46)
Lisa's Life Story (3:05)
Lonesome Cowboy Nando (5:09)
200 Motels Finale (3:48)
Strictly Genteel (6:56)

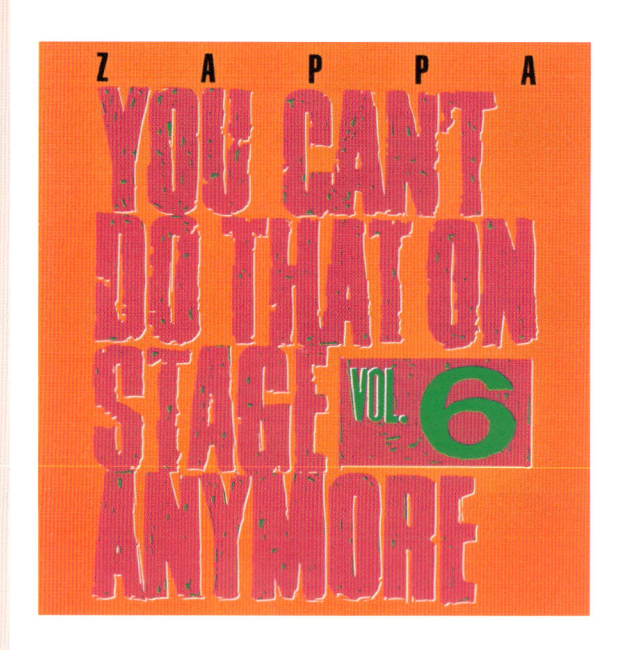

"My personal favourite MK contribution to a Zappa CD occurs in 'Lonesome Cowboy Nando', when I attempt to cram the line 'I describe the little dangling utensils on this thing and tell him to draw it up so that it looks just like a brand new jellyfish' into the same space where I would normally say 'stomp in his face so he don't move no more'. The first time I listened to this song with Frank, he applauded me after that section. One o' them priceless moments."

Mike Keneally

Concluding more than 13 hours of live music, designed primarily to be heard on CD, Volume 6 is another ragbag: no 'original Mothers', more from 84, and a bunch from the final tour.

Thirteen and Take Your Clothes Off feature Shankar on electric violin and were recorded at the legendary Halloween shows at New York's Palladium in 1978.

Lisa's Life Story is a piece featuring 'dramatic soprano' Lisa Popeil and her "quest for the perfect hunk".

Lonesome Cowboy Nando is a mix of the old with the new: part taken from the Just Another Band From L.A. concert in 1971, with Jimmy Carl Black guesting on vocals; and part taken from the very last date of the Broadway tour at the Palasport in Genoa. The song name-checks marine biologist Ferdinando Boero, who named a jellyfish Phialella zappai.

Only YCDTOSAs 1 to 4 were "remastered" for the series' re-release in 1995.

Playground Psychotics
1992

FZ / Mothers

Official Release #60

Originally Released: October 27, 1992

Recording data: September 17, 1970 to December 10, 1971 in Spokane (WA), Edmonton (Alberta), Vancouver (BC), The Edgewater Inn (Seattle), Portland (OR), Tully Gymnasium, Florida State University (FL), Fillmore West (San Francisco), Buffalo (NY), Kensington Palace Hotel (London), Fillmore East (NYC), Pauley Pavilion, UCLA (CA) and Rainbow Theatre (London)

Producer: FZ

Engineers: Mark Pinske, Spencer Chrislu

Tracks:
(A TYPICAL DAY ON THE ROAD, PART 1)
Here Comes The Gear, Lads (1:00)
The Living Garbage Truck (1:20)
A Typical Sound Check (1:19)
"This Is Neat" (0:23)
The Motel Lobby (1:21)
Getting Stewed (0:55)
The Motel Room (0:29)
"Don't Take Me Down" (1:11)
The Dressing Room (0:24)
Learning "Penis Dimension" (2:02)
"You There, With The Hard On!" (0:25)
Zanti Serenade (2:40)
Divan (1:46)
Sleeping In A Jar (1:30)
"Don't Eat There" (2:26)
Brixton Still Life (2:59)
Super Grease (1:39)
Wonderful Wino (4:52)
Sharleena (4:23)
Cruisin' For Burgers (2:53)
Diptheria Blues (6:19)
Well (4:43)
Say Please (0:57)
Aaawk (2:59)
Scumbag (5:53)
A Small Eternity With Yoko Ono (6:07)

(A TYPICAL DAY ON THE ROAD, PART 2)
Beer Shampoo (1:39)
Champagne Lecture (4:29)
Childish Perversions (1:31)
Playground Psychotics (1:08)
The Mudshark Interview (2:39)
"There's No Lust In Jazz" (0:55)
Botulism On The Hoof (0:47)
You Got Your Armies (0:10)
The Spew King (0:24)
I'm Doomed (0:25)
Status Back Baby (2:49)
The London Cab Tape (1:24)
Concentration Moon, Part One (1:20)
The Sanzini Brothers (1:33)
"It's A Good Thing We Get Paid To Do This" (2:45)
Concentration Moon, Part Two (2:04)
Mom & Dad (3:16)
Intro To Music For Low Budget Orchestra (1:32)
Billy The Mountain (30:25)
(THE TRUE STORY OF 200 MOTELS) He's Watching Us (1:21)
If You're Not A Professional Actor (0:23)

"Frank used to carry his Uher tape recorder with us on tour constantly, and Playground Psychotics' basic foundation started during a weekend when we travelled to Spokane, Seattle, to the Edgewater Hotel – which was the foundation for 'The Mud Shark' and the whole story on the Fillmore East album. Frank edited together that weekend into an album called the Official Mothers of Invention Bootleg Album. That was given to Warner Brothers – right after we did Just Another Band From L.A. – as his new album. Warners turned it down, so the album went up on the shelf."

Mark Volman

Zappa had a penchant for the short-lived Flo and Eddie era, and here collects together in concert and off stage recordings, making an audio documentary of that period.

When the Mothers played the Fillmore in 1971, they were joined by John Lennon and Yoko Ono and performed five songs together. A deal was struck whereby they could both release their own versions of the tapes. Lennon issued his (with differing titles and overdubs) the following year as part of the free Live Jam bonus disc that came with his and Ono's Some Time In New York City album. Zappa tagged his mix to the end of the first disc here.

Ending with excerpts from his 1989 home video, The True Story Of Frank Zappa's 200 Motels, the album's title was inspired by the shenanigans on his 1988 tour, which Kaylan and Volman were originally intended to be a part of.

He's Right (0:14)
Going For The Money (0:12)
Jeff Quits (1:33)
A Bunch Of Adventures (0:56)
Martin Lickert's Story (0:39)
A Great Guy (0:30)
Bad Acting (0:10)
The Worst Reviews (0:20)
A Version Of Himself (1:02)
I Could Be A Star Now 0:36

Ahead Of Their Time
1993

FZ

Official Release #61

Originally Released: March 23, 1993

Recording data: October 25, 1968 at Royal Festival Hall (London)

Producer: FZ

Engineer: Bob Stone

Tracks:
Prologue (3:07)
Progress? (4:44)
Like It Or Not (2:21)
The Jimmy Carl Black Philosophy Lesson (2:01)
Holding The Group Back (2:00)
Holiday In Berlin (0:56)
The Rejected Mexican Pope Leaves The Stage (2:55)
Undaunted, The Band Plays On (4:34)
Agency Man (3:17)
Epilogue (1:52)
King Kong (8:13)
Help, I'm A Rock (1:38)
Transylvania Boogie (3:07)
Pound For A Brown (6:50)
Sleeping In A Jar (2:24)
Let's Make The Water Turn Black (1:51)
Harry, You're A Beast (0:53)
The Orange County Lumber Truck (Part I) (0:47)
Oh No (3:22)
The Orange County Lumber Truck (Part II) (10:40)

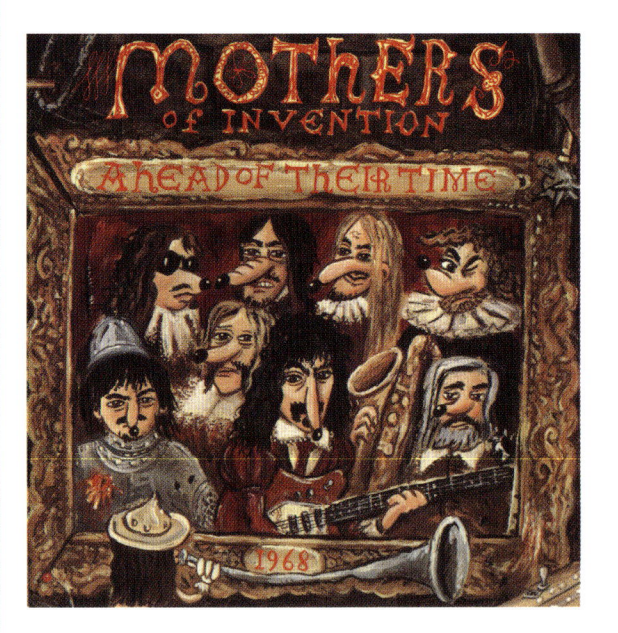

"I've put together an album called Ahead Of Their Time. It's the last Mothers Of Invention album, and it has the entire performance from the Royal Festival Hall in 1968 in London, with all the rock music from the show. We were our own opening act for that show. Everybody in the band was in this play, and the music – which I had written – was supplied by 14 members of the BBC symphony. The performance of that play is contained on one of the Mystery Discs, but none of the rock music from that show has ever been released. I think there's a market for this, since it's probably the most interesting of all the archival tapes. We did the remix from four-track one-inch masters to digital, and it's pretty crisp."

Frank Zappa

While portions of this material had already been seen (in the Uncle Meat and The True Story Of 200 Motels home videos) and heard (on the second Mystery Disc), it was good to get a more complete recording of this legendary performance.

Musically the play contains snippets of Mozart, Tchaikovsky and 200 Motels, while the script uses dialogue based on Mothers folklore. Although some band members get writing credits on the improvised pieces, Zappa is in control of proceedings throughout.

The wonderful cover art by Cal Schenkel reflects the album's title (the Mothers in 16th Century ruffs) and maintains Zappa's conceptual continuity.

With Zappa nearing the end of his life, did this and the previous archival release hint at some hitherto hidden sentimentality? Possibly not, as he purposely waited until a lawsuit brought against him by some former Mothers over unpaid royalties had been conclusively settled before issuing this album.

The Yellow Shark
1993

FZ

Official Release #62

Originally Released: November 02, 1993

Recording data: September 17-28, 1992 at Alte Oper (Frankfurt), Philharmonie (Berlin) and Wiener Konzerthaus (Vienna)

Producer: FZ

Engineers: Spencer Chrislu, Harry Andronis, Dave Dondorf, Todd Yvega

Tracks:
Intro (1:43)
Dog Breath Variations (2:06)
Uncle Meat (3:24)
Outrage At Valdez (3:27)
Times Beach II (7:30)
III Revised (1:44)
The Girl In The Magnesium Dress (4:33)
Be-Bop Tango (3:43)
Ruth Is Sleeping (6:06)
None Of The Above (2:06)
Pentagon Afternoon (2:27)
Questi Cazzi Di Piccione (3:02)
Times Beach III (4:25)
Food Gathering In Post-Industrial America, 1992 (2:48)
Welcome To The United States (6:41)
Pound For A Brown (2:12)
Exercise #4 (1:37)
Get Whitey (7:00)
G-Spot Tornado (5:17)

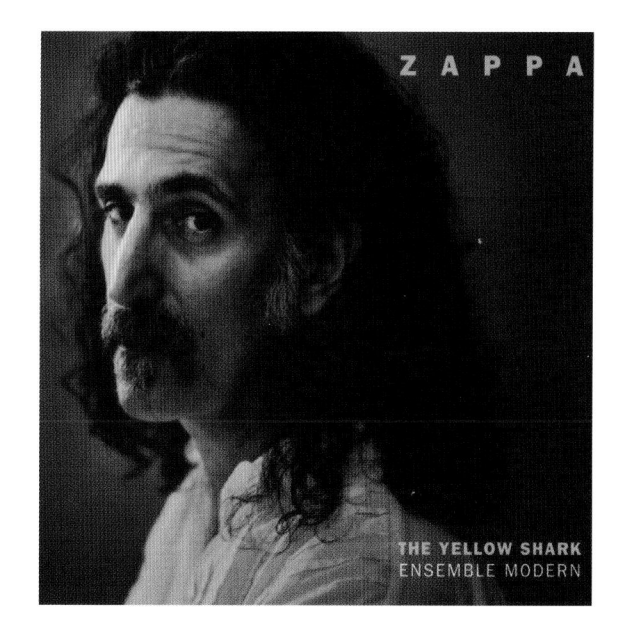

"The musicians had a bit more of an ability to also add what my dad would call 'the eyebrows', meaning they were open to performance suggestions and things that were non – traditional for orchestras."
Dweezil Zappa

In 1991, Zappa belatedly found an orchestra that could do his work justice. The German chamber ensemble, Ensemble Modern, had approached him about performing his compositions at the 1992 Frankfurt Festival (where his music would be celebrated alongside that of John Cage, Karlheinz Stockhausen and Alexander Knaifel). Zappa wrote both new material as well as adapting some older pieces for them with the help of arranger Ali N. Askin.

He found the collaboration 'exhilarating' and this album was taken from a short series of 'Yellow Shark' concerts the Ensemble performed in Frankfurt, Berlin and Vienna. Zappa was unable to partake in all of the shows due to ill health, but did manage to conduct some selections.

He jokingly dismissed one of the new works, Food Gathering In Post-Industrial America, as "programme music" and "a piece of shit", but the whole project was a swansong he was understandably very proud of.

Civilisation Phaze III
1994

FZ

Official Release #63

Originally Released: December 02, 1994

Recording data: 1967 to 1992 at Apostolic Studio (NYC), UMRK (LA) and "Joe's Garage" (LA)

Producer: FZ

Engineers: Dick Kunc, David Dondorf, Todd Yvega, Marque Coy, Spencer Chrislu

Tracks:
(ACT ONE)
"This Is Phaze III" (0:47)
Put A Motor In Yourself (5:13)
"Oh-Umm" (0:50)
They Made Me Eat It (1:48)
Reagan At Bitburg (5:39)
"A Very Nice Body" (1:00)
Navanax (1:40)
"How The Pigs' Music Works" (1:49)
Xmas Values (5:31)
"Dark Water!" (0:23)
Amnerika (3:03)
"Have You Heard Their Band?" (0:38)
Religious Superstition (0:43)
"Saliva Can Only Take So Much" (0:27)
Buffalo Voice (5:12)
"Someplace Else Right Now" (0:32)
Get A Life (2:20)
"A Kayak (On Snow)" (0:28)
N-Lite (18:00)

(ACT TWO)
"I Wish Motorhead Would Come Back" (0:14)
Secular Humanism (2:41)
"Attack! Attack! Attack!" (1:24)
I Was In A Drum (3:38)
"A Different Octave" (0:57)
"This Ain't CNN" (3:20)
"The Pigs' Music" (1:17)
A Pig With Wings (2:52)
"This Is All Wrong" (1:42)
Hot & Putrid (0:29)
"Flowing Inside-Out" (0:46)
"I Had A Dream About That" (0:27)
Gross Man (2:54)
"A Tunnel Into Muck" (0:21)
Why Not? (2:18)
"Put A Little Motor In 'Em" (0:50)
"You're Just Insultin' Me, Aren't You!" (2:13)
"Cold Light Generation" (0:44)
Dio Fa (8:18)
"That Would Be The End Of That" (0:35)
Beat The Reaper (15:23)
Waffenspiel (4:04)

"I think it has a lot to do with Frank knowing that he wasn't going to be able to realize a lot of things that he wanted to do. So then you do what you can. Part of it is an expression of that. I don't think he was in a hurry, as much as he was pragmatic and said, 'I can do this.' I see it as a big time 'Thanks For the Memories,' in some ways."

Gail Zappa

The first studio album of new material since Jazz From Hell was also the first posthumous release from the Zappa Family Trust (ZFT) (on Barking Pumpkin: it was never made available via the distribution deal struck with Rykodisc, and only made widely available by Universal in 2017).

This is the long-awaited third instalment of Lumpy Gravy, with the Abnuceals Emuukha Electric Symphony Orchestra replaced by the Ensemble Modern and a Synclavier. The piano people from those original 1967 sessions re-appear alongside new voices recorded in 1991 – including Moon and her then squeeze, actor Michael Rapaport.

N-Lite is the album's centrepiece, which originally was to have appeared in Act Two; Zappa tinkered with the running order right up until the end, switching this track with Beat The Reaper – perhaps in recognition of his impending demise.

Zappa was planning to stage the work as an 'opera pantomime' in Vienna in May 1994.

The Lost Episodes
1996

FZ

Official Release #64

Originally Released: February 27, 1996

Recording data: 1958 to 1992 at Antelope Valley Jr. College, Lancaster (CA), Pal Recording Studio, Cucamonga (CA, living room in Ontario (CA), Mount St. Mary's College (LA), Original Sound (LA), Studio Z, Cucamonga (CA), Mayfair Studios (NYC), Apostolic Studios (NYC), Zappa basement (LA), The Record Plant (LA), Paramount Recording Studios (LA), Bolic Sound (Inglewood), Whitney Studios (Glendale), Ocean Way Recorders (Hollywood) and UMRK (LA)

Producer: FZ

Engineers: Paul Buff, Spencer Chrislu, et al.

Tracks:
The Blackouts (0:22)
Lost In A Whirlpool (2:46)
Ronnie Sings? (1:05)
Kenny's Booger Story (0:33)
Ronnie's Booger Story 1:16
Mount St. Mary's Concert Excerpt (2:28)
Take Your Clothes Off When You Dance (3:51)
Tiger Roach (2:20)
Run Home Slow Theme (1:25)
Fountain Of Love (2:08)
Run Home Cues, #2 (0:28)
Any Way The Wind Blows (2:14)
Run Home Cues, #3 (0:11)
Charva (1:59)
The Dick Kunc Story (0:46)
Wedding Dress Song (1:14)
Handsome Cabin Boy (1:21)
Cops & Buns (2:36)
The Big Squeeze (0:43)
I'm A Band Leader (1:14)
Alley Cat (2:47)
The Grand Wazoo (2:12)
Wonderful Wino (2:47)
Kung Fu (1:06)
RDNZL (3:49)
Basement Music #1 (3:46)
Inca Roads (3:42)
Lil' Clanton Shuffle (4:47)
I Don't Wanna Get Drafted (3:24)
Sharleena (11:54)

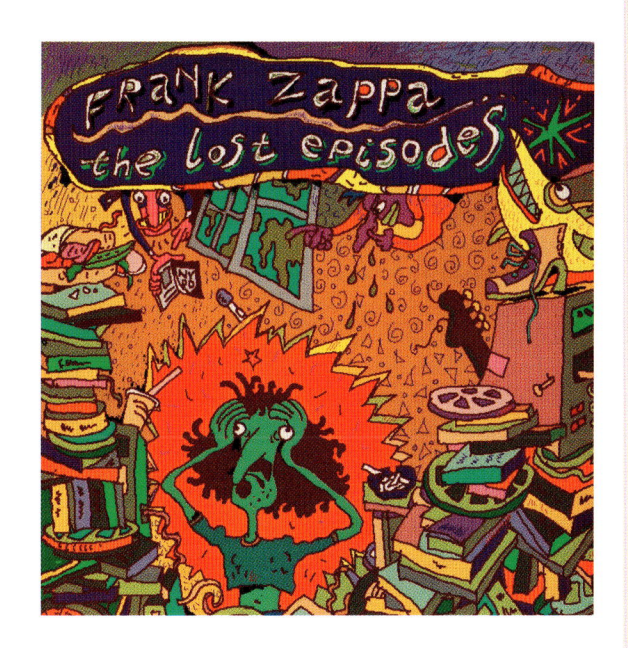

"There's a thing I did with Captain Beefheart here at the house, a little jam session in the basement, called 'Alley Cat'. There's also the original version of 'RDNZL' with George Duke and Jean-Luc Ponty, and a bunch of stuff with Sugarcane Harris like the original version of 'Sharleena' which was ten minutes long, with a fabulous blues violin solo."

Frank Zappa

Before his passing, Zappa was hard at work on potentially three volumes of rare non-road tapes recorded throughout his career. This is the first.

Captain Beefheart's vocals adorn five of the songs, with Lost In A Whirlpool the earliest example of their collaborative efforts – and toilet humour. The Grand Wazoo has the Captain's voice from 1969 backed by Zappa's Synclavier recorded 22 years later.

The instrumental version of Inca Roads was taped at the same session as RDNZL, while Kung Fu was performed a little later by the Roxy-era band.

Basement Music #1 was recorded home alone by Zappa on a primitive rhythm box and synthesizer at the height of his difficulties with Warners when he felt unable to record anywhere else.

I Don't Wanna Get Drafted was released as a single in 1980: an alternate version – Drafted Again – appears on the You Are What You Is album.

Läther
1996

FZ

Official Release #65

Originally Released: September 24, 1996

Recording data: August 1969 to February 17, 1977 at Electric Lady (NYC), Paramount Studios (Hollywood), Bolic Sound (Inglewood), Caribou Ranch (Colorado), Record Plant (LA), Royce Hall (UCLA), Kosei Nenkin Kaikan, Osaka (Japan), The Palladium (NYC), Hammersmith Odeon, London (UK), and elsewhere

Producer: FZ

Engineers: David Dondorf, Spencer Chrislu

Tracks:
Re-gyptian Strut (4:36)
Naval Aviation In Art? (1:32)
A Little Green Rosetta (2:48)
Duck Duck Goose (3:01)
Down In De Dew (2:57)
For The Young Sophisticate (3:14)
Tryin' To Grow A Chin (3:26)
Broken Hearts Are For Assholes (4:40)
The Legend Of The Illinois Enema Bandit (12:43)
Lemme Take You To The Beach (2:46)
Revised Music For Guitar & Low Budget Orchestra (7:36)
RDNZL (8:14)
Honey, Don't You Want A Man Like Me? (4:56)
The Black Page #1 (1:57)
Big Leg Emma (2:11)
Punky's Whips (11:06)
Flambé (2:05)
The Purple Lagoon (16:22)
Pedro's Dowry (7:45)
Läther (3:50)
Spider Of Destiny (2:40)
Duke Of Orchestral Prunes (4:21)
Filthy Habits (7:12)
Titties 'N' Beer (5:23)
The Ocean Is The Ultimate Solution (8:32)
The Adventures of Greggery Peccary (21:00)

Additional tracks on Rykodisc 1996 CD:
Re-gyptian Strut (1993) (4:42)
Leather Goods (6:01)
Revenge Of The Knick Knack People (2:25)
Time Is Money (3:04)

"When the four albums were delivered to Warners, they would not even listen to them. It was weeks before they could find time, or somebody qualified, to listen to the tapes and notice it was a very elaborate thing. And then they said stuff like, 'Well, what if we released these things all at once?' I said, 'Yeah, that would be a great idea.' They go, 'It would?' They're so stupid about it. They should have released it all at once. It would have sold more units; it would have been a really exciting package. But no."

Frank Zappa

After Warner Bros hastily withdrew his live In New York album as delivered, Zappa claimed breach of contract and sued them. To fulfil his contractual obligations, he submitted three further albums, which they swiftly declined.

Believing he was a free agent, Zappa opened negotiations with other labels to release a four record box set containing material from these four sets. A deal with Phonogram led to test pressings being produced, but Warners counter-sued and Phonogram backed-off.

Worried his recording career could be on hold, Zappa played the test pressings on radio, urging listeners to tape it. He then re-edited Läther – and other – material into separate albums that Warners did release.

Läther was eventually released as a three-CD set and is arguably the best one-stop place for a good overview of Zappa's oeuvre, combining as it does recordings of his idiosyncratic guitar soli, orchestral compositions, rock songs and complex almost-jazz instrumentals.

Frank Zappa Plays The Music Of Frank Zappa: A Memorial Tribute 1996

FZ

Official Release #66

Originally Released: October 31, 1996

Recording data: September 27, 1974 to June 1979 at Palais des Sports (Paris), Hala Tivoli (Ljubljana), Kosei Nenkin Kaikan (Osaka), Nihon Seinenkan (Tokyo), Record Plant (LA), Rhein-Neckar-Halle (Eppelheim), The Village Recorders (LA)

Producer: FZ, Dweezil Zappa

Engineers: Spencer Chrislu, FZ, Dave Dondorf

Tracks:
Black Napkins (7:10)
Black Napkins "Zoot Allures" Album Version (4:15)
Zoot Allures (15:45)
Merely A Blues In A (7:26)
Zoot Allures "Zoot Allures" Album Version (4:05)
Watermelon In Easter Hay (6:41)
Watermelon In Easter Hay "Joe's Garage" Album Version (8:42)

"I'm credited with 'Preliminary Research'. That's the album that I helped them compile, except that they replaced one track: for the unreleased version of 'Black Napkins' we had originally chosen the complete 'Pink Napkins' – that's actually a 12 minute track. But after I was gone, Dweezil decided that he wanted all the live versions to be the earliest ones they could find. So they went for a different 'Black Napkins'."

Mike Keneally

After her husband's passing, Gail revealed he had told her he did not want anyone else to perform three of his signature guitar compositions. The album versions of these 'sacred' songs are here placed alongside earlier live renderings, with a blues improvisation thrown in.

Much to his mother's mortification, Dweezil has since performed all three works: she reportedly walked out of the New York Halloween show at which he premiered Watermelon in 2013. Sad, given that in 2012 she had written that this album was "the origin and inspiration for the name of what is now Dweezil's band, Zappa Plays Zappa. And who could do that better?"

Black Napkins from November 1975 is the first released recording of the band that briefly featured Norma Jean Bell on alto sax and vocals.

The manuscript on the cover was provided by the creator of The Simpsons and long-time Zappa fan, Matt Groening.

Have I Offended Someone?
1997

FZ

Official Release #67

Originally Released: *April 08, 1997*

Recording data: *March 19, 1973 to 1985 at Bolic Sound (Inglewood), The Record Plant (LA), The Palladium (NYC), Hammersmith Odeon (London), The Village Recorders (LA), UMRK (LA), Santa Monica Civic Auditorium (CA) and The Pier (NYC)*

Producer: *FZ*

Engineer: *Spencer Chrislu*

Tracks:
Bobby Brown Goes Down (2:43)
Disco Boy (4:23)
Goblin Girl (4:19)
In France (3:30)
He's So Gay (2:45)
SEX (3:44)
Titties 'N' Beer (4:37)
We're Turning Again (4:56)
Dumb All Over (5:43)
Catholic Girls (3:51)
Dinah-Moe Humm (7:14)
Tinsel Town Rebellion (4:24)
Valley Girl (4:50)
Jewish Princess (3:15)
Yo Cats (3:32)

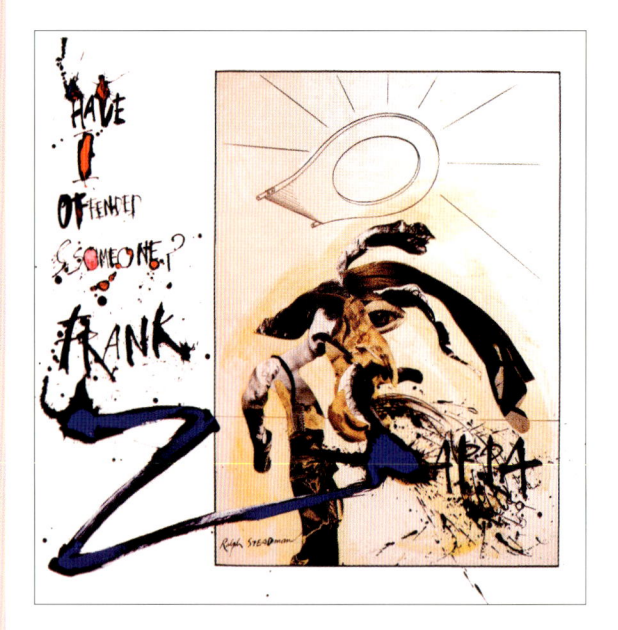

"It's the sexual and politically incorrect songs. I thought 'Why would he put these songs on this', but now I think it's hilarious; because I realise how tempting it is for people to smooth him down or clean him up or something like that, and he fought thirty years against censorship, and God bless him for putting this compilation together. That's Bobby Brown and Titties 'N' Beer and all those songs that might offend mom or something."
    Jill Christiansen (Ryko's 'Zappa Catalog Development Manager')

Pieced together by Zappa, with many of the tracks appreciably remixed. Dumb All Over is the sole 'new' track: a live version from The Pier in New York, recorded the day before the Does Humor Belong in Music? home video, from which this version of Tinsel Town Rebellion is extracted.

Disco Boy sees Terry Bozzio relegated to backing vocalist as his drum track has been overdubbed by Chad Wackerman.

Similarly, David Logeman's drums are here replaced by Wackerman on Goblin Girl, which is also purposely slowed down.

Titties 'N' Beer has once again been edited: as mentioned elsewhere, Warners withdrew the original Zappa In New York album and issued a censored version that removed all mentions of Punky Meadows – including from this song.

The cover art was provided by the famous British cartoonist stroke caricaturist, Ralph Steadman, while the liner notes were penned by Ed Sanders of The Fugs.

Mystery Disc
1998

FZ

Official Release #68

Originally Released: September 14, 1998

Recording data: 1964 to August 1969 at Original Sound (LA), Pal Recording Studio, Cucamonga (CA), Studio Z, Cucamonga (CA), The Saints 'N Sinners, Ontario (CA), The Village Inn & Barbecue, Sun Village (CA), The Broadside, Pomona (CA), Mondo Hollywood party, Seward St. Studio (LA), Fillmore Auditorium (San Francisco), KPFK Studios (LA), Royal Festival Hall (London), Apostolic Studios (NYC), Criteria Studios, Miami (FL), Thee Image, Miami Beach (FL) and The Ballroom, Stratford (CT)

Producer: FZ

Engineer: FZ, et al.

Tracks:
Theme from "Run Home Slow" (1:23)
Original Duke Of Prunes (1:17)
Opening Night at "Studio Z" (Collage) (1:34)
The Village Inn (1:17)
Steal Away (3:43)
I Was A Teen-Age Malt Shop (1:10)
The Birth of Captain Beefheart (0:18)
Metal Man Has Won His Wings (3:06)
Power Trio from The Saints 'n Sinners (0:34)
Bossa Nova Pervertamento (2:15)
Excerpt from The Uncle Frankie Show (0:40)
Charva (2:01)
Speed-Freak Boogie (4:14)
Original Mothers at The Broadside (Pomona) (0:55)
Party Scene from "Mondo Hollywood" (1:54)
Original Mothers Rehearsal (0:22)
How Could I Be Such A Fool? (1:49)
Band introductions at The Fillmore West (1:10)
Plastic People (1:58)
Original Mothers at Fillmore East (0:50)
Harry, You're A Beast (0:30)
Don Interrupts (4:39)
Piece One (2:26)
Jim/Roy (4:04)
Piece Two (6:59)
Agency Man (3:25)
Agency Man (Studio Version) (3:27)
Lecture from Festival Hall Show (0:21)
Wedding Dress Song/The Handsome Cabin Boy (2:36)
Skweezit Skweezit Skweezit (2:57)
The Story of Willie The Pimp (1:33)
Black Beauty (5:23)
Chucha (2:47)
Mothers at KPFK (3:26)
Harmonica Fun (0:41)

"In 1964, Vliet and I were working together in a studio that existed in Cucamonga, California, and we were working on a project called 'I Was A Teen-Age Malt Shop'. It was destined for a program called Repertoire Workshop on CBS, and we had prepared an elaborate demo session and pre-recorded some of the songs that were supposed to be used on the story. The producer of the show came out to the studio to examine the work, whereupon it was immediately rejected."

Frank Zappa

Finally, the two discs included with the first two Old Masters box sets were released together on one CD. Spanning the period from Zappa's earliest experiments at Paul Buff's PAL Studios in Cucamonga (Speed-Freak Boogie) up to tracks marking the end of the original Mothers (The Story of Willie The Pimp), there are some real treats along the way.

Hear primitive studio recordings with Captain Beefheart (Metal Man Has Won His Wings, with lyrics inspired by a DC comic pinned to a board in the studio's hallway), alongside excerpts from what could have been the world's first 'rock opera' (I Was A Teen-Age Malt Shop) and Zappa's second film soundtrack (Run Home Slow, a variant of the theme released on The Lost Episodes album).

Another failed project represented here is a low-budget sci-fi film called Captain Beefheart Vs. The Grunt People, that might've kick-started the career of Vliet. But didn't.

EIHN – Everything Is Healing Nicely   1999

FZ

Official Release #69

Originally Released: *December 21, 1999*

Recording data: *July 1991 at "Joe's Garage" (LA) and UMRK (LA)*

Producer: *FZ*

Engineers: *Spencer Chrislu, Marque Coy, David Dondorf, Todd Yvega*

Tracks:
Library Card (7:42)
This Is A Test (1:35)
Jolly Good Fellow (4:34)
Roland's Big Event/Strat Vindaloo (5:56)
Master Ringo (3:35)
T'Mershi Duween (2:30)
Nap Time (8:02)
9/8 Objects (3:06)
Naked City (8:42)
Whitey (Prototype) (1:12)
Amnerika Goes Home (3:00)
None Of The Above (Revised & Previsited) (8:38)
Wonderful Tattoo! (10:01)

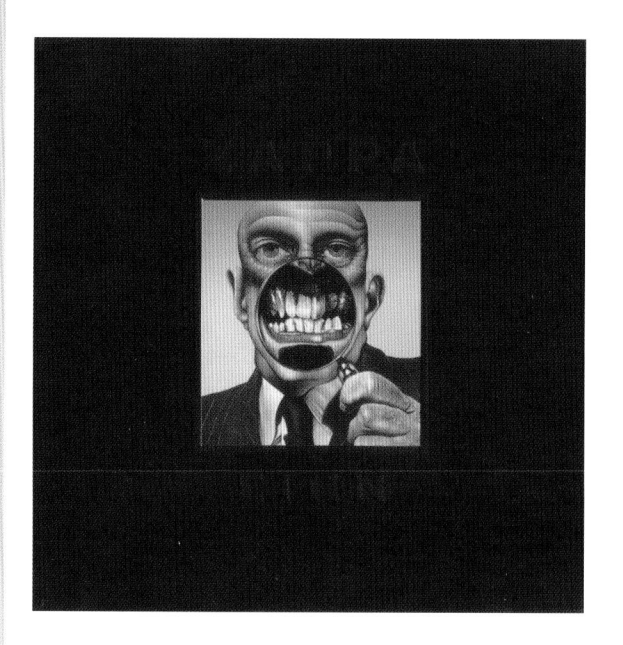

"Because the musicians in this ensemble take everything so seriously – and I mean seriously: if you tell them to scrape their instrument or do something weird to their instrument, they don't look at you out of the corner of their eye, they'll just do it, and do it very seriously. The oboe player was blowing bubbles, and when I suggested that she take her didgeridu and stick it into a pot of water and grunt through it and blow bubbles at the same time, she didn't say, 'You're out of your mind. I'm a lady. I shouldn't do that!' She got the didgeridu, and a couple of the other guys went out and got the little jug of water, and she knew that she was advancing the science of music like every player ever has, but the sound made me laugh so much I had to leave the room while she was recording it. I couldn't believe it. I'd imagined it would be fairly grotesque when I suggested she do it, but when I heard it, I couldn't stop laughing. I was spoiling the tape. I had to leave."
                                                                               Frank Zappa

An album of material mostly culled from Ensemble Modern's fortnight of rehearsals in California in preparation for The Yellow Shark concerts. Although Zappa mixed these tracks, it's unlikely he would have released them this way, if at all.

Like Beefheart quoting from a comic on Metal Man, pianist Hermann Kretzschmar here reads the words from a library card (on the opening track) and letters sent to the editor of Piercing Fans International Quarterly (Master Ringo and Wonderful Tattoo!), from whence the album derives its title.

It's easy to see why Zappa found Kretzschmar's diction amusing, and giving these serious musicians a 'cow in a can' really let them know that humour belonged in his music.

L. Shankar guests on Strat Vindaloo and 9/8 Objects, trading licks with Zappa on the former. This Is A Test pays homage to Stravinsky. None Of The Above includes moments from later rehearsals in Frankfurt.

FZ:OZ
2002

FZ

Official Release #70

Originally Released: August 16, 2002

Recording data: January 06 to February 05, 1976 at rehearsals (LA), Hordern Pavilion (Sydney) and Nihon Seinenkan (Tokyo)

Producer: Dweezil Zappa

Engineer: Spencer Chrislu

Tracks:
Hordern Intro (Incan Art Vamp) (3:10)
Stink-Foot (6:35)
The Poodle Lecture (3:05)
Dirty Love (3:13)
Filthy Habits (6:18)
How Could I Be Such A Fool? (3:27)
I Ain't Got No Heart (2:26)
I'm Not Satisfied (1:54)
Black Napkins (11:57)
Advance Romance (11:17)
The Illinois Enema Bandit (8:45)
Wind Up Workin' In A Gas Station (4:14)
The Torture Never Stops (7:12)
Canard Toujours (3:22)
Kaiser Rolls (3:17)
Find Her Finer (3:48)
Carolina Hard-Core Ecstasy (6:12)
Lonely Little Girl (2:39)
Take Your Clothes Off When You Dance (2:02)
What's The Ugliest Part Of Your Body? (1:07)
Chunga's Revenge (15:41)
Zoot Allures (12:50)
Keep It Greasy (4:40)
Dinah-Moe Humm (6:54)
Camarillo Brillo (3:58)
Muffin Man (3:41)
Kaiser Rolls (Du Jour) (3:00)

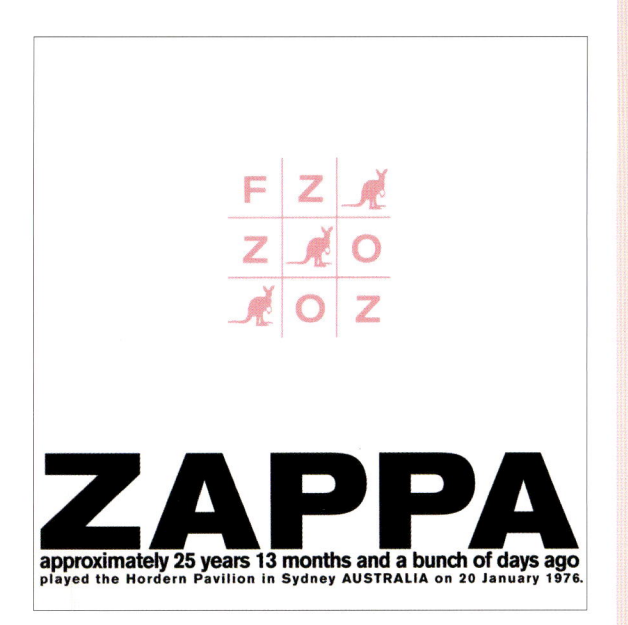

"FZ:OZ consists of a two-disc set of the concert held on January 20th, 1976. The band line-up at the time consisted of Terry Bozzio on drums, Napoleon Murphy Brock on tenor sax & vocals, André Lewis on keyboards and Roy Estrada on bass. The CD was prepared by Spencer Chrislu, myself & Dweezil in 1998. It was one of the last projects worked on by Spence before he left UMRK."

Joe Travers

The inaugural release on Vaulternative Records is a near complete concert: both Honey, Don't You Want A Man Like Me? and Tryin' To Grow A Chin are omitted, but the latter was eventually released on the download-only AAAFNRAA FZ Birthday Bundle in 2006.

Gaps in proceedings caused by tape reel changes are filled with audience recordings, but it's good to hear prototype versions of Enema Bandit and Canard Toujours (better known as Let's Move To Cleveland) by this five piece band.

Brock's vocal prowess is confirmed on the early Mothers songs, plus the two versions of the previously unreleased Kaiser Rolls (the second taken from a rehearsal earlier in the month).

The appearance of Norman Gunston (a popular Australian TV character created by comedian Garry McDonald) during Torture is a nice surprise.

Astonishingly, Gail gives the Australian lady Frank moved into their basement an 'honourable mention' in her liner notes.

Halloween
2003

FZ

Official Release #71

Originally Released: February 04, 2003

Recording data: October 13-31, 1978 at Capitol Theatre, Passaic (NJ), Saturday Night Live (NYC), WPIX (NYC) and The Palladium (NYC)

Producer: Dweezil Zappa

Engineer: Joe Chiccarelli

Tracks:
NYC Audience (1:17)
Ancient Armaments (8:23)
Dancin' Fool (4:35)
Easy Meat (6:03)
Magic Fingers (2:33)
Don't Eat The Yellow Snow (2:24)
Conehead (4:02)
"Zeets" (2:58)
Stink-Foot (8:51)
Dinah-Moe Humm (5:27)
Camarillo Brillo (3:14)
Muffin Man (3:32)
Black Napkins (The Deathless Horsie) (16:56)

Tricks Or Treats:
Suicide Chump (Video) (9:31)
Dancin' Fool (Video) (3:48)
Radio Interview (9:41)

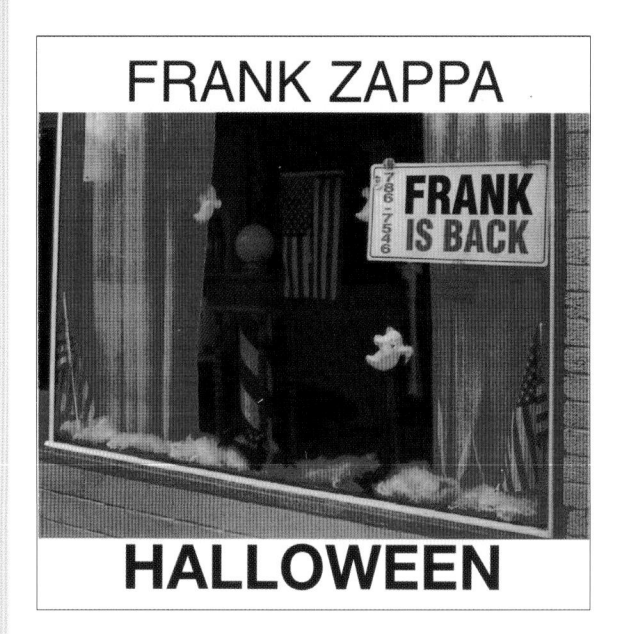

"We were playing in New York at The Palladium, doing our annual Halloween shows. Frank filmed Baby Snakes the year before and Janet The Planet had no idea that she was included in the final film. When Frank saw her, he said 'I'm so glad to see you here; you were so fantastic in my new movie.' She was brought backstage and that is when I first met her. We started dating in April of 1987 and were married in August of 1989."

Denny Walley

At the start, Zappa tells the audience the band is going to play the normal show, with something a bit special later on. What we get here is actually pretty much a truncated version of the standard set-list – an amalgamation of highlights from four of the Halloween 1978 New York concerts.

Ancient Armaments is a longer edit of the I Don't Wanna Get Drafted single b-side. Don't Eat The Yellow Snow is not the whole suite. Shankar joins the band during Conehead.

The playing throughout is magnificent (Zappa's axe work in particular, including on the bonus Suicide Chump video) and the stereo sound quality is spiffy (this is a DVD-A release: 5.1 listening highlights a few naff edits, and it sounds like Dweezil and Travers are fighting over the balance control during Vinnie Colaiuta's drum solo – "Zeets", his nickname). The final track is sublime: worth the admission fee alone.

Joe's Corsage
2004

FZ

Official Release #72

Originally Released: May 30, 2004

Recording data: 1965 to 1966 at locations unknown

Producer: Joe Travers

Engineer: FZ, Bob Stone, et al.

Tracks:
"Pretty Pat" (0:33)
Motherly Love (2:21)
Plastic People (3:05)
Anyway The Wind Blows (2:55)
I Ain't Got No Heart (3:50)
"The Phone Call"-My Babe (4:06)
Wedding Dress Song-Handsome Cabin Boy (1:02)
Hitch Hike (2:54)
I'm So Happy I Could Cry (2:43)
Go Cry On Somebody Else's Shoulder (3:29)
How Could I Be Such A Fool? (3:00)
"We Made Our Reputation Doing It That Way …" (5:34)

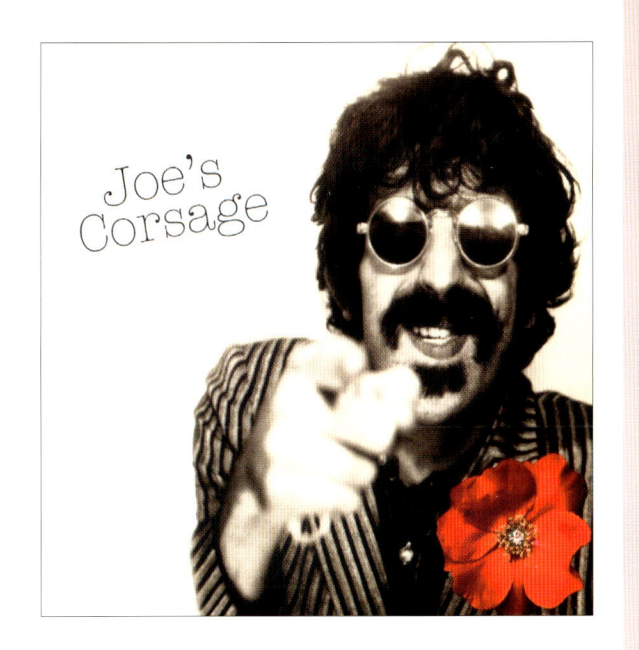

"We kept getting fired for about a year – all the places between Pomona and Torrance …"

Frank Zappa

The first of the Vaultmeister's Corsaga starts with one of three interview extracts in which Zappa gives his standard spiel on how the Mothers got their name.

Motherly Love sports different words from those on Freak Out! and segues swiftly into a Louie Louie plus-one-note version of Plastic People. I'm So Happy I Could Cry is Take Your Clothes Off with trite love lyrics.

Sandwiched between these pre-1966 demos are covers recorded on the bar circuit, like the Righteous Brothers' My Babe and the Wedding Dress/Cabin Boy medley which is considerably pared down from the later percussion dominated studio rendition. Ray Collins was a fine singer, but no Marvin Gaye, which is maybe why Hitch Hike and the other live cuts remained in the Vault until this release.

These old tapes sound surprisingly clear, but it's a shame they couldn't rectify the cut-out on the left channel during Hitch Hike.

Joe's Domage
2004

FZ

Official Release #73

Originally Released: October 01, 2004

Recording data: 1972

Producer: Joe Travers

Engineer: Stephen Marcussen

Tracks:
When it's perfect … (3:18)
The New Brown Clouds (2:44)
Frog Song (17:23)
It Just Might Be A One Shot Deal (1:57)
The ending line … (3:12)
Blessed Relief-The New Brown Clouds (5:03)
It Ain't Real So What's The Deal (13:14)
Think It Over (some)-Think It Over (some more) (5:20)
Another Whole Melodic Section (1:53)
When it feels natural … (1:27)

"Our Corsage series, they're just random examples of stuff that Frank had, intact. We don't do anything to them, we don't try to construct them in any way. There was this one rehearsal tape that Frank carried around with him on the road, and it was a rehearsal of members of the Wazoo band. That's Joe's Domage."

Gail Zappa

A mono cassette recording of a rehearsal, with musicians playing snatches of music (few longer than two minutes in duration) under Zappa's muffled direction: not a great follow-up to Corsage – although you'll note that Official Release #74 came out first.

The most entertaining moment comes near the end, when Zappa and drummer Dunbar sketch out Another Whole Melodic Section (a piece performed by the Mothers in 1969 and the later Hot Rats band, otherwise known as Interlude); only musicologists and hard-core fanatics find anything of redeeming value prior to this.

The Frog Song became It Just Might Be A One-Shot Deal on Waka/Jawaka.

Possibly intended as a 'fuck you' from the ZFT to all the people who had been whining about the paucity of quality releases from the Vault, there's no disputing the Trust's claim that it represents 'material that otherwise wouldn't find a home on a major Zappa release.'

QuAUDIOPHILIAc
2004

FZ

Official Release #74

Originally Released: September 14, 2004

Recording data: March 01, 1970 to November 17, 1981 at FZ's Basement, Paramount Recording Studios (LA), Festhalle Mustermesse (Basel), Royce Hall, UCLA (CA), Kosei Nenkin Kaikan (Osaka), Hammersmith Odeon (London), The Village Recorders (LA) and WLIR (NY)

Producer: FZ, Dweezil Zappa

Engineers: Dick Kunc, Kerry McNabb, Joe Chiccarelli, FZ, Dweezil Zappa, Stephen Marcussen

Tracks:
Naval Aviation In Art? (1:34)
Lumpy Gravy (1:05)
Rollo (6:00)
Drooling Midrange Accountants On Easter Hay (2:15)
Wild Love (4:07)
Ship Ahoy (5:47)
Chunga Basement (11:48)
Venusian Time Bandits (1:54)
Waka/Jawaka (13:23)
Basement Music #2 (2:43)

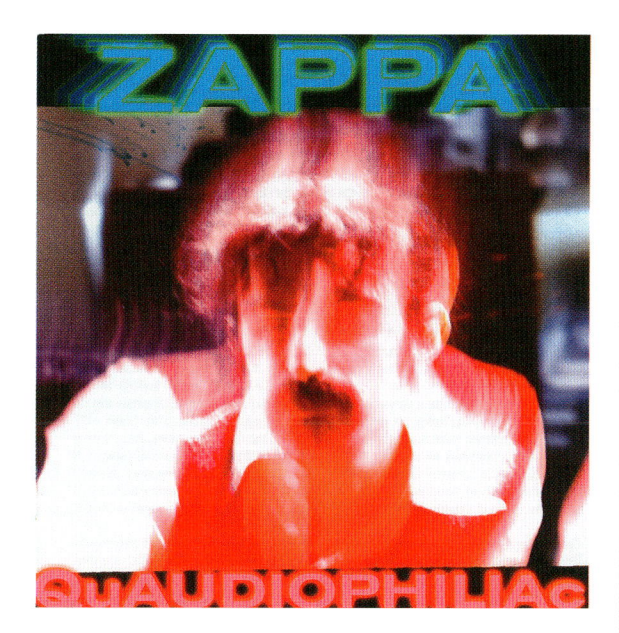

"It is surround sound and is made up of tracks originally mixed/recorded by FZ during the 70s. It is essentially an audio documentary of ideas by FZ about quad and 4 channel mixes and multichannel recordings. Dweezil tweezed these items into a full on programme."

Gail Zappa

All but one of the non-FZ compiled archival releases thus far had been same-band concert or rehearsal collections. QuAUDIOPHILIAc is all from the 1970s, has a theme (all the tracks are quadraphonic mixes created by Zappa) and includes tracks we already have – albeit, mixed for stereo. But like Dweezil's description of Rollo, this is "fucking bitchen!"

Drooling Midrange Accountants has Zappa pontificating about the stifling of creative music over a Mars/Mann run-through of Watermelon In Easter Hay.

Chunga Basement is by the post-Hot Rats Aynsley Dunbar four-piece band and is a little ragged in places. Venusian Time Bandits (also by a four-piece – this time Roxy-era) is essentially a live guitar solo.

Waka/Jawaka is remixed and expanded, with some of the written parts after Dunbar's drum solo replaced by more mini-moog mangling by Preston.

This DVD-A release includes a photo gallery and short video prepared for the 2003 Surround Music Awards.

Joe's XMASage
2005

FZ

Official Release #75

Originally Released: December 21, 2005

Recording data: December 1962 to March 25, 1965 at 314 West G Street, Ontario (CA), Pal Recording Studio, Cucamonga (CA), The Saints 'N Sinners, Ontario (CA) and Studio Z, Cucamonga (CA)

Producer: FZ

Engineers: FZ, John Polito

Tracks:
Mormon Xmas Dance Report (1:51)
Prelude To "The Purse" (2:24)
Mr. Clean (Alternate Mix) (2:04)
Why Don'tcha Do Me Right? (5:01)
The Muthers-Power Trio (3:15)
The Purse (11:38)
The Moon Will Never Be The Same (1:10)
GTR Trio (11:21)
Suckit Rockit (4:11)
Mousie's First Xmas (0:56)
The Uncle Frankie Show (11:42)

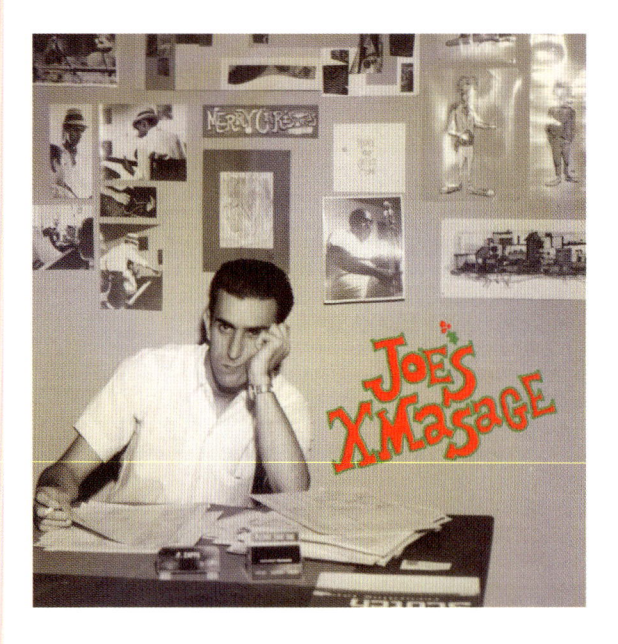

"One of the other great jobs was as a rhythm guitarist in a pickup band at a Christmas dance in a Mormon recreation hall. The room was decorated with wads of cotton hanging on black thread. The band consisted of sax, drums and guitar. I borrowed a fake-book so I could follow the chord changes, since I didn't know any of the tunes. The sax player was, in civilian life, a Spanish teacher from the local high school. He had no sense of rhythm and couldn't even count the tunes off, but he was the leader of the band. I didn't know anything about Mormons at the time so, during a break when I lit up a cigarette, it was as if The Devil Himself had just made a rare personal appearance. A bunch of guys who looked like they weren't quite ready to shave yet started flailing over to me and, in a brotherly sort of way, escorted my ass out the door. I knew I was going to love show business if I ever got into it."

Frank Zappa

The third Corsaga starts with Zappa's first wife interviewing him about a 1962 dance, from which he has just returned.

The alternate mix of Mr. Clean has very loud backing vocals by Zappa, while the piano and drums are completely buried in the mix on the original version of Why Don'tcha Do Me Right.

The Purse – not edited nearly enough! – has Al Surratt rummaging through a teenage girl's handbag.

The Moon Will Never Be The Same is a combination of Poeme Electronique-styled effects, with orchestration à la Integrales. This and Mousie's First Xmas are both stereo sound experiments from the same demo tape.

GTR Trio is the full version of Bossa Nova Pervertamento from Mystery Disc.

In The Uncle Frankie Show, Zappa tells of his plans to submit I Was A Teenage Maltshop to CBS-TV.

All in all, a strange bit of Yuletide nostalgia for us old folks!

Imaginary Diseases
2006

FZ

Official Release #76

Originally Released: January 13, 2006

Recording data: October 27 to December 02, 1972 at Forum, Montreal (Quebec), Palace Theater, Waterbury (CT), Irvine Auditorium, University Of Pennsylvania, Philadelphia (PA), DAR Constitution Hall, Washington (DC), Cowtown Ballroom, Kansas City (MO)

Producer: FZ

Engineers: FZ, Barry Keene, Kerry McNabb, Michael Braunstein, Davey Moire

Tracks:
Oddients (1:13)
Rollo (3:21)
Been To Kansas City In A Minor (10:15)
Farther O'Blivion (16:02)
D.C. Boogie (13:27)
Imaginary Diseases (9:45)
Montreal (9:11)

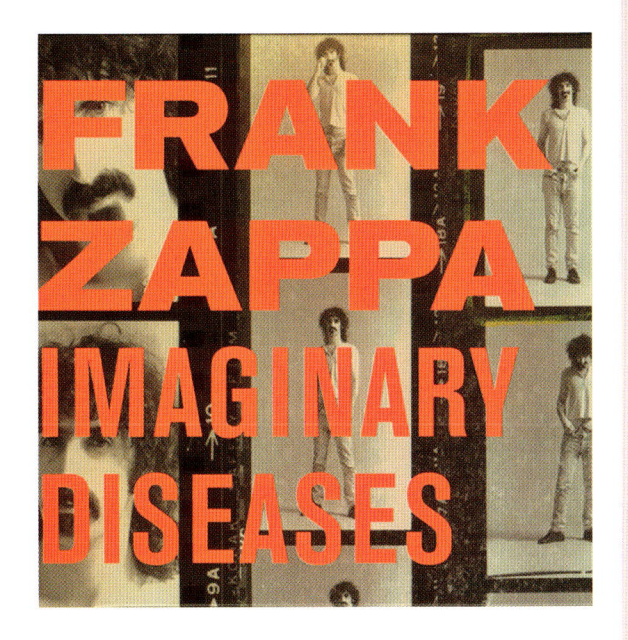

"I remember most of our first concert in Montreal. We came on stage and people started throwing hamburgers at the band to say hello! This was cool, except that Earle Dumler had at least five or six very expensive exotic reed instruments and was in the first row of the horns, so he received the brunt of the carrion onslaught. Dumler was a classical player and had never experienced appreciation from the audience in this form! He swooped up his instruments and carried them to safety off stage. The show was slightly delayed until the audience either ran out of burgers, or realised they would hear no Zappa that evening until they found a less disturbing means of showing their affection for him."

Gary Barone

Starts with the 10-piece Petit Wazoo band tuning up with a little audience participation before moving swiftly into the familiar Yellow Snow end passages.

Been To Kansas City has a Sexual Harrasment-type vamp, with Bruce Fowler and Zappa turning in fine solos.

Prior to its thrilling denouement, Farther O'Blivion features some manic drum fury from Jim Gordon. It also includes snatches from Greggery Peccary and Be-Bop Tango.

At the end of DC Boogie, Zappa asks the audience how they want the piece to end: sadly, the dog food jingle choice is out-voted by the boogie option.

The title track, like some of the other pieces, is largely improvised, but has a pre-arranged beginning and end theme with the horns merrily blowing away; it sits nicely alongside the likes of Regyptian Strut.

The liner notes are by Steve Vai.

We had to wait ten years for the sequel to this album.

The MOFO Project/Object
2006

FZ / The Mothers

Official Release #77

Originally Released: December 12, 2006

Recording data: March 09, 1966 to March 1993 at T.T.G. Studios (LA), Fillmore Auditorium, San Francisco (LA), WRVR (NYC), Mixed Media, Detroit (MI), WDET, Detroit (MI), KBEY-FM, Kansas City (MO), MTV and UMRK (LA)

Producers: Tom Wilson, FZ

Engineers: Val Valentin, Ami Hadani, Tom Hidley, John Judnich, Stan Agol, Bob Stone, Joe Travers, John Polito

Tracks:

Hungry Freaks, Daddy (3:32)
I Ain't Got No Heart (2:34)
Who Are The Brain Police? (3:25)
Go Cry On Somebody Else's Shoulder (3:43)
Motherly Love (2:50)
How Could I Be Such A Fool? (2:16)
Wowie Zowie (2:55)
You Didn't Try To Call Me (3:21)
Anyway The Wind Blows (2:55)
I'm Not Satisfied (2:41)
You're Probably Wondering Why I'm Here (3:41)
Trouble Every Day (5:53)
Help, I'm A Rock (4:42)
It Can't Happen Here (3:59)
The Return Of The Son Of Monster Magnet (12:22)
Hungry Freaks, Daddy – Vocal Overdub Take 1 (3:47)
Anyway The Wind Blows – Vocal Overdub (2:54)
Go Cry On Somebody Else's Shoulder – Vocal Overdub Take 2 (3:48)
I Ain't Got No Heart – Vocal Overdub Master Take (2:37)
Motherly Love – Vocal Overdub Master Takes (3:09)
I'm Not Satisfied – 2nd Vocal Overdub Master, Take 2 (Rough Mix) (2:38)
You're Probably Wondering Why I'm Here – Vocal Overdub Take 1 (Incomplete)/Take 2 (Incomplete) (1:58)
You're Probably Wondering Why I'm Here – Basic Tracks (3:40)
Who Are The Brain Police? – Basic Tracks (3:42)
How Could I Be Such A Fool? – Basic Tracks (2:24)
Anyway The Wind Blows – Basic Tracks (2:48)
Go Cry On Somebody Else's Shoulder – Basic Tracks (3:43)
I Ain't Got No Heart – Basic Tracks (2:36)
You Didn't Try To Call Me – Basic Tracks (3:00)
Trouble Every Day – Basic Tracks (7:11)
Help, I'm A Rock – FZ Edit (5:48)
Who Are The Brain Police? (Section B) – Altern. Take (1:15)
Groupie Bang Bang (3:51)
Hold On To Your Small Tiny Horsies … (2:08)
Objects (4:32)
Freak Trim (Kim Outs A Big Idea) (5:14)
Percussion Insert Session Snoop (3:18)
Freak Out Drum Track w/ Timp. & Lion (4:04)
Percussion Object 1 & 2 (6:01)
Lion Roar & Drums From Freak Out! (5:36)
Vito Rocks The Floor (Greek Out!) (6:09)
"Low Budget Rock & Roll Band" (2:14)
Suzy Creamcheese (What's Got Into You?) (5:49)
Motherly Love (3:12)
You Didn't Try To Call Me (4:06)
I'm Not Satisfied (2:53)
Hungry Freaks, Daddy (3:37)
Go Cry On Somebody Else's Shoulder (2:31)
Wowie Zowie (3:02)
Who Are The Brain Police? (Section A, C, B) (4:32)
Hungry Freaks, Daddy (3:37)
Cream Cheese (Work Part) (8:18)
Trouble Every Day (2:39)
It Can't Happen Here (Mothermania Version) (3:19)
"Psychedelic Music" (2:34)
"MGM" (1:54)
"Dope Fiend Music" (2:06)
"How We Made It Sound That Way" (5:08)

> "The main inspiration for adding people's names into MOFO was because Frank had listed the names of people who helped to influence that music in Freak Out! So I felt that for the people for whom the music exists, and they are going to support it early in, you can have your name and your credit on this too because you deserve it!"
>
> Gail Zappa

The first in a series of 'making of …' audio documentaries comprises: the original Freak Out! album; a second disc of mainly alternate takes and backing tracks; a third (and probably the best of the new bunch) featuring the Lord of Garbage, Kim Fowley, directing the LA freaks and assorted guests, including Terry Gilliam, with lots of great percussion dominated pieces; and a final disc chock-full of interviews.

If evidence were needed that Freak Out! is more than just a bunch of gentle doo-wop parodies, three experimental pieces and a blues-based social critique, this is it.

During some of the early interview segments, Zappa comes across as a pompous ass: did he truly believe the Beatles ripped him off on Lovely Rita, or was it just 'good' PR?

Releasing Groupie Bang Bang in 1966 would surely have generated more of a kerfuffle, with lyrics claiming she "balls better than Epstein do".

The MOFO Project/Object
(Fazedooh) 2006

FZ

Official Release #78

Originally Released: December 05, 2006

Recording data: 1965 to 1986 at an unknown studio, T.T.G. Studios (LA), Fillmore Auditorium, San Francisco (CA) and MTV

Producers: Tom Wilson, FZ

Engineers: Val Valentin, Ami Hadani, Tom Hidley, John Judnich, Stan Agol, Bob Stone, John Polito

Tracks:
Hungry Freaks, Daddy (3:33)
I Ain't Got No Heart (2:35)
Who Are The Brain Police? (3:26)
Go Cry On Somebody Else's Shoulder (3:43)
Motherly Love (2:50)
How Could I Be Such A Fool? (2:17)
Wowie Zowie (2:56)
You Didn't Try To Call Me (3:22)
Any Way The Wind Blows (2:56)
I'm Not Satisfied (2:42)
You're Probably Wondering Why I'm Here (3:42)
Trouble Every Day (5:53)
Help, I'm A Rock (4:43)
It Can't Happen Here (3:59)
The Return Of The Son Of Monster Magnet (12:23)
Trouble Every Day (Basic Tracks) (7:07)
Who Are The Brain Police? (3:24)
I Ain't Got No Heart (Basic Tracks) (2:34)
You Didn't Try To Call Me (Basic Tracks) (2:58)
How Could I Be Such A Fool? (2:11)
Any Way The Wind Blows – 1987 FZ Remix (2:51)
Go Cry On Somebody Else's Shoulder – (Vocal Overdub Take 2) (3:47)
Motherly Love (Vocal Overdub Master Takes) (3:09)
"Tom Wilson" (0:33)
"My Pet Theory" (2:18)
Hungry Freaks Daddy (Basic Tracks) (3:26)
Help, I'm A Rock – 1970 FZ Remix (4:43)
It Can't Happen Here – 1970 FZ Remix (3:58)
Freak Out Drum Track w/Timp. & Lion (4:04)
Watts Riot Demo/Fillmore Sequence (2:07)
Freak Out Zilofone (3:00)
"Low Budget Rock & Roll Band" (2:42)

"Vito and Carl Franzoni were the leaders of this movement although they were quite a bit older than the others. They were ex-beatniks, poets and artists. I had been a fairly straight guy and so had Roy and we just couldn't believe some of these people. Man! The outfits they were wearing were wild! We were wearing our black Homburg hats and we still had our band uniforms on – the green shirts that everybody had to wear. So it was kind of strange, like it was a fancy dress party and not 'real'! So we stopped wearing our uniforms. Frank told us they would have to go but sometimes we'd wear the hats."

Jimmy Carl Black

This again includes the remastered original vinyl stereo mix of the Mothers' debut album, plus material culled from the deluxe four-disc set. But to ensure hard-core fans bought it all over again, it added a few otherwise unavailable elsewhere tracks – viz: Who Are The Brain Police? (mono single mix); How Could I Be Such A Fool? (mono single mix); Hungry Freaks, Daddy (Basic Tracks); Help, I'm A Rock (1970 FZ Remix); It Can't Happen Here (1970 FZ Remix); Watts Riot Demo; and Freak Out Zilofone.

Auxiliary musicians who played during the Freak Out! sessions included Wrecking Crew member Carol Kaye on 12-string guitar, and Mac Rebennack (aka Dr. John), who later complained, "Frank had written me this part to play, five or six notes on the piano over and over. In the background a twenty-voice choir croaked out monster sound effects. I walked out of there and never came back."

"Poop Rock" (0:46)
"Machinery" (1:00)
"Psychedelic Upholstery" (1:44)
"Psychedelic Money" (1:34)
Who Are The Brain Police? (3:39)
Any Way The Wind Blows (2:58)
Hungry Freaks, Daddy (3:33)

"The 'Original' Group" (1:29)
"Necessity" (1:18)
"Union Scale" (1:47)
"25 Hundred Signing Fee" (1:12)
"Tom Wilson" (0:33)
"My Pet Theory" (2:18)
"There Is No Need" (0:43)

Trance-Fusion
2006

FZ

Official Release #79

Originally Released: November 07, 2006

Recording data: October 28, 1977 to June 09, 1988 at The Palladium (NYC), Rhein-Neckar-Halle (Eppelheim), The Pier (NYC), Orpheum Theater (Memphis), Paramount Theatre (Seattle), Memorial Hall, Allentown (PA), Brighton Centre (Brighton), Wembley Arena (London), Johanneshovs Isstadion (Stockholm), Stadthalle (Vienna), Rudi-Sedlmayer-Halle (Munich) and Liederhalle (Stuttgart), Palasport (Genoa)

Producer: FZ

Engineers: Kerry McNabb, Mick Glossop, Mark Pinske, Bob Stone, Spencer Chrislu

Tracks:
Chunga's Revenge (7:01)
Bowling On Charen (5:03)
Good Lobna (1:39)
A Cold Dark Matter (3:31)
Butter Or Cannons (3:24)
Ask Dr. Stupid (3:20)
Scratch & Sniff (3:56)
Trance-Fusion (4:19)
Gorgo (2:41)
Diplodocus (3:22)
Soul Polka (3:17)
For Giuseppe Franco (3:48)
After Dinner Smoker (4:45)
Light Is All That Matters (3:46)
Finding Higgs' Boson (3:41)
Bavarian Sunset (4:00)

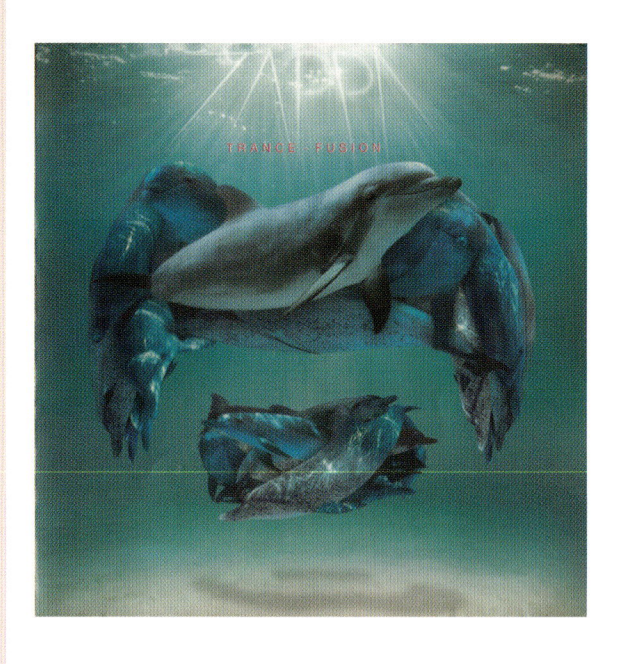

"It's just a guitar record."

Dweezil Zappa

A third album of guitar solos, prepared by Zappa. Interestingly, the first is performed by Dweezil, who is joined by his father after a few minutes on a truncated Chunga's Revenge taken from the second Broadway The Hard Way show in London.

Like Guitar, this album has no inbetweeine tracks. Nine of the pieces are culled from the 1988 tour. Good Lobna, Butter Or Cannons and Light Is All That Matters are all edited from performances of Let's Move To Cleveland on the 1984 tour.

While the title Good Lobna is taken from Episode 9F06 of The Simpsons, Ask Dr. Stupid was a regular segment in The Ren & Stimpy Show, an early 90s animated cartoon series for which Zappa provided the voice of The Pope in one episode.

Trance-Fusion ends with another father/son duet, lifted from a jam that followed a rendition of the Beatles' I Am The Walrus.

Buffalo
2007

FZ

Official Release #80

Originally Released: April 01, 2007

Recording data: October 25, 1980 at Memorial Auditorium, Buffalo (NY)

Producer: Gail Zappa, Joe Travers

Engineer: George Douglas

Tracks:
Chunga's Revenge (8:34)
You Are What You Is (4:12)
Mudd Club (3:02)
The Meek Shall Inherit Nothing (3:21)
Cosmik Debris (3:50)
Keep It Greasy (2:58)
Tinsel Town Rebellion (4:19)
Buffalo Drowning Witch (2:44)
Honey, Don't You Want A Man Like Me? (4:36)
Pick Me, I'm Clean (10:15)
Dead Girls Of London (3:02)
Shall We Take Ourselves Seriously? (1:36)
City Of Tiny Lites (9:58)
Easy Meat 9.26
Ain't Got No Heart (2:00)
The Torture Never Stops (23:36)
Broken Hearts Are For Assholes (3:39)
I'm So Cute (1:38)
Andy (8:14)
Joe's Garage (2:12)
Dancing Fool (3:36)
The "Real World" Thematic Extrapolations (8:53)
Stick It Out (5:36)
I Don't Wanna Get Drafted (2:48)
Bobby Brown (2:42)
Ms Pinky (3:48)

"The tour was first class. Great hotels, never a flight before noon, fun gigs, great people. I guess there was other stuff going on, but I didn't care; I was too busy enjoying it. And too busy cramming, trying to learn the material, because before working with him I was not very familiar with Frank's music."

Bob Harris

At the start of 1980, Vinnie Colaiuta foolishly asked for a raise and got himself fired. He was swiftly replaced by another Christian drummer, David Logeman, but was re-hired by the Fall. Buffalo demonstrates why this might have been, as all of the band members seem to raise their game in Vinnie's presence – including Frank.

A lengthy Torture features jazzy interludes and a fine solo from Colaiuta. Tinsel Town is quite different from the more familiar arrangement. Shall We Take Ourselves Seriously? is much enhanced by Bob Harris' teeny little vox.

In The "Real World" Thematic Extrapolations, Zappa tells what can happen when you go to a disco.

Dead Girls has amended lyrics, inspired by a particular brand of blue jeans popular in the eighties.

With Tommy Mars and Colaiuta playing, you almost don't miss the fact that there's no percussionist.

The elongated Pick Me, I'm Clean is beautifully insane.

Dub Room Special!
2007

FZ

Official Release #81

Originally Released: *August 24, 2007*

Recording data: *August 27, 1974 and October 31, 1981 at KCET Sound Stage B (LA) and The Palladium (NYC)*

Producer: *FZ*

Engineers: *Kerry McNabb, Mark Pinske, Bob Stone*

Tracks:
A Token Of My Extreme (Vamp) (2:29)
Stevie's Spanking (5:54)
The Dog Breath Variations (1:42)
Uncle Meat (2:16)
Stink-Foot (3:58)
Easy Meat (6:51)
Montana (4:24)
Inca Roads (9:46)
Room Service (9:15)
Cosmik Debris (7:44)
Florentine Pogen (10:13)

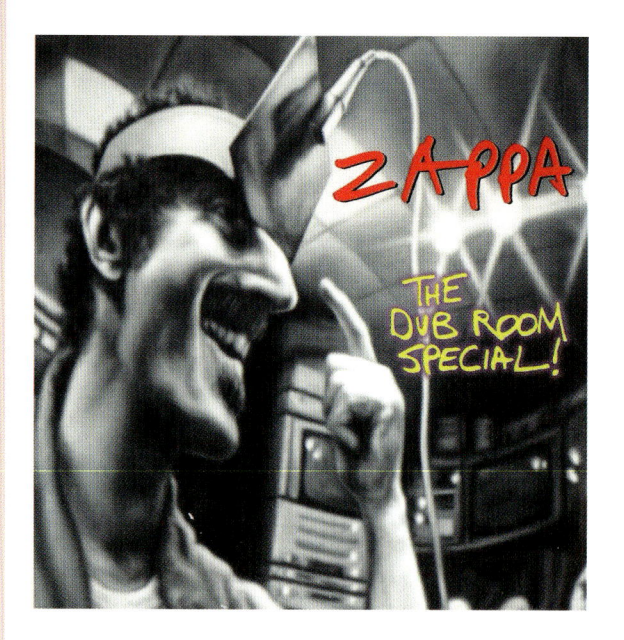

"The 'Room Service' routine, that was all ad-lib. There was a basic format: 'You call me up and tell me what you want,' and we would bounce off of each other. By the time we did that, we had a camaraderie where we would challenge each other without saying, 'I'm gonna challenge you.' We would just challenge each other. Because he would challenge me to see if I was gonna fuck up. I would challenge him to say, 'Okay. Not only am I not gonna fuck up, but I'm gonna throw something different at you every day. Let's see if you can deal with it.' We would kind of look at each other out of the corner of our eyes – because we were basically challenging each other."

Napoleon Murphy Brock

The Dub Room documentary premiered in 1982, when Zappa had prepared this soundtrack album (for vinyl). Twenty five years later it got issued with an "ackshul tape segment" from the UMRK behind the CD tray.

The film was made available as a mail-order-only home video in the mid-80s, and then on DVD in 2005 (when Ahmet's enthusiasm for this soundtrack was noted).

The album includes two tracks from Halloween 1981, with the rest lifted from a 1974 television special.

When Stevie's Spanking fades in after the tush tush Token vamp and the crowd cheers over the Dog Meat intro, you wonder why they didn't just release a disc of the 1974 material – especially as the 1981 concert was issued on DVD less than a year later.

The track running order and audio quality are wonderful, but the Halloween stuff spoils the flow – which is not the case with the DVD.

Wazoo
2007

FZ

Official Release #82

Originally Released: October 31, 2007

Recording data: September 24, 1972 at Boston Music Hall, Boston (MA)

Producers: Gail Zappa, Joe Travers

Engineers: Doug Sax, Robert Hadley

Tracks:
Intro Intros (3:19)
The Grand Wazoo (Think It Over) (17:21)
Approximate (13:35)
Big Swifty (11:49)
"Ulterior Motive" (3:19)
The Adventures Of Greggery Peccary: Movement I (4:50)
The Adventures Of Greggery Peccary: Movement II (9:07)
The Adventures Of Greggery Peccary: Movement III (12:33)
The Adventures Of Greggery Peccary: Movement IV – The New Brown Clouds (6:07)
Penis Dimension (3:35)
Variant I Processional March (3:28)

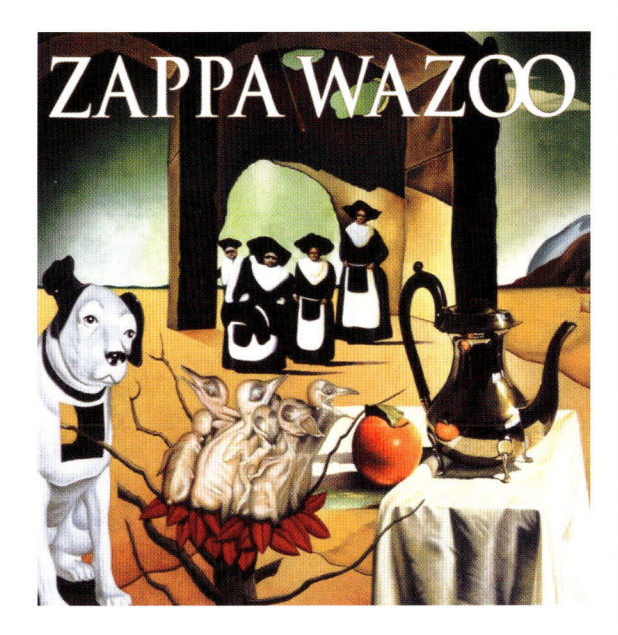

"When the Grand Wazoo did its tour, there was some reel-to-reel tape made of that, and there's some live recordings of that band, but they'll never come out. The quality of that tape is not that good. They're more like souvenirs than real recordings."

Frank Zappa

Ruth Underwood – plus fellow percussionist Tom Raney and cellist Jerry Kessler – can only really be heard during some of the quieter orchestral segments in Greggery Peccary and the middle of Approximate. But that's not too surprising given there are 20 musicians on stage.

The sound is, otherwise, amazing.

Tony Duran gets Grand Wazoo off to a wondrous start, followed by lots of impressive brass and woodwind solos.

The organised madness of Approximate is this set's real highlight, featuring the amazing electric drums of Jim Gordon.

Dave Parlato takes a fine bass solo during a remarkable rendering of Big Swifty.

Aside from being instrumental, Greggery Peccary is unlike the Studio Tan version: rather than being a lengthy structured arrangement, it's largely a series of improvised passages.

Bereft of its lyrics, Penis Dimension is a joy to hear.

Ian Underwood plays jazzy keys throughout, as well as some otherworldly on-stage synth programming.

One Shot Deal
2008

FZ

Official Release #83

Originally Released: June 13, 2008

Recording data: November 11, 1972 to October 31, 1981 at DAR Constitution Hall, Washington (DC), Hordern Pavilion (Sydney), Palais des Sports (Paris), Capitol Theatre, Passaic (NJ), Royce Hall, UCLA (CA), Rhein-Neckar-Halle (Eppelheim), and The Palladium (NYC)

Producers: FZ, Gail Zappa, Joe Travers

Engineer: Bernie Grundman

Tracks:
Bathtub Man (5:43)
Space Boogers (1:24)
Hermitage (2:00)
Trudgin' Across The Tundra (4:01)
Occam's Razor (9:11)
Heidelberg (4:46)
The Illinois Enema Bandit (9:27)
Australian Yellow Snow (12:26)
Rollo (2:57)

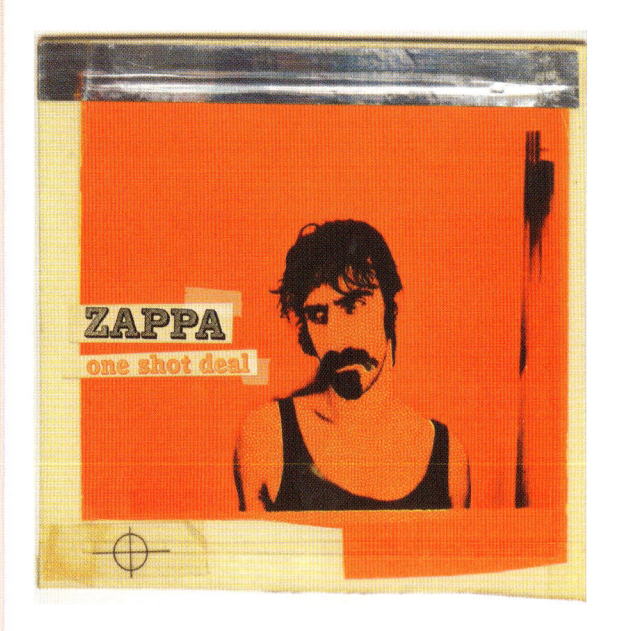

"That guitar solo that is 'Occam's Razor' cut through everything like a razorblade. That track inspired us to compile the rest of the album around it from other goodies that Vaultmeister Joe Travers had unearthed."

Gail Zappa

An unexpected compilation excavated from the Vault. Gail Zappa described it as a sandwich, with Occam's Razor (Zappa's un-Xenochronised solo from On The Bus on Joe's Garage) the meat in the middle.

Bathtub Man is a blues with atypical George Duke and Napoleon Murphy Brock silliness that extends into great solos from Duke and Zappa. Trudgin' Across The Tundra is part of a 30 minute improv by the Petit Wazoo called Seven, the second half of which appears in edited form as D.C. Boogie on Imaginary Diseases.

Heidelburg originally appeared on The Guitar World According To Frank Zappa cassette, and is taken from a live 1978 Yo' Mama. The Illinois Enema Bandit is the Halloween 1981 version from The Torture Never Stops DVD.

Australian Yellow Snow has Jean-Luc Ponty on violin and segues brilliantly into a different edit of the QuAUDIOPHILIAc version of Rollo by the Abnuceals Emuukha Electric Orchestra.

Joe's Menage
2008

FZ

Official Release #84

Originally Released: September 26, 2008

Recording data: November 01, 1975 at William & Mary Hall, College Of William & Mary, Williamsburg (VA)

Producer: FZ

Engineers: Davey Moire, John Polito

Tracks:
Honey, Don't You Want A Man Like Me? (3:57)
The Illinois Enema Bandit (8:42)
Carolina Hard-Core Ecstasy (6:02)
Lonely Little Girl (2:46)
Take Your Clothes Off When You Dance (2:10)
What's The Ugliest Part Of Your Body? (1:16)
Chunga's Revenge (14:18)
Zoot Allures (6:41)

"Norma Bell is a really good saxophone player. She played with Tommy Bolin and Ralphe Armstrong, who was being considered for the gig at the time. He suggested her. She played with us on stage somewhere like Detroit, where she lived, and then Frank brought her along on the road. By the time we got back to LA at the end of the tour she had pretty much succumbed to hanging out with the wrong people and doing a lot of drugs. And so Frank said, 'Forget this!' She wasn't showing up for rehearsals. She didn't last very long. I don't think we recorded anything with her."

Terry Bozzio

This 'less documented line-up' includes Norma Jean Bell (audible tooting her alto sax and warbling on Chunga's Revenge), and an early Illinois Enema Bandit and funky Honey.

Carolina Hard-Core Ecstasy and the early Mothers medley are much the same as on FZ:OZ, though André Lewis has trouble with his organ on the latter, causing Zappa to quote from The Wizard Of Oz and It Can't Happen Here.

Chunga's is the highlight, with solos from Lewis (melodica), Zappa (rhythm guitar) and Bozzio (drums).

Rather than stitch Zoot Allures together, the song fades out then in to mask a tape changeover.

This would be the last time Gail thanked her kids' partners and/or spouses in the liner notes, Ahmet having separated from his actress wife Selma Blair after two years of marriage in 2006. A wise move, as Dweezil and Moon would also go on to divorce their respective spouses later on.

The Lumpy Money Project/Object   2009

FZ

Official Release #85

Originally Released: January 09, 2009

Recording data: January 1961 to 1984 at Pal Recording Studio (Cucamonga), Studio Z, Cucamonga (CA), Fillmore Auditorium (San Francisco), Capitol Studios (Hollywood), T.T.G. Studios (LA), Mayfair Studios (NYC), Apostolic Studios (NYC), Mixed Media, Detroit (MI), West Village (NYC), The New School (NYC), Boston (MA), KBEY-FM, Kansas City (MO) and UMRK (LA)

Producer: FZ

Engineers: Paul Buff, Joe, Rex, Pete, Jim, Bob, Gary, Dick Kunc, Gary Kellgren, Bob Stone, Mark Pinske, John Polito

Tracks:
I Sink Trap (2:45)
II Gum Joy (3:44)
III Up & Down (1:52)
IV Local Butcher (2:36)
V Gypsy Airs (1:41)
VI Hunchy Punchy (2:06)
VII Foamy Soaky (2:34)
VIII Let's Eat Out (1:49)
IX Teen-Age Grand Finale (3:30)
Are You Hung Up? (1:26)
Who Needs The Peace Corps? (2:32)
Concentration Moon (2:22)
Mom & Dad (2:16)
Telephone Conversation (0:49)
Bow Tie Daddy (0:33)
Harry, You're A Beast (1:21)
What's The Ugliest Part Of Your Body? (1:02)
Absolutely Free (3:26)
Flower Punk (3:03)
Hot Poop (0:26)
Nasal Retentive Calliope Music (2:03)
Let's Make The Water Turn Black (1:58)
The Idiot Bastard Son (3:22)
Lonely Little Girl (1:10)
Take Your Clothes Off When You Dance (1:34)
What's The Ugliest Part Of Your Body? (Reprise) (0:58)
Mother People (2:31)
The Chrome Plated Megaphone Of Destiny (6:23)
Lumpy Gravy – Part One (15:57)
Lumpy Gravy – Part Two (17:15)
Are You Hung Up? (1:30)
Who Needs The Peace Corps? (2:35)
Concentration Moon (2:17)
Mom & Dad (2:16)
Telephone Conversation (0:49)
Bow Tie Daddy (0:33)
Harry, You're A Beast (1:22)
What's The Ugliest Part Of Your Body? (1:03)
Absolutely Free (3:28)
Flower Punk (3:04)
Hot Poop (0:29)
Nasal Retentive Calliope Music (2:03)
Let's Make The Water Turn Black (1:45)
The Idiot Bastard Son (3:17)
Lonely Little Girl (1:12)
Take Your Clothes Off When You Dance (1:35)
What's The Ugliest Part Of Your Body? (Reprise) (0:57)
Mother People (2:31)

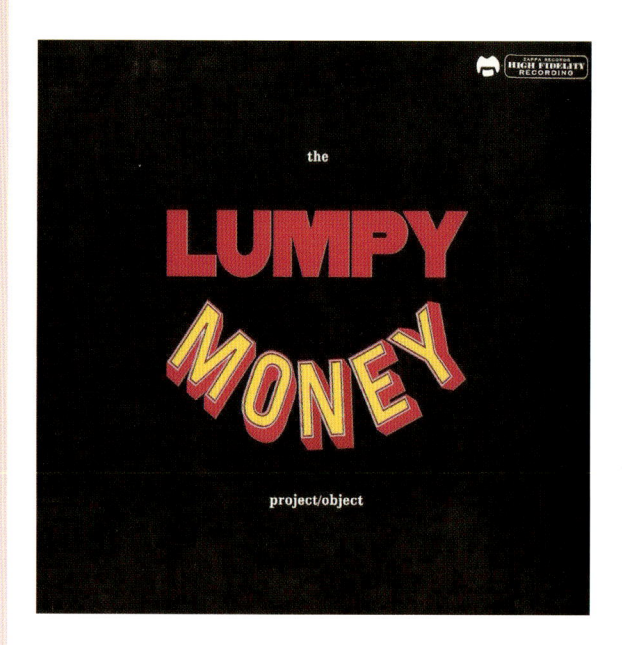

"Before they started making dolls with sexual organs, the only data you could get from your doll was looking between its legs and seeing that little chrome nozzle – if you squeezed the doll, it made a kind of whistling sound. That was the chrome plated megaphone of destiny."
—Frank Zappa

The second 40th anniversary audio documentary examines Phase One and Phase Two.

The first and last discs of this three CD set are of most interest, with Disc 2 consisting of the 1984 remixes of the We're Only In It For The Money and Lumpy Gravy albums (the latter opening with one Thing-Fish a-crooning).

How Did That Get In There? is a big highlight – a 25 minute Zappa construction, some of which is familiar from Lumpy Gravy. The original orchestral mono edit of Lumpy Gravy (Primordial) produced for Capitol Records that opens the whole thing is similarly wonderful.

The interview interruptions on Disc 3 would have been better placed at the very end (like MOFO), as they're listen once or twice affairs.

The instrumental tracks from Money show how great the musicians were, with The Idiot Bastard Son being absolutely belter.

The album ends with a few words from God.

The Chrome Plated Megaphone Of Destiny (6:26)
How Did That Get In Here? (25:01)
Lumpy Gravy "Shuffle" (0:30)
Dense Slight (1:42)
Unit 3A, Take 3 (2:24)
Unit 2, Take 9 (1:10)
Section 8, Take 22 (2:39)
"My Favorite Album" (0:59)
Unit (9:41)
N. Double A, AA (0:55)
Theme From Lumpy Gravy (1:56)
"What The Fuck's Wrong With Her?" (1:07)
Intelligent Design (1:11)
Lonely Little Girl (Original Composition – Take 24) (3:35)

Philly '76
2009

FZ

Official Release #86

Originally Released: December 21, 2009

Recording data: October 29, 1976 at the Spectrum Theater, Philadelphia (PA)

Producer: FZ

Engineer: Frank Filipetti

Tracks:
The Purple Lagoon (3:36)
Stink-Foot (5:53)
The Poodle Lecture (3:49)
Dirty Love (3:37)
Wind Up Workin' In A Gas Station (2:32)
Tryin' To Grow A Chin (4:02)
The Torture Never Stops (13:32)
City Of Tiny Lites (7:47)
You Didn't Try To Call Me (6:32)
Manx Needs Women (1:45)
Chrissy Puked Twice (6:49)
Black Napkins (18:58)
Advance Romance (13:56)
Honey, Don't You Want A Man Like Me? (4:09)
Rudy Wants To Buy Yez A Drink (2:20)
Would You Go All The Way? (2:04)
Daddy, Daddy, Daddy (2:05)
What Kind Of Girl Do You Think We Are? (4:58)
Dinah-Moe Humm (8:10)
Stranded In The Jungle (3:10)
Find Her Finer (3:18)
Camarillo Brillo (4:04)
Muffin Man (6:55)

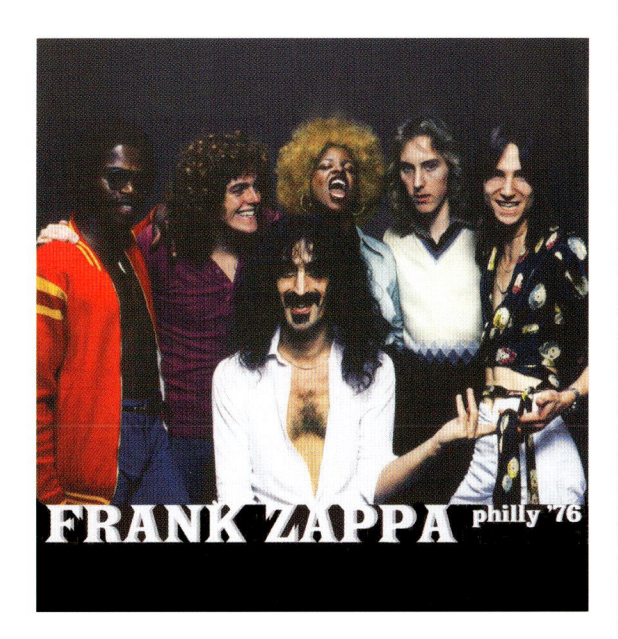

'I was with Frank for almost a year. I was in the band that had Terry Bozzio on drums, Ray White on guitar, Patrick O'Hearn on bass and myself on piano. I was never Bianca Odin or Oden, this name was given me by the people I worked for ... my stage name is and has always been Lady Bianca.'

Bianca Odin

Variations on familiar arrangements include: Eddie Jobson's fantastic violin during an epic Black Napkins; Bianca Odin's soulful lead vocals on Dirty Love, You Didn't Try To Call Me and Advance Romance; and Zappa's upfront singing on the sequence of Vaudeville-era tunes (Flo & Eddie were scheduled to guest, but their guitar player plummeted to his death a few days earlier).

Although Zappa's vocals sounds shaky at the start of this medley, things really take off when Odin joins in. Bozzio and Ray White also get to sing lead – on Tryin' To Grow A Chin and City Of Tiny Lites – which all makes for an incredibly diverse set.

During a funky Tiny Lites, we get to hear White's scat singing and it's evident he and Odin have a great understanding (Lady Bianca's insightful liner notes reveal she introduced White to Zappa).

Throughout, Zappa plugs the imminent release of Zoot Allures.

"That Problem With Absolutely Free" (0:30)
Absolutely Free (Instrumental) (3:59)
Harry, You're A Beast (Instrumental) (1:16)
What's The Ugliest Part of Your Body? (Reprise/Instrumental) (2:01)
Creationism (1:11)
Idiot Bastard Snoop (0:47)
The Idiot Bastard Son (Instrumental) (2:48)
"What's Happening Of The Universe" (1:37)
"The World Will Be A Far Happier Place" (0:21)
Lonely Little Girl (Instrumental) (1:26)
Mom & Dad (Instrumental) (2:16)
Who Needs The Peace Corps? (Instrumental) (2:51)
"Really Little Voice" (2:28)
Take Your Clothes Off When You Dance (Instrumental) (1:24)
Lonely Little Girl – The Single (2:45)
"In Conclusion" (0:25)

Greasy Love Songs
2010

FZ

Official Release #87

Originally Released: April 04, 2010

Recording data: April 1963 to February 21, 1969 Pal Recording Studio, Cucamonga (CA), Apostolic Studios (NYC), Mayfair Studios (NYC), KPPC, Pasadena (CA), WMEX, Boston (MA), The New School (NYC)

Producer: FZ

Engineers: Paul Buff, Dick Kunc, Gary Kellgren, John Polito

Tracks:
Cheap Thrills (2:23)
Love Of My Life (3:10)
How Could I Be Such A Fool (3:35)
Deseri (2:07)
I'm Not Satisfied (4:03)
Jelly Roll Gum Drop (2:20)
Anything (3:04)
Later That Night (3:06)
You Didn't Try To Call Me (3:57)
Fountain Of Love (3:01)
"No. No. No." (2:29)
Anyway The Wind Blows (2:58)
Stuff Up The Cracks (4:35)
Jelly Roll Gum Drop (Alternate Mix – Mono) (2:18)
"No. No. No." (Long Version) (3:06)
Stuff Up The Cracks (Alternate Mix) (6:05)
"Serious Fan Mail" (5:11)
Valerie (3:03)
Jelly Roll Gum Drop (Single Version) (2:24)
"Secret Greasing" (3:36)
Love Of My Life (2:06)

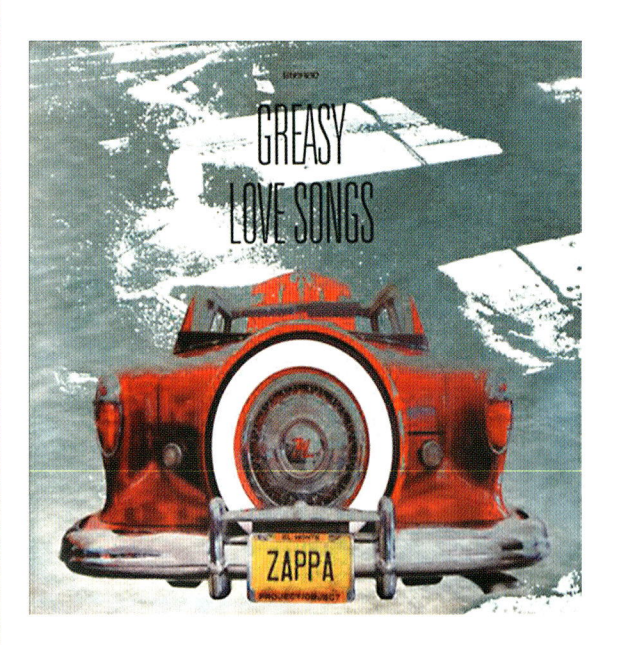

"Frank didn't discuss anything with me. I just went in and did the best singing I could possibly do. The parody was Frank's idea. I think Frank has the tendency to put down what he's doing in fear that it might not be accepted. I've never liked Frank's presentation of an album."

Ray Collins

The third audio documentary is an expanded version of the 1968 stereo mix of Cruising With Ruben & The Jets – though even this does not feature the original drum tracks, as Zappa had Tripp redo them because he didn't like what Mundi had played.

As well as providing 'lewd pulsating rhythm', Jimmy Carl Black is credited with trumpet on Valerie (sic), recorded at the earlier Money sessions.

In the two radio interview excerpts, Zappa tells of how the music got airplay because DJs didn't know Ruben & The Jets was actually the Mothers (who planned to record a more authentic R&B follow-up album), and reads the story of Ruben Sano from the original record's sleeve.

Paul Buff surely deserved a less grudging acknowledgement for playing piano, bass, drums and sax on the 1963 version of Love Of My Life.

Ray Collins would sadly pass away two years after this release.

"Congress Shall Make No Law…" 2010

FZ

Official Release #88

Originally Released: September 19, 2010

Recording data: September 19, 1985 to 1992 at Committee on Commerce, Science and Transportation, Maryland State Legislature and UMRK (LA)

Producer: FZ

Engineers: Spencer Chrislu, Todd Yvega, John Polito

Tracks:
Congress Shall Make No Law (32:46)
Perhaps In Maryland (10:45)
Thou Shalt Have No Other Gods Before Me (2:56)
Thou Shalt Not Make Unto Thee Any Graven Image – Any Likeness Of Anything In Heaven Above, Nor In The Earth Beneath, Nor In The Water Under The Earth (2:31)
Thou Shalt Not Take The Name Of The Lord Thy God In Vain (2:26)
Thou Shalt Keep Holy The Sabbath Day (2:05)
Thou Shalt Honor Thy Father And Thy Mother (2:21)
Thou Shalt Not Kill (2:06)
Thou Shalt Not Commit Adultery (0:55)
Thou Shalt Not Steal (0:39)
Thou Shalt Not Bear False Witness Against Thy Neighbor (1:48)
Thou Shalt Not Covet The House Of Thy Neighbor, The Wife Of Thy Neighbor, Nor His Male Servant, Nor His Female Servant, Nor His Ass, Nor Anything That Belongs To Thy Neighbor (1:13)
Reagan At Bitburg Some More (1:10)

"My nephew, Jade, has the ability to burp very loud and very long, and he can also burp words. So, when he was here visiting in 1987, we had a sampling session with Jade. In fact, he got paid the same as any other musician that comes in here to do samples. I stood him in front of a microphone, and let him do an assortment of burps, and then gave him a list of words and phrases to burp, and some of those were put into the Synclavier."

Frank Zappa

To mark the 25th anniversary of Zappa's testimony before the Senate Commerce, Science and Transportation Committee on "the subject of the content of certain sound recordings and suggestions that recording packages be labelled to provide a warning to prospective purchasers of sexually explicit or other potentially offensive content," this release contains his full statements to Congress and the Maryland State Legislature, plus other relevant quotes. These are intertwined with previously unreleased (and unconnected) Synclavier oddments – mostly from Feeding The Monkies At Ma Maison – and Jade's burps.

The album also commemorated the unveiling of a sculpture in Zappa's hometown of Baltimore, where September 19 was proclaimed 'Frank Zappa Day'.

The package was principally assembled by Gail, who declared it "an educational project".

The naming of tracks after the Decalogue is quite arbitrary – for example, Thou Shalt Not Commit Adultery concerns Michael Jackson making more money for his record label than himself.

Hammersmith Odeon
2010

FZ

Official Release #89

Originally Released: November 06, 2010

Recording data: January 25-27 and February 28, 1978 at Hammersmith Odeon (London)

Producer: FZ

Engineer: Peter Henderson

Tracks:
Convocation/The Purple Lagoon (2:18)
Dancin' Fool (3:43)
Peaches En Regalia (2:36)
The Torture Never Stops (13:52)
Tryin' To Grow A Chin (3:37)
City Of Tiny Lites (7:01)
Baby Snakes (1:54)
Pound For A Brown (20:39)
I Have Been In You (13:55)
Flakes (6:39)
Broken Hearts Are For Assholes (3:54)
Punky's Whips (10:26)
Titties 'N' Beer (4:49)
Audience Participation (3:32)
The Black Page #2 (2:49)
Jones Crusher (3:01)
The Little House I Used To Live In (7:13)
Dong Work For Yuda (2:56)
Bobby Brown (4:54)
Envelopes (2:16)
Terry Firma (4:10)
Disco Boy (6:43)
King Kong (10:10)
Watermelon In Easter Hay [Prequel] (3:55)
Dinah-Moe Humm (6:10)
Camarillo Brillo (3:23)
Muffin Man (6:18)
Black Napkins (5:16)
San Ber'dino (5:54)

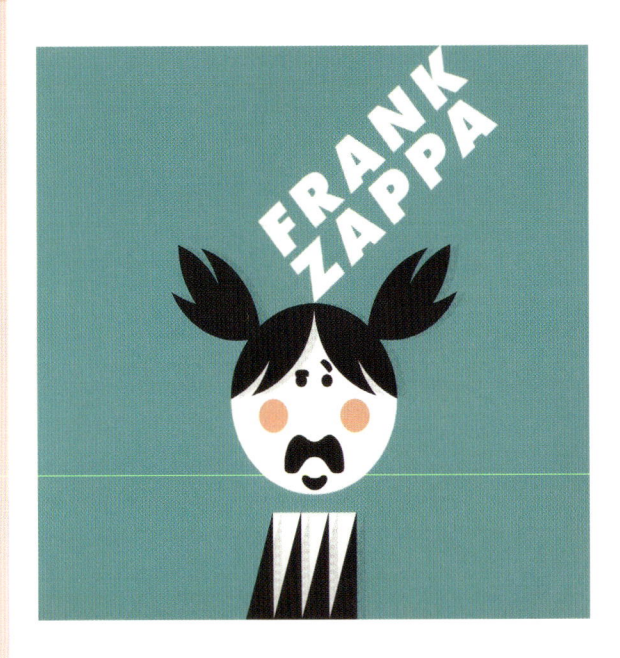

"I remember very clearly being at the Hammersmith Odeon, which is a large theatre in London, and we spent three hours recording things in the theatre because Frank said, 'Well, here I've got a space that I can record in.' He had some of us up in the, some of us were up in the balcony shaking bits of metal and things. Then he would point to someone down at the stage and they'd hit a timpani drum and so on. He was really recording parts that would become xenochrony parts for him. And I'm sure that I'm a part of some of those in his records. It's really hard to tell though what anything's particular source is."
Adrian Belew

Despite occasional audio oddities, this is a great sounding album. Utilising performances from a series of concerts rather than one complete show means we get the best versions and more encores.

Obviously excluded is material from these London concerts used as the backing tracks for much of the Sheik Yerbouti album. So sadly, no Yo' Mama.

This was recorded a year or so before longer improvs stopped being the norm and the set lists became more predictable: Mars is uncontainable – check Pound For A Brown, which includes Hail Caesar Variations – and Bozzio is straining at the reins from which Zappa would shortly set him free.

Dong Work For Yuda swings, Bobby Brown contains the "story of the three assholes", Terry Firma is a nifty drum solo and Envelopes has lyrics.

The author of Frank Zappa: The Negative Dialectics of Poodle Play dances to The Black Page #2 as 'Eric Dolphy'.

Feeding The Monkies At Ma Maison   2011

FZ

Official Release #90

Originally Released: September 22, 2011

Recording data: 1986 to 1992 at UMRK (LA)

Producer: FZ

Engineers: Todd Yvega, John Polito

Tracks:
Feeding The Monkies At Ma Maison (20:12)
Buffalo Voice (11:34)
Secular Humanism (6:37)

Additional tracks on CD:
Worms From Hell (5:31)
Samba Funk (11:29)

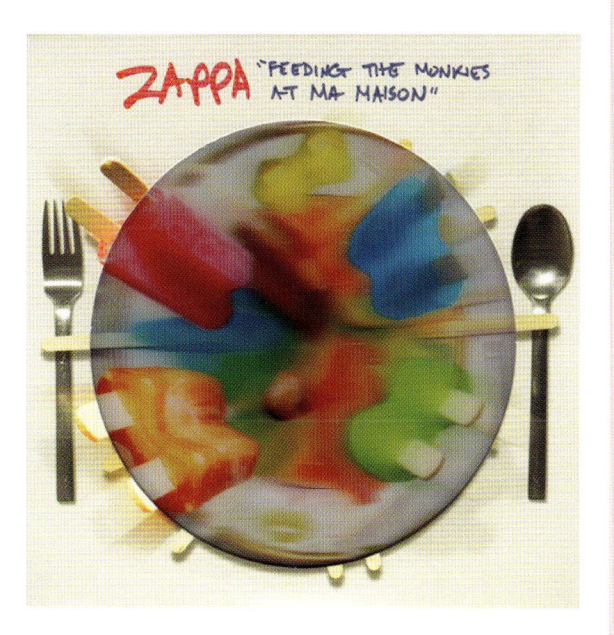

'Imagine making your own mountain and then going to the mountain periodically and hauling your own hunks or marble back to the shop so that you can whack away on them. Sculpture is a subtractive medium, and you start off with more than you wind up with. So the analogy here is that the raw material that I'm working with is whatever is in my imagination versus what samples are at my disposal. And building the mountain is building your collection of samples. After you've recorded the individual instrument, or jackhammer, or whatever it's going to be, you can't deploy it into a composition unless it's been captured."

Frank Zappa

Aside from Moon's (buffalo) voice, this is the sole album of Frank Zappa compositions solely realised on the Synclavier – no guitar or other conventionally manipulated instruments are present.

Containing longer and differently mixed versions of two pieces from Civilization Phase III, it is the title track (at one time named Resolver ED.) that impresses.

28 seconds of Worms From Hell appeared at the start of the Video From Hell home video.

The three track album Zappa intended was released digitally and on vinyl four years later, with a cover painting by John Alexander – titled Feeding The Monkies At "Ma Maison". It is not clear whether Zappa was using the archaic form for the plural of the dry-nosed primate, or perhaps that's just how he hand-labelled the master tape.

Gail dedicated Monkies to Ahmet's new daughter, Halo, as well as Pierre Boulez and Elliott Carter – both of whom subsequently passed away.

Carnegie Hall
2011

FZ / The Mothers Of Invention

Official Release #91

Originally Released: October 31, 2011

Recording data: October 11, 1971 at Carnegie Hall (NYC)

Producer: FZ

Engineer: John Polito

Tracks:
I Just Can't Work No Longer (2:32)
Working All The Live Long Day/Chain Gang (2:20)
Medley #1 (7:28)
Pieces of A Man (2:53)
Buffalo Soldier (4:33)
Medley #2 (2:36)
Medley #3 (3:14)
Hello (to FOH)/Ready?! (to the BAND) (1:03)
Call Any Vegetable (10:36)
Anyway The Wind Blows (4:00)
Magdalena (6:08)
Dog Breath (5:41)
Peaches En Regalia (4:24)
Tears Began To Fall (2:32)
Shove It Right (6:32)
King Kong (30:25)
200 MOTELS Finale (3:41)
Who Are The Brain Police? (7:08)
Auspicious Occasion (2:45)
DIVAN: Once Upon A Time (5:40)
DIVAN: Sofa #1 (3:11)
DIVAN: Magic Pig (1:43)
DIVAN: Stick It Out (4:54)
DIVAN: Divan Ends Here (4:17)
Pound For A Brown (6:03)
Sleeping In A Jar (2:46)
Wonderful Wino (5:46)
Sharleena (4:52)
Cruising For Burgers (3:17)
Billy The Mountain – Part 1 (28:33)
Billy The Mountain – The Carnegie Solos (13:31)

"The Carnegie Hall tapes were originally recorded at 7 1/2ips on a concealed Nagra mono machine using one Electrovoice 664 microphone. These tapes were processed through an Orban Stereo Matrix (ambience generator) and re-equalized to simulate stereo. Our apologies for the recording quality; we felt the solos were interesting enough to warrant the use of the substandard audio replicas."

Frank Zappa

This essentially contains all of the music performed during two sold-out shows at New York's prestigious concert hall. The opening act were The Persuasions, an a cappella group who began singing together in Brooklyn in the mid-1960s that Zappa flew out to LA to record their eponymous debut album in 1970.

Their performance from the first show only is included here (the first seven tracks), though even this was excised when the album was made available to stream and download in 2015. Also missing is an individual photo of Don Preston from the accompanying booklet.

Zappa supposedly dedicated one of the shows to Nigey Lennon, who had a personal and professional relationship with him (as detailed in her 1995 book, Being Frank).

A cover of Zappa's Love Of My Life by The Persuasions' former lead vocalist, Jerry Lawson, appeared on the download-only AAAFNRAAAAAM Birthday Bundle 21 Dec. 2011 album.

Road Tapes, Venue #1
2012

FZ
Official Release #92
Originally Released: October 31, 2012
Recording data: August 25, 1968 at Kerrisdale Arena (Vancouver)
Producer: Gail Zappa
Engineer: John Polito
Tracks:
The Importance Of An Earnest Attempt (By Hand) (3:44)
Help, I'm A Rock/Transylvania Boogie (9:30)
Flopsmash Musics (4:50)
Hungry Freaks, Daddy (3:59)
The Orange County Lumber Truck (20:57)
The Rewards Of A Career In Music (3:29)
Trouble Every Day (5:08)
Shortly: Suite Exists Of Holiday In Berlin Full Blown (9:29)
Pound For A Brown (3:13)
Sleeping In A Jar (3:23)
Oh, In The Sky (2:42)
Octandre (7:40)
King Kong (10:17)

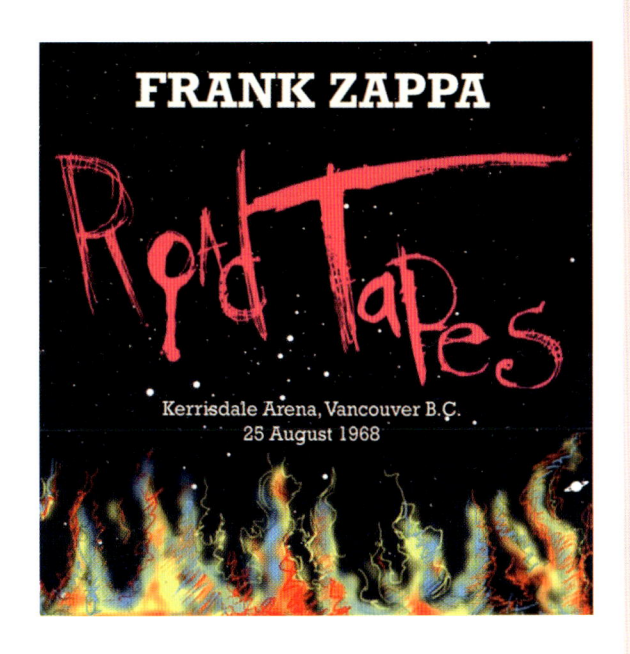

"My guess is that somebody working at the venue ran this off for Frank. The original tape was full of a million inconsistent level jumps. It was a real bitch to get all of the program levelled out to a relatively equal listening level. Also, there were pitch problems. The reel starts at one pitch and progresses to another as it continues on. Lots of corrections. Reel changes seem to always happen at the worst times, but we figured we rather include 'Trouble Every Day' instead of not! The door slam was Gail's idea. Trying to combine the two edit spots was a challenge. Overall, I really think sonically John Polito and I made this a totally listenable object, as the raw tape is definitely not!"
Joe Travers

Inspired by the You Can't Do That On Stage Anymore series, this is the first in a line of guerrilla recordings of previously unheard performances.

The Kerrisdale Arena, which Zappa refers to as the "local electric ice box", is actually a public skating rink.

In The Rewards Of A Career In Music, Bunk Gardner tells the story of how his piano teacher would give a blue star if you made no mistakes during a lesson.

The door slam in the middle of Trouble Every Day can also be heard on MOFO and Joe's XMASage – Gail's go-to sound effect.

At the end of the concert, the crowd call for more and Zappa is aghast at the "unprecedented response for the bullshit that we do".

Almost a year to the day later, after Lowell George had come and gone, the original Mothers would return to Canada to play their final gig together.

Understanding America
2012

FZ

Official Release #93

Originally Released: October 31, 2012

Recording data: March 09, 1966 to April 19, 1988 at T.T.G. Studios (LA), Mayfair Studios (NYC), Apostolic Studios (NYC), Whitney Studios, Glendale (CA), The Record Plant (LA), Fillmore East), Bolic Sound (Inglewood), Caribou Ranch (Nederland), Hammersmith Odeon (London), The Village Recorders (LA), Berkeley Community Theater (CA), Santa Monica Civic Auditorium (CA), Stadthalle (Vienna), UMRK (LA), Committee on Commerce, Science and Transportation, Warner Theatre, Washington (DC), Tower Theater, Upper Darby (PA), Royal Oak Music Theatre, Detroit (MI), Shea's Theater, Buffalo (NY), War Memorial Auditorium, Rochester (NY), Cumberland County Civic Center, Portland (ME), Civic Center, Providence (RI), Rothman Center, Teaneck, (NJ), Nassau Coliseum, Uniondale (NY), Wembley Arena (London)

Producer: FZ

Engineers: Bob Ludwig, et al.

Tracks:
Hungry Freaks, Daddy (3:28)
Plastic People (3:42)
Mom & Dad (2:17)
It Can't Happen Here (3:07)
Who Are The Brain Police? (3:33)
Who Needs The Peace Corps? (2:35)
Brown Shoes Don't Make It (7:29)
Concentration Moon (2:17)
Trouble Every Day (5:08)
You're Probably Wondering Why I'm Here (3:36)
We're Turning Again (4:55)
Road Ladies (4:08)
What Kind Of Girl Do You Think We Are? (4:33)
Camarillo Brillo (3:53)
Find Her Finer (3:34)
Dinah-Moe Humm (6:02)
Disco Boy (4:18)
200 Years Old (4:30)
I'm The Slime (2:34)
Be In My Video (3:37)
I Don't Even Care (3:48)
Can't Afford No Shoes (2:38)
Heavenly Bank Account (3:16)
Cocaine Decisions (2:52)
Dumb All Over (4:03)
Promiscuous (2:03)
Thing-Fish Intro (2:56)
The Central Scrutinizer (2:50)
Porn Wars Deluxe (25:51)
Tinseltown Rebellion (3:43)
Jesus Thinks You're A Jerk (9:18)

"'Porn Wars Deluxe' for me is worth the price of admission (so to speak). I find Understanding America a good starting point to recommend to anyone discovering FZ, made by the man himself."

Joe Travers

Gail made a big hoo-ha about her husband's intent when preventing others performing his music, and would compile much of the posthumous catalogue from his 'build reels' – as if that's what he'd have wanted. But in some cases, Zappa had abandoned these tapes with good reason.

Understanding America is a largely pointless belated compilation of something that seemed like a good idea in 1991 (when he was considering running for President) that he undoubtedly wouldn't have issued in 2012. Bizarrely, it uses the final Zappa-approved versions of tracks issued by Ryko in 1995 at a time when Universal had just rolled out new masters replicating the original vinyl mixes.

Travers is right to single out the elongated version of Porn Wars Deluxe, but the ZFT now had the technology and the archives (eg. a still unissued long version of 200 Years Old) to produce something better than Zappa intended.

Finer Moments
2012

FZ

Official Release #94

Originally Released: December 18, 2012

Recording data: July 1967 to 1972 at Mayfair Studios (NYC), Sunset Sound (LA), Criteria Studios, Miami (FL), Thee Image, Miami Beach (FL), McMillin Theater, Columbia University (NYC), The Ballroom, Stratford (CT), Royal Albert Hall (London), The Ark, Boston (MA), Auditorium Theatre (Chicago), Carnegie Hall (NYC) and Zappa basement

Producer: FZ

Engineers: Jerry Hansen, Dick Kunc, Kerry McNabb, FZ

Tracks:
Intro (1:20)
Sleazette (3:33)
Mozart Piano Sonata In Bb (6:22)
The Walking Zombie Music (3:23)
The Old Curiosity Shoppe (7:08)
You Never Know Who Your Friends Are (2:21)
Uncle Rhebus (17:46)
Music From The Big Squeeze (0:42)
Enigmas 1 Thru 5 (8:16)
Pumped And Waxed (4:19)
There Is No Heaven From Where Slogans Go To Die (4:37)
Squeeze It, Squeeze It, Squeeze It (3:17)
The Subcutaneous Peril (19:41)

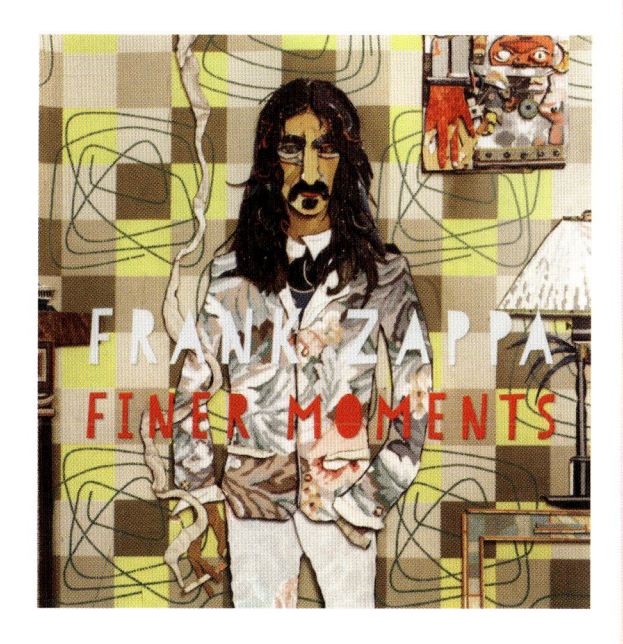

"The vinyl edition was cut directly from the DBX187 encoded 1/4" analog stereo master tapes. NOT from a digital transfer. The digital transfer was done in 2007 which was used for the CD edition, but since the tapes are in great condition we used them again for the 2012 vinyl cutting."

Joe Travers

Another abandoned project that the family decided to resurrect, hot on the heels of Understanding America.

This recycles material both from the Zappa-issued You Can't Do That On Stage Anymore, Mystery Disc and Burnt Weeny Sandwich albums, as well as a huge chunk from the more recent posthumous Carnegie Hall set (The Subcutaneous Peril).

The album's cover art is by Bill Miller, who also provided the artwork for "Congress Shall Make No Law …", and includes the first appearance of Del Casher on a Zappa album!

The first disc primarily features the final incarnation of the original Mothers – now bolstered by Bunk's brother Buzz on trumpet – chiefly taken from their Royal Albert Hall show in June 1969.

Pumped And Waxed is of most interest on Disc Two, being a previously unknown studio recording from 1972, in a similar vein to Zappa's later Basement Music and Synclavier experiments.

Baby Snakes – The Compleat Soundtrack   2012

FZ

Official Release #95

Originally Released: December 21, 2012

Recording data: October 28-31, 1977 to 1978 at The Palladium (NYC) and elsewhere

Producer: FZ

Engineers: Kerry McNabb, Mark Pinske

Tracks:
Baby Snakes Rehearsal (2:11)
"This Is the Show They Never See" (5:52)
Baby Snakes – The Song (2:04)
Bruce Bickford/"Disco Outfreakage" (6:15)
The Poodle Lecture (5:03)
"She Said"/ City Of Tiny Lites (10:28)
New York's Finest Crazy Persons (1:55)
"The Way The Air Smells …"/Flakes (4:01)
Pound Bass & Keyboards Solo (6:36)
"In You" Rap/ Dedication (6:47)
Managua/Police Car/Drum Solo (9:45)
Disco Boy (4:02)
"Give People Somewhere To X-Scape Thru" (6:26)
King Kong/Roy's Halloween Gas Mask (9:01)
Bobby Brown Goes Down (3:43)
Conehead/"All You Need To Know" (5:32)
I'm So Cute/"Entertainment All The Way" (5:15)
Titties 'N' Beer (6:19)
Audience Participation/The Dance Contest (6:36)
The Black Page #2 (2:55)
Jones Crusher (2:53)
Broken Hearts Are For Assholes (3:50)
Punky's Whips (12:10)
"Thank You"/Dinah Moe-Humm (7:19)
Camarillo Brillo (3:26)
Muffin Man (4:59)
San Ber'dino (5:02)
Black Napkins (7:54)
New York's Finest Crazy Persons 2 (4:09)
"Good Night" (1:22)

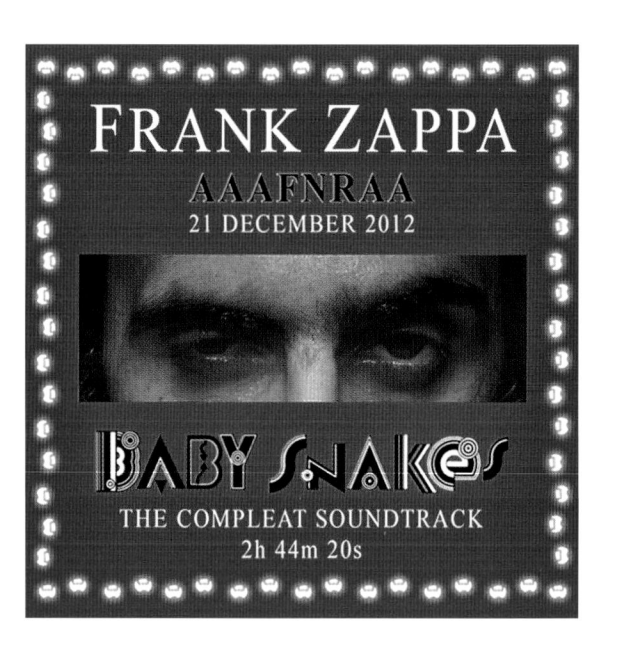

"Baby Snakes is as different from 200 Motels as 200 Motels is from Shane."

Frank Zappa

Baby Snakes the movie premiered in New York in 1979, and went straight to video … eight years later. The DVD was finally rolled-out in 2003.

On what would have been Zappa's 72nd birthday, the ZFT thought fans would now want to download the soundtrack from iTunes and watch the movie in our heads (whilst driving, bathing, jogging, cooking or singing). Alternatively, we could've just played the DVD and unplugged our TV sets: we still wouldn't have seen the cute little drummer, the amazing Mr Bickford's claymation, the band's backstage antics, or people doing stuff that is not normal.

Of course the music sounds great (most notably, Frank's guitar). It's just a shame that we get to hear songs interrupted by the other goings on.

Listening to Zappa and Bickford clicking away in the animation suite is pretty dull, too. Maybe this should be seen as another 'fuck you' to Steve Jobs.

Road Tapes, Venue #2
2013

FZ
Official Release #96
Originally Released: October 31, 2013
Recording data: August 23-24, 1973 at Finlandia-talo (Helsinki)
Producer: FZ
Engineer: Kerry McNabb, Steve Desper
Tracks:
Introcious (5:18)
The Eric Dolphy Memorial Barbecue (1:08)
Kung Fu (1:11)
Penguin In Bondage (4:07)
Exercise #4 (1:58)
Dog Breath (1:36)
The Dog Breath Variations (1:30)
Uncle Meat (2:27)
RDNZL (6:17)
Montana (7:03)
Your Teeth And Your Shoulders and sometimes your foot goes like this …/Pojama Prelude (10:14)
Dupree's Paradise (15:55)
All Skate/Dun-Dun-Dun (The Finnish Hit Single) (14:10)
Village Of The Sun (5:40)
Echidna's Arf (Of You) (4:22)
Don't You Ever Wash That Thing? (9:56)
Big Swifty (12:58)
Farther O'Blivion (22:54)
Brown Shoes Don't Make It (7:33)

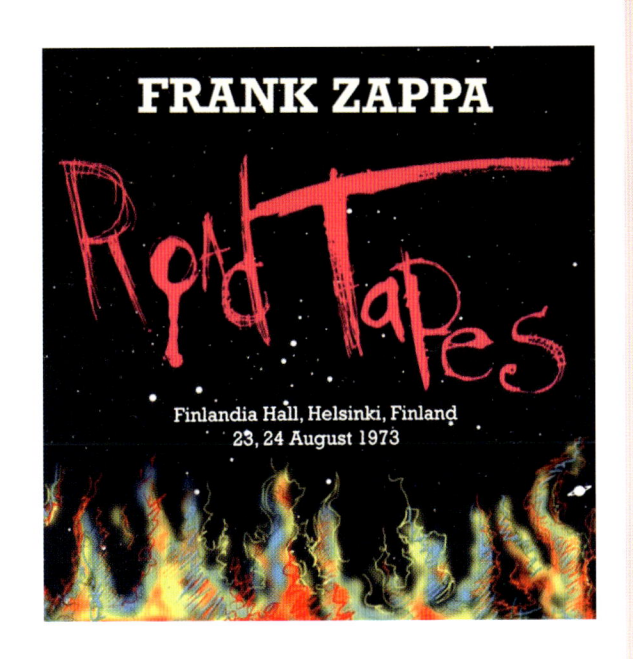

> "These recordings reflect the musical complicity that I had with George Duke. To cite just one example, how he follows me during my improvisation in 'Dupree's Paradise' amazes me today. He plays very rhythmic when I'm echoing some notes of a moment where I am more melodic, or following me in some escapades – very 'free'."
>
> Jean-Luc Ponty

The second in the series is compiled from three shows in the country where I quite want to be, from which the Vaultmeister selected the best sounding performances. Containing lots of lovely long instrumental passages featuring one heck of a band, this was much more like it after the last few releases.

Your Teeth And Your Shoulders is an incredibly long intro into Dupree's Paradise, largely improvised by Duke before Zappa recites some lyrics from the then still to be released Po-Jama People.

In Farther O'Blivion, Zappa tells the audience exactly where 'The Hook' is – a complex little riff you couldn't possibly dance to, followed by a short Ralph Humphrey drum solo!

The album finishes unpredictably with Zappa and Duke sharing vocals on the old Mothers' chestnut, Brown Shoes.

A rendition of Cosmik Debris from these concerts was released by the ZFT for download-only on Mother's Day the following year.

A Token Of His Extreme – Soundtrack   2013

FZ

Official Release #97

Originally Released: November 25, 2013

Recording data: August 27, 1974 at KCET (LA)

Producer: FZ

Engineer: Kerry McNabb

Tracks:
The Dog Breath Variations-Uncle Meat (4:02)
Montana (6:44)
Earl Of Duke (5:49)
Florentine Pogen (11:08)
Stink-Foot (3:58)
Pygmy Twylyte (7:47)
Room Service (12:12)
Inca Roads (9:51)
Oh No-Son Of Orange County (7:10)
More Trouble Every Day (7:17)
A Token Of My Extreme (1:25)

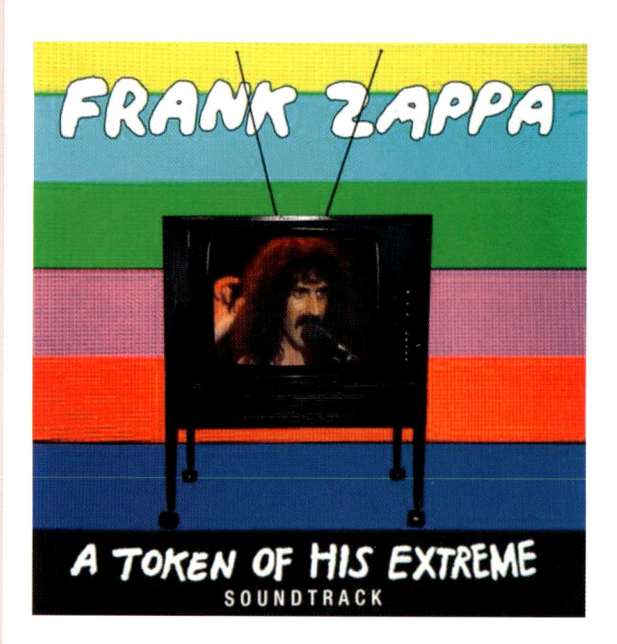

"Perellis had another girlfriend, that he met in Ohio, who had a cockapoo. I believe we were in Ann Arbor, Michigan, and the girl, the cockapoo, and Perellis were in a Holiday Inn, and it was discovered that the cockapoo had worms, and this was Sunday. So in an emergency effort, he wanted to do something about the dog's worms, and called a veterinarian who recommended that they give the dog a Fleet enema. So they wound up filling this bathtub with dog do-do and worms."

Frank Zappa

While still awaiting the arrival of Roxy – The Movie, the ZFT slipped out 'this extravaganza of live music' on DVD and, separately, on this soundtrack CD.

Performed by the same core musicians, much of this recorded-for-TV show had already been issued on The Dub Room Special! CD. But this is an entirely different pocketbook fleecing mix.

The performances of Inca Roads and Florentine Pogen herein had also been used as the basic tracks for those songs on the One Size Fits All album.

Such quibbles aside, this is a fantastic album by a fantastic band.

Room Service affords an opportunity for shout-outs to Herb Cohen and his DiscReet Records partner Zach Glickman, as well as the TV special's producer, Mort Libov.

Earl Of Duke is a keyboard-led improv solely credited to the man Tom Waits referred to as Da Willie.

Coincidentally, Waits is given a name-check by Zappa during Stink-Foot.

Joe's Camouflage
2014

FZ

Official Release #98

Originally Released: *January 30, 2014*

Recording data: *August 25 to early September 1975 at 5831 Sunset Boulevard and Paramount Studios (LA)*

Producers: *Gail Zappa, Joe Travers*

Engineers: *Denny Walley, Joe Travers, John Polito*

Tracks:
Phyniox (Take 1) (2:29)
T'Mershi Duween (2:28)
Reeny Ra (4:13)
"Who Do You Think You Are" (1:39)
"Slack 'Em All Down" (1:26)
Honey, Don't You Want A Man Like Me? (4:16)
The Illinois Enema Bandit (6:27)
Sleep Dirt – In Rehearsal (1:08)
Black Napkins (8:12)
Take Your Clothes Off When You Dance (1:55)
Denny & Froggy Relate (0:31)
"Choose Your Foot" (1:20)
Any Downers? (6:11)
Phyniox (Take 2) (4:18)
"I Heard A Note!" (1:20)

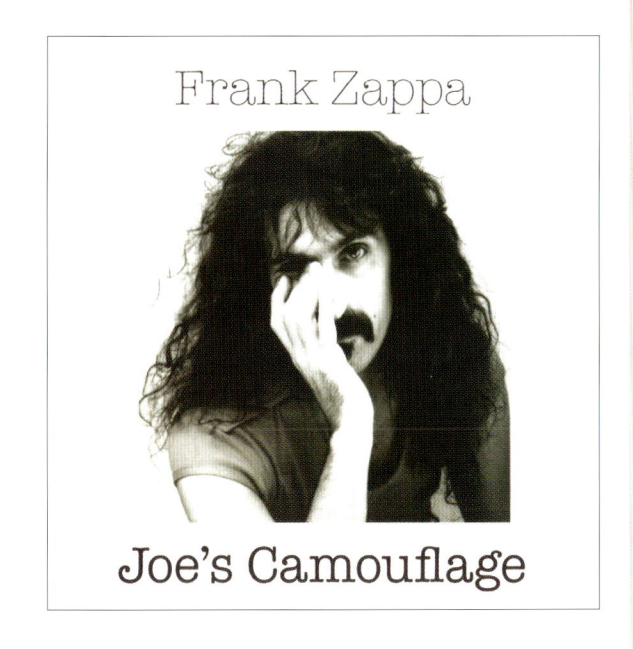

"Frank was trying some other material, but the ensembles didn't work for the entire repertoire. It was just too loose in spots, and then there were some people that were being flaky. Frank then said, 'I've got a solid group here with the five – we're just gonna mold that ...'"
Napoleon Murphy Brock

When Mick Ekers sent Gail an early draft of his Zappa's Gear book, it mentioned some publicity photos from late 1975 showing a band that everyone believed had rehearsed but never actually recorded or toured together. She responded by saying this was "not entirely true – perhaps recorded in rehearsal!"

Shortly thereafter came news of this album, featuring Denny Walley, Robert "Frog" Camarena, viola player Novi Novog, Napoleon Murphy Brock, Roy Estrada and Terry Bozzio.

Five of the tracks are taken from Walley's cassette recordings. Reeny Ra contains the melody from Zappa's unreleased love song to Gail, Solitude. "Who Do You Think You Are?" is briefly disrupted by Moon and Dweezil.

André Lewis gets a special mention in the liners but doesn't actually appear: Novog and Brock share keyboard duties here. Lewis would though join the band after Walley defected to Beefheart's Magic Band, and "Frog" and Novog accepted better offers.

Roxy By Proxy
2014

FZ

Official Release #99

Originally Released: March 15, 2014

Recording data: December 08-10, 1973 at The Roxy (LA)

Producers: FZ, Gail Zappa, Joe Travers

Engineer: Kerry McNabb

Tracks:
"Carved In The Rock" (3:42)
Inca Roads (8:21)
Penguin In Bondage (5:52)
T'Mershi Duween (1:56)
Dog Breath Variations-Uncle Meat (4:14)
RDNZL (5:23)
Village Of The Sun (3:24)
Echidna's Arf (Of You) (4:00)
Don't You Ever Wash That Thing (5:28)
Cheepnis – Percussion (5:24)
Cheepnis (3:35)
Dupree's Paradise (15:12)
King Kong-Chunga's Revenge-Mr. Green Genes (9:13)

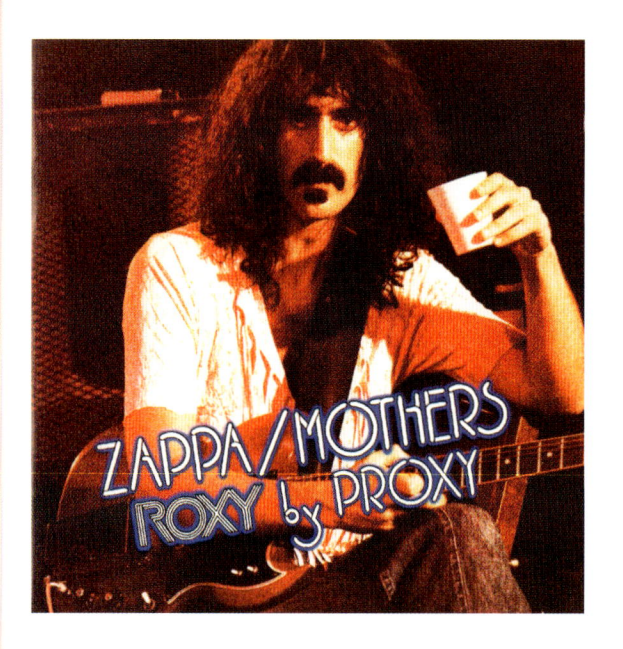

"There is a lot of great music here. Frank loved this band, and I must admit there's a special essence that comes through and reflects the respect we all had for each other. I've managed to see past the flaws and even embrace the unpolished, unadulterated, honest and down-to-earth quality of the recording. Although it's not one of the great Zappa CDs, it is one of the most pleasurable ever to listen to."
Ruth Underwood

On 28 November 2012, Gail Zappa announced the "chance to be part of music business history and become an authorized distributor of a live Zappa record". All she needed was one thousand 'real' fans within the US to stump-up $1K by 28 December so that the world could finally see Roxy – The Movie in time to commemorate the 40th anniversary of the December 1973 concerts.

Contributors/licensees would be able replicate the official product – this here introductory soundtrack/prequel CD – to sell or gift to whoever, in competition with the Zappa Family Trust.

The deadline was extended, and "enthusiastic Zappa fans throughout the known universe without a US passport" were then also allowed to participate.

Gail would later declare that "nobody voted for Roxy By Proxy" and, within days of the few contributors/distributors receiving their CDMasters, the ZFT started distributing production copies of Roxy By Proxy.

Total folly. But a great album!

Dance Me This
2015

FZ

Official Release #100

Originally Released: June 21, 2015

Recording data: 1993 at UMRK (LA)

Producer: FZ

Engineers: David Dondorf, Spencer Chrislu

Tracks:
Dance Me This (2:01)
Pachuco Gavotte (3:27)
Wolf Harbor (8:02)
Wolf Harbor II (6:53)
Wolf Harbor III (6:09)
Wolf Harbor IV (3:38)
Wolf Harbor V (3:09)
Goat Polo (3:04)
Rykoniki (1:59)
Piano (7:09)
Calculus (4:49)

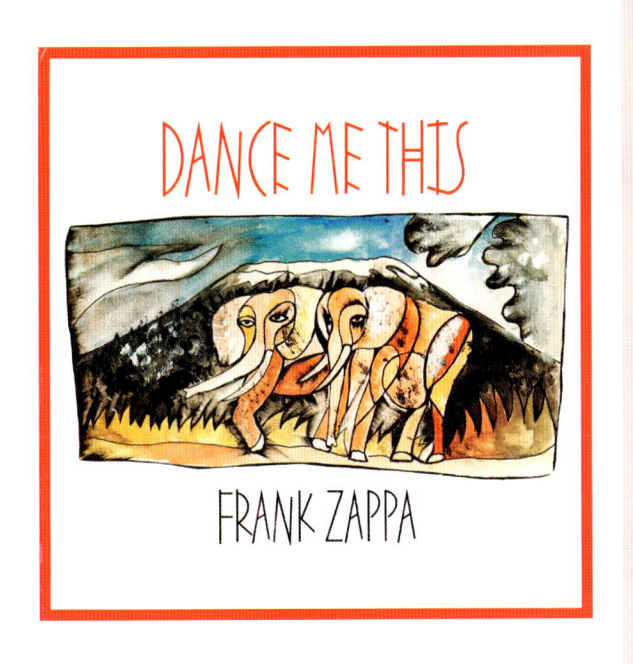

"Frank approached music the way a sculptor tackles a piece of stone. He'd chisel away until it all made sense. This is what he did here. He had compositions which went back a decade or so, and they suddenly came into focus in the context of this album. He would take a small section of notes and work at this – chisel away – until he was satisfied."
Todd Yvega

It was almost as if the ZFT issued Congress ..., Understanding America and the soundtrack albums just to ensure that this – one of four albums Zappa completed in his final year – was the one hundredth official release. That so very few people had actually heard it since its creation all those years ago made it extra special.

Always touted as a Synclavier album designed to be used by modern dance groups, it was a surprise to hear Zappa on guitar on the title track.

Aside from Yvega's 'algorithm & Synclavier asistancy', the only other folk featured (albeit in sampled form) are three Tuvan throat singers: two members of the music group Huun-Huur-Tu plus the late Great Kongar-ōl Ondar.

Following Food Gathering In Post-Industrial America, Wolf Harbor again highlights Zappa's concerns about pollution while Goat Polo references a particularly barbaric Afghan sport.

Now fans only awaited the arrival of Roxy – The Movie.

Frank Zappa: 200 Motels – The Suites   2015

Los Angeles Philharmonic / Los Angeles Master Chorale

Official Release #101

Originally Released: November 20, 2015

Recording data: October 23, 2013 at Walt Disney Concert Hall (LA)

Producers: Frank Filipetti, Gail Zappa

Engineers: Frank Filipetti, Mark Linett, Stacey Hempel, Jeremy Hinskton, David Schwerkolt, Fred Vogler, Richard Landers

Tracks:
Overture (2:17)
Went On The Road (1:41)
Centerville (2:24)
This Town Is A Sealed Tuna Sandwich (10:15)
The Restaurant Scene (4:23)
Touring Can Make You Crazy (2:06)
What's The Name Of Your Group? (11:46)
Can I Help You With This Dummy? (2:33)
The Pleated Gazelle (21:00)
I'm Stealing The Room (13:44)
Shove It Right In (7:26)
Penis Dimension (9:58)
Finale: Strictly Genteel (11:14)

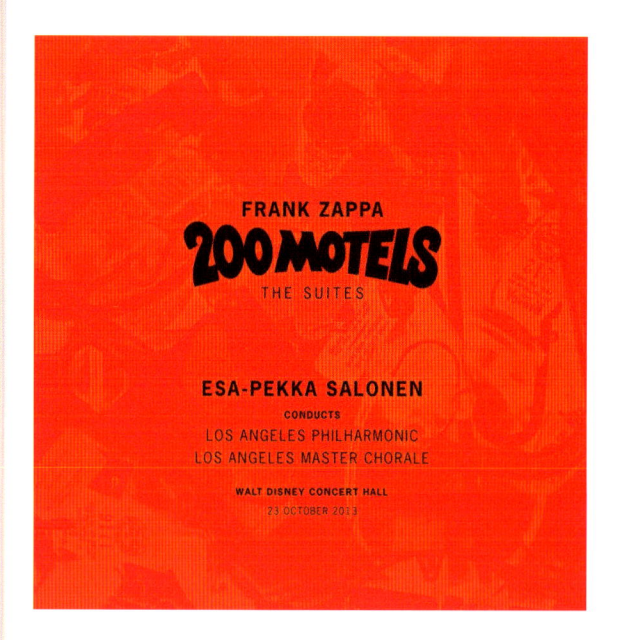

"This marks the 101st Frank Zappa album release and the last record Gail creatively worked on, as well. It was an incredibly important project for her and a real labour of love to see it through to completion. It was an amazing night of music – the performances were extraordinary and the maestro Esa-Pekka Salonen was phenomenal. This is an especially emotional release for my family and I know both Gail and Frank are smiling down with pride at this record. Enjoy!"
Ahmet Zappa

We can all argue about the inclusion (and order) of certain items in the first 100 albums of the Official Discography, but they all had some direct input by FZ. 200 Motels – The Suites however – as co-producer Frank Filipetti states in his liner notes – is entirely "as envisioned by Gail Zappa and [former ScoreMeister] Kurt Morgan".

As well as Ian Underwood (keyboard 1/electric alto sax) and Scott Thunes (electric bass), the album also features Lou Anne Neill.

Neill, who has been the Los Angeles Philharmonic's principal harpist since 1983, was a part of the Abnuceals Emuukha Electric Symphony Orchestra that can be heard on Orchestral Favorites and QuAUDIOPHILIAc, and also contributed to Zoot Allures, Zappa In New York and Tinseltown Rebellion.

Gail, who oversaw this production and the one by the BBC Concert Orchestra/Southbank Sinfonia at London's Festival Hall six days later, passed away the month before the album's release.

Roxy – The Movie (Soundtrack)
2015

FZ

Official Release #102

Originally Released: October 31, 2015

Recording data: December 08-10, 1973 at The Roxy (LA)

Producer: FZ

Engineer: Kerry McNabb

Tracks:
Something Terrible Has Happened … (1:19)
Cosmik Debris (9:54)
Penguin In Bondage (8:22)
T'Mershi Duween (1:56)
The Dog Breath Variations-Uncle Meat (4:14)
RDNZL (4:51)
Echidna's Arf (Of You) (3:54)
Don't You Ever Wash That Thing (7:02)
Cheepnis – Percussion (4:08)
Cheepnis (5:40)
Be-Bop Tango (Of The Old Jazzman's Church) (17:32)

'We worked all the time and it was a happy band. When Napoleon Murphy Brock joined, it was an interesting thing. Napi almost instantaneously knew what Frank wanted. It took me a long time to figure this out, but Napi walked in and he got it! He understood exactly what to do to make Frank smile. Chester on the other hand, when he auditioned, I said, 'He'll never get this gig, because he's too grumpy. He never smiles!' But Frank likes diversity, that's what he wants to do. It was weird putting me in the band; because I was a little straight-laced, black-suit, thin black tie, white shirt-wearing jazz player. Now why would I be in the band? He just loved that kind of dichotomy: something doesn't quite work together and you just see what comes out. It's an interesting way to make music and live life!"
George Duke

The DVD came with this abridged soundtrack CD.

Having released … By Proxy the previous year, it is surprising to see songs duplicated here – but not Village Of The Sun, meaning that Echidna's comes in with a jolt, bereft of its traditional joyous intro/segue. The Proxy rendition of Village is though inferior without the overdubs present on the Elsewhere album, which may explain its celluloid exclusion.

The Roxy footage of Montana and Dupree's Paradise shown before ZPZ concerts in 2006 are also omitted from the movie, but never mind: this is one of Zappa's finest ensembles and such quibbles pale into insignificance given the forty year wait.

Cosmik Debris was still slower than the studio version laid down several months previous, but this band was adept at tempo changes.

Many were surprised by drummer Ralph Humphrey's contribution after Chester Thompson was chosen to join Genesis on the strength of these shows.

Road Tapes, Venue #3
2016

FZ

Official Release #103

Originally Released: May 27, 2016

Recording data: July 05, 1970 at Tyrone Guthrie Theater, Minneapolis (MN)

Producers: FZ, Ahmet Zappa, Joe Travers

Engineer: Bruce Margolis

Tracks:
Tyrone Start The Tape … (1:59)
King Kong (3:37)
Wonderful Wino (4:47)
Concentration Moon (2:34)
Mom & Dad (3:25)
The Air (3:46)
Dog Breath (2:01)
Mother People (2:06)
You Didn't Try To Call Me (4:10)
Agon – Interlude (0:36)
Call Any Vegetable (7:59)
King Kong-Igor's Boogie (20:25)
It Can't Happen Here (3:05)
Sharleena (4:59)
The 23rd "Mondellos" (3:13)
Justine (1:46)
Pound For A Brown (5:07)
Sleeping In A Jar (3:37)
Sharleena (5:49)
"A Piece Of Contemporary Music" (7:03)
The Return Of The Hunchback Duke (including: Little House I Used To Live In, Holiday In Berlin) (10:00)
Cruising For Burgers (3:44)
Let's Make The Water Turn Black (1:42)
Harry, You're A Beast (1:29)
Oh No-Orange County Lumber Truck (11:01)
Call Any Vegetable (11:29)
Mondello's Revenge (1:46)
The Clap (Chunga's Revenge) (13:01)

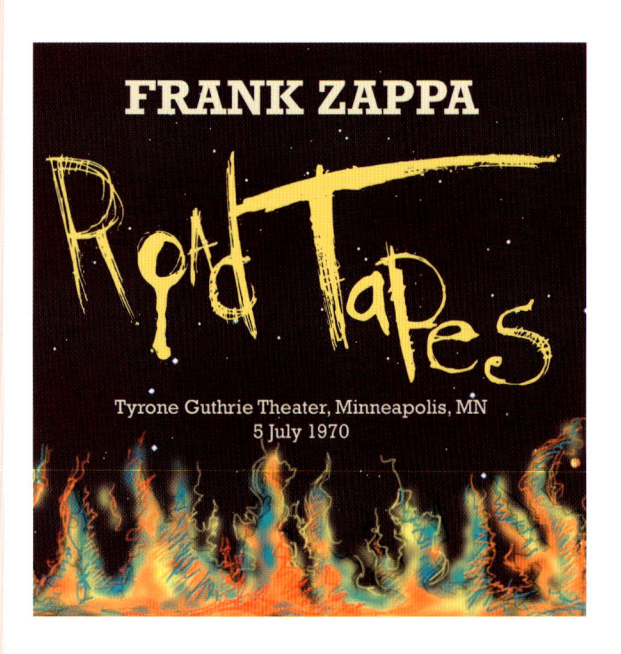

> "They've both been mistaken for Larry Mondello … it used to be Corky the fat little kid that took care of Lassie between Jeff and Timmy. At every concert for six years one of them has been mistaken for that kid on Leave It To Beaver. Their real names are Mark Volman and Howie Kaylan."
>
> *Frank Zappa*

For those reared on the original Flo & Eddie-era albums, this is a bit of an eye opener in that their parts are more constricted, allowing the musicians to fly much more. This was before Jeff Simmons quit and the groupie routines became the norm; hearing the pair sing many of the original Mothers' songs is a real treat – especially the with-words version of Holiday In Berlin.

Like Happy Together on the Fillmore East album, Justine is a song previously performed by Volman and Kaylan (né Kaplan) – but with prototype Turtles, The Crossfires, in 1963.

The Nancy & Mary Music on the Chunga's Revenge album was pieced together from parts of the performances of King Kong/Igor's Boogie and The Clap (Chunga's Revenge), presented here in their lovely fullness.

Like Carnegie Hall before it, this album is culled from two shows recorded on the same day, so some tracks are duplicated.

The Crux Of The Biscuit
2016

FZ

Official Release #104

Originally Released: July 15, 2016

Recording data: May 24, 1972 to June 24, 1973 at Paramount Studios (LA), Electric Lady Studios (NYC), Bolic Sound (Inglewood), GTK (Australia) and Hordern Pavilion (Sydney)

Producers: FZ, Gail Zappa, Joe Travers

Engineers: Barry Keene, Kerry McNabb, Dave Whitman, Steve Desper, Bob Ludwig, Craig Parker Adams, et al.

Tracks:
Cosmik Debris (4:21)
Uncle Remus (Mix Outtake) (3:59)
Down In De Dew (Alternate Mix) (3:16)
Apostrophe' (Mix Outtake) (9:07)
The Story Of "Don't Eat The Yellow Snow/St. Alphonzo's Pancake Breakfast" (3:25)
Don't Eat The Yellow Snow/St. Alphonzo's Pancake Breakfast (Live) (19:26)
Excentrifugal Forz (Mix Outtake) (1:34)
Energy Frontier (Take 4) (3:04)
Energy Frontier (Take 6 with Overdubs) (4:15)
Energy Frontier (Bridge) (8:23)
Cosmik Debris (Basic Tracks – Take 3) (5:11)
Don't Eat The Yellow Snow (Basic Tracks – Alternate Take) (2:12)
Nanook Rubs It (Basic Tracks – Outtake) (0:42)
Nanook Rubs It (Session Outtake) (0:48)
Frank's Last Words … (0:16)

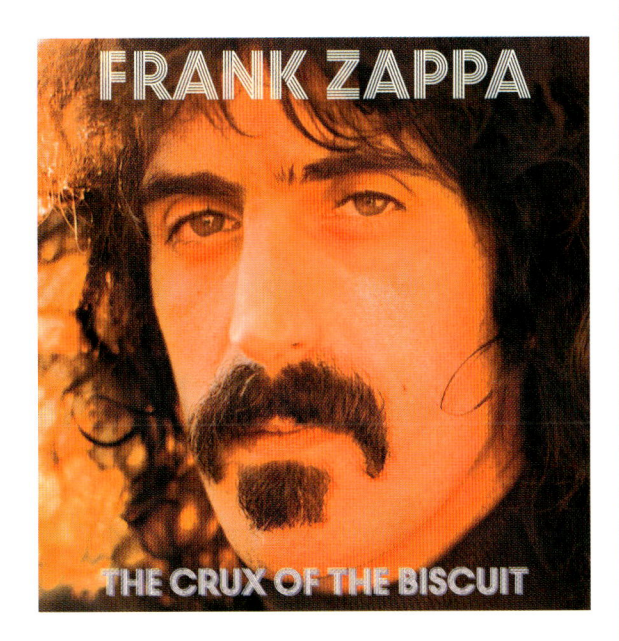

"Whilst in the USA I played a session with Frank Zappa and Jim Gordon that ended up on Frank's album Apostrophe. We had met before and he suggested that it might be fun to work together. For that session he originally wanted me to use a cello on the track, but as my instrument was back in London he hired one from a company in New York. It was so bad that I couldn't use it. That's when he suggested doing something with me playing my EB 3 bass and the track 'Apostrophe' came out of that."

Jack Bruce

This belated 4tieth anniversary of Apostrophe audio documentary features side one of that album as originally envisaged by Zappa, a live performance from Sydney '73 (recorded the day before Australian Yellow Snow on the One Shot Deal album), and various iterations of the piece initially titled Energy Frontier that Zappa split, edited and released as Apostrophe and Down In De Dew during his lifetime.

All of the above, plus the stop/starts of Nanook, mean this collection of alternate mixes and studio outtakes is clearly not an album for newbies. Even the cover photo used here was ditched by Zappa!

A mystery flautist can be heard on takes 4 and 6 of Energy Frontier, but acoustic bass player Dave Parlato says, "I don't recall a flute live when we recorded."

Also includes excellent sleeve notes by the semantic scrutinizer, Simon Prentis, who also wrote the liners for the Rykodisc Läther CD.

Frank Zappa For President 2016

FZ

Official Release #105

Originally Released: *July 15, 2016*

Recording data: *November 18, 1966 to 1993 at T.T.G. Studios (LA), UMRK (LA) and Nassau Coliseum, Uniondale (NY)*

Producers: *FZ, Tom Wilson, Ahmet Zappa, Joe Travers*

Engineers: *Ami Hadani, Dick Kunc, Mark Pinske, Bob Stone, Spencer Chrislu*

Tracks:
Overture To "Uncle Sam" (15:16)
Brown Shoes Don't Make It (Remix) (7:27)
Amnerika (Vocal Version) (3:10)
"If I Was President …" (2:34)
When The Lie's So Big (3:38)
Medieval Ensemble (6:31)
America The Beautiful (3:27)

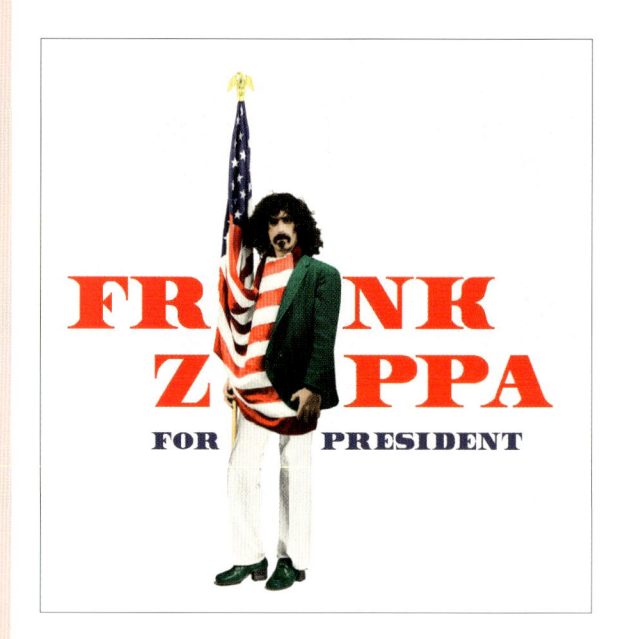

"You haven't really heard Amnerika until you've heard me sing it. We created it together. I still have the tape, and it's funny: I'm laughing, and he's laughing – because he's putting this melody to those words: 'You're crazy!' And he's going, 'Yeah. Isn't it cool?'"

Napoleon Murphy Brock

Issued in the run-up to the 2016 United States presidential election that saw Ahmet Zappa (now the CEO of Zappa Records and executor of the ZFT) firmly behind the Democratic Party's nominee, Hillary Clinton (whose husband FZ used to refer to as 'Slick Willie').

This Joe Travers compilation could be seen as a sort of companion piece to the Zappa assembled Understanding America, though it is comprised of largely unreleased performances – mostly on the Synclavier.

Uncle Sam and Medieval Ensemble are totally realised on 'La Machine', while Napoleon Murphy Brock sings Amnerika and Zappa tells us what he would do if he was President over a Synthesized backing.

When The Lie's So Big and America The Beautiful (the final song Zappa would perform live on US soil) come from the Broadway The Hard Way tour, the latter having been previously issued on 2008's download-only The Frank Zappa AAAFRNAAA Birthday Bundle.

ZAPPAtite – Frank Zappa's Tastiest Tracks   2016

FZ

Official Release #106

Originally Released: September 23, 2016

Recording data: March 09, 1966 to 1986 at T.T.G. Studios (LA), Sunset Sound (LA), Whitney Studios (Glendale), The Record Plant (LA), Bolic Sound (Inglewood), Paramount Studios (LA), The Palladium (NYC), Hammersmith Odeon (London), The Village Recorders (LA), UMRK (LA), Twickenham Film Studio (London) and elsewhere

Producers: FZ, Tom Wilson

Engineers: Val Valentin, Dick Kunc, Brian Ingoldsby, Bruce Margolis, Barry Keene, Terry Dunavan, Kerry McNabb, Davey Moire, FZ, Joe Chiccarelli, Mark Pinske, Bob Stone, Bob Rice, et al.

Tracks:
I'm The Slime (3:35)
Dirty Love (2:58)
Dancing Fool (3:43)
Trouble Every Day (5:50)
Peaches En Regalia (3:38)
Tell Me You Love Me (2:33)
Bobby Brown Goes Down (2:49)
You Are What You Is (4:23)
Valley Girl (4:50)
Joe's Garage (6:09)
Cosmik Debris (4:14)
Sofa No. 1 (2:39)
Don't Eat The Yellow Snow (Single Version) (3:35)
Titties & Beer (7:17)
G-Spot Tornado (3:17)
Cocaine Decisions (3:53)
Zoot Allures (4:16)
Strictly Genteel (6:57)

'This isn't a greatest hits album as Frank didn't really have 'hits,' per se, nor is it a 'best of' since that would be an impossibility to fit so much awesome onto one disc. It's a veritable smorgasbord of musicality for the curious and a buffet of favourites for the fans, ZAPPAtite collects a cross section of my favourite songs composed by my dad, that lean more towards the rock side of his expansive repertoire. I hope you're hungry because this meal for your ears rocks!"

Ahmet Zappa

With the Zappa family now rent in twain, Official Release #102 is (at the time of writing) the last posthumous album on which thanks are expressed to Moon and Dweezil – with the latter publicly confirming he now has nothing to do with the releases.

At least Ahmet saw fit to include arguably his father's most celebrated songs: Peaches En Regalia (from an album dedicated to Dweezil) and Valley Girl (featuring Moon).

This album is divided into three courses – Appetizers, Entrees and Desserts – but only the single version of Don't Eat The Yellow Snow might cause existing fans to salivate (though even this had previously been included on the Rykodisc compilation, Strictly Commercial).

Within weeks of ZAPPAtite's release, Diva launched her own 'Zappa tights' – a collection of ladies' leggings with images of her father, including one pair employing artwork from We're Only In It For The Money.

What larks, Pip!

Meat Light – The Uncle Meat Project/Object   2016

FZ

Official Release #107

Originally Released: November 04, 2016

Recording data: 1967 to February 14, 1969 at Apostolic Studios (NYC), Royal Albert Hall (London), Falkoner Teatret (Copenhagen), Gulfstream Park, Hallandale (FL), Whisky à Go-Go (LA), Sunset Sound (LA) and McMillin Theater, Columbia University (NYC)

Producers: FZ, Gail Zappa, Joe Travers

Engineers: Dick Kunc, Jerry Hansen, Wally Heider

Tracks:

Uncle Meat: Main Title Theme (1:56)
The Voice Of Cheese (0:26)
Nine Types Of Industrial Pollution (6:02)
Zolar Czackl (0:54)
Dog Breath, In The Year Of The Plague (3:59)
The Legend Of The Golden Arches (3:27)
Louie Louie (At the Royal Albert Hall in London) (2:18)
The Dog Breath Variations (1:50)
Sleeping In A Jar (0:50)
Our Bizarre Relationship (1:05)
The Uncle Meat Variations (4:46)
Electric Aunt Jemima (1:46)
Prelude To King Kong (3:39)
God Bless America (Live at the Whisky A Go Go) (1:10)
A Pound For A Brown On The Bus (1:29)
Ian Underwood Whips It Out (Live in Copenhagen) (5:09)
Mr. Green Genes (3:13)
We Can Shoot You (2:03)
"If We'd All Been Living In California …" (1:14)
The Air (2:57)
Project X (4:49)
Cruising For Burgers (2:18)
King Kong (as played by the Mothers in a studio) (0:51)
King Kong (its magnificence as interpreted by Dom DeWild) (1:19)
King Kong (as Motorhead explains it) (1:45)
King Kong (the Gardner Varieties) (6:14)
King Kong (as played by 3 deranged Good Humor Trucks) (0:37)
King Kong (live on a flat bed diesel in the middle of a race track at a Miami Pop Festival … the Underwood ramifications) (7:24)
Dog Breath, In The Year Of The Plague (2:55)
The Legend Of The Golden Arches (3:16)
The Voice Of Cheese (0:26)
Whiskey Wah (1:34)
Nine Types Of Industrial Pollution (6:03)
Louie Louie (Live at the Royal Albert Hall in London) (2:27)
The Dog Breath Variations (1:51)
Shoot You Percussion Item (1:28)
The Whip (5:03)
The Uncle Meat Variations (4:47)
King Kong (10:46)
Project X Minus .5 (1:47)
A Pound For A Brown On The Bus (1:29)
Electric Aunt Jemima (1:46)
Prelude To King Kong (3:39)
God Bless America (Live at the Whiskey A Go Go) (1:11)
Sleeping In A Jar (0:51)
Cops & Buns (5:56)
Zolar Czakl (0:47)

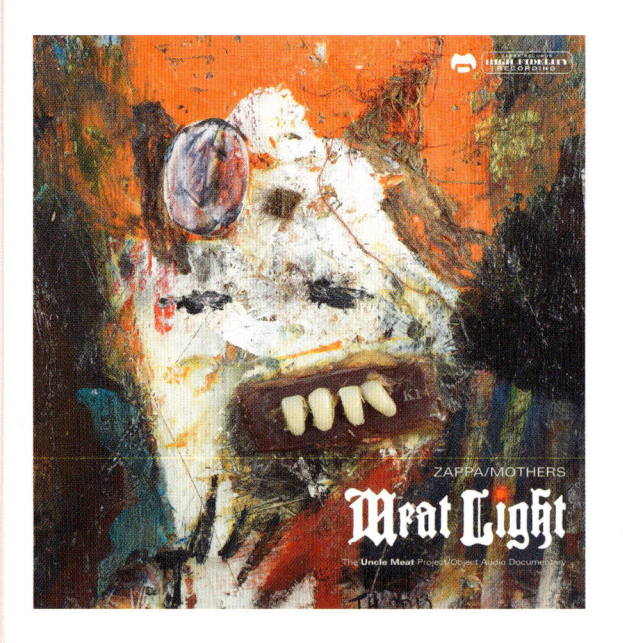

> "When we did Uncle Meat, we had a 12-track Scully recorder, a humungous piece of furniture as big as my fireplace. What we tried to do was play all the individual lines in this orchestral score. We had two wind players, Ian Underwood and Bunk Gardner, who could read. So they would be playing those parts two at a time and we'd be stacking them and bouncing them together. It took days just to do a few seconds of music that way. But it was an experiment that needed to be done."
>
> Frank Zappa

There are many delights to be found on this expanded edition of the Uncle Meat album, but a longer edit of Cops & Buns (a field recording of an early morning police visit to Apostolic that appeared on The Lost Episodes) is not one of them. The exclusion of the film excerpts most certainly is, however!

What we have here is Zappa's original 1969 vinyl mix and also his original sequence, plus a bunch of stuff from the Vault – which is where the real meat is for fans who were around when the album was first issued nearly 50 years earlier (though Meat Light is referred to as a fortieth anniversary release).

In Echo Pie, Zappa proposes The Mothers tour without him if they want to make extra money.

The original sequence contains some nice surprises too, like Whiskey Wah and The Whip.

Includes liner notes written by Ian Underwood.

We Can Not Shoot You (1:16)
Mr. Green Genes (3:13)
"PooYeahrg" (0:32)
Uncle Meat: Main Title Theme (1:27)
Our Bizarre Relationship (1:10)
"Later We Can Shoot You" (0:15)
"If We'd All Been Living In California …" (1:19)
'Ere Ian Whips It/JCB Spits It/Motorhead Rips It (2:30)
The Air (2:58)
Project X .5 (2:38)
Cruising For Burgers (2:23)
"A Bunch Of Stuff" (1:40)
Dog Breath (Single Version, Stereo) (2:55)
Tango (0:24)

Chicago '78
2016

FZ

Official Release #108

Originally Released: November 04, 2016

Recording data: September 29, 1978 at Uptown Theatre (Chicago)

Producers: FZ, Gail Zappa, Joe Travers

Engineers: Claus Weideman, Davy Moire, Craig Parker Adams, Bob Ludwig

Tracks:
Chicago Walk-On (1:20)
Twenty-One (8:26)
Dancin' Fool (3:29)
Honey, Don't You Want A Man Like Me? (4:21)
Keep It Greasy (3:41)
Village Of The Sun (9:15)
The Meek Shall Inherit Nothing (3:29)
Bamboozled By Love (8:32)
Sy Borg (4:36)
Little House I Used To Live In (9:38)
Paroxysmal Splendor (includes: FZ & Pig/I'm A Beautiful Guy/Crew Slut) (7:14)
Yo' Mama (12:28)
Magic Fingers (2:37)
Don't Eat The Yellow Snow (18:36)
Strictly Genteel (8:25)
Black Napkins (8:01)

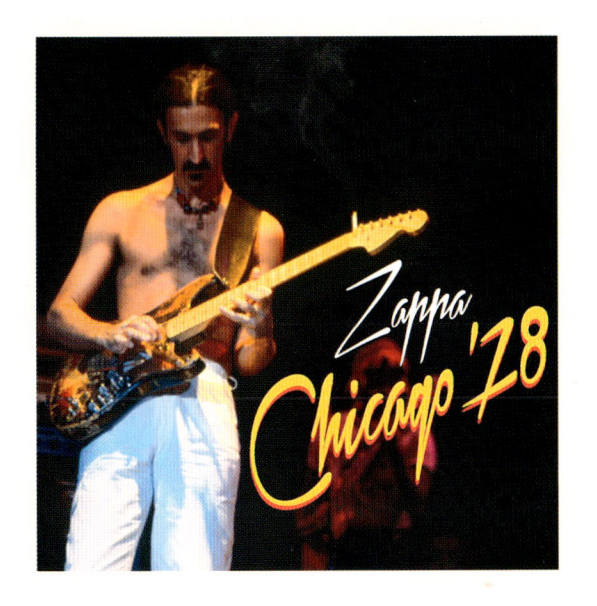

"I flew into LA and we were rehearsing at the old Desilu studios. It was Denny, Tommy, Ed, Peter Wolf ... Frank was looking to replace Adrian Belew, Terry Bozzio and Patrick O'Hearn. He gave me a big bear hug and said, 'Glad you made it. Help me with these guys here. I'll get to you later.' I was there and I pretty much didn't leave. That was on a Tuesday and on Thursday he gave me 20 seconds on my audition and goes, "Okay, let's get back to work.' On Friday, he hired me and Vinnie and Artie Barrow."

Ike Willis

Just over a fortnight after this gig, Willis would be temporarily retired and O'Hearn brought back to bolster the new line-up. Despite its ersatz grey area release cover, the music within is nevertheless tip-top from an excellent group of players. Willis is in great form, his performance on Village Of The Sun and its extended outro being a particular highlight.

The opening vamp (in 21/8, a vehicle for Zappa to solo over) appears on the studio version of Keep It Greasy and in many 1988 versions of Marque-son's Chicken (one such being released as Trance-Fusion). Colaiuta cuts loose at the end of Little House before the medley that is Paroxysmal Splendor, which includes references to Greggery Peccary and Cherry Pink And Apple Blossom White, as well as the pieces listed.

What is interesting is that only seven of the tracks performed were commercially available at the time of the concert.

The String Quartet (3:06)
Electric Aunt Jemima (Mix Outtake) (1:40)
Exercise 4 Variant (4:32)
Zolar Czackl (Mix Outtake) (0:45)
"More Beer!" (0:17)
Green Genes Snoop (1:13)
Mr. Green Genes (Mix Outtake) (3:11)
Echo Pie (2:16)

1/4 Tone Unit (1:06)
Sakuji's March (0:35)
No. 4 (1:52)
Prelude To King Kong (Extended Version) (5:24)
Blood Unit (1:22)
My Guitar (Proto I-Excerpt) (2:12)
Nine Types Of Industrial Pollution (Guitar track, normal speed) (9:53)
Uncle Meat (Live at Columbia University 1969) (4:44)
Dog Breath (Instrumental) (2:50)
The Dog Breath Variations (Mix Outtake) (1:46)

Little Dots
2016

FZ

Official Release #109

Originally Released: November 04, 2016

Recording data: November 04 to December 02, 1972 at Park Center Arena, Charlotte (NC), Township Auditorium, Columbia (SC), DAR Constitution Hall, Washington (DC), Cowtown Ballroom, Kansas City (MO)

Producers: FZ, Ahmet Zappa, Joe Travers

Engineers: FZ, Barry Keene, Michael Braunstein, Kerry McNabb

Tracks:
Cosmik Debris (5:40)
Little Dots (Part 1) (11:00)
Little Dots (Part 2) (12:59)
Rollo (includes: Rollo/The Rollo Interior Area/Rollo Goes Out) (9:04)
Kansas City Shuffle (6:46)
"Columbia, S.C." (Part 1) (8:58)
"Columbia, S.C." (Part 2) (16:40)

(10-30-77 Show)
10-30-77 Show Start (1:40) / Stink-Foot (7:45) / The Poodle Lecture (5:10) / Dirty Love (2:32) / Peaches En Regalia (2:40) / The Torture Never Stops (12:53) / Tryin' To Grow A Chin (3:32) / City Of Tiny Lites (7:36) / Pound For A Brown (10:03) / I Have Been In You (8:35) / Dancin' Fool (World Premiere) (4:50) / Jewish Princess (Prototype) (4:41) / King Kong (8:45) / Terry's Solo #5 (5:07) / Disco Boy (4:01) / Envelopes (2:19) / A Halloween Treat with Thomas Nordegg (6:17) / Lather (3:47) / Wild Love (25:19) / Titties 'N' Beer (7:01) / Audience Participation #5 (8:28) / The Black Page #2 (2:59) / Jones Crusher (2:53) / Broken Hearts Are For Assholes (3:52) / Punky's Whips (12:36) / Encore Rap (1:11) / Dinah-Moe Humm (6:06) / Camarillo Brillo (3:27) / Muffin Man (5:18) / San Ber'dino (6:20)

(10-31-77 Show)
Halloween 1977 Show Start/Introductions (3:11) / Peaches En Regalia (2:42) / The Torture Never Stops (13:54) / Tryin' To Grow A Chin (3:35) / City Of Tiny Lites (8:17) / Pound For A Brown (13:40) / The Demise Of The Imported Rubber Goods Mask (8:33) / Bobby Brown Goes Down (3:49) / Conehead (Instrumental) (8:21) / Flakes (3:04) / Big Leg Emma (1:58) / Envelopes (2:25) / Terry's Halloween Solo (4:38) / Disco Boy (3:55) / Lather (3:58) / Wild Love (30:11) / Titties 'N' Beer (7:24) / Halloween Audience Participation (7:04) / The Black Page #2 (2:55) / Jones Crusher (2:58) / Broken Hearts Are For Assholes (3:52) / Punky's Whips (11:23) / Halloween Encore Audience I (2:07) / Dinah-Moe Humm (6:41) / Camarillo Brillo (3:24) / Muffin Man (5:21) / San Ber'dino (5:01) / Black Napkins (9:19)

"Right before the band went on stage, Jim Gordon pulled Gary Barone into a bathroom off stage and they had a toot or two. Blammo, the door comes down and the Columbia S.C. Police Department busts Gary and Jim right before the band goes on. Here is Jimmie and Gary handcuffed being led past Frank, guitar around his neck as he heads for the stage. Naturally, he shit. No the cops wouldn't wait. Sure they could do without a trumpet, but the drummer!"

Jock Ellis

And so Maury Baker, who was the support act's drummer, sat in with the Petit Wazoo in Gordon's temporary absence for the one gig from which the last two 'invented songs' are taken.

Who knew?

We had to wait quite awhile for this, the sequel to Imaginary Diseases, which Gail had confirmed was in the can many years beforehand – indeed, Zappa himself had played the R&B version of Cosmik Debris on a radio show in the mid-1970s.

The title track had been well known to tape traders, and bassist Dave Parlato deserves a special mention for 'grinding it out'.

Rather than being just the bit tagged onto the end of the Yellow Snow suite, Rollo here is a complete song with its own daft lyrics.

Another piece by this band, Portland Improvisation, was released on Record Store Day the following year on a 10" clear vinyl single (together with Rollo).

Halloween 77 (Box Set)
2017

FZ

Official Release #110

Originally Released: October 20, 2017

Recording data: October 28-31, 1977 at The Palladium (NYC)

Producers: FZ, Ahmet Zappa, Joe Travers

Engineers: Kerry McNabb, Craig Parker Adams, Nicole Lexi Davis

Tracks:

(10-28-77 Show 1)
10-28-77 Show 1 Start/Introductions (3:28) / Peaches En Regalia (2:42) / The Torture Never Stops (13:05) / Tryin' To Grow A Chin (3:37) / City Of Tiny Lites (6:04) / Pound For A Brown (8:05) / Bobby Brown Goes Down (4:33) / Conehead (Instrumental) (9:19) / Flakes (4:03) / Big Leg Emma (1:47) / Envelopes (2:29) / Terry's Solo #1 (4:42) / Disco Boy (3:53) / Lather (3:36) / Wild Love (24:05) / Titties 'N' Beer (7:16) / Audience Participation #1 (0:48) / The Black Page #2 (3:02) / Jones Crusher (2:48) / Broken Hearts Are For Assholes (3:52) / Punky's Whips (9:43) / Encore Audience #1 (1:21) / Dinah-Moe Humm (4:55) / Camarillo Brillo (3:35) / Muffin Man (4:36)

(10-28-77 Show 2)
10-28-77 Show 2 Start/Introductions (3:13) / Peaches En Regalia (2:42) / The Torture Never Stops (12:33) / Tryin' To Grow A Chin (3:37) / City Of Tiny Lites (8:00) / Pound For A Brown (9:19) / Bobby Brown Goes Down (5:36) / Conehead (Instrumental) (9:18) / Flakes (4:10) / Big Leg Emma (1:48) / Envelopes (2:33) / Terry's Solo #2 (4:17) / Disco Boy (3:54) / Lather (3:42) / Wild Love (24:57) / Titties 'N' Beer (7:50) / Audience Participation #2 (2:37) / The Black Page #2 (3:14) / Jones Crusher (2:58) / Broken Hearts Are For Assholes (3:54) / Punky's Whips (9:51) / Encore Audience #2 (2:13) / Dinah-Moe Humm (4:01) / Camarillo Brillo (3:36) / Muffin Man (6:20)

(10-29-77 Show 1)
10-29-77 Show 1 Start/Introductions (4:06) / Peaches En Regalia (2:42) / The Torture Never Stops (12:59) / Tryin' To Grow A Chin (3:34) / City Of Tiny Lites (7:15) / Pound For A Brown (8:26) / Bobby Brown Goes Down (6:06) / Conehead (Instrumental) (5:50) / Flakes (3:53) / Big Leg Emma (1:52) / Envelopes (2:42) / Terry's Solo #3 (3:51) / Disco Boy (3:57) / Lather (3:40) / Wild Love (22:51) / Titties 'N' Beer (6:01) / Audience Participation #3 (2:42) / The Black Page #2 (3:05) / Jones Crusher (2:53) / Broken Hearts Are For Assholes (3:50) / Punky's Whips (9:18) / Encore Audience #3 (1:46) / Dinah-Moe Humm (5:12) / Camarillo Brillo (3:29) / Muffin Man (5:09)

(10-29-77 Show 2)
10-29-77 Show 2 Start/Introductions (4:21) / Peaches En Regalia (2:42) / The Torture Never Stops (11:30) / Tryin' To Grow A Chin (3:36) / City Of Tiny Lites (7:01) / Pound For A Brown (9:05) / Bobby Brown Goes Down (9:12) / Conehead (Instrumental) (6:29) / Flakes (3:28) / Big Leg Emma (1:49) / Envelopes (2:52) / Terry's Solo #4 (4:07) / Disco Boy (3:54) / Lather (3:56) / Wild Love (27:33) / Titties 'N' Beer (8:12) / Audience Participation #4 (5:02) / The Black Page #2 (2:57) / Jones Crusher (2:49) / Broken Hearts Are For Assholes (3:48) / Punky's Whips (9:36) / Encore Audience #4 (2:23) / Dinah-Moe Humm (6:19) / Camarillo Brillo (3:30) / Muffin Man (6:02)

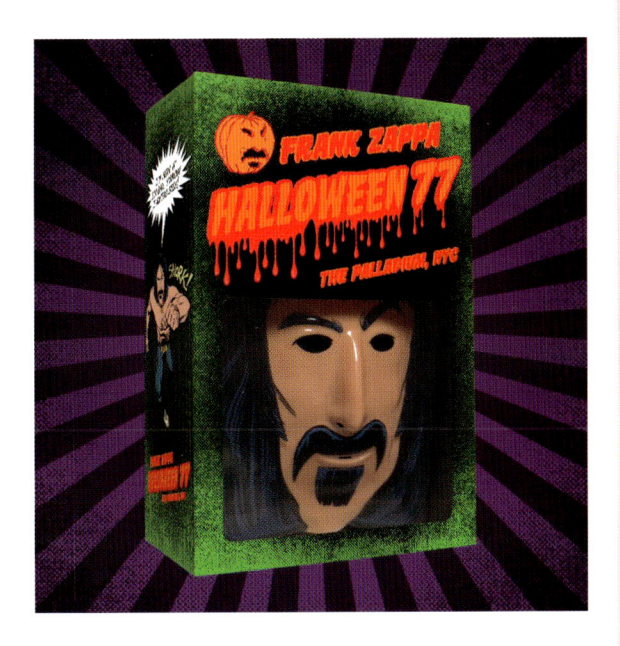

"The toughest chart I ever had to play with Frank was the straight version of 'The Black Page'. It's mainly difficult for the drum chair, but it's a tough chart all around. We actually worked up two arrangements of it: the straight one and the disco arrangement, which was hilarious. Terry would slip into sort of a Latin hustle beat, and I did the ubiquitous bass octaves that had been made popular by God knows how many groups of the era. We'd hold a dance contest onstage; some of that is in the concert film, Baby Snakes. He would bring up members of the audience and have them dance to this arrangement. Peter Wolf and Tommy Mars would play the keyboard chart as written, but Adrian Belew, Terry and I would slip back and forth between the disco and straight arrangements, causing these hiccups."

Patrick O'Hearn

It might seem that listening to six consecutive shows with much the same set list could get boring. But with the different in-between chat, the Pound For A Brown solos (that see O'Hearn occasionally quoting rock classics and In A Silent Way), the extended iterations of Wild Love (wherein Zappa allows Adrian Belew to fly free while he plays rhythm guitar) and Frank's always epic solos during The Torture Never Stops, there's just about enough variation to keep hard-core fans entertained.

This came loaded onto a 'Zappa's Oh Punky' fun size candy bar-shaped USB drive in 24-bit WAV audio (containing one faulty track), together with a cheesy Zappa Halloween mask and costume.

It's most certainly overkill, but in a good way.

It's unlikely Frank would have ever issued this material like this: instead he chose to condense it into Sheik Yerbouti, Baby Snakes, YCDTOSA 6 and Trance-Fusion (Bowling On Charen).

Halloween 77 (3 CD)
2017

FZ

Official Release #110K

Originally Released: October 20, 2017

Recording data: October 30 & 31, 1977 at The Palladium (NYC)

Producers: FZ, Ahmet Zappa, Joe Travers

Engineers: Kerry McNabb, Craig Parker Adams, Nicole Lexi Davis

Tracks:
Halloween 1977 Show Start/Introductions (3:11)
Peaches En Regalia (2:42)
The Torture Never Stops (13:54)
Tryin' To Grow A Chin (3:35)
City Of Tiny Lites (8:17)
Pound For A Brown (13:40)
The Demise Of The Imported Rubber Goods Mask (8:33)
Bobby Brown Goes Down (3:49)
Conehead (Instrumental) (8:21)
Flakes (3:04)
Big Leg Emma (1:58)
Envelopes (2:25)
Terry's Halloween Solo (4:38)
Disco Boy (3:55)
Lather (3:58)
Wild Love (30:11)
Titties 'N' Beer (7:24)
Halloween Audience Participation (7:04)
The Black Page #2 (2:55)
Jones Crusher (2:58)
Broken Hearts Are For Assholes (3:52)
Punky's Whips (11:23)
Halloween Encore Audience I (2:07)
Dinah-Moe Humm (6:41)
Camarillo Brillo (3:24)
Muffin Man (5:21)
San Ber'dino (5:01)
Black Napkins (9:19)

Bonus Section:
King Kong (8:17)
A Halloween Treat With Thomas Nordegg (6:15)
Audience Participation #5 (7:46)
The Black Page #2 (2:59)

"Since it is Halloween, the 'Road Mangler', which is the title Phil Kaufman goes by, will look after the costuming for willing band members. And since you are already in a costume of sorts (a paratrooper's jumpsuit bought at an Army/Navy store on Melrose Ave.), you're happy to oblige. As it happens the entire concert is being filmed to be released as a live concert film called Baby Snakes. So when Phil shows up late in the afternoon with your costume, you try to put on a brave face. The costume he's chosen is a WAC uniform which matches your paratrooper jumpsuit and just so happens to fit you perfectly. At some point during the evening's concert you find yourself offstage changing into the WAC uniform. The film crew surrounds you as you don the now-infamous $500,000 Jimi Hendrix strat and step back onto the busy stage in front of 2,000 people and a host of lights and cameras. It's at this precise moment you realize you're wearing a dress."

Adrian Belew

Here we have the whole Halloween show, plus select tracks from the previous night for those on a tight budget – and less patience than those who bought the costume box set.

When Adrian Belew posted on Facebook that he was writing liner notes for this release, he faced a shitstorm for seeming to side with Ahmet – who at the time was publicly at war with his brother. Happily, this didn't deter him from detailing what it was like to work with Frank.

If you're wondering why this is Official Release 110K, it's because the ZFT gave each of the shows a different suffix – with the exception of the 30 October one, which was not originally intended to be made available as a stand-alone download. So the 28 October show #1 has the suffix 'F', while show #2 is 'R'; and the 29 October shows are 'A' and 'N' respectively. Comprendre?

The Roxy Performances
2018

FZ / Mothers

Official Release #111

Originally Released: February 02, 2018

Recording data: December 08, 09, 10 & 12, 1973 at The Roxy (LA) and Bolic Sound (Inglewood)

Producers: FZ, Ahmet Zappa, Joe Travers

Engineers: Kerry McNabb, Jack & The Boys, Bob Hughes, Doug Graves, Bob Stone, Craig Parker Adams, Nicole Lexi Davis

Tracks:

(12-9-73 Show 1) Sunday Show 1 Start (4:59) / Cosmik Debris (11:33) / "We're Makin' A Movie" (3:16) / Pygmy Twylyte (9:08) / The Idiot Bastard Son (2:19) / Cheepnis (3:44) / Hollywood Perverts (1:07) / Penguin In Bondage (5:54) / T'Mershi Duween (1:56) / The Dog Breath Variations (1:44) / Uncle Meat (2:29) / RDNZL (5:14) / Montana (7:49) / Dupree's Paradise (15:25) / Dickie's Such An Asshole (10:29)

(12-9-73 Show 2) Sunday Show 2 Start (4:08) / Inca Roads (8:27) / Village Of The Sun (4:19) / Echidna's Arf (Of You) (4:01) / Don't You Ever Wash That Thing? (13:22) / Slime Intro (0:59) / I'm The Slime (3:34) / Big Swifty (9:01) / Tango #1 Intro (3:50) / Be-Bop Tango (Of The Old Jazzmen's Church) (18:12) / Medley: King Kong-Chunga's Revenge-Son Of Mr. Green Genes (9:46)

(12-10-73 Show 1) Monday Show 1 Start (5:31) / Montana (6:57) / Dupree's Paradise (21:26) / Cosmik Intro (1:05) / Cosmik Debris (8:05) / Bondage Intro (1:52) / Penguin In Bondage (6:54) / T'Mershi Duween (1:52) / The Dog Breath Variations (1:48) / Uncle Meat (2:29) / RDNZL (4:59) / Audience Participation – RDNZL (3:08) / Pygmy Twylyte (4:05) / The Idiot Bastard Son (2:21) / Cheepnis (4:49) / Dickie's Such An Asshole (10:21)

(12-10-73 Show 2) Monday Show 2 Start (5:13) / Penguin In Bondage (6:33) / T'Mershi Duween (1:52) / The Dog Breath Variations (1:46) / Uncle Meat (2:28) / RDNZL (5:11) / Village Of The Sun (4:05) / Echidna's Arf (Of You) (3:54) / Don't You Ever Wash That Thing? (6:56) / Cheepnis – Percussion (4:08) / "I Love Monster Movies" (2:10) / Cheepnis (3:35) / "Turn The Light Off"/Pamela's Intro (3:59) / Pygmy Twylyte (7:23) / The Idiot Bastard Son (2:22) / Tango #2 Intro (2:01) / Be-Bop Tango (Of The Old Jazzmen's Church) (22:08) / Dickie's Such An Asshole (15:39)

(12-10-73 Roxy Rehearsal) Big Swifty – In Rehearsal (2:50) / Village Of The Sun (3:13) / Farther O'Blivion – In Rehearsal (5:34) / Pygmy Twylyte (6:17) / That Arrogant Dick Nixon (2:19)

(12-12-73 Bolic Studios Recording Session) Kung Fu – In Session (4:50) / Kung Fu – with guitar overdub (1:17) / Tuning And Studio Chatter (3:38) / Echidna's Arf (Of You) – In Session (1:22) / Don't Eat The Yellow Snow – In Session (9:49) / Nanook Rubs It – In Session (5:41) / St. Alfonzo's Pancake Breakfast – In Session (2:46) / Father O'Blivion – In Session (2:31) / Rollo (Be-Bop Version) (2:36)

(12-8-73 Sound Check/Film Shoot) Saturday Show Start (2:20) / Pygmy Twylyte – Dummy Up (20:25) / Pygmy Twylyte – Part II (14:25) / Echidna's Arf (Of You) (3:42) / Don't You Ever Wash That Thing? (6:01) / Orgy, Orgy (3:39) / Penguin In Bondage (6:30) / T'Mershi Duween (1:53) / The Dog Breath Variations (1:45) / Uncle Meat-Show End (4:01)

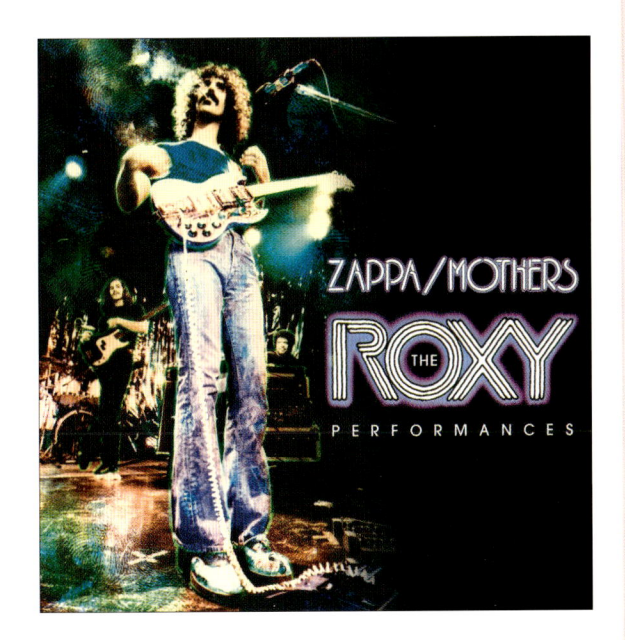

"We wanted to do something special: we've seen all the footage, we know what the nights were like, and it's such an amazing band; I marvel at their ability, their level of excellence and the performances captured those nights. And it's really strange to have lived with the record for so long, and then to hear these alternate versions of tracks you're so familiar with. I'm like conflicted, I don't know which ones I like more, because they were all so good. It just felt like a natural project to do considering I've had people ask me for it."

Ahmet Zappa

As if Roxy & Elsewhere, Roxy By Proxy, Roxy – The Movie (Soundtrack) and selections from the YCDTOSA series weren't enough, hot on the heels of the Halloween 77 box came this: the complete Roxy run of all four public shows, invite-only soundcheck, rehearsal nuggets, plus contemporaneous Bolic Studios session highlights (some of which might have been better suited to The Crux Of The Biscuit, but never mind). And a little more conventionally: seven compact discs, with no doo-dads.

Pamela is former GTO Pamela Des Barres, who eroticises Napoleon Murphy Brock while he sings Pygmy Twylyte.

That Arrogant Dick Nixon is a re-written and overdubbed version of The Idiot Bastard Son, which Frank bottled out of releasing during his lifetime. (Fun fact: Tricky Dicky passed away less than four months after Frank.)

The liner notes include an essay by Jen Jewel Brown, the Australian lady given an honourable mention on FZ:OZ.

Acknowledgements

Mick would like to thank:

Remco Aalhuizen, Morgan Ågren, Carsten Ahrens, Martin Ahrens, Cynthia Albritton, Theo Alers, Daevid Allen, Hans Annellsson, Arf Society & Arf Dossier, Ali N. Askin, Steve Auerbach, Alli Bach, Martin Bahm, Maury Baker, Jörn Bantow, Jan Barfod, Barking Pumpkins Rendsburg, Paul Barnard, Pamela Des Barres, Arthur Barrow, Royse Bassham, Massimo Bassoli, Adrian Belew, Bryan Beller, Petter Berggren, Guy Bickel, Adam Bickerton, Bruce Bickford, Jim & Moni Black, Ingo Bläser, Wolfgang Blaha, Claudia Bock, Rainer von Bock und Polach, Thomas Böhme, Bogus Pomp, Dietmar Bonnen, Mark Bradford, Juliana Brandon, Frank Braukmann, Napoleon Murphy Brock, Tim op het Broek, Arthur Brown, Pete & Sandy Brunelli, Georg Justin Buckesfeld, Pauline Butcher Bird, Guy van Buyten, Robert Froggie Camarena, John Campbell, Bill Carbone, Jason Caren, Paul Carr, Daniel Casanova, Václav Cesák, Scott Chatfield, Mary Jayne & Stephen Chillemi, André Cholmondeley, Valentina Ciardelli, Ted Clifford, Dave Coash, Jim Cohen, Katrina & Dan Cooper, Fried Dähn, Matthias Dankert, Ian Day, Alex Debus, Michel Delville, Thomas Denzel, Joseph Diaz, Jared Terfa Dibaba, Nick Didkovsky, Thomas Dippel, Bob Dobbs, Richard Drakes, George Duke, Christian Eckhardt, Mick Ekers, Robert Elovsson, Håkan Engborg, Sven Eriksson, Annette Ernst, Roy Estrada, Christl Etterer, Peter Feilscher, Jerry Ford, Tom Fowler, Mike Fox, Carl Franzoni, Martial Frenzel, Christian Frerichs, Edgar Froese, Steve Gainsford, Matthew Galaher, Frank Gallius, Gamma & Frankie Gamble, Christopher Garcia, Bunk Gardner, Gary & Jerry, Nigel Gavin, Robin Gelberg, Roland St. Germain, Roddie Gilliard, Philippe Giroux, Jürgen Gispert, Jacopo Giusti, Kerstin & Peter Görs, Luuk de Goede, Sabine & Thomas "Tomgo" Gölz, Frank Goos, Anja Z Gna, Michael Graf, Paul Green, Andrew & Julie Greenaway, Svenja Greier, John Hore Grenell, Stu Grimshaw, Tina Grohowski, Todd Grubbs, Urban Gwerder, Marianne & Beat Gysi, Fred H, Eike & Marina Hagen, Nina Hagen, Achim Haller, Roy & Nick Harper, Thana, Bob & Nate Harris, Norman Hartnett, Hasi Hasslinger, Hellmut Hattler, Warren Haynes, Jürgen Heibutzki, Michael Heinze, Audrey van Hek, Peggy Helwes, Evil Dick Hemmings, Rebekah Heppner, Martin C. Herberg, Martin Herberich, Björn Olav Herheim, Jörg Herrmann, Ulf Hoberg, Christoph Hoermann, Corné van Hooijdonk, David Hopkinson, Bärbel & Peter Hoppe, Paul Hubweber, Shaun Ibbott, Mick Innes, David Ironside, Willi Jäger, Dieter Jakob, Alan Jenkins, Eddie Jobson, John, Paul, George & Ringo, Ian Jump, Thomas Jung, Michael & Thomas Käckenmeister, John Kaminski, Kantina Kasino, Oliver Kassel, Chantal Keijenberg, Lex Kemper, Mike Keneally, Michael Keropian, Ralph Kessler, Reiner Keuchel, Kevin & Pam, Clare King, Helmut King, Mick Kirkup, David Kisyk, Howie Kittelson, Andreas Kleerup, Eric Klerks, Jörg Kleinworth, Georg Klose,

Wolfram Klug, Sebastian Knauer, Michael Knoke, Andreas König, Marcel Koeslin, Dirk Konings, Harald Koob, Bogdan Kostyra, Oliver Kraft, Michael Krampe, Horst Krispien, Michael Kroll, Reinhard Krüger, Joachim Kühn, Claude Kuhnen, Heiko Kujath, Max Kutner, Christian Kutz, Maike Kutz, Wolfhard & Tracy-Lynn Kutz, Peter van Laarhoven, Buzzo Landi, Katja Lange, Bas & Evelien Langereis, Jon Larsen, Ivan Leirvik, Nigey Lennon, Glenn Leonard, Esther Leslie, Bernd Leu, Giorgio Libera, Magnus Liljeqvist, Udo Lindenberg, Tommy Loewe, Gary Lucas, Niklas Lychou, Birgit Mahner, Robbie Seahag Mangano, Ed Mann, Volkmar Mantei, Thomas Maos, Harald Marasus, Bobby Marquis, Zappo Marsik, Robert Martin, John Martyn, Pat Mastelotto, Jessica Mastrodomenico, Anne Maurer, Paul Maurer, Henry Maybauer, Guthrie McDonald, Zap Mcinnes, Ngaio McKay, Dave McMann, Carlos Medina Mendoza, Aad Meijer, Frank Meißner, Marco Minnemann, Dave Mitchell, Steffen Moddrow, Benoît Moerlen, Jan Möbius, Hugo Möller, Mom & Dad, Travis Moody, Georges Moustaki, Mudd Club México, Muffin Men, Kent Nagano, Marko Nakari, Frank Neumann, Mani Neumeier, André Nickel, Michael Nickel, Norbert Niederhäuser, Georg Nilius, Andy Niven, Hansi Noack, Gerd Nöth, Joey Nolan, David Noodler, John Nowak, Poul Friis Nybo, Mats Oberg, Frank Oberländer, Nobat Obermanns, Sandro Oliva, Sílvia Oliveira, Rick Olson, Chris Oppermann, Maru Ortiz, Jerry Outlaw, Steve Outlaw, Dave Owen, Alex Rosco Pakalov, Ed Palermo, Erik Palm, Tim Palmieri, Reinier Parengkuan, Scott Parker, Dave Parlato, Giles Ob Parlett, Alex Pasut, David Pate, Detlef Pawils, Luc Peersman, Andrea Pennati, Michael Petruzzi, Mark G. Pinske, Robert Plant, Jean-Luc Ponty, Wolfgang Porsow & Anne Karlchen, Nolan Porter, Simon Prentis, Don Preston, Reinhard Preuss, Norbert Preuß, Chris Priestley, Prairie Prince, Grace Quinn, George Rademacher, Fritz Rau, Avo Raup, Andreas Rausch, Sannybabe Rehauge, John Reilly, Birgit & Thomas Reinicke, Wiebke Richter, Robert Riedt, Johannes Rienau, Dirk Rösner, Daniel Rohr, Aagot Rokne, Pierpaolo Romani, Robert Ross, Barbara Rossi, Klaus Roßmanek, Jochen Rüdebusch, Mark Ruhrmann, Rupert & Carlotta, Greg Russo, Paul Ryan, Sale Salomon, Gerald Sanders, Beau Sasser, Eric Satie, Bill Saunders, Ulli Schäfer, Burkhard Schempp, Cal Schenkel, Jörg Scherf, Clemens & Rimbert Schickling, Wolfgang Schild, Daggie Schindler, Maggie, Max, Steffen & Tom Schindler, Kirsten Schmidt, Ralph Schmidt, Jörg Schmitt, Thomas Schmitt, Volkmar Schneider, Claus & Michael Schockmann, Annemarieke Schoonderwaldt, Jos Schoone, Peer Schröder, Ulli Schröder, Heike Schürmann, Larry Schulz, Klaus Schulze, Christiane Seebach, Ed Seeman, Dan, Jude, Ellie & Patrick Sefton, Elizabeth & Brian Sefton, Chato Segerer, Remko Serban, Deborah Serrano, Pujit Shingala, Leo Sieg,

Coen Siersma, Günter Sievers, Jeff Silvertrust, Jeff Simmons, Deepinder Singh Cheema, Jon Singley, Eric, Julie & Robin Slick, Dave Smith, Ward Smith, Helmut Sommer, Society Pages, Dar Spanner, Torsten Starke, Thomas Stårvik, Ralph Steadman, Dieter Stein, Andreas Steinhardt, Martin G. Stephenson, Craig "Twister" Steward, Georg Stock, Jean-Paul Stotijn, Rémy Sträuli, Kathrin Strauch, Raimond Strauß, Igor Stravinsky, Spemcer Streeter, Reiner Struck, Erlend Sundin, Simo Superpatata, Jürgen Swakowski, John Tabacco, Wayne Tarasoff, Helen Tate, Nicola Taylor, Angel "Mollo" Tejeda & Family, John Thorburn, Stacy Thunes, Geert Tiersma, T'Mershi Duween, JRR Tolkien, Carola Trabert, Joe Travers, Eric Trøim, Joe Trump, Charles Ulrich, Veronika Ulrich, Steve Vai, Edgar Varèse, Herman van Veen, Siglinde & Harm Vellguth, Don van Vliet, Chad Wackerman, Clint Walker, Denny & Janet Walley, Ben Watson, Stefanie Weber, Matthias Wehrhahn, Gregor Weigmann, Thomas Weller, Katja Maria Werker, Dieter Westendorff, Ray White, Frank Wiedmer, Ike Willis, Donald Roller Wilson, Albert Quon Wing, Frank Wonneberg, Hank Woods, Michal Matragon Worgacz, Jörg Wulf, Wymer UK Ltd., Stefan Zander, Dweezil, Moon & Bob Zappa, Patrice Zappa-Porter, Stanley Jason Zappa, Zappanale, Zappateers, Uli Zeidler, Kerstin & Finja Zeuner (:-*), Kathrin & Olaf Ziedrich, and Daniela Ziegner.

Andrew would like to thank:

All the usual suspects – family and friends, both dead and living, but not some of those thanked in previous books (you know who you are, you pricks); Spike Milligan, Billy Connolly, Monty Python, Mel Brooks, Ren & Stimpy, and Chico, Harpo, Groucho … and sometimes Zeppo, for making me laugh; Kurt Vonnegut, Woody Allen and Joe Orton, for also amusing me, but in a slightly different way; Román García Albertos, and all that make IINK the most valuable resource online for all things Frank; Peter Van Laarhoven and Burkhard Schempp for spreading the word; Jenny Agutter, for the helping hand through puberty; Coronation Street, Chelsea FC and Speedway GP, for regularly entertaining me; Robert Plant, Tori Amos, the Fab Four and Jeff Beck for being mostly alive and still doing it for me; Kevin Crosby and my fellow members of ZERO around the globe; Mick Zeuner, for sharing his dream; Klaus Kühner, for making Mick's dream come true; all 'Mothers' everywhere; and finally FZ, without whom, etc.

Klaus would like to thank:

my beloved daughter and family; my parents – who never understood me, but at least put me on the right path; all friends who have accompanied me or are still walking my path; all those I met once, twice or several times, who touched, stirred, irritated or pushed me, or gave me a swerve; all the artists and aesthetes who have led me to the right places in life; all the literats and writers who have enchanted me with their exceptional words; all the filmmakers and actors who have greatly enriched my visual perception; all the musicians and composers who touched my soul and set my blood racing; all the theorists, thinkers, practitioners and inventors who delighted and enchanted my world; and finally, all the geniuses who have created cross-genre brilliance and timelessness: I bow down to you all.

ADVERTISEMENT

Mappa Zappa
2018

Various Artists

Cordelia Release #7

Originally Released: *June 6, 2018*

Recording data: *1998 to 2018 at "The Office" (Florida), Störtebecker Studios (Hamburg), State Theater, St. Petersburg, (Florida), Hansestudio (Hamburg), The Raven (Corby), SpannerHQ (London), Rancho Frio Studios (Connecticut), The Yellow Hippo Studios (The Hague), Egg Studios (Seattle), and a variety of remote locations worldwide*

Producer: *Andrew Greenaway*

Engineer: *Alan Jenkins*

Tracks:
Transylvania Boogie by Todd Grubbs Group (5:09)
Dead Girls Of London by Gabba Zappa Hey! (2:29)
Wolf Harbor by Evil Dick (4:28)
The Purple Lagoon by Hans Annellsson (3:14)
Tinsel Town Rebellion by Tante Tofu (2:30)
Let's Move To Cleveland by Bogus Pomp (1:56)
Poofter's Froth Wyoming Plans Ahead by The Muffin Men feat. Jimmy Carl Black (2:46)
Phyniox by String Trash (3:54)
Village Of The Sun by Acton Zappa (4:17)
Cucamonga by Spannertate (2:37)
Outrage At Valdez by Fuchsprellen (4:15)
Been To Kansas City In A Minor by Fred Händl (7:01)
D.C. Boogie by Guranfoe (5:45)
San Ber'dino by Caballero Reynaldo (2:44)
What's New In Baltimore? by Zappa Early Renaissance Orchestra feat. Ike Willis (6:10)

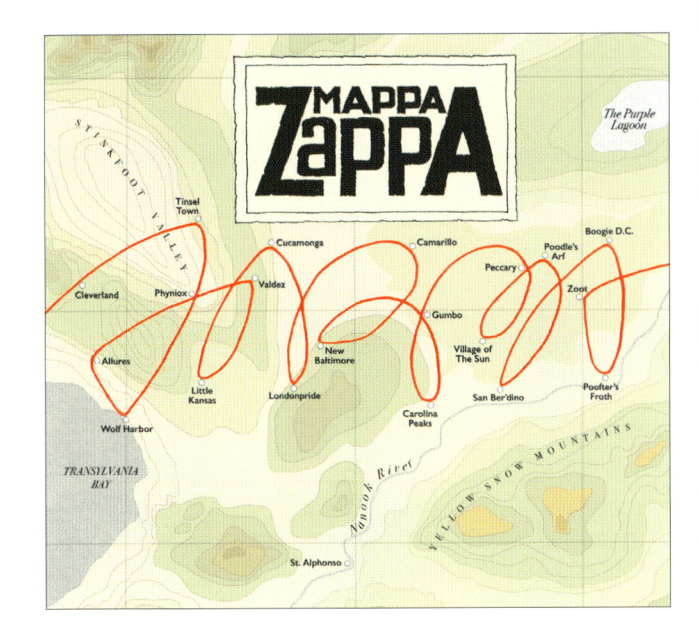

"This version of Wolf Harbor treads the hilarious line between computer music and free improvisation. Imagine the stinking, grey polluted water. Seabirds – drenched in crude oil and tangled in plastic – feasting on the rotting remains of fish poisoned by radiation. Sewage outlets spewing out a noxious cocktail full of used baby wipes, condoms and sanitary equipment. And jazz."

Dr Richard Hemmings

Foreshadowing publication of The Zappa Tour Atlas, Andrew asked 15 bands to record 15 renditions of 15 Zappa songs, all with place names in the title. He then commissioned graphic designer/illustrator Antero Valério to create the artwork for this, the seventh Zappa themed CD he has compiled for Cordelia Records.

It is readily available to purchase, download or stream, and the authors urge you to do this and listen while flicking through Klaus' amazing maps.

The album not only features Mick, as the bass player of String Trash, but Andrew himself makes a fleeting appearance during ZERO's version of What's New In Baltimore? – which is dedicated to late/great Yes bassist, Chris Squire.

Andrew, like all of the artists involved, does not make a penny from this album. But Cordelia Records think that, after manufacturing costs and mechanical royalties, they might be able to break even.

Within twenty or so years.

Zappa The Hard Way
2010

Andrew Greenaway

Wymer Publishing

Originally Released: August 25, 2010

Tracks from the 1988 tour not included in the Official Discography:

Bamboozled By Love (5:41)
– from The Frank Zappa AAAFRNAA Birthday Bundle.
Exclusive download from iTunes.
Released: 21 December 2006

More Trouble Every Day (5:48)
– from The Frank Zappa AAAFRNAAA Birthday Bundle.
Exclusive download from iTunes.
Released: 21 December 2008

I Am The Walrus (03:43) / America The Beautiful (03:16)
– from Beat The Boots III – Disc Two.
Exclusive download from AmazonMP3 and iTunes.
Released: 25 January 2009

My Guitar Wants To Kill Your Mama (3:34) / Stairway To Heaven (10:10)
– from The FRANK ZAPPA aaafnraaaa Birthday Bundle.
Exclusive download from iTunes.
Released: 21 December 2010

Peaches (Vienna 88) (2:50)
– from The FRANK ZAPPA AAAFNRAAAAM Birthday Bundle.
Exclusive download from iTunes.
Released: 21 December 2011

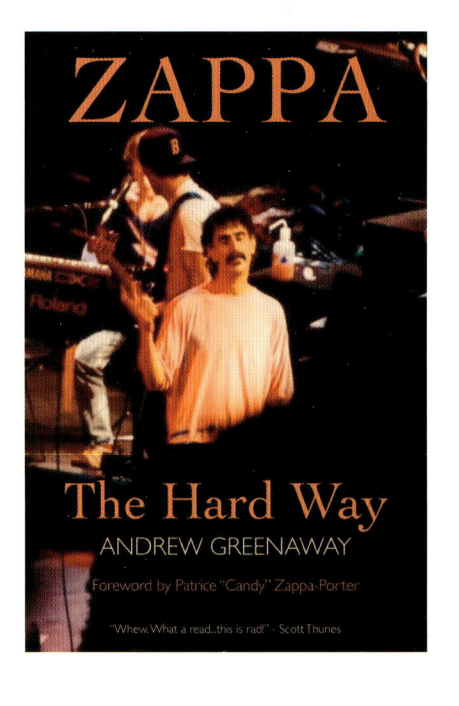

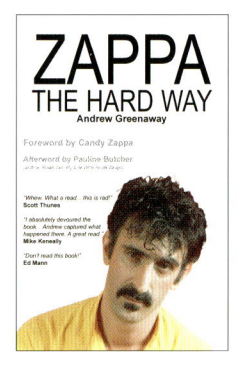

"In 1988, Frank Zappa hung up his guitar and never played with his band again. The reasons given publicly relate to squabbles between members of the band. But was this the real reason? Could it have been an excuse, a cover up for something else – ie. Frank's ailing health? Andrew Greenaway has tackled this anomaly in this excellent book. He shows how it was that these eleven men lived and played in harmony through dozens of concerts because of their respect and admiration for Frank Zappa. And what astonishing concerts they were too. Greenaway manages to convey the brilliance and uniqueness of this band not only through his own descriptions but also from the band members' own praise for the astonishing variety of music they created. But even this respect could not stop cracks opening up. Read this meticulously researched book and find out the answer to why Broadway, The Hard Way was Frank Zappa's last band."
Pauline Butcher (author of Freak Out! My Life With Frank Zappa)

In 1988 Frank Zappa toured with a twelve-piece band that had rehearsed for months, learnt a repertoire of over 100 songs and played an entirely different set each night.

Zappa appointed bass player Scott Thunes to rehearse the group in his absence. In carrying out this role, Thunes was apparently abrasive, blunt and rude to the other members.

While in Europe, Zappa told the band there were ten more weeks of concerts booked in the USA and asked them: "If Scott's in the band, will you do the tour?" With the exception of Mike Keneally, they all said "no".

Greenaway has interviewed the surviving band members and others associated with the tour to unravel the goings on behind the scenes that drove Zappa to call a halt to proceedings, despite huge personal financial losses.

Zappa The Hard Way might just be the best book you've never read in your life!

ADVERTISEMENT

Frank Talk: The Inside Stories Of Zappa's Other People
2017

Andrew Greenaway

Wymer Publishing

Originally Released: *July 21, 2017*

Interviewees:
Arthur Barrow (2001)
Lorraine Belcher (2010 / 2017)
Bruce Bickford (2009)
Jimmy Carl Black (2000 / 2003 / 2008)
Terry Bozzio (1992)
Napoleon Murphy Brock (2002)
Pauline Butcher (2012)
Warren Cuccurullo (1994 / 2010)
Dr Dot (2003)
Roy Estrada (2002)
Bob Harris #2 (2000)
Thana Harris (2000)
Mike Keneally (1997 / 2016)
Nigey Lennon (2000)
Martin Lickert (1993)
Robert Martin (2009)
Essra Mohawk (2011)
Kent Nagano (1990)
Lisa Popeil (2010)
Don Preston (2001 / 2011)
Craig 'Twister' Steward (2015)
Scott Thunes (2006 / 2012)
The Tornadoes (2005)
Steve Vai (1997)
Mark Volman (2006)
Chad Wackerman (2007)
Denny Walley (2008)
Ike Willis (2009)
Albert Wing (2010 / 2016)
Bob Zappa (2015)
Candy Zappa (2001)
Dweezil Zappa (1991 / 2012 / 2015)

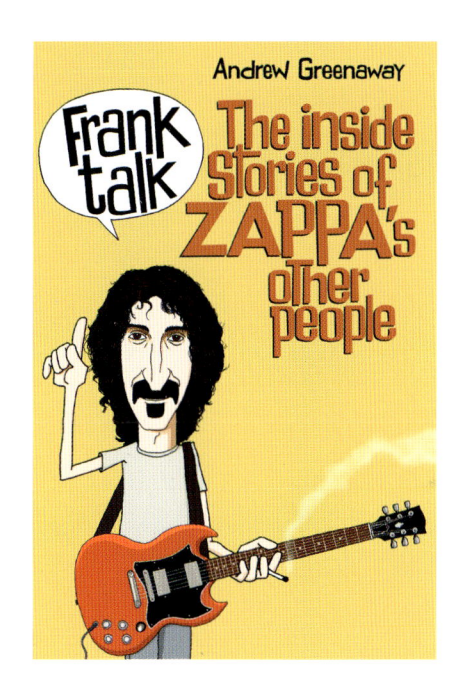

"When it comes to the study of the music and life of Frank Zappa, there can be few scholars who show such inexhaustible energy and such detailed knowledge as Andrew Greenaway. Frank Talk contains a comprehensive selection of interviews with Zappa alumni and associates that cannot help but increase our knowledge of the subject, and Greenaway is simultaneously a benign, good-natured interviewer and a keen investigator with an instinct for a killer question. In this respect, the contributions of Essra Mohawk and Lorraine Belcher make fascinating reading. He also provides a subtle contrast between his entertaining interviews and his precise, detailed footnotes."

Dr Geoff Wills (author of Zappa And Jazz)

Following his highly successful previous book, Frank Zappa specialist Andrew Greenaway's second tome on the influential cult artist is something completely different!

Frank Talk: The Inside Stories of Zappa's Other People is compiled from over 40 interviews Greenaway has conducted during the past three decades with the people who knew and worked with the legendary composer and musician.

From Zappa's own family, through to members of the Mothers of Invention, his major discoveries (like guitarists Warren Cuccurullo & Steve Vai, plus drummer extraordinaire, Terry Bozzio), and the likes of Ike Willis, Scott Thunes, Mike Keneally and Robert Martin from his last touring band.

Augmented with artwork and caricatures created by noted designer Antero Valério, Frank Talk gives an extraordinary insight into this musical genius that is piled on in layers. With Greenaway's recognised knowledge of Zappa this book will undoubtedly compliment his previous title and be every bit as revered.